A GREY'S HARBOR CHRISTMAS

A GREY'S HARBOR CHRISTMAS

A GREY'S HARBOR HOLIDAY ANTHOLOGY

LARK GRIFFING   PIPER MALONE

JENNIFER SIVEC   J.C. WING

Three Quills press

ISBN-13: 978-0-9995217-5-5

Edited in part by Wing Family Editing

Edited in part by Dot and Dash, LLC.

Formatted by Wind Lark Publishing

Cover Design by Wing Family Editing

GREY'S HARBOR SERIES

GREY'S LANDING
A Grey's Harbor Story
by Lark Griffing

GREY'S HARBOR
A Grey's Harbor Anthology
By Carol Cassada
Lark Griffing
Piper Malone
Jennifer Sivec
J.C. Wing

HOPE ADRIFT
A Grey's Harbor Story
By Lark Griffing

HARBOR TIDES
A Grey's Harbor Story
By Lark Griffing

PERFECT SEAS
A Grey's Harbor Story
By Jennifer Sivec

HARBOR SONG
A Grey's Harbor Story
By J.C. Wing

PROLOGUE

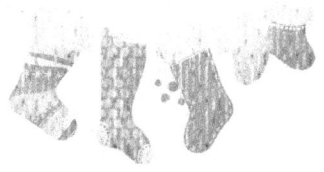

*C*hristmas was just around the corner, and Grey's Harbor was filled with festivity. The quaint iron streetlights that lined Main Street, each held a balsam wreath frosted with a light covering of snow, the velvet tails of the bows blowing gently in the sea breeze. Garlands draped gracefully across the streets making a wonderland of greenery, the quintessential east coast picture post card.

Red noses of mittened children glowed as they piled into the Cathead diner knowing that Maeve would have free hot cocoa waiting for them after an afternoon of Christmas caroling.

The door of the Cathead slammed as the last of the children piled in talking in excited voices, basking in the warmth. Maeve ushered them in as Old Man Detrick cocked his head sideways. A look of concern clouded his ancient eye.

"What's wrong, Deeter?" Tank asked as he handed a mug of cocoa to a passing cherub.

"There's trouble in the wind," Detrick replied. His deeply lined face creased heavily. "Mark my words, there's a storm brewing. Cold and hard." He shuddered.

"Seriously? How bad?" Tank asked, knowing that the reticent man didn't speak up often, not one to stir up drama.

"Bridger better secure the marina, move the boats upriver out of the storm surge. I give it a day, maybe two." With that, Mr. Detrick stood up. He left a five spot on the table and pulled his cap down over his ears. "Might be my last nor'easter," he mused. "At least it's gonna be a doozy."

Joy

By Lark Griffing

For Kathy

CHAPTER 1

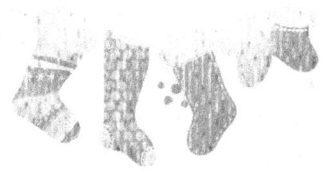

"*H*ello, darlin'."

Joy recognized the soft drawl, a gauzy memory, a voice from the past. *Damn it,* that voice could still squeeze her heart until she almost couldn't breathe. She finished locking up her shop, Joyful Cuts, before she turned to face him. He could wait. After all, it had been how many years?

She finally tipped her face and looked up into the deep brown eyes she remembered so well. Now they were older, wiser, maybe, with crinkles at the corner.

"Hello, Ransom. What brings you here?" No pleasantries. No, 'you look good, how've ya been...' Just a steady, cold, question. She was surprised that it hurt her so much to steel her voice. But damn it, she was steel now. She was a stone cold bitch.

"Had some business to attend to." He waited for her to respond. He was braced for her anger but was surprised when it didn't come. It wasn't often he was surprised. He was the kind of person who could read people, who knew what to expect. Situations didn't catch him off guard. This time he was not prepared for her sigh. *Where was that temper?* Joy was as fiery as her hair.

"That doesn't explain why you're standing here." She straightened to her full height, which still only brought her just to his shoulders. That brought a smile to his lips.

She didn't take kindly to it.

He switched his tactics.

"I just got into town and settled into the Harbor Inn. When I saw Joyful Cuts, I figured it was you. I haven't eaten." He waited, wondering if she would be polite enough to continue the conversation.

She wasn't.

"It's been years, so I wasn't sure where I should grab a late dinner." He watched her closely.

"I'm sure the internet could have given you a listing with lots of suggestions," she said dryly. She decided to make him work for this. She had to admit, she was curious. He looked good, his body still as hard and lean as it had been in high school. He still wore cowboy boots, too. He wasn't a cowboy. So far from it, but he always liked the style, and he didn't give a rat's ass what anyone else thought of it. She always like it, too. They fit him. Just like her motorcycle boots fit her. Of course, she rode a motorcycle. As far as she knew, he didn't ride a horse.

He stared at her, his deep brown eyes hardening. He didn't expect this amount of animosity. He didn't expect her to throw herself at him. Far from it, but hell, it had been years. He was hoping the hurt had mellowed. He should've known better. After all, he discovered all too recently that the scab could be picked, and the wound underneath was raw and festered.

"Come on, Joy," he said softly. "Would you join me for dinner? Old friends catching up. That's it," he promised. *For now,* he told himself. And then, he was going to have to open up a whole world of hurt to her, and it pained him. After all, it was all his fault.

· ⁎ ⁂ ⁎ ·

*L*ila Rose lay on the grungy bedspread trying not to think about just what might be infused in those fibers. She was in a cheap motel right off the interstate. The sound of the trucks' gears changing as they pulled the heavy rigs up the mountain was a steady rhythm. At first she found it annoying, but soon it became comforting, a reminder that her journey was still waiting for her, she just had to merge on the entrance ramp and make her way east.

Her fingers reached for the folder again. The manilla tab was worn from nineteen years of worry. Her momma's fingers must have worried it first, holding the folder, reading the contents, wondering when the time, if any, would be the right time to hand it over to Lila. Lila had only come upon the folder ten months ago when the lawyer had handed over the last of the personal papers and effects he had in his possession. Her parents were gone. Daddy left her eighteen months ago, apologizing that he wouldn't be there to help guide her through college, but cancer was a bitch. She knew it broke his heart. She knew he had planned on protecting her until she was well into adulthood and maybe installed with another alpha male who could take over the watch. Her Daddy, the strong detective, not so strong against those deviant cells.

Daddy's death broke Momma's heart. Momma clung to Lila Rose like the last petal on the homecoming rose bouquet, but Momma had turned grey and finally that petal fell. Not through any fault of her own. Nope. Nature helped that along. An icy curve and Momma joined Daddy. Poof.

Now Lila Rose was contemplating a sheaf of papers that her momma had surely meant to share with her, just hadn't gotten around to it. A sheaf of papers that held secrets. A sheaf of papers that made Lila Rose realize she really didn't know who she was or where she came from.

She flipped past the data sheet, female, 8 lbs., 4 oz, blah blah, and her fingers scratched on the last documents in the folder. The ones that didn't look official. She picked up the blue piece of stationary with the rounded loopy cursive. She had read it a million times. She knew it by heart. But she searched it, looking again for a clue, a feeling, a different emotion. Of course, there wouldn't be one. It would read like it had read the last million times she had read it.

. . .

*R*ose,

   I know you probably don't have that name now, but that's how I think of you. My Rosebud. We were reading Citizen Kane *in high school when I had to leave to stay home. I guess the symbolism kinda stuck.*

   You'll probably never get to read this. I don't even know why I'm writing it except to maybe ask for your forgiveness, or maybe to just cleanse my soul.

   My cousin, Linda, wanted to know why I just didn't abort you. She aborted her baby. She said it was no big deal. Well, it is to me. Why should I punish you for my mistake? You don't deserve to die because I had a fling by the lighthouse. Oh, and by the way, yes, you can get pregnant the first time!

   You kicked me hard today. That still surprises me. It's such a weird thing. I remember the first time I felt you. You were just a flutter, a reminder that my decision was the right one. I will bring you into this world, but, honey, I can't keep you. You deserve a good life. I know there's a momma out there who wants a baby but can't have one. It's not that I don't want you. I'm not ready for you. I can't be good for you. I'm just a dumb kid who did a dumb thing.

   If you ever read this, I want you to know that I love you. I love you, little flutter. I love you enough to try to give you a life you deserve. Be happy. Be good. And if you ever get the chance to stand on the sand and watch the ocean waves roll in, think about your first momma who loved you enough to let you go, like the wave that lapped the shore and washed back into the ocean only to get bigger. If you actually are reading this, you did get bigger and stronger. Just know that is all I wanted for you. I hope I did the right thing by you.

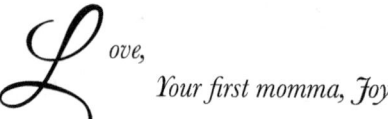

*L*ove,
   Your first momma, Joy

*L*ila Rose did what she always did after reading the letter. She flipped it over to see the back of the paper. To check it. Just like always, there was nothing there. Not a thing.

   She sighed and put the letter back in the folder under the other handwritten paper, a loose-leaf binder sheet, college ruled, yellowed a bit with age. She pulled her glasses off her nose and scrubbed her face with her open palms. Then crawled between the sheets and rolled over to turn off the light. She was tired and was almost asleep within seconds of her head settling into the pillow. The last thought moved through her brain like the sea.

Well, first momma, I did get bigger. And I am like that wave. The thing about waves, Momma, is they come back on shore. I'm coming back. I'm going to find you. I hope you're ready for this wave.

· ·✳· ·

*J*oy stared Ransom in the eyes for half a beat then smiled a slow smile. She knew that would throw him off guard.

"Sure, I'm hungry. I was planning to go to the Mizzen Mast for the fish fry. You remember Izzy?"

Ransom gazed off into the distance, bringing up a hazy image of a defiant teenage girl who didn't run in his circles.

"Vaguely," he said, wondering why it mattered.

"Izzy owns the Mizzen Mast, and she's known three counties over for her fish fry."

"I'm game. You want me to drive?" Ransom asked, slipping into the dominant role he had perfected.

"No," Joy said, enjoying the game.

"Okay, you can drive," Ransom acquiesced, hating the idea of riding shotgun. It went against his grain as a man. He had been accused more times than he could count of being sexist.

Joy looked at him with a sneer.

"You would freeze your ass off if you rode with me dressed like that, besides, I don't have a back seat, and I don't ride anyone bitch." She waited, relishing the quick look of shock on his face. He recovered quickly, looking her up and down.

"Well, darlin', you've got the boots for it, but I don't see a bike."

"Because she's tucked in tight tonight. I walked to work, and we can walk to Izzy's place. It's not far."

"Lead the way." Ransom fell in beside Joy. Usually he enjoyed exchanging barbs with people, but tonight it just made him tired. He didn't want to play this game with Joy. He wanted to be able to talk to her like he always used to when they shared their secrets and their dreams. When they had hopes and plans as they walked side by side, holding hands for miles down the beach. They were wild and free and had the world by the tail. But all that changed, and he let it destroy them. He was bound and determined he wasn't going to destroy her again, but it was going to be damn hard, and she had a wall up that was a mile high. It was going to take a light touch and some time. He just didn't know if he had enough hours left to prepare her for what was to come.

CHAPTER 2

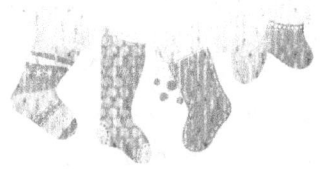

*T*he Mizzen Mast was bustling with activity full of locals gathering for a Friday night out with friends. Izzy's place was the bar in town where people came to unwind, eat good food, listen to good music, and sometimes get counseled by Izzy. The woman knew everything about everybody but was tight-lipped and trustworthy. Izzy and Joy weren't close friends, but they respected each other, and Joy always had the feeling that she and Izzy shared something, a hurt, that bore deeply.

When Joy and Ransom entered the door, Izzy watched them from the across the bar. She nodded at Joy and narrowed her eyes at Ransom, trying to place him. There was something familiar about him, about those square, strong shoulders, trim waist, and tall cool looks. High school. Shit. Joy's old boyfriend. Izzy's brain went into overdrive. Remembering. He'd left town right after graduation and, as far as she knew, had never stepped foot back in the town again.

Izzy's newest waitress descended on Joy and Ransom, leading them off to a corner table, and Izzy's attention was drawn to making an Irish coffee. She was going to have to up her game with the winter cocktails if the weather continued on this cold snap. Christmas was around the corner and Jennifer Wynn had been after

Izzy to add a festive holiday drink. Jennifer complained Irish coffee didn't fit the bill. Izzy slid the Irish coffee to the sweater-clad, blue-haired octogenarian who was flirting with a stooped elderly man in a dusty tweed jacket. They were out-of-towners who had stumbled into Izzy's place and were charmed by the bar on the river. But they were not pleased with the cold raw wind blowing down the estuary from the ocean. They would be heading further south in the morning.

Speak of the devil, thought Izzy as a cold blast swept through the bar. Jennifer walked in on Ryker's arm, her cheeks flushed pink, happiness blossoming on her face. Everyone turned to see who walked in and someone yelled for them to close the damn door.

Ransom looked up from his menu to see who was causing the commotion. Ryker Wynn he recognized immediately, but it was the woman on his arm that shocked him. She looked like Jennifer Creely, or at least what Jennifer Creely should have looked like if she were happy.

Joy read his face.

"Yep, that's Jennifer. Crazy what safety and security will do for a girl," she said dryly.

Score. That wounded him, but he deserved it.

"Hey, Jennifer. Try this." Izzy held out a copper mug for Jennifer as the couple approached the bar.

"What is it? It's pretty and smells amazing," Jennifer said, wrinkling up her delicate nose after getting a strong whiff of peppermint that frosted her nostrils.

"It's my version of a Mistletoe Mule. What do you think?"

"I think it's a perfect holiday specialty cocktail. Are you going to advertise it?" Jennifer asked, sipping the festive concoction.

Ryker tried not to laugh at the pained look on Izzy's face. Looking at the ingredients he couldn't imagine having all that stuff on hand for just a few orders. The locals here were kinda set on tradition.

"I'll have to think about it," said Izzy, not intending at all to go any further than giving Jennifer this one festive spirit.

"Oh, what's that?" a perky blonde asked as she stepped up to the bar and eyed Jennifer's drink.

"It's Izzy's holiday special cocktail. It's a Mistletoe Mule."

"Can I get one of these?" the blonde asked.

"Coming right up," said Izzy as she turned, rolling her eyes. Ryker caught it and shot her a sympathetic grin. "Whatever it takes, huh, Ryker. The customer is always right."

"Damn straight," he said as he raised his beer in salute to his favorite bartender.

* ✴ *

*J*oy watched Ransom finish the last fry on his plate and sit back, obviously sated. He grinned at her, and she couldn't help but smile back. His smile was infectious.

"You're right, Joy, that's the best damn fish I've eaten in years. It takes me back to Pops' fish frys. You remember those?" he asked, his eyes going somewhere else.

Yes, she remembered. Memories flooded back of walking into Pops' back yard, holding Ransom's hand, a broomstick skirt swirling at her sandal-clad toes. A midriff top skimmed her tanned belly, and a small braid with a feather tumbled over her shoulders tucked in the glorious auburn tresses. Pops had two huge propane burners going, one for the beer-battered fish and the other for the battered, thick cut onion rings. Picnic tables covered with Kraft paper and red and white checked paper napkins were filled with people, friends and neighbors, drinking cold beer and teasing Pops, anticipation growing for the first baskets of fried fish.

Pops was in his glory. He loved people, and he loved food. He also loved his grandson and the girl who was always on his grandson's arm. Pops was a happy man.

"I miss him," Joy whispered, knowing that it cut Ransom's heart. Pops dropped dead of a heart attack, alone in his cottage. Ransom was with Joy that night. At the lighthouse. In the dark.

"I miss him every day. He raised me. He gave me everything. I wish I could have given him his golden years."

"He was proud of you. I know that. You never let him down." Joy stopped, remembering. But then, Pops never knew.

"Oh, but I did, and you know it." Ransom held Joy's eyes.

Neither one looked away.

"It's over, Ransom. The past is past. Leave it buried." Joy stood abruptly and tossed a twenty on the table. "I've got to get going. I have an early client in the morning. It was good seeing you, Ransom. Take care of yourself." She turned to leave, but Ransom caught her arm.

"Joy, my business in town…it's going to take a few days."

"Then enjoy your stay," she said tersely, pulling at her arm to free herself from his grip. It wasn't tight, not hurtful, just firm, commanding.

"There are some things we should talk about…"

She shook her head.

"No, Ransom. The time for talking is done. Good night."

She turned and left the bar, letting the cold wind from a brewing Nor'easter blast into the bar. A warning of an upcoming storm on the horizon.

Oh, Joy, thought Ransom. *There's a storm coming, but not the one you're expecting.* He drained his beer and looked in disgust at the twenty Joy left. He wasn't going to fight her about that, but he'd be damned if she was going to pay for dinner. He motioned for the waitress and paid the bill. Then he handed her the twenty and told her merry Christmas. Her young face lit up, and she couldn't thank the handsome man enough. He put his finger to his lips, shushing her, as he left the bar, once again letting winter into the warm space.

Izzy and Ryker watched as Ransom left.

"I've a bad feeling about this," Izzy said, her eyes narrowed.

"Why?" asked Ryker. "Ransom was always a stand-up guy."

"A man like that doesn't come back into town for no reason. He has no family left, no ties to this place. No, he's on a mission, and I'm afraid it's going to cause some heartache. I don't know why, but I just feel it."

"Feel what?" asked Jennifer as she slid back on the bar stool returning from her trip to the powder room.

"I feel like there is a serious storm brewing," said Izzy as another customer struggled with the door and the wind. "In more ways than one."

❈

*T*he cold wind bit into Joy's cheeks and blew down the neck of her leather jacket, cutting through her jeans, chilling her to the core. It had been cold when she left her shop and walked to the Mizzen Mast with Ransom, but in the hour and a half she was in the bar, the temperature had plummeted. She grinned to herself remembering that Ransom wasn't dressed for this weather. She knew he would be freezing on his hike back to the Harbor Inn. *Damn*, she thought, that old hotel was going to take the brunt of the nor'easter's cutting wind. He wouldn't be enjoying the wide porch, staring at the ocean and sipping on a cocktail anytime on this little trip back home.

The night was dark, but she felt at home walking at this late hour on these streets. She was never shy about being out alone at night. She could take care of herself, thank you very much. Besides, the town was safe. Crime was unheard of around here, except for when that out of town guidance counselor caused all that trouble. That was rare, but he was dealt with and life had returned to the peaceful calm of a sleepy seaside town.

She unlocked the door that led to a stairway and her apartment above the old hardware store. The window in the door rattled as she pulled it closed and the old wooden stairs creaked as she climbed them. The sound was comforting, welcoming her home as they had done for the last ten years. She would probably die in this old apartment, she thought as she unlocked the door to her home at the top of the stairs.

Soft light glowed from the floor lamp in the corner. A sleek tabby cat wound his way between her legs in a greeting that was just short of affectionate.

"Evening, Cat." She knew better than to scratch his head. They had been together for years, but he still took time to warm up to her every night.

He meowed softly and walked to his bowl, irritation showing with every stride. He sat in front of his dish and lifted his front right paw, licking it daintily, refusing to look at her.

"I suppose you want me to feed you," she said, opening the cupboard to snag a pouch of something in gravy.

The cat yawned.

She stooped over, ripping the top of the foil packet and squeezing the wet mess into the animal's dish. She stood up and stepped back, watching.

He sniffed the mound, lifted his face and looked at her full of reproach, then turned and walked away toward the bedroom, his tail held high.

"Cat, you're a bastard, you know that?"

Joy pulled off her boots and put them on the mat by the door. She padded down the hall, her socks sliding on the highly polished wood floor. She was tired and she had a seven o'clock client in the morning, a woman who was making an appearance on the local news show in the morning, so she needed to put on the dog. Joy was going to have a hell of a time convincing her to go subtle. Most of her clients knew better than to argue with her. She was always right, in the end. It just took some clients longer to recognize her skill. They always came around. The thing is, the longer it took, the more it cost them. Life was funny that way. She grinned to herself. Maybe it wasn't a bad thing that Laura Lee would take some convincing and several different styles. The thing is, Joy warned them if they didn't listen to her and she had to do the hair twice, the second time the style she had originally suggested, it was going to cost double. Most of the time the client was so grateful she netted a sizable tip, too. She wasn't a bitch to be mean, she just didn't like to listen to people's shit.

She changed into an old pair of sweats and then padded back to the kitchen, putting the tea kettle on. She pulled the thick cream-colored mug out of the cupboard, the one that her grandfather had drunk coffee out of so many years ago. Tonight, it would hold rich gourmet hot chocolate. She needed comfort, and the damn cat wasn't going to give it to her. Within minutes, the water was ready, forcing the steam through the little hole in the spout, filling the apartment with a cheery sound. If fell dull on Joy's heart. She was in a mood tonight. Ransom put her there.

She stirred her cocoa thoughtfully, combining the water and the rich mix, making certain there were no lumps on the bottom, then she carried her mug into the living room and sat by the lamp, curled into the wing arm chair that was positioned to look out the front windows, over the top of the bait shop and out into the dark of the ocean. She could hear the waves crashing on shore, and she knew, in the dark, foam was blowing off the top of those waves, the ocean being stirred into a frenzy by that north east wind.

The cat appeared at her feet and regarded her, not blinking. She glanced at him, then turned her attention again out the window. She knew better than to look. She knew the routine. He jumped to the arm of the chair, stalked across the back cushion and down to the other arm. Stepping fastidiously over her arms and working his way between her chest and the cocoa mug, he turned to lay down on her lap, stopping first to swipe her chin with his turkey and gravy, fish smelling tongue. Then he curled up against the warm mug and began to clean his left shoulder with that same tongue, twisting just so.

"Keep your nasty hair out of my mug, Cat," she admonished him. She stroked the soft fur on his back, and he forced the side of his head against her petting hand, making her rub his cheeks firmly. "Careful Cat, or you're going to have an earful of hot gourmet cocoa. Then the two of us will be pissed about that."

She took a careful sip, relishing the rich, deep flavors. It was peaceful here with her cat on her lap. This was what she had. This was her life. This was her circle. She was usually content with it, but tonight Ransom had come back. Her peace was shattered.

Damn it, she sighed. She had a wall. She was a fortress. No one was inside. Sometimes the cat, but he was an asshole. At least she knew where she stood with him.

But Ransom had come back, and she knew he was going to come knocking on her door again. She knew he had unfinished business. The thing is, she had finished that business nineteen years ago. Without him.

A car backfired in the street causing the cat to vault off her lap, digging his back claws deep into her thigh.

"Damn it," she swore out loud as hot cocoa slopped onto her wrist and into the bloody wounds in her thighs. "I hate you, Cat," she muttered under her breath as she walked across the kitchen, wincing. She ran her hand under cold water, cooling the burn. "Screw it," she announced to no one. "I'm going to bed." Unceremoniously, she dumped the precious cocoa down the drain and switched off the kitchen light. A sharp wind howled, rattling the window. For a moment, she felt like it rattled her bones.

CHAPTER 3

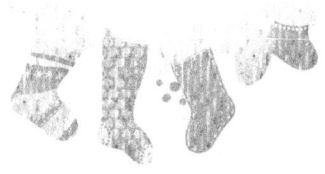

*L*ila Rose pulled off the interstate and drove past the small mall complete with its requisite family chain restaurants. She felt a pang of disappointment. When she saw the sign announcing that she had entered the Grey's Harbor corporation limits, she was expecting a quaint seaside town with picturesque boats floating into a harbor. Instead, she had the same damn interchange as any midwestern town. She felt deflated.

She followed the main road as it gave way to some large, upscale homes parked in subdivisions with nautical names. One even had a bronze captain statue complete with slicker as he hauled on a bronze ship wheel. *Over the top,* she thought.

The scenery gave way to older homes tucked behind long lawns, some with large trees that were currently being tossed by a strong north wind. A minute later, she had glimpses of the sea, an incredibly angry sea. She stopped the car along the road and stared over the bluff and down the dunes to the pounding surf. The dark gray of the waves was ominous. She was hoping to feel welcome. Instead she was beginning to second guess her mission, her soul filling with dread.

A truck pulled up beside her, stopping, and a passenger rolled down the window.

"Are you okay?" A strong man with close cropped hair peered at her from a truck whose passenger door sported the name Wynn Construction. "Do you need some help?"

"No, thank you," she stammered, "I'm just trying to get my bearings."

"Where ya headin'?" the extremely muscular, attractive man asked her.

"Don't scare the girl, Tank," said the driver, smiling at her as he ducked his head so he could see out the window. "Tank looks dangerous, but he's a pussy cat. I'm Ryker. Are you sure you don't need anything?" Ryker asked.

"Well, I assume this road leads into the town of Grey's Harbor, right?" she asked with a tentative smile.

"Yes, ma'am," Tank answered. "Anywhere in particular?"

Lila Rose hesitated for a minute, not sure if it was safe to divulge the information. *Oh, what the hell,* she thought. *Why not?*

"The Harbor Inn," she replied.

"Just keep going. This road will turn into Main Street and take you into the old part of Grey's Harbor. The Inn is on the left as you approach the village. You can't miss it. It's a big white inn with a wraparound porch. Dark blue shutters and door. If you need food, try The Mizzen Mast for bar food, or The Cat's Head Diner. The diner will be open for a little bit longer. It's my personal favorite," volunteered Tank.

"Only because you are in love with the woman who owns it," teased Ryker, putting Lila Rose at ease.

"Thanks for the advice. I appreciate it. Have a great day," she said awkwardly, not sure how to end the exchange.

"No problem," said Tank kindly. "You have a great day, too, and the lady who runs the Inn, Donna Riley, is a sweetheart. You'll like her. Take care." With that Ryker smiled and waved while Tank rolled up the truck window and gave a careless salute. They moved the truck on down the road while keeping an eye out making sure the young girl started her car moving and didn't stay stopped.

Lila Rose checked her mirrors and pulled out, following a considerable distance behind the Wynn Construction truck. The feeling of dread dissipated a little as she realized she'd had her first encounter with some Grey's Harbor inhabitants. They seemed normal. And a whole lot cute, she giggled to herself.

She thought for a minute about what Tank had said. She realized she was hungry. Bar food or diner? She wasn't sure but she wanted to get settled first. The diner might not still be open by the time she was ready. Her stomach growled again. She decided to get a move on.

A few minutes later, the truck in front of her slowed and a lazy arm appeared from the driver side, pointing out a rambling white inn on the bluffs above the ocean. The Harbor Inn. She tooted her horn as a thank you and waved, turning left into the long winding drive. *Nice guys*, she decided. *Probably not serial killers. Probably just normal guys with normal lives and normal families. Unlike mine*, she thought. *Mine was screwed up, and I didn't even know it.*

Her eyes welled up, threatening to spill salty tears down her cheeks. She was determined not to cry, but suddenly the task in front of her felt monumental and terrifying. The bravado she had bolstered herself up with earlier had disappeared into a cold ball in her gut. *Stop it*, she scolded herself. *You've come this far. Suck it up butter-cup, and let's find out just who the hell you are.*

She parked her car in the small gravel lot. A minute later she was walking up the wide steps of the gracious front porch, her small rolling suitcase following her like a dutiful puppy, her backpack slung carelessly across her shoulder looking like a carefree college student on her winter break from college.

* ✳ *

"This is your room," said Donna as she placed the brass key in the lock and turned the ornate doorknob. She pushed the door open allowing Lila Rose to admire the beautifully appointed room. Cornflower blue wallpaper graced the walls while creamy white trim and crown moulding added a grace not seen in modern homes.

"It's so beautiful," Lila Rose sighed. Two windows faced the ocean and a small, mullioned door between them led out onto a balcony. On a summer day Lila imagined she would spend an entire

23

lazy afternoon out there reading a book and soaking in the ocean breeze. Tonight however, the thought made her shiver. This was not a beach vacation. She was on a mission.

"Thank you," Donna replied. "This is my daughter's favorite room in the inn." She smiled indulgently, thinking of her only child who was three states away raising a family. "I always make sure she gets this one when she visits. I put her two rapscallion children in a room at the end of the hall so their momma can get a moments peace." Donna chattered on as she showed Lila Rose the room's appointments, the floral scented soaps, and where the extra towels were in the hall linen closet. She invited her to help herself to whatever she needed. Lila thanked her and smiled indulgently while wishing the woman would just leave her alone. It wasn't that the lady was annoying, it was that Lila Rose was overwhelmed and needed some space.

As soon as Donna left, Lila walked into the bathroom and started running the hot water in the beautiful claw footed tub. She looked over the various travel size bottles, presumably from some local boutique, and selected a honeysuckle bubble bath. She poured the bottle into the running water and sighed as the heavenly scent of heavy summer honeysuckle filled the room. A few minutes ago she was hungry. Now, her tummy had been forgotten, and all Lila Rose wanted to do was slip into that silky water and drown in the sweet scent.

She sank to her chin in the generous tub and closed her eyes. Steam rose around her curling the tendrils of auburn hair that had escaped from her messy bun. She knew she needed to plan her strategy, but this moment, this place put her in a space she hadn't been in months. She felt at peace, if only for a few minutes. She never believed in aroma therapy or the healing powers of certain scents, but she was being converted as she soaked.

Within minutes, Lila's breathing became a steady light snore, and she napped chin-deep in the fragrant water. Her mind began to wind its way on its own, her subconscious coming to the forefront while she slept. She was walking in a garden, the moon lighting her path. She could hear the ocean somewhere to her left, the waves a steady lapping in the dark, soft and comforting.

Ransom was waiting for her at a bench, his face shadowed, the moonlight striking the back of his head shrouding his features in darkness. She moved closer, apprehensive. She was afraid of what he might tell her. Her fear of rejection strangling her. Unable to move forward she lifted her right hand helplessly in a defeated gesture. She would never know her birth mother. She was sure of it now.

Water flowed into Lila's open mouth and she sat up quickly, choking and sputtering. The bath was tepid, no longer steaming its heavenly fragrance. The serene feeling she had earlier was gone, dread snaking its ugly tendrils into her consciousness. She sighed and her stomach growled. As much as she didn't want to move forward, she knew she couldn't stay in that tub forever.

She stood, water streaming off of her slender body as she grabbed a thick blue towel and wrapped herself in its protective warmth. She hugged herself, straightened her shoulders determined to move forward, then rubbed her body vigorously, trying to shed water and doubt at the same time.

· ✳ ·

$\mathcal{L}$ila pulled into the gravel parking lot, her tires crunching on the crushed stone. She looked up at the sign to make sure she had pulled into the right place. The Mizzen Mast. This was one of the places the guys in the truck had suggested. Donna had agreed that it would be the best choice at this time of night.

The front lot was full, so she followed around to the side where she parked near a beautiful deck that overlooked the river. Festive lights lit the railing, twinkling off the water where it ran swiftly by in the dark. As inviting as it looked, the knife-edged wind stopped all but the most die-hard smokers from spending any time out there.

Locking her car, she followed a stamped concrete walk to the front of the building. By the time she reached the front door, she was shaking with cold, her hands aching with the bite of the wind. Chiding herself for not packing warmer clothes or appropriate outdoor wear she made a mental shopping list for the next day. Gloves were on the top of that list. The door abruptly opened and a laughing couple moved past her into the night. The man held the door for Lila, and she stepped into the warmth of Izzy's bar.

The mellow strains of folk music wove through the conversations of the crowd as a lone man sat on a stool in the corner, strumming his guitar and moaning lyrics from an era long before Lila Rose, or even her parents had walked the earth. A bearded man at a table near the musician sat with a smile on his face stroking his grizzled beard. His Vietnam vet ball cap pegged him as a man who would be intimately familiar with the music the younger man was playing. Although the song was unfamiliar to Lila, the sentiment was not...the time's they are a-changin'.

When the guitarist whipped out a harmonica and started whaling, the old vet closed his eyes and cocked his head slightly as if listening to sounds of the past. Lila stared at him shamelessly. The man had walked a long road. His battles were not all obvious, but Lila Rose knew that his soul harbored demons. Hers did, too, but she chided herself. Her demons were nothing compared to this man's horror. She knew it in her heart. It gave her strength.

A woman with a quick smile greeted her. Lila Rose tried not to stare at the ink and the piercings that graced the woman's body. Lila didn't expect it here in a village like Grey's Harbor. It didn't fit her romantic vision of the seaside town. Izzy's lips quirked up, not at all offended. She was used to the stares of strangers. Sometimes she took offense if the strangers had the vibe of an asshole. This girl had the vibe of a lost puppy that may have been kicked recently. Not abused as such, just a surprise kick that left her confused and out of sorts. Izzy had a nose for those kinds of people, and this auburn-haired beauty looked just the type. And the poor thing looked cold.

"Welcome to the Mizzen Mast. Are you looking for some food or just a space at the bar?" Izzy asked kindly.

"A booth, please?" Lila Rose said shyly.

"No problem. I'm Izzy. You're not from here," she said, not unkindly.

"No ma'am, I'm not," Lila said, not volunteering more.

"Passing through?" Izzy prodded as she led Lila to a booth in the corner near the musician who had moved on to missing flowers and children.

"Yes, well, no. Actually, I'm not sure," Lila stammered, her face turning red, accentuating the smattering of freckles across her nose.

For a second, Izzy had a flash, but it was gone before she could put her finger on it. Something familiar.

"Well, it's okay to be unsure. Grey's Harbor is a good place to land for a bit. What can I get you to drink?" Izzy waited.

"I don't suppose you have hot tea?" Lila asked instantly sorry she did as she looked around the bar. "If not, that's fine," she rushed to say.

"I have several kinds of tea," Izzy assured her. "Herbal? Green? Earl Grey, or the old standby Lipton."

"Old standby," Lila said and grinned. She liked this Izzy lady.

"Coming up." Izzy handed Lila a menu and left to get her a steaming mug of tea.

Lila looked over her choices. She was hungry, but she was also beginning to feel queasy, nervous about her next step. She picked up her phone, her palms sweaty.

"Just do it," she whispered.

Shaking, her fingers tapped out the text

I'm in Grey's Harbor.

Where? Came the immediate reply. Her stomach flipped over on itself, and she closed her eyes trying to steady her nerves.

"Hey sweetie. You okay?"

Lila Rose opened her eyes to see Izzy scrutinizing her. She passed Lila the thick white mug of hot tea and sat a bottle of honey on the table next to her.

"Seriously, are you okay? I know we just met and all, but if you need something. If you need help... I'll listen."

Where are you? A chime announced the incoming text. Izzy's eyes took in the screen.

"Look, if someone is after you. If you need a safe house, I can get you help. Just say the word." Izzy's eyes flashed, ready for action.

"No, no. I'm fine. I'm safe." Lila offered a wan smile. "It's not like that. I'm just... I'm going to meet someone for the first time.

I'm going to finally see… my dad." She let that sink in, the words sounding strange on her tongue.

"Ah," Izzy smiled. "Parents separated?"

"Yes, well, no. I don't know." Lila laughed sharply. "You must think I'm a loon," she said looking up at Izzy's furrowed brow.

"Not at all. I'm guessing you're in an uncomfortable place. You want to move forward, but you're scared, and everything you have in you is telling you to run, but you don't want to. How does that sum it up?"

"Perfectly," Lila admitted.

"Have you eaten anything today?" Izzy said noting the pale, drawn face and the trembling hand.

"No," Lila admitted. "I'm starving, but my stomach is in knots."

"Okay, I'm thinking my potato soup with chunks of lobster. Comfort food at its finest."

"That sounds amazing. And maybe a salad, no dressing?"

"Coming right up." Izzy reached over and patted Lila's hand. "Honey, it's gonna be okay. And if things aren't, let me know and we'll fix it. Okay?"

Lila smiled shyly at her nodding her head.

"Now, are you going to answer that text while I get your food or no?"

Lila stared down at her phone and gave a deep breath. Then she tapped the message.

The Mizzen Mast.

CHAPTER 4

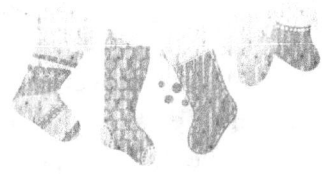

*R*ansom stared at his phone.
The Mizzen Mast.

The bar he was in last night with Joy. His mind reeled as he thought about the fact that his daughter was this close. The daughter he had never met. Never held. Never knew.

But that could change.

She was here.

And no one was stopping him from seeing her.

Where are you staying?

He waited.

Nothing.

Stupid, he thought. Of course, she wouldn't want to tell him that. She didn't know him. Didn't know if he was safe. What an idiot he was. He would never let his daughter meet a stranger, yet here he was, doing just that.

Sorry, I didn't mean to make you uncomfortable.

It's okay.

Do you want to meet now, or do you want to wait until morning? I can meet you there, or not?

He waited, trying to be patient.

I'm going to have some dinner here. At the Mizzen Mast. I'll be here for a little bit.

He took a deep breath. Should he? She beat him to it.

I hate to eat alone

He grabbed his jacket and flew out the door.

· ✳ ·

*J*oy was restless. Her early morning client had finally listened to her after the third hairstyle. As usual, Joy was tipped well, and the client went away happy. The rest of the day was a typical day in the salon. Ladies gossiped with each other, and Joy pretended to listen, nodding at the appropriate time, but her mind was elsewhere.

Luckily, her clients were used to her brusque demeanor, so they thought nothing of the fact that she wasn't totally engaged, which was fine and dandy with her.

As the day wore on, Joy felt more and more edgy. She was sure the approaching storm was playing into her mood, setting her nerves on edge, but it was more than that.

Ransom was back.

He hadn't been back since that night that she told him to go, to walk away. Well, not just told him. More like screamed at him, then said hateful things that she could never take back. That was the night that she shut the door on happiness, when the ache in her heart consumed her. When she knew she had not only lost those she loved, but she lost herself in the process.

What the hell? Tears welled up in Joy's eyes, threatening to spill down her cheeks and start a river that might never stop flowing.

"Joy, honey, are you okay?" Hope Chandler looked in the mirror at the stylist who was running a flat iron through Hope's hair. Hope was startled to see what looked like tears in Joy's bright eyes.

"Yeah, fine," Joy lied, "I think I have a piece of hair in my eye. Hang on." She put the flat iron in its holder and excused herself to the back room where she took a moment to compose herself.

What the hell just happened? She asked herself. *I don't cry. That doesn't happen to me. Not anymore.*

She pulled a spring water out of the mini-fridge and took a long pull on the bottle. She was okay now. It was just a quirk. A moment. She had work to do. She shook her head and moved back to her chair and the waiting Hope.

"All better?" Hope asked, a knowing look in her eye.

"Yep. I got it out. Thanks."

Hope was her last client of the day. Normally, Joy enjoyed her time with Hope who was one of the kindest women she knew, but today, she just wanted everyone gone. Her mind kept circling back to Ransom. She needed to think about this. It was really odd that he showed up after all these years. She didn't trust him. Something was up.

Hope paid and left, giving Joy a quick hug.

"I hope everything is okay, Joy. If you need anything, just let me know. Okay?" Hope held Joy's eyes with hers, making certain Joy knew she was sincere.

Joy was gruff, but she'd been raised right and was polite. She also recognized sincerity.

"Thanks, Hope. I appreciate that, but I really am fine. Just a weird day. I think the nor'easter has me jumpy.

"It has us all jumpy. I know Bridger has started moving boats trying to make sure they are safe from any storm surge. He says it's going to be a bad one."

"I think Bridger's right. I wonder about the timing of this."

"No kidding," said Hope coming to a realization the same time as Joy. "Oh no, Alexandria and Gabe's wedding…"

"Uh oh. This could get interesting," Joy said as she started thinking about the updo's she would be doing for the wedding.

"Maybe it'll blow over," said Hope. "Finger's crossed." She gave Joy another quick hug and stepped out the door into the cold.

Joy turned the lock as she closed the door. She turned the sign to closed and moved through the shop making sure everything was sanitized and secure. Then she pulled her coat off the hook in the back room and made her way out the into the night.

※

*T*he wind lifted Joy's long auburn hair, whipping the ends into tangles, but she didn't care. She flipped up the collar of her leather jacket and wound the wool scarf around her neck, cutting out the cold. She needed to walk.

She made her way down Main Street ignoring the festive decorations of the season. The garlands that draped across the streets twinkling with white lights were being tossed wildly like a grotesque carnival ride. The old-fashioned lamp posts were twisted with garlands of fresh greens and red ribbons which were beginning to show tattered ends from the never-ending onslaught of the wind.

She continued down the street toward the Mizzen Mast. She hadn't eaten all day, but she still wasn't ready. As she reached the boardwalk that led to the beach she turned toward the ocean.

In minutes she was on the open beach, the wind buffeted against her chest, actually making her stagger. She caught her breath with the cold, ducked her head against the wind and trudged into the frozen sand.

The waves roared around her, crashing in sets, one louder than the other. Clouds raced through the sky obscuring the moon one minute then flying away, allowing the beach to be lit up in the full moon's brilliance only to be plunged in darkness again with the next layer of clouds.

Joy knew not to get too close to the pounding surf. Not only was it freezing and getting wet could be a death sentence, but a rogue wave could hit the beach further than any of the others and knock her down, pulling her out to sea.

Cat wouldn't like that. After all, who would open the stinky pouches and pour the disgusting gravy mess into his dish? The thought of caring for her cat brought fresh tears flooding her eyes.

There was another time when Joy cared for something. Something precious. But she gave that away. She gave up her chance to care for and love and be loved back. She destroyed that. Once she did that, the cutting of the final ties was easy. She turned her back on Ransom. She forced him away. She couldn't look in his eyes and remember.

A sob tore through her throat bubbling up from the depths of her soul. Once that sob escaped, another one followed until her body was wracked with shudders, tears racing down her cheeks, matting her eyelashes, making her face even colder.

She didn't know how long she stood there. She just knew that with her last hiccup, she was spent. There was nothing left in her soul. *Like a bad hangover*, she thought. *Ya think you have nothing left in you and then you dry heave some more.* She drew a shuddering breath and tried to settle herself, but there was nothing left to settle. She was an empty husk, dry, and dusty.

She turned and walked back to the board walk then turned away from the Mizzen Mast. Food no longer interested her. She just wanted to crawl in bed and sleep. To escape the present and just sleep.

CHAPTER 5

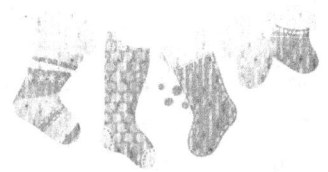

*R*ansom tore open the door to the Mizzen Mast and scanned the crowd. She was here somewhere. He didn't want to appear too eager, not wanting to scare her, but he had waited so long.

Izzy's head snapped up from the bar, sensing a change in her atmosphere. Ransom Wheeler stood in the doorway, haunted eyes searching.

Click.

It all fell into place. She knew exactly who the young stranger reminded her of, and she also knew why she had felt that the storm was about to get worse.

"Hey, Ransom. Here for dinner?" Izzy asked. She waited a beat before she finished, "or are you looking for someone?"

Ransom's eyes snapped to Izzy's.

"She's over in the corner." Izzy gestured with her chin. "Take it slow. She's skittish and confused. It's none of my business, but I suggest you put on the kid gloves and don't push."

"Thank you, Izzy. Joy said you were good people. She was right."

"I can also be a force to be reckoned with. Don't hurt the people I love."

"You know Lila Rose?" he asked, confused.

"No, but I love this town and the people who belong to it. That includes Joy and now Lila Rose by proxy, doesn't it?" she said, her meaning clear.

"You know?"

"It wasn't hard to figure out. She has Joy's beauty. Now go introduce yourself to your daughter."

⋅ ⚹ ⋅

*L*ila Rose looked up from her steaming bowl of potato soup to see a tall, lean man walking toward her. He hands were shoved in the front pockets of his low-slung jeans. His dark brown eyes were intense, and his longish brown hair looked like he had run his hands through it just recently because it was slightly messy, but still fell where it belonged.

He stopped in front of her table, hesitant to come any closer. He gave her a half smile, then shrugged and lifted his hand in a half-hearted wave.

"Lila Rose?" he asked, although he already knew.

"Ransom." She didn't ask. She was looking at her birth father.

He nodded.

"Yes, ma'am, I'm Ransom. I'm the man who fathered you. I won't presume to say I'm your daddy. I didn't get that privilege, nor will I take that honor from the man who did the job for me."

"Thank you," she whispered. "I loved him. He was a fine man and a wonderful father." Her eyes filled with tears.

Ransom didn't know what to do.

"I'm sorry," she said, and she roughly swiped at the tears with the back of her hand. "Please, sit." She gestured toward the seat opposite of her. He slid into the booth, his eyes never leaving her face, drinking in every inch of her; the curve of her mouth, the long lashes, green eyes, the sun-kissed freckles. Joy, only softer, more vulnerable. Like Joy before.

"What?" she asked, becoming uncomfortable with his scrutiny.

"You're beautiful," he said softly. He smiled, his heart breaking at the time he'd lost, the lifetime that had passed.

"Thank you," she said.

It was quiet then. Neither one knowing how to progress.

Izzy broke the silence.

"So, Ransom, would you like some potato soup, too? It has chucks of lobster."

"Yes, please. That sounds wonderful. Some bread or rolls, too?" he asked.

"That's a lot of carbs," Lila Rose suggested.

"No such thing," Ransom shot back. Izzy nodded in agreement. "And Izzy, do you have root beer?"

"I do. Naked Beach Brewery has a root beer. Non-alcoholic and delicious."

"Sounds perfect. I'll have that," Ransom smiled at her, grateful for her perfect timing and intrusion to end the awkward silence.

"More tea, Lila Rose?"

"I'm thinking I might like a root beer, too, please."

"Coming right up." Izzy winked and patted Lila's arm.

A minute later Izzy plopped two bottles on the table after lifting the caps. Mist poured from the frosty necks. Lila Rose stared at the label.

"Randy Rockfish Root Beer?" She sputtered laughing at the hand drawn picture of a fish in sunglasses, lounging in a chaise on the beach oogling a girl in a bikini walking by.

"Yeah, the boys at Naked Beach are a goofy bunch. They get more outrageous with each new name. I thought they would quit after Sperm Whale Ale, but no such luck." Izzy shrugged and left to get Ransom's soup.

Ransom tipped his bottle toward Lila Rose. She clinked his and grinned. He grinned back. The ice was broken. Now they could go on and get to know each other

CHAPTER 6

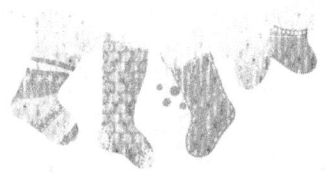

$\mathcal{R}$*ing.*
Joy moaned, swimming up out of a deep sleep.

Ring…Ring

The cat sighed, angry he was being disturbed by the offending sound.

Ring.

"What?" Joy said out loud, reaching out an arm for her phone but contacting an angry cat instead, who bit her hand then jumped off the bed before she could retaliate.

"Asshole, cat," she yelled.

Ring.

"What the hell? What?" She said into the phone still disoriented and pissed at being awakened. She glanced at the clock as she waited for the human on the other end of the line to recover from her gruff greeting. It was only ten o'clock pm.

"Hello, Joy? Are you okay?"

Ransom.

Damn it.

"Yeah," she said, not wanting to volunteer more.

"Joy, we have to talk."

"No, we don't."

"No, we really do. It's important. Really, really important."

"Ransom, there is nothing you can say to me that will change my mind." She moved to ring off, but his next words stopped her.

"Joy, do you know what I do for a living?"

Her heart started pounding, but she didn't know why. All she knew was this sounded dangerous. Like it was going to hurt her.

"Did you hear me?"

"I did, and no, I don't."

"I find missing children." He let that sink in.

Now her heart was racing, beating against her chest, actually causing pain. She couldn't catch her breath. *What was he saying? What was he implying?*

"And?" She couldn't believe she asked him.

"And we need to talk. Can I meet you? Is there a place we can go... to talk?"

She didn't want it. She didn't want him back in her world. She didn't want him tainting her space.

"You can come here," she heard herself say, and with those words she knew she was lost. She would never be okay again.

She realized she was holding her phone, but Ransom was no longer on the other end. He was on his way and nothing could stop what was coming.

· ⁎ ·

She pulled on a pair of ratty sweats and a beaten up hoody. It was old, but it was comforting. It wasn't inviting. It didn't suggest. It was a lifeless lump of cotton fleece that matched her, covered her, held her.

She waited for him, sitting in her chair, looking out the window, straining to see the ocean in the distance. She knew it was there. That's all that mattered. To know that out there, even though she couldn't see it that the sea was still there, alive, thriving, a force to be reckoned with. She counted on that. Even if she turned her back and walked away, the ocean would still be there. Waiting for her.

· ⁎ ·

a soft knock at her door, and a voice.

"Joy?"

"It's unlocked," she said, not leaving the chair. Not meeting him halfway.

The doorknob turned and Ransom stood in the open doorway waiting politely to be invited in. When it didn't happen, he stepped into the room and closed the door. In his hands he held two paper coffee cups.

"I brought you coffee. I added chocolate syrup and cream, just like you used to like. Do you still drink it that way?"

Despite herself, the corner of her lip tipped up ever so slightly. He remembered, after nineteen years, he remembered. She had given up the habit, but the memory comforted her, so she reached out her hand and accepted the peace offering.

"Thank you," she said and she took a tentative sip. It was perfect. Of course.

When he handed her the cup, his fingers brushed hers. It hurt him to feel how cold her hands were. She looked broken, wounded, and he wanted to take her in his arms and fix it, but he knew that was impossible. She wouldn't allow it, and he wouldn't hurt her again. He should never have left. Even though she had insisted, he should have stayed. He was young. They were stupid. He was idealistic. She was realistic. Those two things didn't work. He felt betrayed.

Now, he realized why she did what she did. She was right. They weren't ready. But still, he could have made it work. But he didn't. He left. He should have fought.

She raised her eyes to meet his. His tough, feisty, fiery, redhead was a broken bird in her nest, unwilling to move. He crouched in front of her, setting his coffee on the floor. He took hers from her hands and set it down next to his. Then he took her hands in his and began to speak.

"I left Grey's Harbor, left you, left everything and walked away. I needed to find myself, to find a new start." He waited, making sure he had eye contact. That she was listening.

She was.

"I landed in a small town in Tennessee where I did odd jobs and day labor. I lived on an old lady's back porch in exchange for yard work and grocery runs. Once I got on my feet I went through the training and became a police officer.

"After a few years there, I was restless. I knew there was more, so I applied to another police force and moved to a larger town. Bigger challenges, bigger problems. I made detective and began working the seedier side of life. I saw things that scared me. I saw girls, runaways who could only make ends meet by working the streets. I was put on a task force investigating human trafficking. I made it my purpose to find those missing girls. To try to bring them home, or at least bring them into the light. The whole time I did this, I thought of our baby, my daughter. I wondered where she was, who she was. I hoped she was happy, but I was afraid. What if this happened to our girl? What if she wasn't safe? It made me a little crazy. The funny thing is, I couldn't find her. I found lots of girls, but not my own." He paused, taking a deep breath. "Then, one day, she found me."

He stopped talking and watched Joy react to that. She was hanging onto every word. He handed her the cup so she could take a sip. She obliged. He carefully put the cup down and took her hands again. He spied a small footstool off to the side. He stood and slid it with his foot so he could sit, easing the cramping in his thighs.

"The thing is, I left her a letter. Just like you did."

Joy gasped, her face changing. He'd never told her that. She didn't even know it was an option. He kept that from her.

That was unforgivable.

Ransom watched the transformation. The jaw hardening. Her eyes narrowing. Her nostrils flaring slightly.

Good. She was angry. It meant she felt something.

"Why didn't you tell me?" Her voice was steel.

"Because you wouldn't have liked it. Because you already removed me from her life and from yours. Because I had a choice, too. Joy, you gave away our baby. I made sure I didn't abandon her." He was angry, too, but the minute the words left his mouth he knew they were the wrong ones. They were the right ones for him, but the wrong ones for her to hear.

"I. DID. NOT. ABANDON. HER." She spit the words at him, those magnificent green eyes flashing. She was good and pissed now. The fight was on. "I gave her a life. I gave her hope. I gave her all the things I couldn't give her myself."

She had half risen from the chair, her hands balled in fists, rage radiating from her.

"God damn it. I LOVED HER!" And then she broke. Her fists dropped to her side and she slumped, still standing, bent, broken, and sobbing for the second time in twelve hours her body shuddered in pain.

Ransom stood and wrapped his arms around her, pulling her to his chest. He reached to smooth her hair, but she straightened and fought like a wildcat, tearing at him with her nails, pounding his chest, ripping at his clothes, anything she could do to hurt him, to wound him so he could understand her pain.

He did understand. It was Joy that didn't. The pain wasn't only hers. She didn't have a monopoly on broken. She ripped his soul from him, but he stood there and took it, because that is what he did, and when she was spent, panting, face wet with tears, he gathered her again and rocked her against his chest. This time she collapsed into him and cried quietly against his shirt.

"I loved her, too, Joy," he said softly. "Losing the both of you destroyed me." His arms tightened around her, trying to let her feel his love. Love that had never completely died. Love that still sparked, that was still reserved for her, and for his little girl.

**

"*Y*ou have a cat?" Ransom asked his lips brushing the top of Joy's glossy hair. She hiccupped a little and nodded. "But you hate cats."

"Yeah well, life happens," she muttered. "He needed someone..." her voice faded off.

And so did you. He stroked her hair, his heart squeezing, knowing he should have never left her.

"What's her or his name?" he asked.

"Cat. He."

"Cat? You named him Cat?"

"No, well, yes. I mean that's what I call him when I address him." As it came out of her mouth she realized just how lame it sounded. She sighed. Giving a name makes it yours. It's better not to name it. Her heart squeezed at the thought of Rose. Her Rose. The baby she named. The baby she gave away. And damn it, the tears flowed fresh.

Ransom looked down at Joy's tear stained face and turned her, leading her to the couch where he deposited her. He saw a hand crocheted throw tossed over the back. Pulling it off, he tucked it around her and under her chin. The coffee was ice cold. That wasn't going to help, so he reached down to pick up the cat, intending to put it in her lap to give her comfort.

"NO! Don't!" But it was too late. With lethal claws extended, the cat swiped at Ransom's hand leaving four lines bubbling with blood. "He doesn't like that."

"No kidding," Ransom said ruefully. He regarded the cat.

The cat regarded him, licking his front claws. There was a gleam in his eye.

The bastard liked the taste of blood.

"Did you ever consider a nice dog instead?" Ransom asked from the kitchen where he was rummaging around looking for tea in the cupboard.

"Not really. Cat and I have an understanding. We share a roof. In the evening, I pet him and provide him a lap."

Ransom put the kettle on the stove and came back to sit on the couch next to Joy. She reached over and lifted his hand, looking at the wound her cat had inflicted. Ransom held perfectly still. Her soft fingers held his hand lightly. He had forgotten just how good that felt.

She had a cat.

He had nothing.

Silence hung in the air, neither of them wanting to pick up the thread of conversation that lay untangled on the floor between them. Ransom was surprised Joy didn't jump on the fact that he knew where their daughter was. He was very wary of her next reaction. He wasn't even sure if she could handle the knowledge that their daughter was in Grey's Harbor wanting to meet her birth mother. Needing to meet her.

He couldn't screw this up.

The tea kettle whistled, its cheerful sound at odds with the mood. Ransom sighed. There were three days left until Christmas. This should be the most joyful time of the year, and he had just helped to destroy a woman, a woman he had loved with every fiber of his being. A woman he still loved even if he was unwilling to admit it out loud.

CHAPTER 7

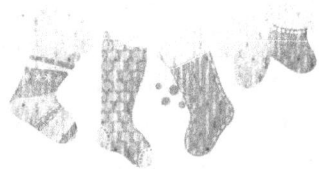

"So, you know where she is?" Joy looked out under her lashes, her fingers entwined around the mug of tea, the throw tucked around her. She looked young and haunted. She looked beaten.

"I do." Ransom waited, watching her.

"Does she know about me?"

"She does. She has your letter." He wanted to tell her so much, but it wasn't his place. His conversation with Lila was his. It was up to Lila to let Joy in. He wouldn't intrude or impose himself in that story.

"Does she hate me?" The words were barely a whisper, and when Joy had finished them she felt faint with fear. Despite the warmth from the mug, her fingers were frozen, her soul, ice.

"No," but then, he didn't know that. They didn't talk about that, but he couldn't not say it. He had to make that true.

"There's something you don't want to tell me." And now her voice was dead, all hope spent. She knew Ransom. Despite the years lost between them, she still knew him. They had been one. They had been the world to each other.

"Joy, it's not my story to tell. It's not my place. The two of you have to come to that place together."

"I don't know if I can." When the words left her mouth, she realized just how true they were. She had dreamt of meeting her daughter, of finding that beautiful child she had given away. Well, if the truth be told, the child who had been taken from her arms while she tried to hold tightly to the warm bundle without crushing the precious contents. Her fingers clutching, begging for the baby to be placed back in her arms so she could take in the sweet smell of her head, feel the faint breath from her perfectly bowed lips. When the case worker turned and left the room, Joy had collapsed to the floor, inconsolable. No one could reason with her. She sobbed on the hard terrazzo squares in the cold hospital, her body sore, bleeding, and her breasts aching for the child who would never suckle there.

Her mother, hurting herself as she watched her granddaughter being removed from her life turned to her daughter, straightening her back as she spoke. "Okay, nothing's to be done about it. Time to move on. Get off the floor, Joy, and get back to living." With that she turned and walk out of the room, leaving her daughter to mourn on the floor.

Deck the halls with boughs of holly, fa la la la la la la la la....

Outside, snow had begun to fall, swirling madly in the north wind while the youth group from Grey's Harbor Methodist Church bravely tried to carol down Main Street, their sweet voices lifting up to Joy's lit window.

'Tis the season to be jolly, fa la la la la la la la la

Joy snorted, cynicism dripping, the walls beginning to build around her again, protecting her from the pain that had been at the fringes for nineteen years.

Ransom stood and walked to the window. Eight children of varying ages and heights huddled together singing the happy carol. He waved down at them and mimed applause. They happily waved back and turned to move on, seemingly oblivious to the miserable weather they were fighting, the adult chaperones were not faring as well. Their shoulders were hunched against the wind, visions of hot toddies floating in their heads.

Ransom moved back and sat on the couch next to Joy. *What the hell*, he thought as he moved his arm around her shoulders and pulled her close. She didn't resist. Together they sipped their tea and didn't talk, each lost in their own thoughts. The wind howled, rattling the windows, and the snow continued to pile up outside.

· ✳ ·

*R*ansom woke up to an extremely warm lap and a dead arm. Joy snored softly against his chest. Cat lay on his lap looking into Ransom's eyes, daring him to move. A clock somewhere in the apartment chimed three times.

Cat blinked and yawned allowing Ransom to contemplate the cat's fangs.

His body was cramping up, but he didn't want to disturb Joy, and he wasn't taking a chance with Cat . He considered easing them all back against the arm of the couch so he could lay down and stretch out while still holding Joy, but he couldn't figure out how to do it without disturbing the vicious beast in his lap.

"Getting stiff?" Joy's voice floated up to him, sleepy, vulnerable.

Sheesh woman, he grimaced. "Kinda," he admitted. He didn't want her to move. He was enjoying the memories of them sleeping together, always entwined like they couldn't get enough of each other's bodies. But if he didn't move, he was going to have a charley horse, and that would not be the way he wanted Joy to extricate herself from his arms, nor the cat for that matter. He had a feeling startling the cat would be a very bad idea.

Joy sat up, her tousled mane framing her face, sleep messy, and very sexy. Her question came back to him and his body responded.

The cat looked surprised.

Cat stood, staring Ransom in the face, and started kneading his lap, delicately extending his claws, just enough to make a point.

"Damn you cat," Ransom swore as Cat gracefully jumped to the floor, leaving an exclamation point with his back claws on Ransom's privates.

Joy giggled.

The cat smiled.

Joy stood and stretched, reaching for the ceiling, her sweatshirt raising with her arms, her flat belly exposed. Ransom remembered that belly button. He remembered his hands spanning her waist, marveling at how tiny she was, and then amazed at how her belly grew, full and round, holding their baby. He wanted to touch that belly again. He wanted to blow softly against that sexy slit of a navel.

"Damn." Joy stood staring out the window.

"What's wrong?" Ransom jumped up, concerned at the new distress in Joy's voice.

"We're buried."

"What are you talking about?" Ransom walked over to the window where Joy was now, her arms hugging her midriff. She shivered.

"We're buried in snow," she said, stating what was now obvious to both of them. The snow was coming down so hard the buildings across the street were obliterated from view. Wind drove the flakes hard against the window, plastering the wet mess against the frame, making small drifts along the outside sill. The Christmas decorations on the streetlights no longer looked festive but bent under the high winds and heavy snow. The cars parked on the street, those belonging to the down town dwellers in the antique apartments above the old businesses, were completely buried under the white stuff.

"It looks like we got three feet," Ransom said in awe. "That's unheard of here."

"No kidding," Joy murmured, realizing that it could be days before the roads were cleared, as the town of Grey's Harbor had no need of a snowplow. Deep snow was rare, and when it happened, the county plows did the job when they got around to it, if the snow hadn't melted first.

"The wedding," Joy said, suddenly realizing what all this snow meant.

"What wedding?"

"Alex and Gabe. They're getting married today. I'm doing Alex's hair."

"I have my doubts about that happening," said Ransom as he gazed down the street. Huge drifts snaked between the buildings and across the road like the dunes on the beach, the crossroads making a channel for even bigger drifts. Nope, no one was going anywhere. Ransom's mind flipped to his daughter. He hoped she was tucked in safe and sound at the Inn. He wanted to text her, but it was 3:30 in the morning. She had taken care of herself so far, she would be fine, he reassured himself.

Joy sighed. She didn't want to think about Alex's hair or a wedding for that matter. All the chatter of a bridal party was the last thing she needed right now. What she needed was to think about her daughter. What Ransom had told her. What it meant.

She shivered again, but not from the cold. She was exhausted and her nerves were strung tight. Ransom came up behind her and slid his arms around her.

She stiffened.

He dropped his arms.

"I'm sorry, Joy. I didn't mean…"

"It's okay. I don't know what to feel right now. I don't know what to think or what to do. Do you know how many years I waited for you to come back to me? How I would catch a glimpse of a man in cowboy boots and my heart would hope it was you, but I knew it wasn't. That it wasn't ever going to be you. You walked out on me, Ransom. You walked out when I needed you the most." She didn't turn to look at him. She was still looking out the window, not trusting herself to look into his eyes.

"I know, Joy. I'm sorry. I wish I never would have left, but I was hurting, too. I think I hurt more that you could ever imagine. I know you were her momma, but damn it, I was her daddy. I was supposed to protect her as she grew up. I was supposed to teach her to ride a bike and skip stones, and surf fish. I was supposed to fix the skinned knee. I was supposed to make sure her boyfriends treated her right and I was supposed to run off the bad ones. That was my job, and it was taken from me."

"I was supposed to fix her skinned knee," Joy said softly.

"What?"

"That was my job. The knee fixin'. The boyfriend thing was yours." She sniffled, realizing everything they had lost together.

He put his arms around her again and this time she let him.

⁕⁕⁕

"You did agree," Joy said as they lay together in her bed. There was no way Ransom was going anywhere that night, and they both needed sleep. They didn't need to share their bodies, but they did need to share their memories, so they lay under the covers and talked as their eyelids got heavier and their burdens a little lighter.

"I know. I didn't think I had a choice."

"I didn't think I did either." And for the umpteenth time that night, tears slid down her cheeks. Her eyes were gritty from crying and her heart couldn't possibly break any further.

"Come here," Ransom said as he pulled her into his chest, settling her tiny frame against him like they had done so many times so many years ago. "Sleep honey. We'll figure out what to do next in the morning."

"Together?" she asked, as she fell asleep and wasn't any longer responsible for what words escaped her lips.

CHAPTER 8

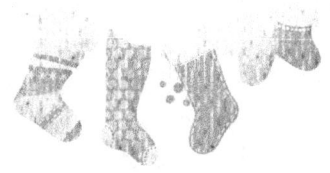

$\mathcal{L}$ ila Rose's eyes flew open. The room was filled with a strange light and the sound of wind screaming outside mixed with the crashing of the waves on the shore. She was astounded to see the windows were completely covered in snow and the tip of her nose was cold. She snuggled under the down comforter, grateful for the warmth.

Today was the day.

At least, that was her plan. Today was the day she was going to meet her birth mother, whether her birth mother wanted to meet her or not. Lila Rose still wasn't sure how she was going to do it. Ransom told her he would break the ice for her. She wondered how he told Joy. What kind of shock it had been. Part of her wanted to do the telling, but most of her was grateful Ransom had taken that burden from her.

The windows rattled, demanding to be noticed. It seemed that there was a snowstorm, but this was the North Carolina coast. *How bad could it be?*

A big gust of wind and a loud bang outside begged to differ. Apparently, it could be very bad.

Lila rolled over and pulled the covers over her head. She needed to get up and take a shower. Donna told her breakfast would be available from seven until nine. Usually, Lila Rose didn't eat break-fast, but the scent of cinnamon wafting into her room made her stomach rumble. Coffee and a cinnamon something sounded really good.

Her hand snaked out from under the covers and snagged her cellphone from the nightstand. A quick check revealed a disap-pointing lack of text messages. Ransom hadn't gotten back to her. A twinge of nerves started. She hadn't really faced the fact that her birth mother might not want anything to do with her. What if Joy didn't want her life disrupted? Ransom never said if Joy was married or had a family. *Oh God, what if she was a horrible secret that Joy needed to keep hidden from her husband and children?*

A tear slipped down Lila's cheek. She really hadn't considered what showing up on her birth mother's doorstep might mean to the woman's life. She had been so shocked herself to discover she had been adopted and had another mother somewhere, but she hadn't thought beyond her own needs and wants. Now she felt really bad. Despite the bravado she had bolstered herself up with the last couple of months, she was not that tough. She was a kind, caring young lady who usually put others first. Since her parents died, she moved through life in a haze, just trying to survive and keep herself together. This was the first time in her life she had been selfish.

She slipped out of bed, placing her bare feet on the floor. Instantly she recoiled. The floor was freezing. In fact, the room was really freezing. Was she nuts, or could she see her breath? No, not nuts. That was a little frozen cloud in front of her face. *What the hell?* She didn't bring slippers, so she dug into her overnight back and pulled out a pair of cabin socks. Her feet were grateful. Something must have happened to the heat. She wondered if that meant some-thing had happened to the hot water, too. She decided to throw on her leggings and a heavy sweater, then go downstairs to figure out what was going on. Now she was really looking forward to that cup of coffee and cinnamon something.

*****

"There you are dear." Donna ushered Lila Rose to the giant dining room, gesturing to a sideboard laden with breakfast food. A large coffee urn held promise. "I hope you like dark roast. We like our coffee strong around these parts, and this is one of our local roaster's best darks."

"Dark roast is perfect." Lila Rose's eyes darted around knowing full well there was no hope of chocolate syrup anywhere, but a mocha would be perfect on this snowy morning. When she had descended the staircase, she looked out the landing window and was blown away by the amount of snow that had fallen. Not only was the world blanketed in white. It was literally buried. She spotted her car in the parking lot, but a drift had obliterated the front end. She wasn't going anywhere today. That hit her hard. She stood on the landing and just stared. The knowledge that she wasn't going to meet her birth mother because of the storm had deflated her, and now she really could use some damn chocolate syrup.

Donna's voice brought her back to the present.

"We have some sausages in the first chafer and Belgian waffles in the next. There's some real New England maple syrup for those waffles, or, if you're like me, you like them topped with whipped cream and chocolate sauce. She gestured to a small silver pot with a ladle. Lila Rose peeked in it. *Hallelujah, chocolate syrup.* "I also made my famous cinnamon rolls, so that rounds out the sweet tooth offerings. If you prefer eggs, I make them to order, and there is oatmeal available, too."

Lila glanced around at the other diners, some seated at the large family style table, others sitting at smaller tables placed in the room adjacent to the formal dining room. A fire blazed merrily in the huge fireplace in the front room, while large windows afforded views of the snow-covered dunes and the raging sea.

"Why is it so cold upstairs? Is the heat out?"

"No. It might be chilly because the crazy weather, but it shouldn't be cold. I'll have maintenance check for you, but with this storm, it's tough to keep this old place cozy. Help yourself to breakfast. Did you want eggs before I check your room?"

"No, I think I'm going to just have coffee and a cinnamon roll but thank you."

Donna scurried away while Lila Rose picked up a lovely blue mug off the pegs on the wall rack. She poured her coffee and took it over to the warm chocolate syrup, adding half a ladleful. Then she topped it with a squirt of whipped cream. She took a sip. *Damn, that was good.* She moseyed down the sideboard taking in the scents of the various breakfast foods but stopped short in front of the cinnamon rolls. She couldn't believe the size of them. She had never seen any rolls so big. Creamy icing lay thick on the tops, and as she placed one on her plate, she marveled at the soft elastic texture. She knew she was in for a treat.

· ❋ ·

*L*ila wandered through the dining room and found a small room to the side that was empty of people but showcased a small ornate fireplace. *How many fireplaces did this place have?* She crossed to a wing chair next to the roaring blaze and sank into it gratefully. Peace and quiet was what she was looking for. A small side table with coasters was a perfect place to set her breakfast. She smiled to herself. Her mom would be happy that she took care to use the coasters, especially as a guest. Her heart pinged. She missed her mom. She was still miffed that Mom never told her that she was adopted, but then again, think of Mom. What would it be like to admit to your child you're not her real mom? *No, not true. She is my real mom. Joy is my birth mom. Big difference.* She sighed into her coffee. *I wish you would have just told me, Mom.*

"Excuse me, but are you okay?" A warm, deep voice brought her out of her thoughts. She swiped at her tears and looked up into the troubled deep brown eyes of the man who stood in front of her, holding a mug of his own.

"Yes, I'm fine thank you. Just had a moment," she stammered, not sure what to say to this stranger.

"Do you mind if I share the fire?" He gestured at the second winged chair on the opposite side of the little side table.

"No, not at all. Please, sit."

He settled into the chair and took a sip of his coffee, looking over the rim, studying her. She considered the cinnamon roll, then threw caution to the wind and dove in.

"How is it?"

She looked up at him and grinned.

"It is absolutely amazing. I hate dry cinnamon rolls, but this one is moist and elastic. It's a piece of heaven."

"Really? Well that's my department, so I'll have to give one a try." He reached his right hand toward her. "I'm Dave."

She took the proffered hand and shook it solemnly.

"Lila Rose," she said. "How is heaven your department?"

"Well, I'm not a funeral director, so what's left?"

"Priest? Father Dave?"

"Close. Reverend Dave." He set his coffee down and made his way back to the sideboard where he snagged a cinnamon roll for himself. Glancing over at Lila Rose, he picked up a second napkin.

"Here you go." He grinned as she looked at her sticky fingers knowing she was wondering how she was going to handle that gracefully.

"Thanks," she said, her freckled face coloring slightly while she wiped the gooey icing from her fingertips. "I have to admit, I'm a bit discombobulated lately." She took a sip of her coffee, embarrassed that she admitted that to a stranger.

"We all get that way once in a while." He smiled, encouraging her to keep talking. "And you're right, these are amazing."

She smiled back at him and took a sip of her coffee.

"So, what's got you all out of sorts?" He settled back and studied the pastry in his hand.

"Considering my life has completely turned upside down, it's not a surprise." She shocked herself that she actually said that. "And now I'm sitting here wondering where I should go from here. I'm in a strange town, nowhere left to go, everyone I loved is gone, and I don't know if my real mom wants to meet me or not." *Shit, there go the tears.* She dabbed her cheeks with the sticky napkin leaving a smear of frosting under one eye.

"Well, that would be enough to mess with even the strongest of souls," Dave said as he produced a clean napkin and gently wiped her tears and the spot of frosting he found incredibly endearing. "Why don't you start at the beginning? I have nowhere to go at the moment, and it looks like you could use a friendly ear. I'm a pro at that."

Lila Rose stared at the fire, thoughts swirling in her head like the snow outside the windows. It would feel so good to unload, and who better than a kind stranger who she would never see again? She took a deep breath that escaped her lips with a slight shudder.

"My parents died not too terribly long ago." She raised her hand to wave off his condolences. "My heart is broken, but I am dealing with that like any other person would. I thought I was alone in the world, with no one, and that was scary. But then I discovered some things in my mom's personal papers. Apparently, I was adopted. My parents never told me." She stopped needing to gather her thoughts.

"You feel betrayed." It was a statement, not a question.

"I do."

"That's completely normal, and that doesn't make you disloyal to the memory of your parents."

Lila Rose stared at the reverend. He hit the nail on the head. It wasn't just that she felt betrayed. She felt guilty for feeling betrayed, like she was letting her dead parents down.

"Yeah, you're right, but that's easy to say. It's hard to shake that feeling."

"Expect that to take a while. Let yourself have time to come to grips with that, just like you're giving yourself time to heal from their deaths. Bereavement covers a lot of events, not just a death."

"With the adoption papers were two letters. One from my birth mother and one from the man who conceived me. My mother just signed her first name, my father not only signed his name, but he gave his address at the time. He lived here, in Grey's Harbor. I was conceived here, in this little seaside town." She gave a short bitter laugh. "It should seem romantic, a quaint little seaside town, a high school romance, but here we are in a town buried in snow, bitterly cold, the sea a beast out there and it's Christmas and I'm alone, so there's that." She shook her head. "And now I sound like a whiny brat."

Dave sat his coffee down and took her hands in his. They were so small, and frozen. He put them together to help warm them between his. He looked at her steadily until she brought her eyes up to meet his, hers bright with tears.

"Lila Rose, you are never alone. I have faith in God, and I hope you do, but I also have faith in people. There are good people everywhere, but you need to reach out."

"I found my father," she whispered. "He met me last night."

"He still lives in Grey's Harbor? That was fortunate."

"No, he didn't...doesn't. I was able to track him down, and I contacted him. He agreed to meet me here. I told him I wanted to meet my birth mom. He said he would help me do that, and I agreed to come here, to meet him, and I hope, to meet her. She never left Grey's Harbor."

"So, where do we stand?" he asked, determined to help this lost child, because that is what she looked like right now.

"I have no idea. When I left Ransom last night, he said he was going to talk to my birth mom, kinda break the ice for me. I haven't heard from him since."

Ransom. Dave had only ever heard of one person with that name. Pops' grandson, Ransom Wheeler. Dave had been just a kid when his parents used to take him to Pops' fish frys. He remembered marveling at the older boy, Ransom's, cowboy boots, always wishing for a pair of his own. One Christmas, Santa brought him a pair. They weren't nearly as spiffy as Ransom's, but boy was he proud of those boots. Who was the girl that was always on Ransom's arm? He looked over at Lila Rose, and suddenly it hit him. Joy Stewart, the wild girl with the long red hair and the infectious laugh. Lila Rose was the spitting image of her mom.

"What do you think I should do?" Her voice brought him out of his reverie to the present and the worried eyes looking to him for direction. A gust of wind rattled the windows and Lila shivered. He was looking at a fragile, broken girl who was trying very hard to hold it together.

"Well, the weather is awful, so I'm not surprised that you haven't heard anything yet. Have you tried calling Ransom?"

"No. I wanted to wait, to give him time, but maybe a text?" She looked to him for approval.

"I think a text would be appropriate. Maybe just ask if everything is okay." He let go of her hands and encouraged her to complete the task, making note of her trembling fingers.

"Okay, I sent it. Now I wait. So," she continued brightly, "tell me about you."

Dave recognized that she wanted to take attention away from the phone and the waiting for a reply.

"Well, I grew up here in Grey's Harbor. I left to go to seminary. I'm here to attend a wedding this afternoon, but I don't know…" his voice trailed off as he looked out the window. "I think today is up in the air for a lot of people." He smiled at her and his eyes crinkled at the corners.

He must smile a lot. The thought startled her, coming out of nowhere.

"I guess both of us are just going to have to wait to find out what today holds, huh?"

She smiled and nodded, suddenly feeling a tiny bit better.

CHAPTER 9

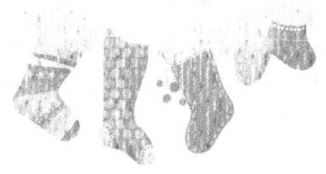

"Crap!"

Joy jumped out of bed and headed for the shower at record speed.

"What's wrong?" Ransom, disoriented, looked around for danger wondering just what he needed to protect Joy from.

"I need to do a bridal party!" she yelled from the bathroom as she turned on the shower.

"Wow, do you realize how that sounds?" Ransom teased as he slid out of bed and worked the kinks out of his back. His eyes were closed as he stretched. That's why he missed the slipper hurtling its way through space before it connected neatly with his forehead.

"Don't be an ass," she yelled as she jumped in the shower.

Ransom walked to the window and noted the lack of any snow removal taking place. He doubted Joy was going anywhere to do a bridal party.

He made his way to the kitchen and started to scrounge around, trying to scrape together something for breakfast. Her cupboards and refrigerator were seriously lacking. Eggs, bagels, and muenster cheese. It was a start.

"Don't tell me you're making bagel sandwiches without ham."

Joy came up behind Ransom. She smelled of flowers and spice. *Steady.* He told himself.

"I didn't see any ham."

"Move." Joy bumped him aside with her hip and opened the deli drawer. "Ham."

She moved to grind some coffee beans and Joe melted butter in a skillet. They worked in a companionable silence, slipping into a rhythm they had known many, many years before.

Her back was to Ransom as she poured the coffee. She stopped and stared, watching the cream swirl into the coffee in the mugs. Without turning around she asked, "Will she see me? Does she want to see me? I want to see her." She was bound and determined not to cry, but she was going to lose that battle.

Ransom came up behind her and slid his arms around her. "Yes, she will see you. She wants to meet you."

"Okay. I'll have to cancel appointments, figure out how long I'll be gone. People are going to be pissed, but this is important."

"Joy, you don't need to cancel appointments."

"I can. I'm doing okay, so I can afford a vacation. I haven't had time off in a long time, in fact, I can't remember when, but I can travel, meet my daughter." She was babbling.

"Joy, sit. The sandwiches are done and staring at the coffee isn't going to make it any more ready. Let's eat." He led her to the small table in her kitchen and pressed her into a chair. Her fingers picked at a rag rug woven placemat in muted colors. Fitting, he thought. Like Joy, muted, like the light inside had been switched to dim. He wished he could change that.

"First, no one is going anywhere today." He glanced out the window. The snow had slowed but the wind was still howling. "This town needs to be dug out first."

"Well, there is a wedding today, and I need to get out in order to do the bridal party's hair."

A phone rang somewhere in the apartment. Ransom instinctively reached into his pocket, but he had left his phone on the nightstand at the side of the bed. Joy got up and hurried to the bedroom, retrieving both of their phones. She was talking into hers. His was dead.

Damn. What if Lila Rose was trying to reach him? Of course, he didn't bring his charger with him.

Joy hung up.

"Well, the bride is trying to get into town. Somehow someone with a plow is going to make that happen. I don't need to be at the farm for a while, so I have time to figure out how I'm going to make it happen for me."

"The farm?"

"Yeah, the wedding is being held at Spencer Farm."

Ransom thought quietly for a minute while he and Joy munched on their breakfast. Joy's voice broke into his thoughts.

"So, you never told me. Where do I have to go to see my daughter? How long will it take me to get there? Do I need to book plane tickets, or…?" She looked at him expectantly.

He took a deep breath. This could go either way.

"You don't have to go anywhere, Joy. Your daughter is here. In Grey's Harbor."

Joy's sandwich stuck in her throat. What was he telling her? Her daughter? Here? How long had she been here?

"How long were you going to keep that from me?"

"Joy, I came here last night, remember?"

"Yeah, but it seems like you left out a very important detail."

"When should have I told you? When you were hitting me? When you were looking at me like I was a monster for leaving her a letter?"

"No," she said softly, "When we were in bed last night. When we were talking. When we were remembering. You could have told me then."

"I could have. But Joy, it's time you start seeing my side, too. My daughter, our daughter reached out to me. I met her for the first time last night. She asked to meet me here in Grey's Harbor, where she was conceived. Where her parents gave her life. I agreed. I knew you hadn't left. Believe it or not, I've kept tabs on you." He raised his hand as she started to protest, anger flashing in her eyes. "I wasn't trying to get in your business. I just needed to know you were okay. That you were still there. I needed to know that."

She sighed. Exhausted again, the day had just begun and the

idea of getting through it hung before her, a challenge she wasn't sure she was willing to meet.

"I told Lila I would talk to you. Let you know that she wanted to meet you. Joy, she's scared. She's young. She's alone in the world, and she's afraid of what she will find when she finally meets you. I told her I would break the ice for her, but I am not going to be the person who explains either of you to the other. That's something you two have to do on your own."

"I know," Joy said, shuddering, suddenly chilled. She sipped her coffee. Ransom saw her hands shake. He reached over to cover hers with his as she sat the cup down. "Joy, I'm here for the both of you. For however long it takes and for however long you need me. I've got the both of you, and I won't let either of you fall. But you have to come halfway, and so does she. In fact, she has traveled a long way to be here, to meet us. She has spunk, that's for damn sure."

"She gets it from you," Joy said with a sad smile.

"No, honey. She gets that from you, and we both know it." He stood up from the table and picked up her empty plate, kissing the top of her head without thinking. It was a natural gesture, one they had done many times in the past. Instead of stiffening, Joy looked up at Ransom and gave him a wan smile.

"I think this is going to be a very long day."

"I think you might be right."

* ✽ *

"*J* need to get my phone charged. I don't suppose you have something that will charge this?" Ransom handed Joy his phone.

"I actually might. If I don't here, I probably have something at the shop. I know that sounds weird, but I keep lots of different chargers so my clients can use them. Let me check the extra ones I keep at home here in my drawer." She opened a door in the kitchen that revealed a small pantry and utility closet. There was a plastic drawer cart. She pulled open the second drawer and extracted several different chargers all neatly coiled and secured with a rubber band.

She offered them to Ransom.

"Bingo." He smiled at her. "You never ceased to amaze me, lady." He plugged it in next to the coffee maker and pushed the end into his totally dead phone. He was getting antsy wondering about Lila. If she was okay.

"I need to get over to my shop and gather my supplies, then I need to figure out how I'm going to get to Alexandria's place. I don't need to be there for a couple more hours, but it might take that long just to make it out there. Then, as soon as I get done with that, I want to meet my daughter." She said the words firmly. Ransom recognized that tone. Joy wasn't messing around. She had made a decision and expected it to be respected.

Ransom's phone beeped, then the sound of several text message alerts went off. He snatched the phone from the counter. Two were from his partner at work, filling him in on a case they had been working on, and the last one was from Lila.

Did everything go okay? Are you okay?

"What?" Joy studied his face. She knew him so well. "Is something wrong?"

"No. Nothing's wrong. It's just our daughter wondering how it went when I told you about her. What do you want me to say?"

"The truth, of course," she said without hesitation.

"And what would that be?" he asked, slightly amused.

"Well, I suppose it wouldn't be a good idea to tell her that I beat you up, my cat tried to kill you, and we slept together."

He was surprised at the joke and the amusement in her eyes.

"Yeah, how about I let her know that we talked it out and that you would like to meet her? Does that work for you?"

"Yes, it does. Ransom, where is she?"

Are you at the Harbor Inn? I assume you are safe and holed up there.

Yes, I'm at the Inn. I don't think I can get out. The front end of my car is covered in a snow drift. Did you talk to Joy?

· ✽ ·

"What's wrong, Lila Rose?" Dave watched the girl's face turn pale as she watched the text messages roll in on her phone.

"Nothing, It's just, Ransom finally texted me back. He talked to Joy. I don't know if she wants to see me. He didn't say." Her hand was trembling, and she felt a little sick to her stomach.

Joy and I had a lot to talk about. It was very emotional for her. I'm sorry I didn't text you earlier, but my phone battery died.

That's okay. I understand, and I understand if she doesn't want to meet me. I'm sure I'm a shock. I mean, if she has to explain me to her husband or her children. I understand.

Dave watched a tear slide unnoticed down her cheek. He wanted so badly to wipe it away, but he didn't want to intrude on this moment. Obviously, the text conversation was intense. Still, he was drawn to this beautiful woman, her frailty, her need to be wanted. He felt an intense desire to protect her.

"Lila?"

She shook her head, afraid she was going to fall apart. The phone rang in her hand, startling her so much that she dropped it on the floor.

"Oh, shit… Oh, God, I'm sorry, Father, Reverend." She stuttered as she tried to retrieve the ringing phone. Dave calmly handed it to her and smiled, trying to put her at ease.

"Hello," Lila answered, her voice quiet, shaken.

"Hello, Lila?" A woman's voice came through the phone. "Lila, this is your, well, the person…Lila, you're my daughter. Let's get this straight. I have no reason to hide you, be ashamed of you, or not want to see you. You do not need to be explained. You are the child I gave birth to. The child I gave up so that you could have a better life than I could have ever given you, and the child that I have loved and regretted letting go of every single day of my life. And more than anything in the world, I want to meet the woman you grew up to be." The woman stopped talking and waited.

Lila sat shocked, her green eyes wide, her hand frozen holding the phone to her ear.

"Lila? Are you there?"

"Um, I'm here. I just wasn't expecting you, to hear your voice, to meet you like this. I don't know what to say except I can't wait to meet you, too."

Dave grinned from ear to ear. *What a Christmas gift,* he thought. *A mother and child reuniting.*

CHAPTER 10

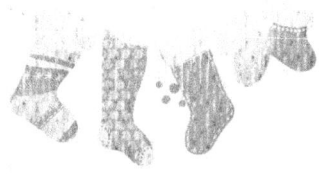

"*R*ansom, I have managed for nineteen years without you."

"I understand that, and you seem to have done an admirable job, but I'm here and my job is to protect people. You know, sworn to protect and serve."

"I don't need protecting. Thank you very much. I'm going to walk over to my shop and get the things I need. Then I'm going to fire up my Jeep and head out to the farm where I will make a bunch of cackling hens look fabulous. What are you going to do?"

"Follow you out there."

"Like hell you are."

"It's a free country. You really can't stop me."

"I probably could," she threatened, danger flashing in her eyes. For a minute, Ransom thought he might just be in trouble, but he held her stare and she burst out laughing. "You are such a chauvinist pig."

"A fact I have never denied. Seriously", he said, taking her hands in his. "Let me follow you and make sure you get there safely. Then I'm going to take care of some things and head over to the Inn."

"Are you staying there, too?"

"I am. Lila doesn't even know that. I haven't been back there since we met."

"I could meet you there. After the hair thing and the wedding thing. I have to show up, but can I meet you, meet her, after."

"Let's plan on dinner. Things just seem to go easier with food. Now, what do we need to do? You said you have a Jeep, so you're not too worried about the snow? Do you have a shovel?"

"I probably have one at the shop. Once in a blue moon I have to shovel the sidewalks."

"Good. I want you to take it in the Jeep with you. If anything happens, you can shovel yourself out."

"How 'bout I take some kitty litter, too?" She said with a crooked smile. "Remember when you taught me that trick?"

"Yeah. We were making out down by the river. We didn't even realize we were in the middle of an ice storm until we decided to leave. We weren't going anywhere."

"But you had picked up a bucket of litter for Pops' cat. I've never forgotten that."

"I haven't forgotten that either, but it isn't the kitty litter that is the highlight of that memory." His mind flashed to the memory of Joy's lightly freckled breasts in the light of the radio while Journey serenaded them as they explored each other's bodies. It made his body want her badly. Not the time or the place, he reminded himself.

They smiled at each other, sad for the time they had lost, the lifetime they had thrown away.

· ✳ ·

"Joy, these tires aren't in the best of shape."

Ransom shook his head as he looked at the old Jeep as Joy stowed her kit in the back.

"They're fine. You are being a worry wort. The farm isn't that far. The Jeep will handle the snow just fine and you'll be behind me. It's all good," she soothed him. Her mind was ticking through everything she packed, making sure she had everything she needed to transform the ladies' locks into the perfect updo's. She was slipping into business mode, and she didn't need to be distracted. This was how she made a living, and she took her work seriously.

70

Ransom retrieved his truck from where he had left it in a public parking lot. He used the shovel from Joy's shop to dig out around the tires. Once he was satisfied, he hopped in and shifted into four-wheel drive. He had to guess where the driveway crossed the sidewalk and move into the street. He guessed wrong and felt the truck drop down over the curb. *Strike one*, he thought.

The truck pulled through the snow until he got to the lot where Joy had her Jeep. She was done checking over her kit and ready to go. He dug out around her tires and put the shovel on the floor in her back seat. Then he stepped back to watch her move out of the lot. The Jeep blasted through the snow like a champ. He caught a glance of Joy, grinning wildly, her auburn hair blowing in the wind from the open window. She reached a hand out and waved at Ransom, and she four-wheeled through the snow and made her way down the street. Ransom jumped in his truck to follow her.

The ride to Spencer Farm was uneventful. Ransom relaxed when he realized the wild, carefree girl he dated in high school had grown into a levelheaded woman who had put a curb on the reckless side that dominated their youth. *She wasn't the only one*, he thought with a wry smile. Together, they had done their fair share of tearing up the town and performing death defying feats, or at least in their minds they were death defying. The most reckless had been making love at the lighthouse without protection. The one act that had changed their lives forever.

Joy turned into Spencer Farm and started up the driveway. The road leading to the farm and the driveway had been freshly plowed as Alexandria had promised it would be. Bridesmaids were arriving, some of them driving themselves in four-wheel SUV's, others being dropped by friends or husbands whose trucks could get through the snow. Ransom figured Joy was in good hands, so he waved goodbye and headed to the Inn to check on his daughter and get a shower.

· **** ·

*J*oy smiled and nodded at the appropriate times, listened to the chatter of the girls who were not only excited about the wedding but sharing stories of how the storm had made this day seem like it wasn't going to happen. The town was pulling together to make sure this wedding took place. Joy's mind was on her daughter and Ransom. She was going to see them tonight. Have dinner with them, and finally get to know her daughter.

Her fingers worked by themselves, muscle memory taking over, while her thoughts took her elsewhere.

"Joy, did you hear me? You're staying for the wedding, right?" asked one of the bridesmaids.

"Of course. I have a change of clothes in the Jeep." She didn't want to stay, but she knew she was going to have to. These were her friends, and friends of friends. These people were the town, the people who had supported her when she needed it most. When she was alone, hurting and trying to make a living.

Three hours later, Joy had finished her work. She stayed on hand to fix a strand here, spray a little there, while the photographer finished up with the candid and posed photos. Then she slipped out to her Jeep to stow her kit and grab her clothes to change. In a few minutes, she was dressed as a guest instead of the help. She took a minute to arrange her hair, touching it up with a curling iron so soft loose curls fell over her shoulders and down her back. She swept on a light coat of eye shadow and a soft blush of lip gloss and she was done. She was never one for much make up. She may be in the industry, but she didn't embrace the overuse of product. Satisfied, she joined the guests in the barn and tried to turn her attention to the festivities instead of thoughts of her daughter.

· ✻ ·

*J*oy gathered her coat and glanced around trying to locate Maddy Grey. She had a huge favor to ask, and Maddy Grey was just the person who could get the job done. With her connection to a colony of artists who stayed as guests at Maddy's mansion turned artist colony, Joy felt certain the idea she had cooked up during the wedding could become a reality. She spotted Maddy and made her way through the crush of guests. Once she explained what she was looking for Maddy went to work.

A few phone calls later, an introduction, and Joy was on her way to meet an artist who could make Joy's idea a reality.

She made her polite goodbyes, wished the bride and groom the best of luck and escaped the party, walking into the crisp evening. The winds had died and the weather was calm. Blankets of untouched snow spread across the world, clean and fresh. The sun was setting and a subtle pink light touched the top of the drifts. *Was the world always this beautiful?* Joy thought, *or am I just finally seeing it again?* A smile settled on her lips. She was going to see her daughter, and she was going to bring her a special gift. Her heart was light and her soul felt peace.

It was dark when Joy left the artist retreat that Maddy Gray had created from Mirabelle Grey's Victorian mansion. She clutched to her chest a box which contained a beautiful silver bracelet that the jeweler in residence had put together for her as she waited. Joy willingly paid the price and gave Jay a sizable tip and a peck on the cheek for his help. Everything was falling into place. She was on her way to meet her daughter. The child she only held for a short time those nineteen years ago.

She put the precious gift on the seat next to her and headed into town, to the Inn and to her daughter. As she rounded the curve at the bluff, where the road hugged the bluff and during the day, the view of the ocean was all you could see, the headlights of a car appeared in her lane. Quick instincts saved Joy from a head-on collision. Snow covered roads tilted her on her side and sent her skidding across the road and over the bluff. The last thing Joy remembered was reaching for the box that contained the bracelet and thinking about how her mother died on a curve of a road covered by a sheet of ice.

CHAPTER 11

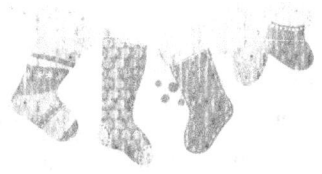

*I*t was Christmas Eve. The night was quiet, stars shone bright in a velvety black sky, the salty sea air unusually crisp. The Harbor Inn's windows glowed warmly against the dunes, snow covered wreaths hanging in every window, electric candles on every sill welcoming guests. Pine boughs graced the railings of the wrap around porch and festively decorated Christmas trees twinkled through the windows in all of the rooms, each its own theme. Joy clutched the package in her mittened hands, the glossy red bow and cream and black checked paper held promise of a cherished gift. She hesitated at the door of the Inn wanting to go inside, but her feet felt stuck.

The door opened and Ransom stepped out. Somehow he knew she was there, on the porch, fearing the future.

"Hey," Ransom said, looking at the gift in her hands.

"Hey, yourself." She smiled shyly. "Is she here?"

"Of course she is. She's waiting to meet you."

"We were supposed to do this yesterday. "

"It wasn't meant to be. Things happen for a reason. Just accept it." He took her elbow and carefully steered her through the door, making sure he protected her right arm and the cast that encased it.

Christmas music played softly in the background. Guests

murmured in tightly knit groups snacking on hors d'oeuvres and Christmas cookies, mulled wine, and hot cocoa for the children. The air was spiced with cinnamon and balsam fir and the warm scent of the wood fires burning merrily in all the fireplaces.

Ransom led Joy through the dining room and into a small side room. A dainty Christmas tree covered in starfish stood in the corner. A fireplace was ablaze, its mantle covered in a thick garland with large white iridescent glitter coated starfish nestled inside the needles, sparkling in the tiny white lights that were hidden among the branches.

In the wing chair next to the fireplace sat a girl. A beautiful red-haired girl with perfect bowed lips. The perfect bow that Joy remembered as she looked down at her daughter in her arms that very first time over nineteen years ago.

"Lila." It was a statement, not a question. The girl stood, looking shy and uncertain.

"Joy?"

The girl lifted her hands slightly in a gesture resembling a hug, then let them fall to her sides. Joy crossed the room quickly and reached out toward her daughter. Ransom held his breath. Lila reached toward her mother and grasped the fingers of her left hand, then gently pulled her mother toward her and gathered the woman into her arms. It was Lila that comforted Joy and brought her home to her.

· ⁎ ·

"*I* wanted to give you something." Joy awkwardly handed the gift to Lila.

"You didn't need to. I didn't get you anything," Lila said shyly.

Joy waved her protests away and settled into the companion chair next to Lila, watching her daughter carefully open the package, her eyes shining with excitement.

"It's beautiful," Lila exclaimed, as she lifted a silver bracelet from the glittering tissue. She inspected the shiny snake chain with the two silver tags. She read the inscriptions on the tags. The first one, Lila. The second one, Rose.

"Lila Rose," Lila said softly.

"I hope you don't mind," Joy said swiftly. I named you Rose when you were born. I knew you couldn't keep the name, that you would get a new name when you were adopted." She stopped talking, all of the sudden feeling silly.

"I have the letter. You wrote it to Rose. I know that's what you called me, and I love that name." She reached for Joy's hand. "But do you know what my full name is? Do you know what my adoptive parents named me?"

Joy shook her head, unable to speak.

"My name is Lila Rose." She smiled at Joy. "My mother kept the name you gave me, and I'm so glad she did."

Joy stared at her daughter in disbelief, tears streaming unchecked down her cheeks and once again, Lila Rose comforted her mother.

"Okay, ladies. There has been enough crying in the last few days to last me a lifetime," Ransom teased. "And I'm hungry. Can we pull ourselves together and eat?"

Joy pulled herself away from her daughter, wincing at the pain in her back and shoulder.

"Considering I haven't eaten since yesterday at the wedding, I have to agree with you. Lead the way."

Lila helped Joy to her feet and the two of them followed Ransom to the front room where a table waited for them. White linens graced the table, silver candlesticks held white tapers and the glow of the old fashioned colored lightbulbs on the massive tree cast soft colors in the room.

"No wine for the nineteen year old or the drugged up mom, so we have some sparkling grape juice." Ransom filled their goblets and held up his glass. He cleared his throat which was unexpectedly tight. "To the two most important ladies in my life. My world wasn't complete until today, and now I have a lifetime to catch up on. I hope you both will allow me to always be a part of your worlds." Ransom's gaze held Joy's, a question in them. She smiled and gave him a slight nod then raised her glass to her lips.

"We have a lot to work out," Joy said after she swallowed her sip. "I don't know what you want to do, Lila, but I am here to support you and to cheer you on, and Ransom, I don't know what to do with you, never did, but I think we have a better chance of figuring it out this time". She smiled across the table, feeling the familiar pang in her heart when she looked in his eyes.

"I want you in my life. My parents were the best parents a girl could ever wish for. The fact that they were taken from me is wrong, and it hurts so badly, but I have something that most people don't. I have another set of parents. I know you did what you did because you thought it was for the best. Who knows if it was or wasn't, but what was meant to be was. Now here we are. I want to know everything about you, who you are, what you think, and Joy, I want to meet your cat. Ransom told me all about him. I think he is just misunderstood.

"More than anything, I want to be part of this family, whatever we make of it, and I want to try out Grey's Harbor as my home. If that's okay with you, Joy?"

"Lila Rose, that is more than okay. Remember you said you didn't get me anything? Well, you just gave me the best Christmas gift I could ever get." She reached across the table with her good arm and took her daughter's hand. Ransom placed his on top of theirs and decided then and there he just might have to come back to Grey's Harbor himself.

The End

Leave a Light On

On

EDWARDS

J.C. Wing

CHAPTER 1

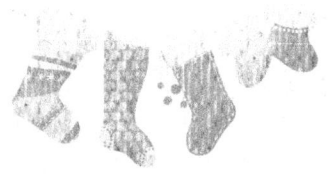

The Grey's Harbor Public Library had been closed for hours, but Magnolia Jane, the lead children's librarian, was still hard at work. It was only two days before Christmas, and the holidays were a busy time for someone dedicated to the younger generation. She'd organized a Secret Santa gift exchange, holiday parties, food, gifts, coloring contests and several visits from the jolly fat man himself. It had been another hectic day in Magnolia Jane's portion of the library, and she couldn't go home before all the preparations were complete.

"Goodnight, Mrs. Mason."

Magnolia Jane looked up to see Jeannie, one of the regular custodians that came in each night to clean the library. She'd already donned her coat, and a knit cap sit snugly on her head. The local weatherman had been predicting a storm for the last several days, and the wind had arrived as scheduled early that afternoon. The normally gentle breezes coming from the Atlantic had grown blustery, and the humidity in the air had turned cold. The last time Magnolia Jane looked out the window, flakes had been falling from a white cotton sky. That had been hours ago, and the sun had long since tucked itself into bed.

"Goodnight, Jeannie. Be careful on your trip home. Stay warm."

Jeannie smiled and gave her a nod. "Will do. You do the same."

The lock on the back service door had already been engaged, which meant that once Jeannie had used it to get outside and to the parking lot behind the building, the heavy door would shut and lock on its own. Magnolia Jane heard the chair creak beneath her as she stretched the ache from her lower back, and she thought, not for the first time, that she needed to either invest in a more comfortable chair or get upper management to.

The door shut with a definitive "*thunk*", and Magnolia Jane clicked through the files on her computer. She had some funding from the library for the events she planned, but she always put in quite a bit of her own money to make those events extra special. She looked down at the budget she'd been working on and calculated how much this next round of celebrating was going to cost her.

Her phone went off and Magnolia Jane stood, swiping it from the desk as she made her way toward the kitchen. "Hi." She smiled at the anticipation of hearing his voice on the other end of the line.

"Did you bring your skis to work with you today?"

Magnolia Jane pulled a mug from one of the cupboards. "I knew I forgot something. I even set them by the door and I still left without them."

"You think I'm kidding," Trey said," but have you looked outside lately? There's six inches of snow out there. Easily. I fell asleep in front of the TV and woke up to a white out."

Magnolia Jane put the mug down and made her way back into the main part of the library. She stood near the circulation desk, her eyes lifted to the large windows high above the main entrance and watched as a flurry of snowflakes fell against the backdrop of the streetlight that shone in through the ice encrusted glass.

"Well, would you look at that."

"Looks like we'll have a white Christmas."

"Oh, damn …"

"What? This is incredible. We rarely ever get snow like this."

"The wedding."

There was a moment of silence while Trey caught up. "Oh," he said, drawing the word out. "At Spencer Farm."

"That's the one. It's tomorrow."

"They'll figure it out. If this had happened the day before our wedding, we wouldn't have let it stop us." That momentous occasion had taken place almost eight months earlier on a warm day at the beginning of May. The only storm that threatened the ceremony back then was the one raging in Izzy's heart. Sometimes, the past can rear its ugly head and cast shadows of fear and doubt on the present. Sometimes, those shadows need the light of the future to chase them from the darkest corners.

"Yeah," Magnolia Jane conceded. "You're right. But wow … look at it come down."

"I was thinking I should come and pick you up."

Magnolia Jane smiled as she shook her head. She drove a Blazer, and Trey knew both she and her truck were more than capable of driving the seven miles between the library and their house in the middle of a blizzard. She wouldn't even need help digging the snow away from the tires before she climbed behind the wheel.

"You just wanna play in the snow."

"Yes, ma'am," Trey laughed, "I really do."

"Okay, then," Magnolia Jane told him, finding it easy to give in. "Give me twenty minutes to finish things up here before you come and rescue me."

"You realize the library will be closed tomorrow, right?"

"Sure," Magnolia Jane nodded. "And for the next few days probably, but everything will happen, it will just be postponed for a bit. I still need to make sure everything is ready to go."

"I love you, library goddess."

"I expect nothing less."

Magnolia Jane's attention was diverted from the falling snow outside the window when she heard a loud bang behind her. She turned in the direction of the noise and wondered if the wind she saw blowing hard outside hadn't knocked a lid loose from a dumpster out back.

"See you soon."

"I'll be ready."

She heard another noise. She pushed her phone into her pocket and moved toward the back of the building. Something was definitely going on outside, but Magnolia Jane wasn't sure it had to do with the wind. It sounded like someone was trying to get into the building. She flipped the light switch and watched as the handle on the door wriggled.

"Jeannie?"

She wondered if the woman had forgotten something, or perhaps her car was stuck and she needed help. Magnolia Jane smiled and shook her head thinking she still might be digging snow away from tires even though her Blazer would remain parked in the library lot overnight.

"Hang on, I'm coming."

Magnolia Jane pushed the door open and felt it hit something on the other side.

"Oh!"

Jeannie slipped and tried to right herself, her arms windmilling as she struggled to maintain her balance.

Magnolia Jane reached out and grabbed Jeannie by the arm, keeping her from spilling over. "I'm sorry," she said. "You probably couldn't hear me through this big, thick door, could you? I didn't mean to knock you over."

Jeannie finally found her footing and raised her chin. Her eyes caught Magnolia Jane's and she heard the younger woman gasp.

"You're not Jeannie …"

Magnolia Jane felt a quick flash of panic, her mind pulling information from the self-defense classes she'd taken in college as she stepped away from the stranger. Her body grew rigid, and every muscle tensed, ready to fight.

"Marjorie?"

Magnolia Jane had never heard the voice, but she knew the name well enough. It wasn't hers, of course. It belonged to the woman who had given birth to her. The woman who had abandoned her in Grey's Harbor when she'd been four years old.

CHAPTER 2

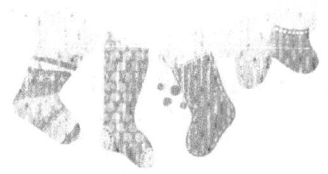

"Oh my god ..." the woman breathed. She shook her head and snow fell from her dark blonde head. She stared at Magnolia Jane, her hands out like she wanted to touch her. Magnolia Jane took another step back. "How is this possible? How are you here?"

"What?" Magnolia Jane asked. "How am *I* here? I work here. I'm supposed to be here. I thought Jeannie needed help. How in the hell are *you* here?" The wind whipped around the two of them, swirls of snow rising in the air like icy cyclones.

"You know who I am?"

Another big gust rose and shoved the two of them hard like an invisible hand. The woman stumbled, grabbing onto Magnolia Jane's arm. Magnolia Jane tried to regain her balance, but between the weight of the woman pulling on her and the wind pushing her in the same direction, she had nowhere to go but down. They both fell in a pile, landing on the floor as one last burst of wintry air pushed its way into the building, blasting against their faces. Then the heavy door slammed shut with a loud bang, locking the storm outside. They remained on the floor for a moment, trying to catch their breaths.

"Yeah," Magnolia Jane finally said. "I know who you are, and Aunt Iz wasn't kidding."

"Damn it. Can you move your … yeah … oh, lord, that hurts." She was grimacing in pain, and Magnolia Jane tried to untangle her arm from the scarf she assumed used to be around the woman's neck. "Wasn't kidding about what?"

"You bring a certain amount of drama with you wherever you go."

"She said that?"

Magnolia Jane moved away from the woman and stood up. "She did. And damn if this doesn't prove just one more time that she's always right. Come on," she said, offering a hand.

The woman looked up and caught her gaze. She blinked a few times and shook her head. "I know you're not Marjorie, but I swear, you're the spittin' image."

"Yeah," Magnolia Jane said with a shrug. "I've heard that before."

"Have you?"

"Only forty or fifty times. I'm Magnolia Jane. M.J. if that's too much of a mouthful. And you're Olivia."

"Your grandma." She bit the corner of her mouth. "Ironic. I never thought I'd be okay with anyone calling me that. Makes me sound so old."

"Don't worry about it," Magnolia Jane assured her. "Stay young. I don't know you at all well enough to call you grandma. I'll stick with Olivia for right now." She wiggled her fingers. "You can stay down there if you want, or you can let me help you up."

Olivia resituated herself. "There's something wrong with my ankle. It hurts to put weight on it."

"Okay," Magnolia Jane said. "Which one is hurt?"

"The right one."

Magnolia Jane stepped in front of Olivia, putting both of her feet in front of Olivia's left one. "Take hold and push against my feet as leverage." She crossed her arms and held her hands out. Olivia grasped them, locking her thumbs with Magnolia Jane's, and let her granddaughter pull her off the ground. "Okay, now be careful." Magnolia Jane slipped her arm around Olivia's waist, her shoulder beneath the woman's armpit so she could support her. "Good thing about a library is there are plenty of comfortable chairs to sit in."

Once she'd helped Olivia to a chair near her desk, Magnolia Jane turned and studied the woman. She knew what she had to do, she just wasn't excited about doing it. She pulled her phone out of the back pocket of her jeans.

"You're not calling the cops, are you?"

Magnolia Jane's brow furrowed. "Why would I do that? Are you here to rob the place? Maybe you're here to make off with that big batch of Christmas goodies we have in the kitchen. Kris makes some killer cookies but breaking into the library to get at them seems a bit extreme."

Olivia heaved a sigh. "You inherited Izzy's witty sarcasm I see."

"Speak of the devil," Magnolia Jane said when her aunt picked up the phone. "Hey, Aunt Iz. This nor'easter is a crazy one, isn't it? You're not gonna believe this, but it just blew Olivia Edwards right through the back door of the library."

⁙

"*J*ust what in the hell is goin' on here?"

Izzy and Trey showed up at the same time, but the two of them came in through the front door. It was obvious to Magnolia Jane that Trey had no idea the drama he was about to walk in on, but he knew Izzy well enough to know to hold the door open for her so she could storm through it and to otherwise keep his mouth shut.

"Jeannie had left not fifteen minutes before," Magnolia Jane began as a gust of cold air pushed past the pair and Izzy's Doc Martens tracked snow into the entry way of the library. "I figured her car wouldn't start or it was stuck, so when I heard banging on the back door, I opened it."

"Apparently, Jeannie escaped just fine."

"Yes, ma'am."

"Well, where is she?" Snow glistened in Izzy's jet-black hair, and the humidity had kicked her natural wave up a couple notches, the

87

strands looking like a disorganized halo rising wildly around her head.

"By my desk. She's hurt."

"Is that so?"

It wasn't a question Izzy really wanted an answer to, so Magnolia Jane didn't provide her one. Izzy brushed past her, pulling her gloves off as she thundered through, and Magnolia Jane looked up to find Trey's eyes. He was still in the dark, but the look on his wife's face told him something serious was going on. He opened his arms and she immediately walked into them. He held her tight, his chin propped on the top of her head and the snow from his coat wetting the front of her sweater.

"My grandma's here."

His forehead creased in confusion. The only woman Magnolia Jane referred to as her grandma was Bailey Edwards, her grandpa Mateo's wife. They'd both known Bailey their entire lives, and there was no circumstance he could think of that would involve her and the feeling of impending doom he'd just stepped into. "Your what?"

"My grandma, Olivia," she said, snow melting against the warmth of her cheek. "Aunt Izzy's mom."

"Holy shit …" Trey breathed. Mateo's *first* wife. Izzy was always a force of nature, but now her current state suddenly made all the sense in the world.

Magnolia Jane nodded. "Yeah," she said in agreement. She felt Trey hug her a little tighter, and she drew strength from his embrace. She had a feeling she was going to need it.

"What are you doing here?" they heard Izzy demand.

Magnolia Jane pulled away from Trey, but he caught her fingers in his own, following her quickly toward the voices deeper inside the building.

Olivia had shed her coat, and it lay over the arm of another chair, the melting snow dripping from the fabric and pooling on the ground beneath it. Her wet hair was flattened against her head, and strands stuck to the sides of her face.

Magnolia Jane did some quick math in her head. Olivia was about sixty-eight if her calculations were correct. *Abuelo* was close to the same age, but he'd always seemed so alive, so vibrant to

Magnolia Jane. She didn't know this woman sitting in front of her, but she was having a hard time putting her and Mateo together. Many years had passed since the two of them had been a couple, and Izzy had reminded her not so long ago that life is overflowing with both good and bad things. Magnolia Jane was aware of a lot of what had occurred in Mateo's life. He'd had some heartache to be sure, but she knew he'd be the first to say that the years had been good to him. Magnolia Jane suspected that Olivia would claim the opposite of her life. She wore disappointment and emotional angst on her frame like an off color, ill-fitting dress.

"What, do you own the town of Grey's Harbor now? You've gotten that powerful and affluent since I left? I need your permission to come and visit?"

Magnolia Jane could almost feel the heat radiating from Izzy's body and worried about how the next few moments were going to play out.

"Don't you dare," Izzy told her mom, walking closer to where Olivia sat. "You chose to leave, and that was fine. It was probably the best thing you could've done, but things are different now, and I'm not about to put up with your brand of bullshit again. You talk to me and tell me the truth, or you don't say one damn word. Either way works just fine with me."

The two of them stared at one another.

"It's Christmas," Olivia said.

"Come on, Mom," Izzy said, her voice calm but angry. "Is that really the best you can come up with? There's been what, twenty-five Christmases between this one and the last time we saw each other? What makes this one so special?"

Olivia was shivering. Her hair and clothes were wet, and Magnolia Jane thought her lips looked a little discolored. It was obvious to her that Olivia was struggling. She believed Izzy deserved answers, but she wasn't sure Olivia was physically capable of delivering them at the present time.

"Aunt Iz," Magnolia Jane spoke up, "I'm not trying to let Olivia skate here or anything, but she's nearly frozen through—"

"And I hurt somethin' terrible," Olivia interrupted.

"What hurts?" Trey asked, moving closer to Olivia's chair.

"It's this damn leg," Olivia complained. She looked up and studied Trey as he pushed an ottoman forward.

"Mind if I lift it? I'll be careful."

"You a doctor?"

"No, ma'am," Trey said, giving her a smile. "But I've been injured more times than I can count. I might be able to help." He spread his hands and watched her, not wanting to touch her before she gave her consent.

"Alright, then."

Trey carefully lifted Olivia's leg and rested it on the ottoman. The woman's jeans were sopping wet, and her boots were holding more water than they were keeping out.

"I can already tell there's a lot of swelling." His fingers probed Olivia's leg, and when he moved down toward her ankle, the woman jumped in her seat. He hadn't pressed very hard, which let him know something serious was going on beneath her boot. He turned and looked up at Izzy. "It's her ankle. If I take this boot off now, it'll swell up even bigger most likely. That probably shouldn't happen until she's settled in for the night."

"Great, so, where are you staying?" Izzy asked her mom, impatience laced in her words. "Let's take you to wherever you're going so the rest of us can get ourselves home."

"I tried to make a reservation," Olivia told her.

"Where?"

"The Harbor Inn."

"Tried?" Izzy asked, scrolling through the contacts in her phone.

"Who are you?" Olivia asked Trey, not one for subtleties. Izzy found the number she was looking for and made the call. She found she couldn't be still and began to pace the area around Magnolia Jane's desk.

"Trey Mason, ma'am," Trey answered. Olivia's eyes narrowed when she recognized the surname. Everyone in and around Grey's Harbor was well acquainted with the Mason Paper Company because a great number of them worked for the corporation. It had been that way for many, many years.

"And my husband," Magnolia Jane added. Trey gave her a smile.

"Your husband." It was a statement, not a question, and Izzy's eyes kept moving toward her mom. Grey's Harbor had been a hard place for Olivia Edwards to live. Izzy had no way of knowing what kind of life her mother had made for herself once she'd packed up and moved on, but while she'd been here, she'd been a Have Not. The Masons had always been Haves, and it had always irked her that Izzy and Gabriel Mason had been good friends in high school.

"This shit should have ended a long time ago," Izzy said, voicing her thoughts aloud. "Why are you here?" She stared at her mom, then paused and took a breath. "Hey, Donna," she said, straining to bring her voice back to a normal pitch. "This is Izzy. Hi. I'm sorry to call so late, but I was wondering if you might have a room available?" There was another pause as Izzy listened to Donna on the other end of the line. "The wedding ... yes, of course, you've got all the guests there." She turned and caught Magnolia Jane's gaze. "Yes, ma'am, I am playing for the ceremony." She nodded, absent mindedly. "Thanks, Donna, that's nice of you. I look forward to seeing you there, too." Magnolia Jane watched as Izzy's jaw clenched. "Oh," she said into the phone, "the room. Yeah ... an unexpected visitor showed up tonight." Her eyes moved back to Olivia. "I'll take care of it." A storm of feelings much like the whirl-wind of snow that fell outside churned up in her gut. She'd take care of it just like she always had.

CHAPTER 3

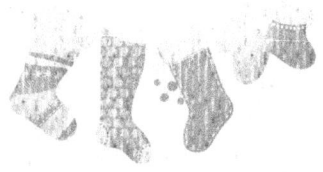

*I*zzy held her phone tightly in her hand as she watched the snow continue to fall. Her first thought was to call Mateo, but she realized she was falling back on childhood behaviors. Back then she'd needed an adult to help her. Now, she was the adult. Whatever mess Olivia had gotten herself into—and Izzy was sure that Olivia was in a mess because she wouldn't have shown up in Grey's Harbor otherwise—it would be up to Izzy to fix. Or not. She hadn't had that option as a kid. She did now.

"Did I hear you say there was a wedding going on?" Olivia asked.

Izzy looked back at her mom. "At Spencer Farm tomorrow."

"And you're playing your cello?"

The tone in her mother's voice further irked Izzy, much as it had when she'd been a child. She felt it spark in her chest. What she'd said hadn't been the issue as much as how she'd said it, and Izzy remembered the way Olivia would pick fights just because it entertained her. "I am," she said simply.

"I'm surprised folks invite you to play at weddings, what with all those tattoos and piercings. When I look at you, the word 'cellist' is the last thing that comes to my mind. You look like a criminal, not a musician."

Instantly, Magnolia Jane's back was up. "How dare you—"

"It's okay, M.J.," Izzy said, her arm raising, crossing over Magnolia Jane's middle as though they were in the car and Izzy had to step suddenly on the brakes. Izzy's eyes never left Olivia's face. She fought hard to maintain her cool, but she'd lied to her niece. Things were definitely far from being okay. "Seems like Olivia here is just picking up where she left off," she said, her voice strained. "She was always real good at ruffling feathers. What is it, Mom? What shit have you stepped into now? What do you need help scraping off the bottom of your shoes?"

Magnolia Jane watched Izzy's face. There was a long history between these two women. Izzy had shared things with Magnolia Jane but seeing the two of them together was a lot different than hearing stories. Izzy's place was at the heart of Grey's Harbor. She knew and cared about the people who lived there. She was well educated in all the family histories that made up the town, she kept many people's secrets, and she protected those who came to her for help and advice. She was brash, stubborn and didn't have an issue with calling people out. She was brutally honest and expected the same in return, no matter how hard that made things. She had a foul mouth, and she was fluent in sarcasm. She was also the kindest, most generous person Magnolia Jane had ever known in her entire life. The pain Olivia had caused her eldest daughter ran deep, and Magnolia Jane's desire to protect Izzy nearly overwhelmed her as they stood there in the middle of the library.

"You haven't cleaned anything up for me in a very long time, Iz," Olivia said, her eyes holding fast to her daughter's. "You're acting as high and mighty now as you used to when you were young. Always thinking you had the right answers, always feeling superior to everyone else."

"Let me make myself as clear as I can," Izzy told her, dropping down in a crouch in front of Olivia so they were eye to eye. When she spoke, her words were measured and precise. "You didn't know me back then, and you sure as hell don't know me now. I put up with a lot growing up, but I will be taking no more shit from you, do you understand? None. There are no hotel rooms available, and I'm not about to impose on anyone else on your behalf, so if you want a place to stay tonight, I'll take you home with me. If and when you finally choose to tell me why you decided to come back to Grey's Harbor, I'll figure out how to deal with that. Until then, I'm gonna need you to keep your mouth shut so we can get ourselves safely out of this storm."

Izzy and Olivia held each other's gazes. There'd been a big chunk of time carved in the middle of the match the two of them began when Izzy had been a child. It had been a long time out, but they'd never quit or declared a winner. Neither one of them had ever taken off the gloves, and now they were dancing around the ring again.

"I'm going with you," Magnolia Jane said.

Izzy stood up and stepped away from Olivia's chair, her eyes still on her mother's face. "You think we might need a referee?" Izzy was only half joking.

Magnolia Jane's gaze moved between her aunt and her grand-mother. "Maybe," she answered honestly. "I'd just feel better being there."

"Well, my Jeep is that way." Izzy pointed toward the front of the library. "I need a minute," she said, bouncing her phone off her thigh.

"Here," Magnolia Jane said, handing Izzy her keys. "Hit the lights and lock up for me. We'll get Olivia ready to go."

Izzy took the keys and Trey held his left hand out to Olivia. "Careful," he told her. "Not too much weight on that foot now." He pulled her up and Magnolia Jane tucked her shoulder beneath Olivia's other arm. The two of them made their way to the front door with Olivia limping between them.

The air hit the three of them so hard when they pushed the door open that Magnolia Jane heard Olivia gasp. She squinted against the onslaught of icy snow, and the wind instantly froze her cheeks and nose.

"You picked a fine night to blow back into town," she said, her voice raised so that Olivia could hear her. "You know what else Aunt Iz always said about you?"

"I can't begin to imagine."

"Well," Magnolia Jane said, about to fill her in. "You always had impeccable timing."

· ✳ ·

*I*zzy maneuvered the Jeep through the snow stacked streets, her high beams cutting a bright path that was filled with huge, lacy flakes.

"It was nice of you to give me the front seat," Olivia said over her shoulder to Magnolia Jane.

"Age before beauty," Izzy told her, her eyes moving up and catching Magnolia Jane's in the rearview mirror. The girl smiled and Izzy tried to let the image soak into her soul.

"This isn't the most comfortable car."

"It's not a car," Izzy said, slowing for the light on Main Street. "It's a Jeep. If I had a car, I'd be snowed in at the Mizzen Mast and I might have avoided this whole reunion."

Olivia ignored the jab. "You work at Jack Forester's bar?"

"I own Jack Forester's bar." Izzy moved the Jeep along the street, the wind pushing it sideways as the meaty tires bit into the snow. The heat was pouring through the vents, but Olivia still shivered. She felt frozen down to her bones, and no amount of warmth seemed to penetrate.

Izzy turned down Blue Fin Road. "Jack hasn't lived here in a long time," she said. "He left more than twenty years ago," she paused. "Not too long after you did. Difference is, I still get a Christmas card from him every year."

The comment hung in the air and Magnolia Jane sat quietly in the backseat. It had already been a long day. It looked like it wouldn't be ending anytime soon.

When Izzy pulled into the driveway in front of her bungalow, she heard a surprised sound escape Olivia's throat.

"You still live here? God, I hated this house. I hated everything about this house."

Light poured through the four panes of wavy glass set in the thick oak door at the front of the house. A wreath hung there adorned with pinecones and fresh holly that now looked a bit worse for the wear beneath the heavy snow that covered it. Yellow light shone through the glass, looking buttery and warm as the nor'easter continued to rage and beat against the little blue bungalow both Izzy and Magnolia Jane had grown up in.

"Welcome home," Magnolia Jane quipped as Izzy brought the Jeep to a stop.

The front door opened, and Bennett stepped outside, his hair covered in a knit cap and his large build made even bigger by the thick coat he wore. Hohner, Izzy's hound dog, ran past Bennett, howling a greeting at the familiar Jeep. He galloped in the thick snow, his floppy ears flying in the icy wind.

"That's a very big dog," Olivia said, watching the pair move through the snow and wind. "That's a very big man," she added.

"And they both love Aunt Iz, so keep that in mind, Olivia. They play favorites."

Bennett opened the door, shielding Olivia from the worst of the wind. "I'm Bennett," he said. "Iz told me your ankle is injured. This weather isn't really the kind I want to be out in for any longer than I need to be, so if you don't mind ..." He leaned in, scooped Olivia from the seat, and held her close to his body. She cried out, surprised, then leaned her head against his chest when he turned, and the blowing snow blasted her in the face.

"That's one way to do it," Magnolia Jane said.

"God bless him," Izzy muttered as she got out of the car and raced toward the house, pushing the door open so Bennett and Olivia could come inside. Hohner and Magnolia Jane followed.

Olivia saw the front door as she was being carried through it. The name *Edwards* was still stamped on a small doorplate that was affixed just below the Christmas wreath. The letters were a bit worn, but it looked much the same as it had all the years she lived in the bungalow. She'd wanted to remove it countless times. It represented Mateo and then later, Izzy. Although it had once been her own name, it tasted bitter on her tongue. Especially here in Grey's Harbor. Especially in this little bungalow she'd been incredibly happy to run away from. She swallowed the sourness in her mouth and was happy to hear the sounds of the storm muted when the door was shut behind her.

"Straight to the guest bathroom," Izzy instructed, and Bennett carried Olivia easily through the house.

Olivia's eyes were wide as she looked around. "The guest bathroom?" she asked.

"Oh, Mom," she heard Izzy say behind her. "This tattooed, pierced, bar owning cellist has done a lot with her life in the last twenty some years. Updating the house was just the beginning."

CHAPTER 4

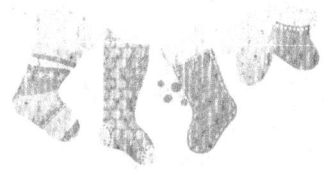

*O*livia soaked in the oversized tub, steam rising from the water that covered her tired, battered body. She remembered when Izzy and Marjorie would come sit on the toilet seat and talk with her while she bathed. She thought about it now and realized that maybe she had been the one who had done most of the talking.

She lay back, her head resting against the lip of the tub. Izzy had called this the guest bath, but this had been the bathroom she remembered from years ago, indicating that maybe the house now had more than one. Everything was in the same place, of course, but it all looked different. The tub was larger, deeper, and the vanity wasn't the same old clunky stained wood with the chipped basin. The walls were painted a deep blue, like the depths of the ocean, and the sconces above the sink emitted a bright but soft light in the room. The chrome faucet gleamed, and everything smelled clean.

She'd never been the best housekeeper, especially in the days she called this place home. It had never felt big enough, extraordinary enough, special enough. Somewhere deep in her heart she always knew that Mateo had wanted these walls to protect her, provide shelter and love for her, and, for a while, they had. But her soul had been restless. She'd always wanted more, and this little place became a prison of her own making instead of the haven it was meant to be. She'd lived in denial and expected her children to love and adore her even though she'd never worked very hard at being a good mother. She'd done a lot of soul searching as of late, and if she hadn't come to the conclusion already, it had been made very clear to her this evening that she hadn't been worthy of love and adoration. If Izzy had felt those things for her as a child, she certainly didn't feel them now.

Her whole body ached, but her ankle throbbed. She lifted it from the water and saw that it was swollen and sporting several horrible shades of black and dark purple. Over the last few years, she'd become good at hiding her injuries. This one had been different. This one had pushed her over the edge. This was the one that made her decide it was time to run.

She sat up and worked shampoo into her shoulder length hair. It had just been professionally cut and colored, and it was still thick like it had been when she'd been younger. The scent of honeysuckle filled her nose as the lather grew beneath her massaging fingers and she closed her eyes. She soaped up a washcloth and cleaned her face, then slowly washed her body, wincing when the fabric ran over the handful of sore spots beneath her skin. She'd run out of energy, and she felt exhausted down to her soul. She sighed, unable to hold the tears in any longer, and she began to weep. Once she got started, she found that she couldn't stop. Emotion took over, and soon her body was shaking, her sobs loud and mournful as the tears poured from her eyes.

"Mom?"

Olivia felt panic mix in with the sadness, the overwhelming exhaustion, and the feeling of utter helplessness. She tried to call out, to tell Izzy not to come into the room, but she couldn't find her voice. She'd pushed herself to a breaking point, and her body was no longer capable of carrying out any more instructions.

"Mom?" Izzy asked again, a note of anxiety carrying out the word. When she still didn't get an answer, she pushed through the door.

Olivia tried to cover herself with her arms, tried to shrink beneath the water and layer of dissipating bubbles, but her brain couldn't seem to send the command to her body. Instead, it shuddered and shook with her sobs, and she could barely see the image of her daughter as she rushed into the room.

"Why didn't you answer ..." Izzy was in the middle of scolding Olivia, but the words stopped short as she witnessed the sobbing, shaking woman who huddled in the bathtub. Izzy stared down at Olivia, who seemed to have shrunk since the last time she'd seen her. Now, without clothes, the change in Olivia was hard to ignore. She'd never been skinny. Her body had been shapely, pleasantly plump. She'd had beautiful curves and creamy skin that tanned easily beneath the warm sunshine. What Izzy saw now along the landscape of her mother's body made her angry. There was a large bruise on the side of Olivia's left breast, and a chain of purple wrapped around her upper arm. Her right hip was discolored, and the knee below it was double the size of the other one. Izzy reached down and scattered the bubbles, uncovering the ankle Olivia had been favoring. The injury to it looked stark against the white of the tub, and it had lost any semblance of its original shape. Izzy was no medical expert, but it was obvious to her that the ankle was broken. Olivia herself was broken.

"Mom ..." Izzy reached out, her hand faltering when Olivia winced. Izzy moved the wet hair away from Olivia's face and saw the tell-tale outline of what looked to have been a substantial black eye. She hadn't seen it in the library, but it was unmistakable now. "You came to me for a reason. Is this it? Is this what you need me to help you with?"

Olivia's body was still shaking. "Yes ..."

Izzy forced herself to look at Olivia. She knew there was a mess. She'd had no idea what kind. She'd never seen her mother this tenuous, this vulnerable before. Izzy had so much residual anger, resentment, and frustration in her heart, and so much of it had been placed there by this woman in front of her. There had been so many fights, so many hurtful words, so many broken promises. When Olivia left Grey's Harbor, Izzy had cried, not only in defeat, but in relief. They'd never been what the other needed. They'd never been able to coexist without friction and static between them. It had felt hopeless, and while she'd been sad to see her leave, Izzy had long since run out of ways to make their volatile and hurtful relationship survive. She'd decided her only option was to let her go.

"Who did this to you?"

Olivia's first impulse was to lie. It had become a habit, almost like breathing. This time she was honest. "Darien Johansen. My husband."

"How long?"

"Almost four years."

"You want it to stop?"

Olivia's eyes moved around Izzy's face. She realized how beautiful her daughter had become, with her wild bobbed hair and her wide, dark eyes. Olivia had never been into tattoos or piercings, but when she looked at Izzy, she had the strangest sense that all the things Izzy had added to her skin over the years belonged there. She was fierce. In Olivia's heart, she'd always known that. That's why she'd come.

"Yes."

Izzy took a deep breath, then she made the only decision that felt right in her soul. "Okay," she said, "but I need the truth. I need all of it, not pieces and parts, and you can't lie to me. Understood? This won't work if you lie to me."

"No lies," Olivia agreed.

"I can help, but you're the one who has to decide." They held eyes. "And you're going to have to keep deciding, over and over again."

"I need out." Tears were leaking from Olivia's eyes again. "I can't live like this anymore."

"That's what you've decided right now. This second. If you really want out, you have to make that decision every minute. Every day. Every week. If you don't, he'll do this to you again and again. You're the only one who can change this. No one else has that power."

Olivia watched her, a tear falling from her chin into the bathwater. "You talk like you've got some experience."

"I do," Izzy said without hesitation. "We're both addicts, Mom. My drug is alcohol, yours is men. They're different, but they're exactly the same."

Olivia shivered. The water around her had cooled, and her ankle was screaming so loudly she could barely concentrate on anything else. She reluctantly agreed when Izzy told her she needed to take photos of her bruised body, then surrendered even further when Izzy told her they needed to tell Magnolia Jane.

"Come here, M.J.," Izzy said when Magnolia Jane walked into the room. Izzy held out her hand when she saw the look that came over her niece's face. She knew hers had probably looked similar when she saw the bruises all over Olivia's body.

"Oh, Olivia," Magnolia Jane breathed. "Oh, no …" She took hold of Izzy's hand and fell to her knees next to the tub.

"Your grandma is running from an abusive marriage. She needs help. I've agreed to do what I can for her. You're not obligated by any means, but you and I don't keep secrets from one another. I needed to make sure you knew what was going on."

Magnolia Jane reached into the tub and took Olivia's hand. The woman's fingers were puckered and cold, but she held tight to her granddaughter's hand.

"We're a package deal, me and Aunt Iz," Magnolia Jane said without hesitation. "I'm here. I'll do whatever I can."

Izzy nudged Magnolia Jane's shoulder with her own. "I might not have given birth to her, but she's mine. We're a hell of a lot stronger together than we ever will be apart." She was quiet as she studied Olivia's face. "I can't pretend things are okay between us, Mom. I'm still dealing with a lot of the shit that went down between us. There are a lot of folks that attend A.A. meetings that know a whole lot about you. I'm not over it. I'm still angry. I'm still hurt. All of that is still there. Maybe it always will be. I don't know. What I do know is that no one deserves to be treated like this." Her eyes moved down Olivia's body, snagging on each mark, each bruise, and settling on the misshapen discolored ankle before she closed them and dipped her chin. She felt Magnolia Jane shift beside her.

"If the two of us are strong together, just think about how unbeatable the three of us will be."

Izzy squeezed Magnolia Jane's hand and nodded her head knowing they would have to be. There was no other choice in the matter. She opened her eyes and looked at Magnolia Jane, giving her hand another squeeze. "Our first step is to get Olivia out of the tub." She turned to her mom again. "Nor'easter be damned. We've got to get that ankle taken care of."

* * *

The closest hospital was in the next town over. Magnolia Jane sat in the passenger's seat while Olivia sat sideways with her injured leg up in the back. The borrowed sneaker she wore on her left foot remained mostly dry thanks to Bennett, who had carried her as quickly to the Jeep as the weather would allow, but her hands felt like ice. She tried to burrow them in the pockets of the coat Magnolia Jane had given her, but her body was twisted strangely to keep her leg elevated, and the seatbelt kept her from doing so. Izzy drove as quickly as she could through the blizzard, her gloved hands gripping tight to the steering wheel as the snow and wind blew forcefully around the Jeep.

"I feel like Han Solo flying the Millennium Falcon," she said. "The way the snow is rushing straight at me."

"That makes me Leia," Magnolia Jane smiled. "I'll take it."

"Or Luke."

Magnolia Jane shook her head. "Nope. Leia. No discussion."

"Mom, I guess that means you're Chewbacca." Izzy looked up into the rearview mirror and caught Olivia's eyes. "You used to yell a lot like him back in the day."

Olivia held Izzy's eyes. She reached up and pulled at the uncomfortable seatbelt. "I wouldn't mind that Wookiee costume he wore right about now," she said. "Will the heat go up any higher?"

Magnolia Jane reached over and turned the knob up a notch.

"I need to know what you're going to say to the doc," Izzy said. "I know telling me wasn't easy, but it's going to get harder from here. At least for a while."

Olivia had heard everything Izzy told her. She even agreed with it, but she wanted to live in denial a while longer. She wanted to say something mean, to deflect how she really felt. The first thing that flew from her mouth was always either sarcastic, biting or rude. It had been that way since as far back as she could remember. Her daddy called her insolent and too big for her britches. Never once did he stop to realize she'd learned everything she knew from him. The men in her life had often been turned on by her smart mouth at first, but eventually, they grew tired of it. There was a difference between feisty and mean. Most of them hung in there for a while before they gave up and left. Her latest husband had retaliated, beat that cheeky, back talking mouth into silence and submission.

"You've got the photos?" she asked.

"Yes, ma'am," Izzy answered.

Olivia bit her bottom lip so hard that tears came to her eyes again. "Then I'll tell him the truth."

"M.J.," Izzy told her niece, "we're gonna need a lawyer."

"I'll call Sam Chapman," Magnolia Jane said quickly. She'd had reason to talk to Sam a lot in the last year due to some legal issues Trey had found himself in. "If he can't help us, he'll know someone who can."

"Good. I have no idea what needs to be done here, but I'm thinking a restraining order is probably a good place to start."

Magnolia Jane turned and gave her grandmother a reassuring smile. Olivia was struck again by the resemblance she saw to Marjorie in the girl's face. She knew that coming back to Grey's Harbor was going to be difficult, but she'd had no idea how deep the pool of memories she'd be forced to swim in would be. She was having a hard time keeping her head above water.

Marjorie had been just sixteen when she left Grey's Harbor the first time. During her return trip four years later, Olivia had seen her for less than fifteen minutes. Once Marjorie had decided to go, she stayed gone. Seeing Magnolia Jane here in front of her brought Marjorie right back again.

Tatum, Marjorie's best friend, had invited her to go to California with her family for spring break their sophomore year. Tatum's family had planned a trip to Disneyland, but all Marjorie could see in her mind was the Hollywood sign and her ticket to fame and fortune. Three days after they'd arrived, Marjorie disappeared. Distraught, Tatum's family called the police. When the girl was found two days later and Olivia received a call from the station, she told them she wasn't breaking any North Carolina rules by dropping out of school. According to the law, Marjorie had every right to petition the court for emancipation, but Olivia told her not bother. She gave her daughter her consent to leave home.

"You'll be happier out there, baby girl. Grab a shooting star and take off across the sky."

Thinking about that now, Olivia wondered how that had all gone down without her being charged with abandonment or child endangerment. She knew she hadn't parented either one of her children well. Thank goodness Izzy had always had Mateo in her life. He'd been good to all three of them, but the truth was getting harder and harder to deny. She had let both her girls down. No wonder Izzy still struggled so hard to forgive her.

"Hello, Sam?" Olivia blinked and the memories cleared. "This is Magnolia Jane Mason. I'm sorry to be calling so late, but I'm afraid my family is in trouble and we need your help."

CHAPTER 5

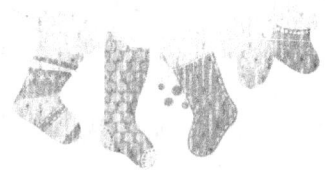

*I*zzy crawled into bed and felt Bennett roll over. Instead of letting her settle her head against the pillow, he brought her closer to him, taking her into his arms and cuddling her against his chest. The tears came before she could stop them. Bennett held her while she cried. He rained kisses on her hair and pressed the tops of his warm feet up against the bottoms of hers which were ice cold.

"His name is Darien Johansen. He's the CEO of Auerbach International, which owns and runs something like twelve highly established hotel chains all over the world."

"Like Hilton and Marriott?"

"Exactly like that. He works in one of the corporate offices in Vienna, Virginia, which is where he and Mom live. It's the wealthiest county in all of Virginia, which is exactly what attracted her to it, and their house sounds twice as big as Wren and Gabe's with a cleaning service, gardeners and a full kitchen staff."

"The exact opposite of what she ever had here."

"And precisely what she coveted the whole time I was growing up. It's only thirty minutes outside of Washington, DC, and she and Darien are always invited to all the swanky parties hosted by men who make a ton of money and their wives who like to help them spend it. She's a trophy wife with a large expense account at her fingertips and lots of people around to kiss her ass. That's what attracted her to Darien and his lifestyle. It's maybe what kept her there, at least at first. But it turns out that Darien's a mean son of a bitch who likes to use his fists and pretends that his wife is his personal punching bag. She's got a broken ankle now, and more bruises than I can even count. Her hip and her knee are badly swollen. Oh, Bennett," she paused, "seeing her naked in that tub … she's so thin, and she looks so fragile, like if I breathed on her too hard she might just break in two. She's been in and out of the hospital with other injuries over the past four years. The physical damage he's done makes my head want to explode, but I think he's messed her up mentally even worse."

Izzy sniffed and Bennett reached up to run his fingers through her hair, pulling the wild strands away from her face.

"Maybe she's stronger than you think," he told her. "She came all the way from Virginia to the coast of North Carolina with a single bag and a broken ankle to get away from him. She took a huge risk. She came back to a town she always hated, bared her soul to the person she probably loves most in the world, and the person to whom she's been the most horrible to. She's always hated the fact that she needed you in the past, but you're the one she came to when she needed help the most. I don't know, Iz. She sounds pretty damn brave to me."

Izzy's feet were much warmer now, and her body fit so well against Bennett's. It was three in the morning, and she'd been awake for nearly twenty hours. She'd been so keyed up, believing she'd never calm down enough to rest. The house was quiet. The wind had stopped blowing, and the snow had stopped falling. Hohner was snoring in his bed, and Izzy could hear the steady beating of Bennett's heart. The memory of his voice still floated around her head, and the words he'd spoken still held their shape. Without meaning to, Izzy closed her eyes. Her breathing slowed, her brain decided to calm its whirring, and she slept.

· ✻ ·

*B*ennett came up behind Izzy and wrapped his arms around her waist. Izzy leaned her head against him, let him cradle her against his chest. She could smell his shower still lingering on his skin, and he felt warm against her back. When he began whistling, he did so quietly. Izzy recognized the first line of the song almost immediately, and when Bennett saw her reflection smiling at him from the mirror, he started over so she could fill in the words.

"Fly me to the moon, let me play among the stars ... Let me see what spring is like on Jupiter and Mars. In other words, hold my hand ..."

"In other words," Bennett picked up the lyrics, turning Izzy around in his arms. "Baby, kiss me ..."

She obliged, standing up on her toes to deepen the kiss. "Old Blue Eyes."

He felt her smile against his lips. He'd have been disappointed had she not said it. "Sure," he told her. "Or Tony Bennett."

Izzy kissed him again, feeling his beard against her skin. She wished there was more time. She wished there weren't eight inches of snow outside. She wished her mother and her niece weren't sitting in the living room and able to pick up on noises coming from the master bedroom.

"Or Tony Bennett," she agreed. "Kiss me once more."

"How about twice for good measure." Izzy smiled, but then Bennett covered it with his mouth. "We taking my truck or your Jeep?"

"I can't sit still."

Bennett kissed the tip of her nose. "The Jeep it is then."

· ✳ ·

*O*livia was quietly snoring in Bennett's leather recliner, the volume turned low on *It's a Wonderful Life*. Five freshly painted toenails in a bright shade of holiday red poked out of the fleece blanket tucked around her lap.

Magnolia Jane sat at the kitchen table sipping warm hazelnut coffee with a heavy dose of sweet cream and flipping through a catalog while she talked on the phone.

"I wish you were with me," Trey told her. She could hear his windshield wipers as he cleared the glass and the sound of snow beneath the tires of his truck.

"Me, too," she replied, flipping a page. She'd already filled him in on what had happened the night before. "I'm glad that at least one of us is showing up to the wedding, though. Thank you. I didn't feel good about leaving Oli here by herself. She needs to take her meds every four hours, and she needs to eat. She's a little wonky on the pain killers. I don't want her to try to get up and hurt herself even more."

"Oli?"

Magnolia Jane sighed. "I can't call her 'grandma'. It doesn't feel right. But neither does 'Olivia'. She's part of my mom, and I never got my mom, so I feel like I want to get to know her. She's in bad shape, Trey. She was mean at the library, but her life is so messy. Aunt Iz promised to help her."

"And where Aunt Iz goes, you go." He wasn't teasing her, and she knew it. He was merely stating a fact.

"Yeah. I've seen the recent damage that's been done to her body. She's dealt with this for years and it makes me want to cry, Trey, it really does. Aunt Iz has told me quite a bit about her. Not a lot of it was good, and I see glimpses of the woman that raised her and my mom every so often, but for the most part, when I'm with her, she just seems broken."

"And Iz is really good at putting broken things back together again."

Magnolia Jane felt Hohner lean back against her leg. He'd been half lounging at her feet since she'd poured her coffee, but the urge for a late morning nap had overcome him. He'd been one of those broken things once, and Izzy had given him the time, love, and encouragement he needed to become whole again.

"Let me know how the wedding goes?"

"I will call you on my way home if not sooner. Any chance I'll see you tonight?"

"I hope so. When Aunt Iz gets back, we'll figure out what happens next."

Hohner's head popped up and Magnolia Jane heard Olivia cough in the living room.

"I love you."

Magnolia Jane bent down and rubbed one of Hohner's ears, silently praising him for his attention to detail. "I love you, too. Be careful."

When she and Hohner padded into the living room, Magnolia Jane saw that Olivia was awake.

"I'm in here droolin' on myself."

"If I were on Vicodin, I'd drool, too. Enjoy it while you can. We've got tissues." She reached out and gently touched Olivia's toes. "I think they're dry now. And cold. Let's cover you up. Did you have a good nap?"

"I can't believe how tired I am."

"Your body is healing," Magnolia Jane told her. "Sleep is good for you. So is food. I'll be right back."

While Magnolia Jane prepared lunch, she thought about how exhausting it must have been for Olivia to live in constant fear. She hoped that maybe Olivia was able to sleep now because she knew someone was looking after her. The thought made her happy and sad all at once.

It had been late when they'd gotten Sam on the phone the night before, and he wasn't sure he could get to the hospital during the storm. While they waited for the nurse to take Olivia for x-rays, Izzy and Magnolia Jane listened to Sam talk to his client over the speaker on Izzy's phone.

Six months earlier, during a brutal argument, Darien pushed Olivia out of a moving vehicle and broke her collar bone. Olivia didn't share the details of exactly what happened, and neither Izzy nor Magnolia Jane were sure they wanted to know. The important part of that experience for Olivia was that it had been the catalyst that prompted her to leave.

When one of the nurses who had cared for her in the ER, a beautiful black woman named Kara, called to check up on her the next day, Olivia lied just like she had so many times before. Yes, she was okay. Yes, she felt safe in her home. She and her husband's relationship was just fine. She couldn't believe how clumsy she was. She just hadn't seen that water on the floor. Thank you so much for checking in.

A few minutes later, when Kara texted her a number for a website about domestic violence funded by the department of Health and Human Services, Olivia knew she either needed to become a better storyteller, or she needed to do something about her situation. She committed the address to memory, deleted the text from her phone, and went straight to the library where she logged onto to one of the public computers. As she clicked through the pages, she came to the slow and painful realization that she had become a statistic. She was the one in four adult women who wound up the victim of physical violence by an intimate partner. She'd been lying to everyone for the last several years, including herself.

She followed the guidelines on the webpage and started putting together a go bag. Over time, she filled it with cash she secretly squirrelled away. She packed clothes, toiletries, and legal documents, like her birth certificate, her Social Security card, her passport, and her insurance cards. When she couldn't think of a good place to hide the bag, she gathered her courage, called the hospital and asked to speak to Kara. The woman quickly agreed to keep the bag hidden in an old milk box on her porch she hadn't used for the last ten years, leaving it accessible to Olivia no matter what time of day she might need to get to it.

On December twenty-first, two days before she showed up in Grey's Harbor, Olivia decided she needed to get to that bag.

Olivia and Darien had attended a party at an affluent business partner's home. She hadn't been feeling well and decided to take some cold medicine to help clear her stuffy head. When she was offered a drink, she hadn't thought twice about accepting, but, according to Darien, she'd acted strangely, and several of his colleagues mentioned it. He'd fumed in the car, so Olivia knew she'd be made to pay for her mistake. It had been much worse than she'd imagined.

The argument started in the bedroom. He berated her for the dress she'd chosen to wear, although it had been one he'd picked out for her himself. It made her look fat, he said, made the other wives wonder what she did all day while her husband was hard at work. When he reached for the crystal butterfly clip that sat perched above her left ear, he yanked a handful of hair out with it, tossing it all toward the lit makeup mirror in their dressing room. Then he accused her of being messy and swiped his arms along the surface of the vanity, sending makeup and jewelry flying across the room and breaking her mirror and several perfume bottles when they shattered against the wall.

Afraid, Olivia turned and ran from the room. He and his angry voice followed her, accusing her of acting flighty and giggling like a schoolgirl. He told her Tom Cargill claimed she'd even hit on him. It didn't matter that Tom had an over inflated sense of self-importance and habitually reported that wives flirted with him. It was a joke among the men, and most of the women, too. It held no weight, but Darien used it to help fuel the fire of his rage.

Olivia made it to the top of the stairway on her own, but she had help with the trip down. After Darien shoved her, watching her roll precariously down the hardwood treads, hitting her head and body against the railing and landing in a heap in the foyer, he'd called her stupid and useless, then stomped back to the bedroom and slammed the door. It had the sound of finality to it that Olivia needed. She dragged herself to one of the guest bedrooms on the main floor that night and slept with a chair wedged beneath the doorknob. Once she saw Darien drive his white Mercedes down the long driveway and turn left onto the main road, Olivia said her goodbyes.

She wrapped her swelling ankle and forced it into a pair of boots. Then she took her car, retrieved her bag, and headed to the grocery store where she shopped every week. She pulled the battery from her phone, then threw them both into the trash can in the parking lot. From there, she took a cab to the metro station south of town and headed into DC. She boarded a train and spent the next nine hours traveling south. Her ankle throbbed while her thoughts spun around in her head. By the time she got to Grey's Harbor, her stomach was so tied up in knots, she spent an hour in the bathroom of a gas station throwing up the chicken salad sandwich and stale chips she'd forced herself to eat for dinner.

Olivia hadn't been paying attention to the weather reports and had no idea a record-breaking nor'easter was heading in the same direction she was. And she couldn't have known there was a wedding taking place in Grey's Harbor the day after she arrived and that the Harbor Inn would be at capacity. It had been happenstance that she'd been hobbling past the library, trying to keep out of sight in case someone she'd known all those years ago might recognize her, and saw the woman come out of the back door. It had been pure coincidence, or Olivia believed now, fate that Magnolia Jane had been the one to open that door to find her on the other side.

She really had no plan once she arrived in Grey's Harbor. She knew she had to leave Virginia. She knew she had to run. Her heart told her to go home, although Grey's Harbor had never truly felt like home to her. She only fully understood once she'd arrived that cold and stormy night that home was Izzy.

"You are not going to believe this soup," Magnolia Jane said, Hohner close at her heels as she brought two steaming bowls of potato soup, half a loaf of crusty bread and the butter dish all balanced on a cutting board. She put everything on the coffee table, then set a wooden tray table in place over Olivia's lap. "Would you like some butter for your bread?"

"Yes, please," Olivia nodded. She took the spoon Magnolia Jane offered her, then smelled the soup when the bowl was placed in front of her. "Oh," she said, after taking a bite, "there's chunks of lobster in here."

Magnolia Jane cut two slices of bread and buttered them before placing them on Olivia's tray. "It's amazing, right?"

"It's delicious."

"Aunt Iz made it. She serves it at the bar. People are crazy for that soup."

Olivia took another bite. "I can see why."

The two of them ate in silence for a few minutes, Hohner gratefully accepting the crusts of bread that Magnolia Jane handed down to him.

"I know I've already said it, but you look so much like your mother. It's remarkable."

"Most people that knew her tell me that."

"Are there many around still that remember her?"

Magnolia Jane brought her legs up and crossed them on the couch. On her feet she wore pink fuzzy socks, and she cradled her soup bowl with a hand covered in an over long sweatshirt sleeve— this one light blue with a University of North Carolina Tarheels logo on the front. Her long, dark hair was resting on the crown of her head in a messy bun, and her pretty face was free of makeup. "Sure. There's Aunt Iz, of course, and Gabe and Wren—"

"Wren?" Olivia interrupted. "Your mom is still friends with Wren Murphy?"

"Wren Mason," Magnolia Jane corrected. "She's my mother-in-law now, but she helped Aunt Iz raise me. I doubt there are two closer friends than the two of them on the entire planet."

Olivia set her spoon down and she picked up a slice of bread. She played with it rather than eating it, and Magnolia Jane watched her. "Your husband, is he running the Mason Paper Company yet?"

"Trey," Magnolia Jane reminded her. "I doubt Gabe will be retiring any time soon. He works with his dad. Eventually, he and Brett, his younger brother, will take over."

"Of course they will."

Magnolia Jane heard a touch of resentment in her grandmother's voice. She remembered what Izzy had said about the Haves and the Have Nots and the way Olivia had always felt about her status. She'd hated the bungalow and the fact that her husband had been a lowly auto mechanic. She'd hated the fact that she had to work behind a makeup counter at the mall, and that the priciest thing she'd been able to afford were perfume samples pilfered from her place of employment. She'd never been happy with the fact that she was richer than most in the things that really mattered. She'd had a man who loved her, she had a family, she lived in a beautiful place near the ocean, and she was surrounded by townsfolk who would have loved and accepted her had she allowed them to. Instead, she'd longed for material possessions, strayed from her marriage, gotten pregnant with another man's baby, and had been treated like a child by her oldest daughter who'd been forced to step into the place of mature adult.

"This house …"

"It's different now than when you left."

Olivia nodded. "I'm sleeping in the same room, but it's not at all the way it used to be."

"Aunt Iz remodeled and added a master suite and another bathroom. I was little when she did that. Maybe seven or eight. I still remember what it used to look like, but not very well."

"Izzy and Marjorie used to share your room," Olivia said, aware that Magnolia Jane was certainly privy to this information. She felt the need to talk, to reminisce, and Magnolia Jane seemed open to the idea, so Olivia continued. "It was painted yellow, and your mother had posters all over her half. Drove Izzy crazy."

Magnolia Jane smiled. "She told me about that."

"They fought a lot, those girls." Olivia's hands moved from the tray. "At least Marjorie did. Izzy was always trying to make peace, but it went against everything Marjorie was, so to her it always felt like a fight."

Magnolia Jane watched Olivia. She'd thrown fewer barbs since they'd brought her back from the hospital. She felt a little less prickly, but Magnolia Jane was still on guard. She reminded herself that the woman was on pain killers. She remembered when Trey was going through his shoulder surgeries and the way the pills he took changed aspects of his personality. She wasn't sure she could trust the Olivia sitting here in Izzy's living room. She realized how desperately she wanted to, and that's what she clung to.

"Oh," she said, remembering. She set her nearly empty bowl on the couch and stood up to retrieve a black wooden frame that rested on a set of bookshelves on the other side of the room. "This is one of Aunt Iz's favorite photographs. She's got so many of them. Wren went to this big scrapbooking retreat years ago and bought more stuff than she knew what to do with. She asked me to gather as many pictures as I could find, and she surprised Aunt Iz one Christmas with half a dozen books she put together."

She handed Olivia the frame. Mateo had always been camera happy. He'd stuff quarters into those big photo booths and the two of them would cram inside, laugh and go through a series of poses, then wait for the strip of black and white snapshots to slide from the side of the big metal box. He often set up the timer on the collection of cameras he'd owned over the years, ask his family to pose and wait for the flash. There had been thousands of candid shots he'd taken, pictures of first steps, playing at the park, music recitals, blowing out candles.

It only took a few moments inside the bungalow to see that Izzy had become a shutter bug just like her father. There were no photos of Magnolia Jane as a baby encased in the numerous frames scattered around shelves and other horizontal flat places. It was like those few years had been lost, had never been recorded. Neither Izzy nor Olivia had even known Magnolia Jane existed until she showed up holding tight to Marjorie's hand that fateful day so long ago. Olivia had only met her briefly, hadn't even held the child. She looked down at the photo in the frame and could hardly tell which one of them she was seeing behind the glass, Marjorie or Magnolia Jane.

Quickly, she realized it was a shot of Mateo, Olivia, Izzy and Marjorie. She and Mateo had been divorced for at least four or five years when the photo had been captured. It seemed strange to Olivia as she studied the people staring back at her. She remembered that Mateo had come to pick Izzy up. She'd been about eleven at the time. It had been over winter break, and she'd helped Rosemarie, the secretary at Steve's Auto Shop where Mateo worked, for several weeks on Saturdays and Sundays to earn some spending money. The two of them were going on one of their many father/daughter outings, this time to do some Christmas shopping. When Mateo came inside, he saw that both Olivia and Marjorie were at home and invited them to go to lunch.

Olivia traced each figure in the photograph with the tip of her finger. They were all in front of the oversized Christmas tree they set up at the mall every year. Izzy had opted not to visit Santa, but she'd waited in line so that Marjorie could sit on his lap. They both held candy canes and grinned at the woman Mateo had asked to snap their picture. Marjorie was propped on Mateo's hip, Izzy standing in front of him with Olivia next to her. The four of them were smiling.

They looked like they belonged there together. They looked like a family.

"This is Izzy's favorite?"

Magnolia Jane nodded. "One of them. She's had it framed since as far back as I can remember."

"The fact that I'm it surprises me."

Magnolia Jane studied her grandmother's strong profile. "There's probably a lot about Aunt Iz that would surprise you if you actually got to know her."

Olivia moved her head and met her granddaughter's eyes. She studied the young woman. When she looked at her, it was Marjorie she saw. She'd only just met Magnolia Jane and didn't know what kind of a person she was on her own.

Olivia sighed, the frame gently falling to the tray. Is that what she'd done to Izzy all those years? She'd had the same thought the night before while in the bath. It nagged at her, wouldn't leave her be. When Olivia looked at her eldest, from the time she'd been an infant until she graduated from high school, what she saw was Mateo. Olivia had been so hard to please. No matter what she had, she wanted more. Mateo had given her everything he'd had to give. She knew that now. In so many ways, she realized she'd known it back then. Still, it had never been enough. Izzy resembled her father in countless different ways. Olivia had lived with Izzy for eighteen years, seen her every single day, but now she wondered if she had the slightest idea about what kind of person Izzy actually was. She closed her eyes and laid her head against the back the chair.

"Oli? What's wrong?" Magnolia Jane reached down, put the backs of her fingers against Olivia's forehead. They were warm against her skin.

Olivia remembered the times Izzy had taken care of her. She'd resented Izzy for it. Izzy had made sure that Marjorie had good food in her belly. She kept the electricity, water, and heat on, made sure the phone stayed connected every month. She baby sat her little sister. Truth be told, she'd baby sat Olivia, too. Olivia wanted to be treated like a queen. She wanted to be doted on. She wanted to be loved. Izzy had done that, but it hadn't been the kind of love Olivia craved.

"You look just like your mother," Olivia said again, her eyes still closed, "but you take after your aunt."

Magnolia Jane smiled, but Olivia didn't see it. "Thank you."

Olivia had lost Marjorie. She didn't want to lose Izzy, too.

"So," she said opening her eyes and looking at Magnolia Jane again. "Tell me about this Bennett fella. Is he a good guy?"

"Definitely," Magnolia Jane chuckled. "He's worked with Aunt Iz for nearly four years now. He supplies all the meat for the Mizzen Mast. Owns his own company."

"He lives here in the house?"

Magnolia Jane nodded. "He does."

"What about his family?"

"He's got two boys. Henry is about my age. He works in IT in Raleigh. Harrison is studying marine biology in Florida."

"You've met them?"

Magnolia Jane squinted her eyes. "I have. What's with all the questions?"

"Well," Olivia said, taking in a deep breath. "Both you and your aunt have said some things and I've been thinking pretty hard about them."

"You were actually listening?" She smiled when Olivia gave her side eye.

"I've been told I don't know Isabella that well. I think that's true."

Magnolia Jane laughed again. "It's true, you don't," she stated, "or you would know that *abuelo* is the only one that ever calls Aunt Iz 'Isabella' and gets away with it."

"*Abuelo* ..." If Olivia wondered whether Mateo was still around, that one word removed all doubt.

Magnolia Jane nodded but didn't comment. She heard the wistfulness in her grandmother's voice and decided it was best she left it alone. She glanced at her phone, checking the time. "You about ready for another pill?"

Olivia nodded her head and Magnolia Jane stood, gathered up the soup bowls, stacked them on the cutting board and took it all back to the kitchen. Hohner whined, curious as to where she might be going. His ear twitched, listening to her movements in the kitchen. His face softened when she walked back into the living room with the pill bottle.

"Here you go." Magnolia Jane handed Olivia a fresh glass of water and her medication. Olivia dutifully swallowed it and put the glass down on the tray her granddaughter had moved to the side of the chair.

"I know you don't owe me any favors," she said. "But I was wondering if you might be willing to help me get to know my daughter."

Magnolia Jane reached down and squeezed Olivia's hand. This woman was one big question mark. There was a lot of pain her aunt still held in her heart, and Olivia was the cause of a lot of it. She would never betray Izzy, but as Magnolia Jane thought about it, she decided she might be able uphold her loyalty to Izzy and help her newfound grandmother at the same time.

"Yes, ma'am," she said softly. "I'd be happy to do that for you."

CHAPTER 6

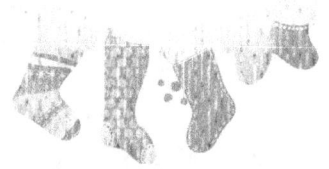

*B*ennett held Izzy in his arms and led her around the makeshift dancefloor. He was a big man, nearly twice her size, but she felt sure and strong against him as they danced. The reverent crowd had grown louder and more boisterous as the quiet of the ceremony came to an end and the party to celebrate the wedding kicked into gear. Izzy had done the opposite, turning quieter and more reserved. Bennett could almost hear the click and whir of cogs as they turned in her head.

"How's my girl?"

Izzy felt the vibration of his words in his chest. She took a deep breath, focused on the pine scent of the soap he liked to use. Her brain hadn't rested once since she'd gotten Magnolia Jane's phone call. When she and Bennett arrived at Spencer Farm earlier that day, she gathered her family around her. Mateo, Bailey, Wren, Gabe, and Brett, and together she and Trey told them about what had happened in the library the previous night. When she relayed the conversation she'd heard between Olivia and Sam Chapman, no one questioned the reason why she'd decided to take her mother in and provide her a safe place to hunker down.

"What's the long-term plan?" Gabe asked.

"I don't know," Izzy explained. "Right now, we're waiting on the restraining order. The holiday is slowing that process, but Sam's working on it. Bennett and I have asked mom to stay with us at least until she recovers."

"Or maybe indefinitely," Bennett added, catching Izzy's eye. That actually hadn't been discussed yet, and Izzy hadn't gone that far in her own mind. She turned to look at Bennett and saw that he was already watching her. "She's pretty fragile right now," he said. "I don't know her like the rest of y'all do, but from what I've heard she isn't usually like she is now."

"She's still got the old Olivia zing to her," Izzy replied with a bit of irritation in her voice.

"She was slingin' some mud around the library," Trey said.

"I'll bet that went over real well with M.J." Wren shook her head. "Is she at the house with Olivia now?"

"She is," Trey nodded. "Iz had to hold her back a couple of times last night, but when I talked to her a half an hour ago, she sounded like she was feeling grateful for the chance to maybe get to know Olivia a little bit."

"I don't know what's going to happen," Izzy said truthfully. "None of us do. It's like me when I was trying to figure out how to get my feet underneath me without alcohol. I fell down. A lot. This road we're on, it's gonna be a bumpy one." She sighed. "Bennett's right. She's fragile. She's also everything Olivia used to be, so I see this frail little bird, but then she strikes like a snake, fangs out. I'm trying to balance those things while dealing with the anger I have for what's been done to her and trying to find some forgiveness for all the shit that happened in the past."

"*Oh, mi dulce niña.*" Mateo gave Izzy a closed mouth smile. "*Estoy orgullosa de ti cariño,*" he told her, pulling her into a hug. Mateo had always been the first person to tell Izzy he was proud of her. Even now in her mid-forties, she found the sentiment affirming.

Tears came to Izzy's eyes as she hugged her dad. He was the one who knew best what Olivia was like. Bennett had said the night before that Olivia had come back to the one person she'd hurt the most. Izzy thought maybe she and Mateo shared that particular title. Olivia had cheated on him during their marriage. She'd gotten pregnant and had a baby that didn't belong to him. He'd divorced her, but he hadn't left. He continued to pay for the house she lived in, he'd been there for Marjorie, was the only father figure the girl ever had, and he'd done his best to take care of them even after Izzy had gone to New York for college. He'd been in a loving relationship, married to Bailey for almost twenty-five years. It didn't take away what had happened between Mateo and Olivia, but it provided a thick cushion. At least in Izzy's subconscious mind. She realized now that she'd been so consumed by how her mother's return was affecting her that she hadn't considered what it might be doing to her dad.

"*Te amo, papá*," she said against his chest.

Mateo's grip on his daughter tightened. "I love you, too," he said. "We all do."

"We're here for you, Iz," Gabe told her, reaching out to squeeze her arm.

"You just let us know what you need," Bailey said.

Izzy took a fortifying breath, then slowly pulled away from Mateo. "Thanks, Bailes."

"Hey," Wren said. Izzy turned and was gathered up in another set of arms.

"Y'all are making me cry."

"It's a wedding," Brett said. "Everybody cries at weddings."

"You alright with me crashing at the house tonight?" Trey asked when Izzy stepped away from Wren.

"Since when do you need an invitation?" she asked, looking at Trey. "Bring food. The occupancy rate is climbing." Izzy felt someone tap her on the shoulder and she turned.

"I think they're about ready for you," a member of the wedding party told her.

Izzy sniffed, wiping at the corner of her eye. "Thanks," she said. "Looks like it's showtime." She turned to Bennett, her chin lifted. He gave her a smile and a kiss before she headed to find her cello.

She'd played beautifully as always. Mateo closed his eyes when her bow touched the strings. A smile lifted the corners of his mouth upward and didn't leave his lips until long after the bride had reached the groom.

Music played now, but it wasn't the classical version.

"You didn't answer," Bennett said as they spun in lazy circles apart from the crowd.

"I'm sorry." She'd been using Bennett as a shelter, a place to ground herself. "What was the question?"

"How are you?"

He felt Izzy breathe against him. "I'm a mess," she admitted.

"Hmmm …" he pondered aloud. "I don't know. You're not nearly as messy as you think you are."

"I feel messy," she countered.

"Talk it out," he urged.

She was quiet as they danced. He led and she didn't have to think about where her feet were supposed to go. "I'm still shocked, you know?" She felt him nod. "Surprised. Furious. Scared." She paused. "Grateful."

He thought about what she'd said while he held her against him. He wanted to be Izzy's refuge. He wanted to help carry her when she needed carrying. Even if it was only for a few minutes. Izzy stood solidly on her own two feet, and she liked it that way.

When it felt as though she'd run out of things to say, Bennett spoke. "Izzy Edwards, you are the most remarkable woman I've ever met."

"Damn straight I am."

Bennett dipped his chin, smelled the faint vanilla scent that clung to Izzy's hair. "I don't know if this is the right time for this. So much has happened in the last two days. I've had it planned for a while now, and, well, I think I love you even more at this moment than I did when the idea came to me."

Izzy pulled her head back and Bennett saw that her eyebrow was raised. The one with the shiny silver hoop in it. He leaned over and pressed a kiss to her forehead.

"Yeah," he said with a nod. "I'm just gonna stick with it." He stepped back and slowly dropped to one knee. Her eyebrow was still raised, and Bennett pulled a small box from the inside of his jacket pocket.

"Bennett …" Izzy looked into the clear amber of his eyes. She could see Christmas lights behind him, all around the two of them, shining and glittering, throwing a soft cheerful glow into the big space. It reminded her of another winter, of Rockefeller Plaza, and the enormous Christmas tree she couldn't get enough of.

At first, she thought she might not be able to take a breath. A fluttery feeling began in the pit of her stomach, and she waited for the panic to overtake her. She watched Bennett's face. That handsome, bearded face, and … then he smiled at her, and she realized that her legs were not about to give away beneath her. It took a few more seconds for her to realize that the sensation in her stomach wasn't panic after all. As a matter of fact, it felt a little like the velvet wings of butterflies moving against her insides. They weren't frantic. She searched for a way to describe the sensation. Was that excitement she felt?

"Huh," she said, tilting her head to the side.

Bennett's smile widened. He continued to watch her, waiting.

"You asked me how I felt earlier."

"Yeah."

"I need to add to the list." She reached out and traced his bottom lip with her fingertip.

"You ready?"

She couldn't help but smile. "To be clear, I'm not wearing a dress."

"I think I've heard that somewhere before. Wear whatever makes you happy. Marry me." He opened the box to show her the ring, but she never looked at it. Her gaze still hadn't moved away from his eyes.

"Yes," she said, grinning.

Bennett half stood, wrapping his arms around her legs just beneath her butt, and brought her to his full height with him. She pressed her palms against his shoulders to balance herself and felt his beard brush against the neckline of her sweater. He spun her around and Izzy laughed.

Music was playing around them, but as Bennett brought her boot covered feet back down the ground, he began to whistle. After the first line Izzy gave him a nod. "Ah …" she said, the grin still on her face. "Keep goin'." He obliged, their feet moving again in time to the notes. "We'll hold hands and touch 'n' hug, he talks so sweet to me. 'Cause he knows a lot about love and stuff, and he's gonna marry me ..."

"He is," Bennett told her, reaching up to move the hair out of her eyes.

"I'm glad you stayed away from any talk about goin' to the chapel."

"I figured we might end up skipping that tradition."

She nodded. "I like that idea."

"It was a teenage wedding, and the old folks wished them well didn't really suit us, either."

Izzy laughed again. "We are the old folks. Totally doesn't fit." She brought her hand to his face and ran her fingertips through his beard. "Dolly was a solid choice. Absolutely perfect."

"Perhaps the timing could have been better."

"No," Izzy said without hesitation. "The timing was perfect, too." She continued to dance against Bennett as a thoughtful expression crossed her face. "Life is crazy. Bad stuff happens all the time, and we can't control any of it. Seems like we're always picking up the pieces ... women cheat on their husbands, tear their families apart ... mama's leave their little girls ... people drink and drive and leave lives in ruins, and men break bones and leave scars on the bodies and hearts of those they've promised to cherish the most." Her hand slipped down until it rested on his chest. "It only seems smart to reach out and grab at the good stuff when we see it shining in front of our eyes, doesn't it? We take the bad, we sure as hell should take the good, too, and hold onto it with all we've got."

Bennett pulled the ring from the box, their feet still moving. The collection of silver bands Izzy wore on her left hand had changed over the last year. Bennett slipped a simple but elegant platinum solitaire on the one finger that bore no jewelry.

"You're my good, Iz," he told her. "I'm holding on with all I've got, and I'm not ever letting you go."

CHAPTER 7

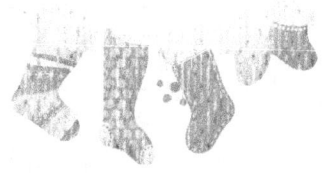

*T*he bungalow had an attached garage, but Izzy never parked her Jeep there. Instead, she used the space for storage, and that's where she kept the large freezer that Bennett kept filled with ground beef, steaks, lamb, pork, chicken and even duck. When Izzy walked into the front door, she knew right away that Magnolia Jane had gone through and found something to cook for dinner.

Hohner heard the Jeep drive up and let out a long, continuous howl as he ran from the kitchen to the front of the house.

"Good lord, girl, whatever that is smells delicious," Bennett called from the front door where he was unlacing his snow caked boots. "Hello, Miss Olivia," he said sending a smile in her direction. "You've got some color in your cheeks this evening. You look beautiful."

"Hi, Mom," Izzy greeted with a smile. "Hello, Hohner, my good, good boy." She rained kisses on the dog's soft, wrinkled head.

"Is he always like this, or is it my Vicodin makin' things feel off kilter?"

"Bennett? Off kilter?" Izzy laughed. "This is one of the steadiest men I know."

There was a knock on the door and Izzy moved out of the way as Trey walked in the house.

"And here's another one," Bennett said.

"Oh, wow," Trey said, taking a deep breath into his lungs. "That's the smell of homemade potpies. My wife's been cooking this afternoon." With his shoes off, he turned and looked at Olivia. Trey had a natural charm about him, one that made it difficult for people—specifically women—not to like him. He wore his dark blond hair in messy spikes, and his eyes were the color of the summer sky. He'd been raised with manners and an easy-going smile, and he used both on Olivia as he moved closer to her.

"Hi, Oli," he said as he bent to place a kiss on her cheek. "I see Spencer loaned you her Rutgers University sweatshirt. That red looks terrific on you. How are you feeling?"

"Spencer?" Olivia asked the exact same time Izzy said, "Oli?"

Trey chuckled and looked back at Izzy. "That's what Spence has been calling Olivia. I figured it was okay that I did, too."

"I like it," Olivia said, her lips lifting in a small smile. "Now, Spencer."

"Well," Trey said, facing Olivia once more. "Since we were little, I've called her by her last name. I'm not sure why, to be honest with you, but it's a habit I haven't been able to break. I'll probably always call her that."

"You'd better," Magnolia Jane said walking into the room. "I'm glad you're here." She threw her arms around his neck and he pulled her to him. The kiss they shared was passionate, but not inde-cent, and Olivia kept her eyes on them. "You're staying, right?"

"Yes, ma'am."

"Excellent answer."

"Was Trey right?" Bennett asked. "Did you really make potpies?"

"A whole slew of them. There's salad and warm cinnamon applesauce, too. Come on, Oli," Magnolia Jane said, pulling the blanket from Olivia's lap. "And after dinner, I challenge y'all to a game of Scrabble."

"Oh, hell no," Izzy stated, coming to help get Olivia out of the chair. "The game of the night is poker, word nerd. I'll warn you, though. I'm feelin' pretty lucky right now."

"I don't know," Olivia said, getting her crutches underneath her. "I do a hell of a lot better at poker than I do Scrabble. You might have some competition, Iz."

"And if she loses," Bennett said from behind them, "she can always blame it on the Vicodin."

∗∗∗

The jar of pennies that sat on the kitchen table was only a third full. Most of the coins were heaped in the middle, with dwindling piles in front of each player.

"Izzy wasn't kidding," Trey said, leaning closer to Magnolia Jane. "She is lucky tonight."

Magnolia Jane ran her fingers over the small amount of coins she'd managed to keep. "It's a good thing we're only playing for pennies."

"And they're not even your pennies," Izzy shook her head.

"This is the only safe way to play poker with you," Magnolia Jane laughed.

The sweep of headlights coming through the kitchen window made everyone look up. The clock hanging above the sink said it was after eleven. Izzy's phone sat on the table in front of her, as did Magnolia Jane's. Both of them had been silent, which meant their loved ones were most likely well and accounted for. Izzy, dismissed it, figuring it was a neighbor arriving home.

"One more hand," Olivia said. "That's about all I have left in me."

"I remember you used to beat the pants off Dad when I was little. He was always so even tempered. Game nights were the only times I really remember him getting angry."

"Angry?" Trey asked. "I don't think I've ever seen Mateo angry."

The laugh that bubbled from Olivia was almost evil. "You bet your ass I beat him." Her response made Bennett chuckle.

"I think I'm growing to like you very much, Miss Olivia."

There was another sweep of headlights and Izzy looked toward the window. When she heard a car door slam, she stood up. She parted the curtains and the light intensified. There was a car parked in front of the house, and Izzy could tell the engine was still running by the plume of exhaust that billowed in the air around the glow of the headlights.

"Anyone expecting company?" she asked. "I can't see it very well, but I don't think I recognize that car." She turned and caught Magnolia Jane's eyes.

"Come on, Oli," Magnolia Jane said. Trey stood and helped Olivia out of her seat. She almost lost her balance when the sound of someone beating on the front door rang through the house, but Trey kept her on her good foot.

Hohner exploded into a long fit of barking, his claws scraping against the floor as he lumbered into the living room. Normally, Izzy would call for him to be quiet. She didn't this time. He turned, looked at Izzy, expecting her to scold him.

"Good boy, Hohner," she told him.

He punctuated her sentence with another long howl followed by a series of deep throated barking.

"Center of the house," Izzy called to Magnolia Jane. It was like going through a hurricane. They'd been through that drill a hundred times. Go someplace without windows. Both Magnolia Jane and Trey knew exactly where they needed to take Olivia.

"It looks like a sedan. Maybe a Lexus or a Mercedes," Bennett said, looking out the window Izzy had just vacated. "It's a light color."

"Shit ..." Olivia said, the grip she had on Magnolia Jane tightening. "It's Darien."

"We knew this might happen," Magnolia Jane told her. "That's why you came here. We've got you."

"I'm calling the cops," Bennett said as Trey pushed through the bathroom door and flipped on the light.

"Let's sit," he said, his voice calm. "Here you go." They lowered Olivia onto the toilet seat and Magnolia Jane closed and locked the door.

"He's not getting in here, Oli," she said, her back pressed

against the wood. "Aunt Iz won't let him get past the porch. I promise."

"Olivia Johansen!" Izzy heard from outside as she came from the master bedroom and walked quickly through the house to the front door. Hohner was jumping all around her, filling the room with his deep, baritone bark as she pushed her feet into her partially unlaced Doc Martens. "Come on out of there now. It's time to go home."

"Who the fuck does this guy think he is?" Izzy asked. Hohner continued to bark, his big body restless as he paced in front of the door. She turned when she heard Bennett on the phone. He took a look at what she held in her hands and moved the phone from his face.

"Iz—"

"No," she told him. "You get the police here and I'll take care of the rest. This is my home, Bennett, and she's my mom. He's not gonna bully her here. I won't fight you on this."

She could tell Bennett wasn't happy with the situation. They both knew he didn't have any recourse. After a few seconds, Bennett continued his phone call.

"Olivia!"

Hohner's agitation grew at the sound of the stranger's voice. He sensed that his house and his loved ones were in danger, and he was vocal as hell about protecting them.

"Good boy," Izzy told him, peeking through one of the glass panes in her front door. She could see the man outside approaching the house. She flipped the porch light on, and the man slowed but didn't stop. She got a good look at her mom's latest husband.

He was tall, at least six feet. His hair was mostly gray, the color of steel, and he wore a red plaid rancher's jacket and blue jeans. Izzy guessed that none of his three-piece corporate suits worked well for herding wayward wives. His hands were empty as far as she could tell. She was glad hers weren't.

She opened the front door and Hohner took off like a shot. The dog's approach caught Darien's attention, but he didn't look afraid. Instead, he put his hands out as though he was going to stop the hound by brute force. Izzy had seen the marks he'd left on her mother's body. If he was capable of that, Izzy had no doubt he'd have any issue hurting a dog.

"Stop!" Izzy commanded, her voice calm but firm. Hohner pulled back, whining. He bobbed from foot to foot on the edge of the porch, eager for a chance to get at the intruder. He howled and barked, but he did as Izzy ordered. She followed Hohner out onto the covered porch. The air was cold and bit at her skin. She held the heavy gun in her hands. She planted her feet, the left one in front, and her body turned slightly.

"You Darien Johansen?"

Hohner whined.

"I am."

"Then I suggest you stay right where you are. This is private property, and I don't plan to invite you inside."

"I believe you got something in that house that belongs to me."

Despite the cold, Izzy felt heat climb up her neck and into her face. "That's where you're mistaken."

"You telling me that my wife isn't here?"

"I didn't say that," Izzy told him. "She's here but she doesn't belong to you. And there's no way in hell she's going anywhere with you ever again."

Izzy's voice was steady, but Hohner sensed the anger in it. It set him off again and he began to bark. She barely heard Darien laugh over the noise, but she thought it sounded humorless and mean.

"You think you're gonna be the one to stop me from taking her? Look at you. You're just a little thing standing up there trying to look big and tough."

Anger flared in Izzy's chest. She racked the gun, the sound sending Darien two steps back. She imagined lifting it and sending a bunch of holes through the arrogant, abusive excuse for a human being who stood in front of her. "I've got Carolina's 'Stand Your Ground Law' and a big ole shotgun here that says different. It's okay if you wanna try me, asshole. Give it a go. I'm not afraid to use either one of 'em."

Izzy heard something behind her. Voices. She heard Bennett and Magnolia Jane. She didn't dare turn around, wouldn't take her eyes off Darien. Then she heard Olivia.

"I'll tell him myself, Izzy."

Her voice was much too close. "Mom, get back in the house."

"Well," Darien said as Izzy watched him. He took another step forward and Hohner growled deep in his throat.

"Stay," Izzy demanded. "Both of you." Her eyes bore into Darien's stubborn face. "Mom, please."

"It doesn't look like she's listenin' to you, sugar. Olivia, here, she's an obstinate one. Doesn't take to bein' told things. She needs to be shown."

Mateo had taught Izzy not to point a gun at anything she wasn't willing to kill. She moved the Browning up and settled the butt against her shoulder, pointing the barrel straight at Darien's head. "I swear to god you come any closer and I will paint that pretty car of yours with the sorry contents of your hard ass skull."

Darien stared up at Izzy in silent challenge. She saw a muscle in his jaw twitch. "I see the apple didn't fall far from the tree now, did it? You're a firecracker just like your mama."

"Leave," she said. "Now."

Magnolia Jane and Trey still stood on either side of Olivia, their hands both holding her up and holding her back. The anger that had been hiding beneath the layers of fear was starting to burn hot. She wasn't alone anymore. She didn't have to battle this beast by herself. The realization empowered her, made her feel stronger emotionally even though her body was beaten and sore.

Bennett had positioned himself between them and Izzy, his phone up and recording. He knew he and Izzy would have to deal with whatever outcome this night presented to them. If they ended up having to defend her in court, he wanted to make sure he had the evidence to do so. All of them stared down at Darien Johansen as Hohner continued to whine and bark.

Darien moved his gaze to Olivia. "Come on, now," he demanded, the false playfulness now absent from his tone. "Pack your things and let's be on our way. I've already lost two days work tryin' to gather you back up. I don't intend to miss much more."

"I'm not going back to Virginia with you," Olivia said over the noise Hohner was making. "Not now, not ever."

"Oh, I think you will," Darien told her.

"I have a restraining order against you." Izzy was glad Olivia hadn't mentioned the fact that it hadn't been freed of red tape yet. If Darien decided to think about that at all, he probably would've been able to figure that out. He wasn't in the thinking kind of mood. "I've got a lawyer, too, and a bunch of pictures of the bruises you gave me. The last ones anyway. I won't be abused anymore, Darien. I'm done. I've had enough."

"You ungrateful, lying bitch. After all I've done for you," Darien said through clenched teeth. He moved forward, his hands balled into fists.

Izzy moved with him. "Not another step." She thought she heard the sound of sirens. They were close, and she silently thanked Bennett for making sure Grey's Harbor's finest made as much to do about their arrival as possible.

"Fuck you," Darien spit and lunged forward. Hohner didn't wait for permission. He sensed an eminent threat, and he leapt off the porch straight at Darien. In that split second, Izzy knew she couldn't fire the gun. At least not where she'd intended to. She couldn't risk hitting Hohner. Instead, she pivoted slightly to her left and reminded herself to keep her feet planted. She squeezed the trigger slowly, aiming for the ground and the inches of snow that covered it. A shot rang out, snow exploding near the woodpile and noise bursting around them, bringing everything to a standstill. Hohner took advantage and brought Darien down hard on his back. Izzy felt a sharp pain from the kickback bloom in her shoulder and the gun suddenly felt twice as heavy in her hands.

Seconds later, Sheriff Chapin screeched up in front of the house, his sirens blazing, lending more earsplitting chaos and a dizzying disco effect of red and blue lights flashing along the front of the bungalow and the cars parked there. His patrol car slid on the ice and snow and hit Darien's expensive sedan, nearly running over the man who was splayed on the ground with a growling 120-pound hound dog on top of him.

"Hohner!" Izzy yelled bringing the shotgun down and resting the butt next to her foot. "Hold!" Seeing that Darien was trapped and gasping for air, she turned to look behind her. "Everyone okay?"

She heard affirmative noises from all four people on the porch, then turned to see the sheriff, his gun drawn, approaching Hohner and Darien.

"Hohner, come!"

The dog was reluctant to obey, but he did, backing away from Darien slowly, his teeth still bared and a menacing growl coming from his throat.

"Good boy," Izzy told him when he turned and ran up the porch steps. "Good, good boy." She reached out, felt the soft fur on his head beneath her shaking palm, and felt like she might be able to breathe again.

Magnolia Jane looked up and watched the colored lights pulse against Olivia's pale face. "I told you he'd never make it past the porch."

CHAPTER 8

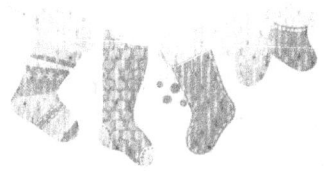

$\mathcal{T}$he room was lit by a night light in the shape of a lighthouse. It had been a gift from Mateo, and it had been shining its beacon within the bedrooms of the house since Izzy had been a little girl. This room had been the one Olivia and Mateo shared. They'd made love in this room, and they'd fought in this room. They'd conceived Izzy here, and this is where they'd decided to end their marriage. It only seemed fitting to Olivia that it was this same ceiling she stared up at when she made another big decision in her life.

Magnolia Jane was on one side, Izzy on the other. The bed was only a queen, but they all three fit just fine on the mattress. There was nothing about the room that looked like it had when Olivia had lived here. The walls were painted a soothing sea foam green, and the window was covered by thick wooden blinds the color of honey. The bed was leaned against a different wall, and there was a small flat screen television that sat on top of the tall six drawer dresser. All the furnishings were simple but tasteful. There was nothing frilly or fancy about the décor, but it all held such warmth. There were framed photos scattered atop the short bureau, and some that hung on the walls. Most of them were of Magnolia Jane, highlighting days, both big and small that, together, added up to what looked like a remarkable life. Others had captured Izzy on her own, some with Wren, Gabe, and Mateo. Bailey, her stepmom, was in many of them. Olivia had spent the last two days studying them all, soaking up a photographic history of the family she found herself eager to call her own.

"Thank you."

Olivia spoke softly, but both Magnolia Jane and Izzy heard her. She held Izzy's right hand and Magnolia Jane's left as they lie together on the bed.

"You're welcome," both of them replied at once, then Magnolia Jane laughed. "Jinx," she said.

"Jinx," Izzy replied.

They didn't know what had happened once Darien had been cuffed and taken away in the back of the sheriff's car. It was possible that the restraining order had been pushed through, in which case, they could argue he'd broken it. That wouldn't hold up for long considering the fact Darien hadn't even known about it at the time. He'd come with the intent to take Olivia from Izzy's home, and it was obvious that meant by force if necessary. Sheriff Chapin tacked on resisting arrest and disorderly conduct, but all three of the women knew that it wouldn't be long before Darien was a free man.

His car, however, was not. It had been involved in a police related accident, therefore it had been hauled off by a tow truck and impounded. Sheriff Chapin told them he'd try to find enough reason to keep Darien in custody for at least twenty-four hours and give them at least that much time to figure out what steps they needed to take next.

The law was a bit murky when it came to the shotgun. Izzy had every right to protect her property and family, and because there was recorded history that indicated Darien was a habitual abuser, Sheriff Chapin didn't think she would hear any static on the matter. Besides, she hadn't shot the intruder. She had four witnesses that attested to the fact that she hadn't aimed at him, and none of them thought the woodpile was going to make a formal complaint.

"I'd like to stay."

Izzy rested her cheek on her mother's shoulder and tried not to think about it too hard. She grabbed at the first thought, the first feeling that came to her. "I'd like that, too."

"Me, three," Magnolia Jane added.

The pain pill Olivia had taken once things had calmed down had her firmly in its grasp. She could barely keep her eyes open, and after a few minutes passed, Izzy could tell by her breathing that Olivia had fallen asleep. She let go of her mother's hand and gently rolled from the bed. Her right shoulder was feeling the aftereffects of the evening's events, and a headache had begun at the base of her skull.

"You sleeping in here?"

"Just in case she wakes up. I don't want her to be afraid," Magnolia Jane answered.

Izzy gave her a tired smile. "'If you weren't you, then we'd all be a little less we'".

"Let me guess," Magnolia Jane grinned. "Socrates? Mother Theresa? Oh, maybe Martin Luther King, Jr.?"

"Nope," Izzy said, walking around the bed to kiss Magnolia Jane's forehead. "Winnie the Pooh."

Magnolia Jane knew that, of course.

"I love you, Aunt Iz."

"Oh, my heart, I love you right back."

· ✳ ·

*H*ohner followed Izzy through the house. She tested the lock on the back door, then again on the front door, even though they'd already been checked half a dozen times. She knew that if Darien wanted Olivia badly enough, he could get into the house. It was all about control for him, and right now, he was not in control. Olivia was in a very dangerous transition right now. Izzy wondered how long it would be before she didn't check the locks multiple times before she went to bed.

The door to the master suite was cracked. Hohner, excited that Izzy was finally moving in the direction of his bed, brushed past her and pushed the door open with his nose. Light spilled out of the room and Izzy saw Bennett sitting up in bed, shirtless, his normally neat hair mussed. He looked as tired as she felt, and she realized they were about to have a conversation she dreaded having.

"Hey," he told her.

"Hey."

"How's Olivia?"

Izzy had taken her boots off again when they'd all come back into the house earlier. She padded into the bathroom, shook out a couple ibuprofen and swallowed them with a handful of tap water. She thought about brushing her teeth but decided she was too tired for something so strenuous. She took her jeans off, and sat on the toilet, wondering how she was going to get back up again and make it to her bed.

"The meds kicked in. M.J. is sleeping in there with her tonight. She told me she wants to stay." She stood, flushed, then kicked her jeans out of the way before smacking the light switch with her palm and trudging toward the bed.

"I was thinking that might be the plan."

"What's your plan?" She sat on the edge of the bed facing away from him. She'd known earlier when she told him she wouldn't fight about protecting her family that there might be repercussions. She'd meant it then, and she felt the same way about it now. That didn't mean the thought of losing him didn't break her heart.

"If tonight happened all over again, would you do it any differently?"

Izzy's bare legs were getting cold, but she didn't move. "No," she said honestly.

"Well," he said, and she felt a tightness in her chest. "I proposed to you this afternoon, and I'd do it again tomorrow and then next week and again next year had you not said yes to me already."

Izzy turned, bending her left knee and sliding her right foot beneath the blankets.

"I was afraid for you tonight," he told her. "I didn't want anything to happen to you, but what you did didn't surprise me in the least little bit. You fight for those you believe in, Iz. It's one of the things I love about you most. You scared the shit out of me, and I wanted to yell and scream and tell you to stop, but I knew it wouldn't do any good. You're who you are, and I wouldn't want you any other way."

She searched his amber colored eyes and found only the truth there. She felt the tightness around her heart ease, and the next thing she felt was the warmth of his fingers as he began to pull the hem of her t-shirt upward.

"Careful," she said quietly. "Kickback."

"Let me see." He helped her take her shirt off, then reached around with both arms to unhook her bra. His lips found the curve of her neck and shoulder as he pulled the garment from her body. "You're bruising," he told her. "I'm afraid it's going to get worse before it gets better."

"I haven't shot that gun in a long time."

"It looks like it hurts."

"I took something."

"I've got something for you, too."

She smiled as he reached back and extinguished the bedside lamp. Then he showed her just how much he loved her.

CHAPTER 9

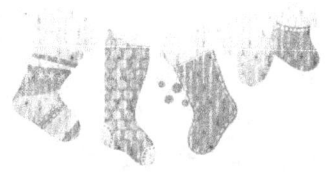

S now was still piled up around the Mason's big three-story house, looking stark and white against the brilliant blue of the Christmas sky. The air felt crisp and clean, and the sun had already started its work of melting what the nor'easter had left behind.

Multi-colored twinkle lights outlined the frame of the tall, sloping roof and the shape of the numerous windows of the house. Izzy remembered the day Wren and Gabe had moved in. They'd gotten married and signed the deed to the house during what Izzy called her hazy period. She'd been trying to hang onto her sobriety back then, and it had gotten away from her several times. While her friends had been putting down roots, Izzy had been doing her best not to drink herself to sleep at night in the tumble-down bungalow Olivia and Marjorie had run away from. The walls to the Mason house had always been strong, secure, and looking at it now while Bennett opened the passenger door of her Jeep, she felt a renewed appreciation for it and everyone that was gathered inside.

"You ready, Miss Olivia?"

"I'm sure I can walk," she told him. He could tell she didn't really want to walk, and he smiled at her.

"Now, if someone offered to carry me around, you better believe

I'd take 'em up on the offer. My advice to you is milk that cast for all it's worth."

Olivia laughed and Izzy saw it reach her eyes. Izzy's breath caught. She was sure she'd seen that happen before, but she knew it had been a long, long time ago. For a moment, she saw that hopeful, beautiful spark Mateo must have fallen in love with at that festival in Raleigh.

"All right," Olivia agreed. "I won't argue with you about it again."

There was an obvious bond between Olivia and Bennett forming. Something about the two of them just worked, and she watched him carry Olivia easily up the shoveled walkway.

"Hohner, be careful!" she yelled as the dog bounded out of the backseat and nearly sideswiped the pair trying to get to the front door. His nose was working overtime, and Wren was one of his favorite cooks.

"Can I help with these?" Trey asked, peeking into the back of the Jeep.

"Don't ask, just grab," Izzy told him. "Hand that bag to me, will you?" she asked as Trey opened the swinging door and lifted the window. "Perfect."

"You doin' alright, Iz?"

She turned and caught Trey's eyes. When she didn't answer right away, he smiled at her. "I respect the hell out of you, you know that? I've heard stories from y'all about what Olivia was like when you were growing up. I wasn't there then, but I was last night. You're a badass." Izzy couldn't help but laugh. "I'm serious," Trey told her. "You reminded me once again just how important family is, and I consider myself lucky as hell to be a part of yours."

"You better hug me quick," she said, feeling tears come to her eyes. Trey gathered her up in his arms and Izzy pressed her forehead against the front of his shoulder. "Ah ..." she winced, and Trey felt her body tighten.

"What happened?" he asked, moving his arms away.

"No," she said quickly. "Just hug me gently. I may be a badass, but that shotgun has a powerful kick." Trey hugged her again, this time without as much enthusiasm.

"Those gifts aren't gonna bring themselves inside now, are they?" Wren hollered from the front door.

Trey laughed again. "Leave the heaviest ones for me. I promise I won't tell anyone and ruin your rep."

The two of them gathered everything from the Jeep and made their way to the front door. Izzy could smell apple cider, ham, and Wren's famous cinnamon rolls as she walked into the foyer. Hohner was busy making the rounds, saying hello to Brett before bounding over to Mateo, who was always reliable for a good ear rub. Bennett had put Olivia down in Gabe's chair and her foot was elevated.

"You're getting to be a pro at recliner surfing," Magnolia Jane joked, making sure her grandmother was comfortable.

"It's been a long time," Wren said, sinking to her knees beside the chair. "It's so good to see you again." Izzy saw Olivia's eyes shine with emotion, and the older woman looked as though she wasn't sure what to do. Wren saw it, too. She leaned forward and gathered Olivia up in a warm embrace. "I'm really glad you're here with us," she said gently in Olivia's ear.

Hohner had moved on to Gabe who was feeding the dog a hearty slice of ham. Mateo, free from ear rubbing duty, came and put his hand on Olivia's shoulder. When Wren stood up, Izzy watched her mom look up at her dad.

"Hey, Liv."

She heard a quiet *click* beside her and turned to see that Magnolia Jane had her phone out.

"Hi, Mateo."

He leaned down and kissed her cheek, lingering there for a moment.

"Oh, I swear," Izzy mumbled, blinking the sting of tears away.

"The last few days have been a lot," Magnolia Jane said.

Izzy looked up to see Bennett standing near the tree. He was watching her, and he cocked an eyebrow when she caught his gaze. She took a deep breath, and a smile found her lips.

"There's about to be a little more," she told her niece. Magnolia Jane looked at Izzy, then over at Bennett. Izzy nodded her head.

It had been one hell of a year. She'd watched Trey bounce back from a career ending injury. She'd seen the young woman she helped raise marry the man of her dreams, she got back the mother she'd lost, the mother she'd always wanted but never really had while she'd been growing up, and she'd finally come clean about her painful past and opened herself up to a future she never dreamed possible.

"Can I have your attention please?" Bennett said in his booming voice.

"Speeches already?" Gabe asked.

"It's too early to be thanking anyone for your gifts," Mateo joked. "We haven't opened any of 'em up yet."

Magnolia Jane looked back at Izzy, her eyes wide. "Oh my god …" she said in an excited whisper.

And soon, she'd be saying, "I do".

"And by the way," she told her niece. "Don't even think about tryin' to get me to wear a dress."

The End

Hearts Full of Hope

By Jennifer Sivec

THE RETURN

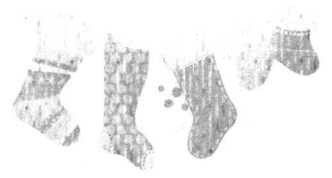

*M*icah and Mikayla Grey sat in the airport waiting for their flight to take them to a place neither of them had been for years. They sat in silence, Micah's leg bouncing up and down while Mikayla played with her long dark hair.

It had been a grueling few months for both, commuting back and forth to Boston and taking care of their ailing mother, Mary. Micah had been traveling from Manhattan while Mikayla had a longer trip from California.

They always met in the middle while one was coming and one was leaving, both there for the same reason. Hoping to ease the pain of a woman they both adored for different reasons.

The cancer had been a bitch, tearing them apart with every visit as they watched their once energetic and robust mother deteriorate into barely a slip of her former self. She had insisted they stop torturing themselves as they came home to care for her, taking turns for weeks at a time, but their love for her gave them no choice. While their father had worked and given them an adequate amount of love and attention, Mary had been their entire world, understanding and accepting them completely. Their beauty and flaws were the same to her when she looked at her children, and they never felt less than loved when they were with her.

As they sat waiting to board the plane to Grey's Harbor, Mary's urn in the bag on the seat next to her, Mikayla tried her best not to chew on her manicured nails.

Mary had loved Grey's Harbor more than any place on earth and talked about it often. She had grown up there with her parents, her mother being one of many Greys in the harbor. They were all descendants of Sullivan Grey who'd had a slew of children after he'd settled in the area in the 1700s.

While her parents had done their best to mold her into a proper young lady of one of the wealthiest families on the harbor, Mary had rebelled.

It was one of the things Martin Landers had loved about her the most. At twenty years old, she had captivated him with her carefree spirit and he had been smitten. At thirty-four, he never thought he would ever find anyone who would interest him. He couldn't imagine wanting anything more than making partner in the high-profile law firm he had been working for in his beloved city of Boston. When he met Mary on a trip to Grey's Harbor to deliver papers to her father from the firm, his life had changed forever.

Mary had been a beautiful wild child and he was an uptight young man who never thought he would marry, until he saw the future in her bright blue eyes.

Once married, Mary had agreed to leave her beloved Grey's Harbor to move to Boston on the condition she could visit anytime she wanted. As the children grew, she took them as often as she could, with Martin accompanying them any time he could tear himself away from his work.

Mary was her happiest at Grey's Harbor and even more so when her beloved husband was by her side with her children. When he died, Mary did her best to find reasons to go on, but she had lost her heart when his stopped beating.

"I never regretted moving here for your father just like he never minded that it was tradition that you keep the Grey name," she'd repeatedly told her children throughout their lives, but it was no secret that she missed the sounds of the sea and the salty smell of the ocean inside of her nose. She had wanted to go back to visit one more time, but her health declined far quicker than she anticipated.

"It is just as well," she had told them in her final days, in one of the lucid moments. They did their best to keep her comfortable even though the doctors couldn't find anything specific wrong to explain her deterioration. "I've had the happiest of lives, now I want you both to go and live yours."

Her final words stayed with Micah and Mikayla as they held Mary's hand and watched her go peacefully on a Sunday night.

She'd only had one final request before they went on with their lives. She asked that they take hers and Martin's ashes and scatter them at their beach home in Grey's Harbor. "I want us to be together in the place where we met that I loved the most. You can bring my grandchildren to visit."

She had never disguised her disappointment that neither of her children had settled down and started a family, but she knew she was partly to blame. Mikayla had inherited her free spirit, never able to find the right one to settle down with while Micah had shared her love of theater after spending countless hours in the dark with her, consuming this transcendent art and every aspect of it.

He had become consumed with the grittiness and beauty of storytelling on the stage and followed his passion into theater which took up most of his waking hours. Yet, she still hoped they would find the great love she had experienced, that had resulted in the birth of her second greatest loves; her children.

The brother and sister had gone to the harbor many times throughout their lives and considered it their second home, though Micah had found it more difficult to get there in recent years. They were fortunate to have hired a wonderful family who lived on the harbor permanently and looked after their home.

Mikayla had been there the month before Mary had revealed her illness to them but hadn't found her way back since and was both excited yet saddened to be going back.

As heartbreaking as it was to have lost both their parents within a year, they were comforted to know they were together. Theirs was the rarest of loves that none of their own relationships could even come close to, always ending up in bitter disappointment.

As the plane taxied on the runway taking off for North Carolina, Mikayla tried to be brave although she hated flying. She had much improved on the many flights she had taken over the past year but still needed to take a tranquilizer before the flight, which she always washed down with a double vodka and tonic much to Micah's disapproval.

She especially hated flying during this time of year when the weather was so cold and unpredictable, but they were lucky that it was cooperating, and for early November, there had strangely been very little snow. Mikayla was thankful that in Grey's Harbor it would be warmer. She hated the bitter cold winters in Boston.

She had never anticipated going so far from home, but her first big love had led her to sunny California. She hadn't intended to stay but one failed relationship after another had kept her there. She had always considered moving to be closer to Micah, who she could never seem to live without, but she was a hopeless romantic and love was a revolving door. She thought it might be different with the one she was seeing now, but his last words to her had been, "if you're going to Boston to see your mother again, then don't expect me to be here when you get back."

She had thrown all of his clothes out of her second-floor window in response, then packed her own bags and left for the airport.

The flight attendant came by and asked them if they would like a drink.

"I'll take a Bloody Mary, make it a double, please." She ignored Micah's eyes on her.

"It's a little early, don't you think, Miki?" He raised an eyebrow.

"I am flying. In the winter. So, no, dear brother, it's not too early." She stuck her tongue out as she said it.

Micah wondered if he would be carrying her off the plane. He shook his head and smiled at her. It wouldn't be the first time he'd had to carry her off somewhere, and he was certain it wouldn't be the last. She made his life very interesting, but he'd missed their time together and was struck by how little of it they had as adults.

They had gone their own separate ways upon graduation, and even though they texted or video messaged multiple times throughout the day, they still felt lost without the other. People always assumed it was the twin thing, the two of them deeply attached to one another their entire lives.

Living so far apart proved difficult at times but he'd always known that he wanted the grit of a city like New York to rub off on him. His parents had always accepted that he would one day live on the stage and indulged him in every way they could, even building him a small outdoor theater in their back yard where he would create his own productions. There had never been a question of where his future lie, and Mary and Martin loved telling everyone who would listen about how he had been entertaining them since he was two years old.

"I don't even remember how long it's been since I've been back to the harbor," Micah mused as he watched his sister try and refrain from downing her drink.

"I have no idea." Mikayla furrowed her perfectly groomed eyebrows. "I was just there last summer for a few weeks."

"Has it been since high school? I know I didn't go much after that. I was too busy running theater camp."

"Theater camp," Mikayla fluttered her lashes and stuck out her tongue. "God, you're such a nerd."

"Hey, don't make fun. Theater camp kids get a lot of tail." Micah grinned mischievously.

"Yeah, well, so do normal kids. On the beach. In the summer. I got laid at the harbor, for the first time." Mikayla smiled at the memory.

"Oh, yeah. It was that guy who had his eye on you all summer your sophomore year and I was pissed because I thought you were too young for him." Micah frowned. They had fought several times about her spending so much time with him that summer, but he had eventually gone away and the fighting stopped.

"You have to admit, he was really hot." Mikayla closed her eyes and for a quick moment she was back in his arms, running her fingers down his muscular back.

"If you say so," Micah screwed up his face. "I was just gonna punch him in the face for taking advantage of my little sister since he was three years older than you, but then you said you really liked him."

"I did really like him. I wrote him every day for the entire school year. I thought he might be 'the one.'"

"Then what happened?" Micah couldn't remember.

"We just stopped writing. That was it, and I just moved on with my life to date so many losers and idiots." Mikayla rolled her eyes dramatically but not before Micah could see the quick flash of pain in her eyes.

"What was his name? I don't remember."

"Oh God, it's not even worth mentioning now." Mikayla waved him away as though she had forgotten. "It was... Noah. Noah Redding."

REMEMBERING

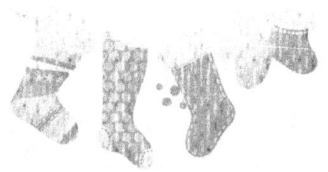

The flight was smooth and uneventful, and Mikayla sat back and closed her eyes.

Her mind drifted as it often did, back to her first love. He was the only boy she had ever truly fallen in love with, and every time she went back to Grey's Harbor, she hoped she might see him. But she was always disappointed, and her heart ached as she lost hope that she would ever see him again.

His daddy had owned a fishing charter with dreams of buying more but the summer after she had met Noah, the hurricane had destroyed his boat and their family disappeared. She had tried finding him over the years, but it was as though he had never existed, and she gave up, accepting that he was probably married with three kids living in a quaint suburb somewhere.

She had met Noah on the beach one afternoon when he had a rare afternoon off. For once, his daddy had made his younger brother pitch in on the charter and do all the work, and they had run into each other by accident. He had actually run into her, not paying attention as she lay on the sand soaking up the sun on their private beach.

He had nearly trampled her without realizing it.

"What are you doing?" she barked at him. "This is private

property!"

She remembered how his cheeks had turned slightly red under his tanned skin, his thick dark hair glistening in the sun.

"Sorry," he mumbled. "I've just been walking. I wasn't even paying attention to where I was going."

Her heart softened immediately.

She heard her mother's voice telling her to be nice. Mary had been telling her that her entire life because she knew her daughter's immediate tendency was to bristle when meeting new people.

"Where are you from?" Mikayla asked, ashamed of herself for being so snippy.

"I'm from here... Grey's Harbor," he said looking sheepish. "I work a lot with my dad, but he gave me the day off today. He said it was time my lazy brother did something for once," he laughed, making Mikayla's heart skip.

"So, you live here all year round?" She sat up interested, as she patted the towel next to her, beckoning him to sit.

"Sure do." He sat next to her and Mikayla couldn't help but notice the smattering of tiny dark freckles across his nose and how close he was. Their arms were nearly touching and the thought of it made her heart speed up.

"So, what does your daddy do?"

"He owns a charter fishing boat, and we take people out deep to fish, " the boy said proudly.

"That sounds like fun!" Mikayla loved boats, especially big ones. She was the only one in her family who didn't get motion sickness, almost as though she was made for the sea. She had never been fishing even though she had begged her daddy to take her so many times, but he refused. He wasn't the outdoorsy type, and he drew the line at fishing, even when it was for his little girl.

Mikayla gave him a pass. He might not love the ocean, but she knew he loved them.

"What's your name?" Mikayla asked the boy who looked her in the eye for the first time, the depth of his brown eyes taking her breath away.

"Noah. Noah Redding. Yours?" Noah held out his hand, making Mikayla giggle.

"Mikayla." Mikayla purposely didn't say her last name.

"Mikayla…." Noah prompted.

"Just Mikayla."

"What's your last name?" Noah's face was inches from hers.

"What does it matter?" Mikayla tried to ignore how her heart fluttered.

"You could be a serial killer." Noah's expression was serious.

Mikayla tried not to laugh. "I assure you, I'm not a serial killer."

Noah sat back. "Hmmm… if you weren't, you would just tell me."

"Grey." Mikayla whispered it.

"That wasn't so difficult, was it?" Noah teased. "You could still be a serial killer."

Mikayla let out a sigh of relief as Noah pretended not to notice. She hated when people made a big deal about her name, and she was happy to see that Noah's expression hadn't changed, not even the tiniest bit.

She took in his tan skin and handsomely rugged physique and assumed that he knew his way around a fishing boat.

"So ... are you a fisherman? Do you usually catch a lot of fish?" Mikayla looked down at his hands that seemed roughened from hard work. She fought the urge to touch them.

"I don't wanna brag and say I'm good, but I'm not bad," he grinned at her.

She decided that she liked him.

He was unlike any of the boys she was used to and whether he knew it or not, they were going to be spending a lot of time together that summer.

"So does your daddy let you have a lot of time off then?" She asked trying not to sound too hopeful.

"He usually doesn't, but he's decided this summer that it's my brothers turn to do a little bit of hard work because he's convinced he's been too easy on him. So, I am getting a bit of a break, but I still plan to help out anywhere I can. It's my last summer here since I'm going off to college." He stared ahead at the ocean.

"You've graduated already?"

"Last year." He looked down at her, and suddenly Mikayla felt self-conscious in her two-piece bathing suit that she had spent so much time shopping for.

"Oh… well, I'm going to be a sophomore next year… but I'm really mature for my age." Mikayla knew her words were coming out far too quickly, her face feeling warm.

Noah smiled but didn't say anything.

"What does your mama do?" Mikayla asked breaking the silence.

"I don't have one anymore. It's just the three of us now." Noah's voice carried a trace of sadness.

"Oh, I'm so sorry. I didn't know."

" How would you know? We just met," he teased, making her smile awkwardly.

"Can I ask… What happened?"

"She had cancer. She died when I was barely five, so I don't remember her much. Other than she gave great hugs and kissed me all the time." He smiled broadly.

"Those are great memories," she thought about her own parents who weren't as affectionate but still let her know she was loved.

"So, what's your daddy like?"

"Oh… He's… Something else. You'll have to meet him. You'll see what I mean."

Mikayla tried to catch her breath at the thought of seeing Noah again.

They sat in silence staring at the ocean.

"Do you want to go swimming?" Mikayla suddenly jumped up putting her hand out for him to grab.

"Sure!" He looked around as though he had forgotten something. "I… Don't have a towel."

"That's OK. You can use mine."

As they raced each other toward the water Mikayla wondered if she could ever remember feeling so free. As their bodies crashed into the waves they erupted with laughter as they caught each other's eyes and the happiness and joy scattered around them like sunlight.

Mikayla knew in her heart that no matter what happened for the rest of the summer, she would never forget this moment for the rest of her life.

ARRIVAL

$\mathcal{T}$he plane landed without incident in Gilmore, the largest city outside of Grey's Harbor.

Mikayla breathed a sigh of relief as she walked off the plane, her legs feeling slightly wobbly. As much as she travelled, she still hated flying.

"Second home, sweet home," Micah chirped excitedly. He hadn't been to Grey's Harbor in far too long, and despite the grim task in front of them he was happy to be there.

"You're awfully chipper," Mikayla laughed. She hadn't seen her brother so happy in a long time.

"Wow, it's warm," he unbuttoned his collar.

"I love the weather here. I don't know why I moved to California," Mikayla smiled.

"I know why you moved to California. Which jerk was it, again?" Micah teased.

"Be quiet, brother dear. Or I'll start to bring up some of your jerks. Oh wait, were there any? I don't remember." Mikayla swatted him playfully.

"You definitely got me there." Micah fell over as though she had wounded him. They both knew he rarely dated. It had become a joke between them that she dated enough for both of them.

"Do you want me to carry that bag of yours?" Micah asked grabbing the handle of her luggage.

"I would never dream of asking you to pull my luggage." Mikayla didn't hide her admiration for her handsome brother. She loved how chivalrous he was and thought guiltily that if she had only been honest when she had the chance, that he might've been able to have the love he'd deserved.

She shook the thought from her head but knew it would resurface again many times. It always did when they were in the harbor.

"You're so weird," Micah laughed. Grey's Harbor brought out the strangest things in his sister that he could never understand. He wasn't sure if it was the ocean air that made her behave so oddly or if it was the one place she could be herself.

Either way, he was never sure what to expect. It was one of her favorite places on earth and he often wondered why she didn't settle there even though she'd told him why.

"You'll never visit me if I move to the harbor," she had told him repeatedly. He would never say but she knew it was too difficult for him, the memories often thick with sadness and regret.

They found the counter for the rental car and waited, becoming more exhausted by the minute.

Micah had called ahead to have the house opened up by Mrs. Murphy who had been taking care of their home for years. When Micah called, she was devastated to hear about Mary's passing.

Mary Grey and Erin Murphy had become friends throughout the years with only ten years separating them. They were more than employer and employee, and Erin was the only one Mary entrusted with the care of the house all year around.

"I think that Mrs. Murphy may be getting on in years. Perhaps we should consider another option at some point," Micah mused as they drove toward the harbor.

"No way!" Mikayla disagreed. "She loves that house. She would never agree to that! Plus, the money has been good for her family, and I'm sure when the time comes she'll let us know when she can't take care of it anymore."

"You're right. The money has been good for her and her family, and she's been good to us as well. So, did you ever reach out to

Maddy Gray about refurbishing the windows in the home like she did at Emerson's?" Mikayla remembered they had talked about that the previous year.

"No, I completely forgot. I'm sure we'll run into her while we're here, and I can ask her then." Micah had been excited to discover new family members. The Greys were scattered throughout the harbor and the siblings enjoyed learning more about their heritage as they grew older. They had even gone to the Grey museum where they discovered Madeline Aubuchon and the story about how she had jumped off the lighthouse and how Maddy was her descendent.

"Hopefully, we will see Emerson and Lillian, too. I understand she has Sawyer's daughter there for lengthy visits, too."

"How did you find all that out?" Micah looked stunned.

"Social media, my dear brother. Something you refuse to be on."

"Social media is a waste of time, and I refuse to be a part of something that contributes to disconnection and depression." Micah and Mikayla disagreed vehemently about social media.

It was one of many things they did not see eye to eye on but could debate about for hours.

"Oh, you're so silly. I like it because I get to find out things, like Gavin's twins and Maddy's new baby, and I get to witness and watch the ones I love thrive and grow."

"But you know it's not real. You only see what they want you to see." Micah countered.

"True, but I wouldn't want to see every moment or hear every thought in someone's head, but when they share pictures of their babies I can't help it," Mikayla squealed.

Micah laughed.

His sister had always been a sucker for babies and puppies, and he loved that about her.

"Speaking of puppies, where is the princess?" Micah hadn't even thought about it until that moment, but Mikayla rarely went anywhere without her miniature dachshund, Heidi.

"She will be joining us in Grey's Harbor," Mikayla's blue eyes glistened gleefully.

"What? How?" Micah was stunned.

"You wouldn't think that I could ever go that long without

seeing my precious princess, do you?" Mikayla scolded him. She loved her dog nearly as much as she loved her brother. Although she often reminded him that it was a very close tie and that he could lose his ground at any moment. She even made him video chat Heidi when they talked, which was nearly every day.

"You're something else," Micah pretended to be shocked but he smiled as he did so.

Mikayla could never go very long without her best friend, other than him, and Micah knew that anything his sister wanted, she always got.

HOME SWEET HOME

$\mathcal{A}$s they got closer to the house, Mikayla clapped her hands excitedly. She always got butterflies any time they drove to the harbor. The warm memories of childhood began to envelop her as she began to take in the familiar sights and smells.

"It never changes," she mused.

"What never changes?"

"The feeling I get when I come here. The overwhelming sense of happiness when we pull into the harbor. It never dissipates." Mikayla smiled wistfully.

"You always say the same thing, sister dear," Micah laughed. "I don't know why you don't just live here."

"I don't know why either." Mikayla had considered moving to the harbor numerous times over the years, but Micah was the one who stopped her.

He always returned reluctantly, but there was too much heartache and devastation there for him. She had lost much, too, but they dealt with it differently like the opposite sides of the coin they were.

While Micah's haunted him, Mikayla drowned hers out with the noisiness of broken hearts and unfinished relationships. She knew deep down that it was the reason he had never opened his heart to anyone again, and she did her best to pay for the sins he knew nothing about.

She had even considered moving to New York to take care of him, but she knew she would only be in his way. He had dreams and aspirations and she had yet to discover hers.

The harbor has always been home for her, like a soft and warm blanket making her feel safe. She had tried going to school, and then decided she wanted to, like Micah, try her hand in acting. When she moved to California, she had even auditioned for a few commercials and television pilots and gotten an agent, but nothing had worked out. She never would've even tried it if she hadn't dated that hot actor who later came out of the closet, but by then she had already moved on.

She knew she never would survive in Manhattan. She couldn't understand what Micah saw in a city filled with millions of people. She hated the noise and the constant traffic, but he loved the energy and everything there was about it.

As they pulled into the driveway, Mikayla could barely contain herself. She threw open the door of the rental and leapt out of the car.

"Hey!" Micah yelled. "At least wait until I stop the car!"

Mikayla ran to the front door and was met by Mrs. Murphy who held all eight pounds of a black and brown dachshund in her ample arms.

Mikayla let out a squeal as she grabbed Heidi and showered her with kisses on her soft black and brown face. Heidi was equally as thrilled to see Mikayla, and she barked excitedly, almost dancing in her arms as she did so, covering her face with sloppy little kisses.

"Well, hello, Mrs. Murphy. I'm sorry you have to witness this disgusting and very wet expression of happiness," Micah laughed as he leaned over and kissed the older woman on the cheek.

He'd always been fond of her but tried to hide his surprise at how much she had aged since he saw her last.

"Oh, this makes me so happy! It's so good to see you kids, though under such sad circumstances." Mrs. Murphy reached out and hugged him warmly, a hint of an Irish brogue tickling his ears.

"How is your family?" Micah asked politely.

"They are doing well. My oldest boy, Christopher, is going to college, and my girl is managing one of the clothing shops in town. They like her so much, they may let her manage a second one." Mrs. Murphy's voice was full of pride. As a single mother it hadn't been easy, but she had worked hard to give her children the life she'd never had.

"You've done well by them. Thank you so much for getting the house ready for us." Micah reached into his pocket and handed her a check.

He turned to watch Mikayla who was busy playing on the floor with Heidi.

"Oh, Micah, this is way too much," Mrs. Murphy protested as she tried to hand him the check back.

"No, please take it. It's the holidays and we appreciate you taking such wonderful care of the house and getting it ready on such short notice." Micah hugged her gratefully.

"Yes! Thank you so much!" Mikayla said without looking up, her focus on Heidi.

Mrs. Murphy laughed. "That Heidi is a sweetheart!"

As Micah walked her to the door he hugged her one last time. "We'll let you know when we will be on our way. I will likely only be here for a few days, but sister dear might be here much longer."

"Just let me know whatever you need. The fridge is stocked, and you should be good here for a couple of weeks." Mrs. Murphy gave them both a little wave.

Mikayla looked at Micah and smiled broadly. "Home sweet home, brother dear."

"Maybe it is time you consider this being home." Micah raised an eyebrow at her.

"We'll see. I don't know, it will all depend on what princess Heidi says." Micah eyed the soft brown eyes of his fur-niece and chuckled. "I have a feeling that Heidi will be happy wherever her mommy is."

"For now, let's just settle in." Micah flopped on the couch and kicked off his shoes, his long legs hanging over the arm. The furniture and everything else was in pristine condition. When he closed his eyes and took a deep breath, he felt like he was ten years old again, waiting for his mom and dad to walk them out to the beach to spend the day.

He swiped at the tears that has squeezed their way out of his right eye.

He hadn't cried in years. Not even at his parents' funerals. He had no problem invoking tears on stage and breathing emotion and whatever misery was required into the characters he brought to life, but when it came to his own personal life he had closed himself off a long time ago.

It was the summer of his eighteenth birthday and the year he lost his love in the harbor. Unlike Mikayla who had opened her heart to many loves throughout the years, he had only the one.

The loss had been devastating and brutal.

"It's just summer love," he remembered his mom smoothing his hair and trying to ease his troubled heart. He had wanted to believe that was all she was, but to him it had been so much more.

He thought about his lost love often, channeling all of his emotion into the stage. While he spent time with women on occasion, they were only a distraction from his life in the theater.

The one girl he could never manage to get out of his heart haunted him still.

Heidi ran up and leapt at the couch, her short legs frustrating her as she barked at him to pick her up.

"Your rat is bothering me," he yelled for Mikayla and was answered with silence.

He reached over and picked the tiny ball of fur up and laid her on his chest, her brown eyes looking directly into his.

"If you tell anybody I did this, I'll deny it," he told her as he massaged her long ears. She laid down and took a deep breath, closing her eyes. The warmth of her small body soothed him for a moment and he let out a long sigh.

He'd always wanted to get a dog, but he was gone too much, and a dog in a five story walk up without a yard to play in didn't make any sense.

They had always grown up surrounded by dogs, their mother loving any stray that came her way as well as the short legged long eared dachshunds she had such a fondness for. While their dad had accepted this to be his fate, he did not share the same love and passion for their four-legged siblings. Micah and Mikayla grew up knowing that Martin's love and passion for their mother allowed for anything.

It had been comforting.

Micah slowly drifted off to sleep. Heidi snored gently as she lay on top of him, his arms wrapped protectively around her.

As usual, he began to dream the same dream.

Grace.

She was waving goodbye from the backseat of her father's car, tears streaming down her face, her hand against the back window, reaching for him. Micah ran after the car as fast as he could but it wouldn't stop. Finally, his legs gave out and he fell to the ground, dirt and gravel hitting him in the eyes.

He watched as the car disappeared and she with it, and Micah knew that it was the last time he would ever see her again.

GHOSTS

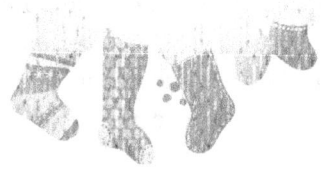

*M*icah sat straight up in the pitch dark, disoriented. He was drenched in sweat and the smell was all wrong. His head was thick with sleep, and for a few sluggish moments, he sat there trying to remember what was happening.

Slowly, he remembered that he was in Grey's Harbor and why. He looked around for Heidi, but there was no sign of her, and he knew she must've gone to find Mikayla. He turned his neck to the side and winced. The long hours on the couch provided an ample cramp in his neck.

He stood up slowly, reminded that he was no longer as young as he once was.

As he walked toward the room that had always been his, he paused along the way to peer at the photos that lined the hallway filled with happy memories and miniature versions of him and his sister morphing through time as they grew older.

He smiled at the picture of his mom and dad sitting on the sand, the house as a backdrop smiling at one another, completely oblivious to the world.

Micah had been proud of that photograph. He had begged her to take it with his dad's new camera when he was ten. Once he had a taste of it he always had a love of photography after.

That picture made him happy, but sad at the same time. He'd always wanted someone to look at him the way his parents looked at one another. He thought he had found that once but without warning it was ripped from him without any explanation.

Other than her, he had never met anyone who made him feel that way and he reasoned with himself that it had just been young love. As he continued down the hall, he listened for a moment at Mikayla's door and there was nothing but silence.

He had always done that as long as he could remember, pausing by her door throughout the years. There had been moments when he had heard crying and others when there had been silence. As the big brother he could never ignore the crying, and she was always grateful for that.

As he opened the door to the room that had always been his he was pleased to see it was exactly the same, and as he flopped down on the bed and closed his eyes, he drifted off to a sweet nothingness.

· ·*⁎* ·

*M*icah felt like he had only been asleep for a few minutes when he heard a rapid knocking on his door.

"Wake up sleepyhead!" Mikayla yelled through the door.

The smell of coffee brewing and bacon cooking made his stomach grumble immediately.

He looked at the clock and rubbed his eyes.

9 AM.

He slept far later than he usually did, the sun shining through his windows as the pitter of little feet echoed through his room. He looked down to see Heidi doing circles in front of the bed looking up at him, as though welcoming him to the day.

"Good morning, little princess." He bent over to pick her up and scratched her ears to which she made an appreciative grunting noise.

His heart warmed a little more toward the furball as she began to lick his face gratefully.

He carried her carefully as he wandered into the kitchen and tried to wake up.

"Here's your coffee, brother dear. Black like your soul." Mikayla sat a steaming mug in front of him and he sipped it slowly, allowing the dark liquid to penetrate his brain.

"So, I see you keep trying to steal my little princess away from me. I walked in to find her sleeping on your chest and now you've imprisoned her," Mikayla scolded him teasingly.

Heidi hung on Mikayla's every word.

"So... is today the day?" Micah asked seating himself on a tall stool at the breakfast nook.

"No, sir. It's too beautiful a day to scatter ashes. We have to wait until there's a storm. Mom always loved storms at the harbor, and she would never want to be scattered in the sunshine." Mikayla was very adamant. "Besides, I thought she might want to spend some time with Dad."

Micah looked over at the fireplace mantle to see that Mikayla had set the two urns next to one another. They'd had Martin's shipped but Mikayla had insisted on carrying Mary's.

"Okay." Micah didn't give up a fight as he sat Heidi gently on the floor and attacked his eggs.

His sister watched in amusement. She thought that he looked like a man who had never eaten before. "Then we need to look at the forecast for the next couple of days, because I can't stay here forever. Unlike you, I have many obligations."

"I thought you were between shows," Mikayla pouted. "I was looking forward to a nice Thanksgiving with you."

"I am between shows and I never committed to Thanksgiving here. That's still a few weeks off, and I'm sorry sister dear, but I have a lot of responsibility at home. I'm not just living off of the Grey money like you are." Micah's tone was a bit harsher than he meant it to be and Mikayla grew strangely silent.

It was the biggest difference between them that often caused friction.

Micah always had plans and aspirations, while Mikayla had none. It was part of her charm as well as the most frustrating thing about her. She was in many ways the epitome of the spoiled little rich girl, yet with a heart of gold.

She had been told several times in her relationships that she lacked substance which infuriated her because she knew that all she lacked was ambition.

She had often spent her days reading and studying things that caught her interest, but she could never hold onto anything for too long.

Micah always told her that she knew a little about everything but not enough about one thing.

He loved his sister, but her lack of direction concerned him greatly. What frustrated him the most was that she had scored a 1500 on her SAT, close to the highest you could get, but it didn't seem to faze her. While he had struggled and sold his soul for his grades, she had breezed through with honors without as much as breaking a sweat. Her mind was brilliant but she lacked direction, and it frustrated anyone who had ever loved her, especially their parents.

Their dad had been convinced that Mikayla would take over the firm and was heartbroken when he realized there was no chance of that.

"You're going to have to take care of your sister, Micah," his dad had made him promise as he lay dying.

Micah had somehow always known that she would need him. It was why Micah had kept her so close, even though they lived on opposite coasts. The medication helped tame her brilliant but manic mind, but it hadn't always worked that way.

Their dad hadn't told them until they were old enough to understand why Mary would switch from high to low, his love for her often dismissing the swings until it became too destructive for them to ignore any longer.

Micah saw a lot of that in his sister, which was why he made sure to talk to her every day.

He thought back to the incident in college when she had disappeared for nearly a week, and he had been out of his mind with worry. When he finally found her, she had stayed in the hospital for several weeks and had dropped out of school. She had never gone back, much to everyone's disappointment, but she had said it was never a good fit.

Years went by and they were finally able to strike a balance with her medication. She had done well ever since, but Micah was terrified to imagine what life would be like for her without him. Or without the security of the life they had been afforded by their dad's hard work and their mom's family name.

"I made you this beautiful breakfast and then we are going to spend the day at the beach. I thought we might even want to swing by the marina and say hi to your old friend, Bridger."

"No sister, first we're going to have to stop and get some clothes for me." Micah hadn't planned to go from New York to Boston to Grey's Harbor in the middle of November, and he had only packed for the cold Boston winter. He thought about all of the heavy clothes he had packed and didn't look forward to sweating to death.

He knew there were clothes in his drawers and the closet in his room, but he hadn't worn them in many years. They would do for now, but he was going to need an update if he was staying for more than a week.

"Yes!" Mikayla clapped her hands. She loved to shop and knew the perfect place. The shopping district in the harbor had grown and she loved any excuse to go shopping. "Hurry up, brother dear. I have big plans for you and our day."

As Mikayla skipped out of the room, Micah groaned. He hated shopping and he knew that he was going to be at his sister's mercy for the rest of the day.

Heidi looked at up him sympathetically.

"Be thankful you're a dog. At least you can go out in public naked." Micah winked at her, dreading the day ahead.

BROTHER DEAR

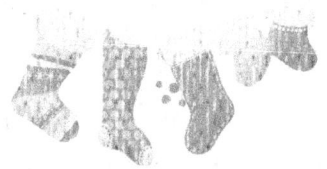

*a*s they made the quick drive into town, Mikayla thought about how she loved any time she had with her brother.

She had been disappointed when he said he wasn't planning to spend Thanksgiving with her, and while she understood, she had hoped deep down that he would.

I'll make him, she told herself.

She missed him far more than she ever wanted him to know. Due to the demands of his life, there were limitations to the amount of attention he could give her. He was her person, even more so now that both of their parents were gone. Still, she knew there was only one thing that could ever change his love for her but swore she would take it to her grave.

As they got out of the car and wandered through the streets of Grey's Harbor, she was struck with how desperately she wished that she could see him every day.

Her perfect brows knit together, and her face darkened as she pushed away the one thing that she had kept from him. If he ever found out, he would never forgive her. She had kept the secret buried so deep that even a few glasses of wine or a martini wouldn't let it slip.

"You okay?" Micah asked, peering at her face with concern.

"I'm fine. I was just thinking about how many bathing suits I would need." Mikayla forced herself to smile.

"I always forget how much I love this place until I'm actually here." Micah took a deep breath of the sea air as they strolled past the Cathead diner, one of their mom's favorite places.

Mikayla paused, breathing in the aroma of the Cathead as the door opened.

"There's nothing like Maeve's meatloaf or clam chowder," Mikayla sighed dreamily.

"If you want to go there after we shop, we can certainly do that." Micah smiled.

"Oh, we'll be going there quite a few times before we leave." Mikayla was suddenly bursting with happiness.

"How much shopping do you need to do, Miki?"

"I don't know... probably a lot!" Mikayla started toward the shopping district where she had spent hours with her mom growing up. Her mom had always been indulgent of Mikayla's love for fashion. She'd even encouraged her to study it, which Mikayla had for a semester and then become bored with it as she did everything.

As she stared down the street at the shops, she swiped at a tear that escaped her eye as she thought of her mom. They'd had many happy memories there.

"I was thinking that if you have a lot of shopping to do, maybe I'll take a detour and see if that old theater is still in operation." Micah's voice was hesitant but hopeful.

Mikayla's heart skipped.

She thought about what the theater had meant to her brother, and the part she'd had in ruining it for him.

"Sure," she waved him away. "I don't need you to watch me try on all of the clothes, and I do mean all of the clothes, I will be buying. I thought you needed to buy some things?"

"You know my size. Just grab a few things for me. Nothing too flashy." Micah bent over and kissed her on the cheek gratefully. "Thanks, little Miki."

He turned on his heel and started down the familiar road that would take him to the place he had fallen in love with not only theater, but also his first and only love in life.

Mikayla watched him walk away and fought the urge to run after him. She knew that as he walked down the road he would be thinking of Grace.

She thought about the blonde hair and the biggest green eyes she'd ever seen and wondered where she might've ended up. It had been so long since she'd last seen her, she imagined she could be anywhere in the world.

As Mikayla wandered into a newer shop she didn't recognize, she absently ran her hands over the soft material of the brightly colored t-shirts that were displayed.

Her mind wandered back to Grace.

Her dad had owned the Allen Theater. It was the only one in the harbor and the first place she had ever seen *Fiddler on the Roof,* *Music Man* and *Romeo and Juliet.* While Mikayla had enjoyed the experience, Micah had consumed it.

It was where his passion for theater took root in him and grew. He had been enthralled as a young boy with the actors on the stage and watched hungrily as they wove together a story that refused to escape his young mind. Their mom had loved theater and was thrilled that Grey's Harbor had one that was so active and esteemed.

The Allen Theater had an excellent reputation and showed plays all year around, attracting tourists and residents alike. It had no trouble enticing elite acting troupes for their show, which gave Grey's Harbor an advantage over many of the other seaside towns because of the culture it added.

Micah had insisted on seeing multiple shows any time they were at the harbor, and his mom obliged. She even donated a large sum of money every year to ensure the theater would always stay afloat, and she organized a fundraiser for the elite of the harbor. Her financial contributions helped ensure the theater's success and when he was old enough, it gave Micah the opportunity to get behind the scenes of any production he wanted.

Then he had met Grace, and he began to spend every waking moment at the theater, falling in love in every way.

Until the theater suddenly closed, and the Allen's disappeared forever, leaving Micah with a gaping hole in his heart that he had never gotten over.

Mikayla thought about the secret she could never let Micah know, her stomach in knots, and suddenly she no longer wanted to shop.

"Can I help you, miss?" A fresh-faced girl who couldn't be older than twenty approached.

"No, I'm just browsing." Mikayla turned toward the T-shirts and attempted to steady her voice.

"Okay, just let me know if you need help. My name is Ophelia."

That voice.

Mikayla jerked her face toward her, searching for anything familiar and was struck with sudden recognition.

"Ophelia, that's an ... interesting name," Mikayla tried to keep her voice light.

"Yes... my mom's favorite play was *Hamlet*, although I wish she wouldn't have named me after a character that drowns herself," the young woman laughed easily, her bright eyes dancing as she did so.

"You look familiar. What's your last name?" Mikayla tried to quiet her heart from pounding so hard in her chest.

The girl looked surprised. "My last name?"

Mikayla suddenly felt weak.

"I mean ... what is your mother's name? "

Ophelia's smile disappeared slightly. "It's Grace. Grace Allen."

Mikayla gasped loudly and rushed out of the store without another word. She looked up at the sign on the storefront and felt like she was going to hyperventilate.

State of Grace.

She hadn't even noticed the name when she'd walked into the store.

She continued briskly down the sidewalk and finally settled on a bench, her heart beating a thousand miles a second.

How could Grace possibly own that shop?

The secret she had been hiding from Micah often kept her up at night, and being at Grey's Harbor always brought it to the forefront of her mind. It was easier to drown out when she travelled and the sights and smells of the harbor were far from her mind.

She hadn't been to the harbor with Micah for many years, and suddenly she felt as though everything was crumbling around her. Her chest was caving in, and she knew that if she didn't do something, she was going to have an anxiety attack.

Shot! I need a shot!

Mikayla hadn't been drinking much lately because it interfered with her new medication, but she needed something to take the edge off.

Just one, she promised herself as she tried to remember her way to Izzy's place, the Mizzen Mast.

Just one.

MEMORIES

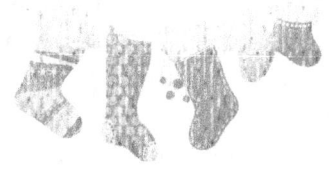

$\mathcal{A}$s Micah neared the theater, his heart began to pound.

He hadn't been able to go there for many years and had kept a picture of it in his mind. Walking the familiar path to the theater brought back many sad memories of a life and dreams he once thought were the most important thing in the world.

He closed his eyes and for a brief moment he thought he could smell her perfume. He shook his head and the scent was gone, that soft mixture of lavender and vanilla that seemed to awaken a part of his brain that was otherwise dead.

His friends in New York had been trying to set him up with someone for years, but he had refused. The occasional casual night or two was all he could muster, his heart always reaching for someone who no longer existed in his life.

He had tried to find her multiple times but was told she had moved far away from the harbor. He'd heard that her father had passed away a few years after they'd moved away which broke Micah's heart. It had only ever been her and her father. Her mother had died when she was a baby, leaving an emptiness in her soul that remained until she met Micah.

Her father had tried to fill the hole in her heart by teaching her every aspect of the theater, most of which she taught to Micah.

Micah thought about her full lips and how soft they had been on his, and the way her deep green eyes could make his heart stop in his tracks. Their love had been deep and seemingly otherworldly, romanticized by the plays they watched and the theater they adored.

"Can you feel me in here?" she always asked, as she'd place her tiny palm on his chest.

"Always," he would say, and he meant it.

When he arrived at the dilapidated building, he felt something in his heart crack. The For Sale sign in the front even looked worn as though the realty company had given up on finally selling it, too. Located on a lot that didn't have the best access, it had been perfect for the mystique of the theater but not ideal for much else.

He closed his eyes and thought about how the theater had once been a beautiful grand building, that even walking in made you feel as though you were about to embark on a wonderful adventure. He had been to that theater countless times from the age of five to seventeen and had met Grace for the first time when they were six, then again when they were fourteen. Even though they lived in completely different worlds, they wrote to each other every night while they were apart, and when they were together when they were on the harbor he spent every waking moment with her from the time they were fourteen until they were seventeen.

Four magical summers spent together.

Four years of the deepest love he had ever known.

His parents thought it was just a phase and encouraged him to date other girls when he was home, but he had refused. Grace was his girl, and he knew from the moment he saw her that they would be together forever.

She was his forever.

His soulmate.

He had whispered those words to her more times than he could remember.

When his parents realized that they were serious, his father began to get concerned. Marty often found reasons to let Micah know that he didn't approve of his relationship.

"Those theater folks are weird," he said on more than one occasion.

When they heard rumors that the theater was struggling when Micah and Mikayla were seventeen, Marty refused to express any concern, though Mary, who had supported the arts and loved the Allen Theater, was heartbroken at the thought of it closing.

She had spent years supporting the theater but construction and several years of lower attendance had an impact on the Allen Theater.

She had loved the sounds and smell of the building as much as he did, as well as the incredible stories that were played out on the stage.

Micah scrubbed his face, trying to erase the memories. What happened after had nearly broken him and he knew that revisiting the theater would only bring it all back.

In the four years he and Grace had been together, Marty had refused to go to the theater or meet Grace's dad, until he ran out of excuses and finally relented. Grace and Micah had been excited and nervous about their fathers meeting, but it had been a disaster, neither one of them overly impressed with the other. Micah knew his dad could be aloof with people that he didn't understand, and Grace's dad could be awkward as well. Clay Allen was proud of his theater, and even though he made good money from the elite families in Grey's Harbor, he didn't have much need for people with money.

He only cared about the art and not the money, which was ultimately his downfall.

"Micah, my boy. People have to make their own way in life or it's just not an honest existence," Clay had told him many times. He had allowed Micah to work on sets since he was fourteen, and with Grace's help had taught him the ropes of the theater.

Marty resented that Clay had taken his son under his wing.

It was behind the scenes, building the sets, spending long hours together that Micah had fallen in love with Grace. And it was under the stage after a beautiful performance of *Romeo and Juliet* that they had first consummated their love, and many times after that.

He had been desperately in love with her, but when the struggling theater was on the verge of closing, Grace and her father packed up and left without a goodbye or any explanation.

He had been utterly heartbroken.

He swiped at his eyes, still surprised that the memories could bring him to instant tears, but he had unsuccessfully tried to purge her from his heart for many years. It was the reason he had avoided the harbor and had refused to visit the skeletal remains of the place where the only love he'd ever known had died.

As he stood outside of the theater, he felt something within shift.

He thought about his company back in New York and wondered if he might belong here instead. He stared at the dilapidated realty sign on the lawn shoved into the overgrown grass and he quickly stored the number in his phone.

He turned away and began walking toward the shopping district hoping to be distracted by Mikayla and her love of spending money on frivolous things. He loved his sister, but he wanted more for her than she even wanted for herself.

He shook his head once again and tried to push away the memories. When he was in New York it was easier to do, but the sight and the smell of the familiar building made it much more difficult to get rid of.

He thought about Grace once again and wondered if she ever came back to the harbor, or if she ever thought about him. He laughed at the irony of his miserable life as he imagined her married with five kids and a happy life.

Once again, he imagined that he could smell her familiar scent in the sea air. He quickened his step toward the only person he knew that could make him forget his pain and tried to ignore the suffering of his soul that always surfaced when he was at Grey's Harbor.

SISTER DEAR

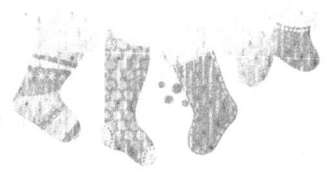

"*W*here are you?" Micah texted Mikayla after he scoured the streets for her for nearly an hour, poking his head in every shop.

He watched for the bubbles on the phone and waiting for the response but there was none.

"Miki…" Frustrated he continued to walk until he finally saw an answer.

"Maeve's."

Of course, Micah sighed. He knew she couldn't have possibly finished shopping. Shopping trips with Mikayla were usually an all day marathon, and he wondered if there was something wrong with her.

He found his way quickly to the Cathead and opened the door, the savory smell of meatloaf and other deliciousness hitting him square in the face. God, he sighed as his stomach rumbled. It had only been a few hours since he had eaten breakfast, but he knew he wasn't leaving without eating as much of Maeve's good cooking as he could.

He looked around the sparkling clean dining room and quickly found Mikayla sitting alone in a booth.

"Are you done shopping already?" He noticed there were no shopping bags.

"No," she started to say more but stopped. "I just got hungry, that's all."

Micah noticed her red cheeks and red rimmed eyes but didn't ask. The faint smell of caramel and vanilla hung in the air around her and he knew immediately that she'd been drinking. He thought better of delving into her emotions, which would only be met with anger.

She had always been that way and he knew when to leave her alone and let her take the lead.

He wasn't happy that she had been drinking already, especially on her medication, but there were dark places in her soul that she didn't always want to share with him right away.

"Did you order already?" Micah glanced at the menu, but already knew what he was going to order.

Mikayla nodded.

"Micah! Mikayla! How good to see the two of you. It's been awhile." The waitress's voice was familiar, and Micah looked up to see the same woman who had been working at the Cathead for years standing at their table. Her name escaped him, and he felt awful for not remembering. He smiled broadly hoping she wouldn't notice and gave her a warm greeting.

After a little small talk, he ordered and waited anxiously for their food to come.

"Well... since you asked where I went, I went to the Allen theater," Micah mused out loud. He paused, waiting for her to respond, and when she didn't he continued. "It's sad, really. Everything is overgrown and it looks like nobody has taken care of it for years. God, I loved that place."

Mikayla nodded again, her eyes suddenly wet with tears that refused to fall.

Micah pretended not to notice. He'd seen it before and knew she was on the verge of breaking down, which usually involved causing a scene.

"It made me think of Grace." Micah's voice broke. "If she saw that today, it would break her heart. "

"Why don't you have a girlfriend?" Mikayla blurted out far too loudly.

Micah looked around at the other diners who were trying not to look at them. "Mikayla!" His voice was sharper than he meant it to be, and he instantly regretted it as his sister's cheeks immediately turned red.

"I'm sorry..." she practically whispered trying to control her voice, "...but why don't you have a girlfriend?"

"We've been over this a million times. " Micah tried to hold back his anger. "I've tried to date but I haven't found the right person. It just doesn't work out for me and honestly, I'm too busy to even think about settling down or being serious with someone. Some people are meant for relationships and others aren't. I guess I'm one of the ones who isn't."

"I don't believe you," Mikayla challenged him, her eyes burning into his. He tried to look away. He hated when she gave him that look as though she was reading deep into his soul. "You are a romantic. You are the stuff relationships are all about. It doesn't make any sense that you wouldn't have fallen in love a hundred times, and had babies, and done all of the things that love makes you do. Instead you've poured all of your love into a theater that can't possibly love you back."

"I'm happy with my life," Micah lied. "What about you? You jump from man to man, always claiming that you are in love only to let it die a few months in. You date the absolute worst human beings and then you wonder why it doesn't work out. You're a smart, beautiful, intelligent woman. Why hasn't it worked out for you?"

The twins stared at each other intensely.

They barely even noticed when their food arrived, the familiar waitress immediately sensing the tension as she dropped off their plates and scurried away.

Mikayla broke the stare first as she looked down at her plate. She fumbled with her fork then took the biggest bite of meatloaf she could fit in her mouth. Micah couldn't help but burst into laughter as he stared at her tiny face with her large cheeks.

Mikayla did her best to chew and not choke, her eyes welling with tears from the laughter that threaten to erupt and explode her meatloaf all over the table. Micah reached across the table and grabbed his sister's hand.

"Listen, I'm sorry. Being here to spread Mom's ashes has me all weirded out. I shouldn't have said those things. It was mean and hurtful."

"No, I'm the one to blame. More than you know. The reason I couldn't shop anymore was because…" Mikayla wiped her mouth and swallowed once more to get the last remnants of meatloaf down her throat. She took a big gulp of water and Micah stared at her waiting patiently. "The first store I went into… The salesgirl looked so familiar. I had to ask her who she was."

Micah's mouth went dry.

"Who was she?"

Mikayla hesitated. As she stared into the longing on her brother's face she considered lying to spare his feelings. She loved him more than anyone in the world and couldn't stand the thought of his heart breaking again. It might be better for him not to know as she wrestled with the inner demons that had kept her secret for so long.

"It was … nobody. I thought it was a Grey… a relative that we hadn't met yet, and then suddenly I got a little nauseous and I thought I better eat."

Micah leaned back disappointed.

Mikayla took another large bite of meatloaf and chewed thoughtfully as she did her best to avoid his gaze.

"You know, for a delicate little thing you eat like an animal," Micah said finally, failing at being humorous.

"You're right, you know." Mikayla swallowed her food. "We're both just very emotional right now, and it's been a hard few weeks. I think we just need to do this thing and then figure out what we're going to do next."

Micah nodded. Even though she was tipsy, she made sense.

He didn't want to do the thing. He had been avoiding even thinking about it since the plane touched down. His thoughts shifted to what they had to do, what his mom had requested them to do, and he pushed down the sadness that threatened to overcome him.

He realized that he hadn't even taken a bite of his food yet as the waitress approached the table. She looked at his untouched plate, concerned.

"Is something wrong?" She pointed it is dish.

"No!" Micah said quickly. "It's perfect. I'm just not as hungry as I thought I would be."

"Do you want me to put it in a box?" The kind waitress started to reach forward.

"No, thank you. I'm going to eat it." He picked up his fork and took a big bite to show her that he meant it. She smiled politely and walked away.

They ate the rest their meal in silence, both of them cleaning their plates. Mikayla even used her roll to sop up the rest of the juices, dropping her fork with a satisfied look.

Micah marveled at how much his sister could eat.

As they paid, leaving the waitress a generous tip, and exited the Cathead, Micah was surprised that he hadn't seen anyone familiar. It was the first time he had been there that he hadn't run into someone he knew.

"It's off-season and getting closer to the holidays, so everyone is probably staying home," Mikayla didn't realize how she had read his thoughts.

"You're probably right. I was hoping we might run into Tank or Jaxx, but to be fair they have no idea we're here." Micah thought about how he had spent some of his best summers with his old friends. Grace had gotten along well with them, and when they weren't at the theater they were with his summer buddies.

Then again, Grace had always gotten along with everyone. People were drawn to her warm demeanor and her beautiful smile and it was hard not to love her.

Micah ignored the stabbing pain in his heart as he pushed the memory away.

As they walked down the sidewalk arm in arm from the Cathead, slowly trying to digest their dinners, Micah heard a voice that made his heart drop.

"Oh my God, Micah Grey? Is that you?"

Micah was terrified to turn around, his mouth suddenly dry.

He knew that if he did, and it wasn't her, he might not be able to stand it, and as he looked over at Mikayla, he realized she was frozen, too. But as he caught her eye and she stared into his, he saw something he didn't expect.

Pure fear.

THE SECRET

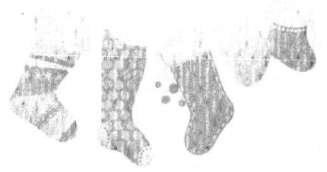

*M*ikayla lay in bed tossing and turning.

They had walked back to the beach house in silence, and when they returned, she went directly to her room without a word to take a nap.

Heidi was restless, too, as she licked her face relentlessly.

Half awake but half asleep, she felt like she was walking through a fog even though she knew she was lying in bed. She was wandering through the house, in the dark, and suddenly she froze. She could hear her dad's voice and it felt like a punch in the gut. It had been far too long since she'd heard it and realized how much she missed him.

Usually mild-mannered and serious, he was yelling, and Mikayla wasn't prepared for the words she was hearing.

"I know that you don't understand, Mary, but this cannot be allowed any longer." She peeked around the corner and her dad's face was red.

She had never seen or heard her parents fight before and she wished that Micah was home, but he was with Grace, like he'd been all summer.

"You're overreacting, Marty." Mary tried to reach out and placed her hand on his, but he jerked his hand away.

Mary looked like she had been slapped in the face, her eyes brimming with tears that refuse to fall.

"We've let this happen under our noses, and I let it go because I thought it was just young love, but now it appears they're serious. I blame myself for not listening to you and not taking control of this when I had a chance, but now it's too late."

"How did you even find out?" Mom asked as she paced back-and-forth.

"I found out because I saw the girl buying a pregnancy test in the drugstore, so I followed her out and asked what she was buying it for. She immediately started crying, and while I wanted to feel bad for her, I couldn't. She's going to ruin his life."

Mikayla covered her mouth with her hands so that her parents wouldn't hear her gasp.

Grace was pregnant with Micah's baby!

She thought about what that meant for her seventeen-year-old brother. Daddy was right, it would ruin his life.

"But just because she bought one doesn't mean it was positive!" Mary tried to sound hopeful.

"She said that it was the third one she'd bought. She wanted to be sure." Marty's face was lined with worry.

"Oh." Mary sat back in her chair heavily. "Does Micah know?"

"Not yet. I made the girl promise not to say anything. I think I scared her and I don't think she will." Marty's voice was unconvincing.

"What are we going to do?" Mary's voice was edged in desperation.

"Tomorrow, I'm going to visit her father, and I'm going to offer to bail him out of the financial mess he's made of the theater, and give him an added incentive to take the girl and move far away."

"You can't do that! You'll break Micah's heart!" There was a sharp edge to Mary's voice that Mikayla had never heard before.

"Think about what a baby would do to Micah at this age! The boy has no skills or ability to do anything. And he's not going to live off of me after what he's done to embarrass this family and ruin his life. No! It would be better if he thinks that they just suddenly moved away."

Mikayla had never heard her father speak so harshly before and he sounded like a complete stranger

Mary began to cry, and Marty gently put his arms around her and stroked her hair.

"I'm sorry I yelled, bunny. You have to trust me. This is what is best for all of us."

Mikayla could hear Mom's voice muffled against Dad's chest. "I understand."

Suddenly, Mikayla was back in bed, the blankets thrown on the floor and Heidi laying on her chest. She felt like she couldn't breathe. Ever since she saw the girl in the shop she had known right away who she must be.

A week later, after the argument between her parents, Grace and Mr. Allen had packed up and were gone, the Allen Theater closed forever.

Mikayla had felt so guilty, a ball in the pit of her stomach all summer.

She hadn't been able to eat or sleep, her mom finally taking her to the doctor because she had lost fifteen pounds.

Micah had been too lost in his own pain to notice, and even though their parents had done their best to comfort him, he refused. He was in pain and wanted to absorb himself in it.

Mikayla was thankful that he hadn't noticed how miserable she was. She hated that she knew, and from that day on, there was a distance between her and her father that hurt him, although he never said it.

She had always been a daddy's girl but listening to him that night, knowing that he would do something that horrific to her brother, stole all of her trust.

She thought about the girl in the shop.

She had been Grace's twin, beautiful and delicate with bright green eyes and blonde hair, but she also reminded her of Micah. Mikayla knew that if he ever saw her, he would recognize himself immediately. When the girl opened her mouth, she sounded just like Grace, and Mikayla had suddenly remembered how much she had loved Grace, too. When she left, there was a deep hollowness in their soul that they both felt.

Grace had often invited Mikayla to the theater with them to work on various projects. She had been part of their little group and they had shared many inside jokes, often at Micah's expense.

"You're the sister I never had," Grace would tell her and then give her a hug.

When her dad had made the Allens go away he hadn't considered that he was taking them away from her, too.

Mikayla knew that if Micah ever found out what their father had done, or that she had any knowledge of it and didn't tell him, he would never forgive her. After all, they always told each other absolutely everything. Mikayla even knew all about the late-night trips under the stage but had never said anything.

She was a secret keeper.

After the Allens disappeared, their father became especially compassionate with Micah, taking an interest in nearly everything he did.

Mikayla wondered if it was the guilt that drove him to be a better father to a son he had barely taken an interest in before, or if he finally realized what he'd been missing. Micah had been surprised at his father's sudden interest in him because he had always accepted that he was invisible. It had always been painfully obvious to everyone, especially him, that his father preferred Mikayla. Much to Micah's surprise, after Grace had shattered his heart, his father had even gone as far as to encourage and celebrate his success in the theater business.

At first, Mikayla thought their father was pretending to appease his guilty heart, but as the years went on she realized that somewhere along the way, he had discovered his love for his son that was nothing like he had dreamed he would be.

Mikayla didn't want to ruin Micah's perception of his father and their perfect relationship. Until his dying day, their dad had taken joy in their time together.

Mikayla knew she could never ruin that for Micah, so she had buried the betrayal deep down as far as she could and prayed with all of her heart that he would never find out what she had done.

As they had walked down the sidewalk from the Cathead arm in arm, a woman had called Micah's name.

They froze. But when they turned around, they saw that it was Emerson Grey who was excited to see them both. Mikayla couldn't believe how much she sounded like Grace as she tried to hide the relief she felt from Micah.

"Oh, Mikayla, I didn't realize that was you. I thought Micah had found himself a young lady. That's what I was hoping anyway." Emerson had kissed Mikayla on the cheek and Mikayla tried not to step back. She knew that Emerson must smell the alcohol on her breath and was ashamed.

"Not yet, Em," Micah had smiled.

Emerson had always been one of his favorite Greys, even though he could never keep straight how they were related. Second, fourth, eight cousins. Who really knew? There were so many scattered around the harbor, it never seemed to matter.

If Emerson smelled the whiskey on Mikayla she didn't show it, and Mikayla was grateful.

"What are you two doing here, and why didn't you let anyone know you were coming?" Emerson scolded.

"We actually came to scatter Mom's ashes. That's what she wanted." Mikayla's voice quivered as she said the words out loud.

"I'm so sorry. I adored your mom. She was the absolute best." Emerson wiped a tear away from the corner of her eye. "Should we have a service?"

"No," Micah said a little too quickly. "She just wanted us to do it."

"I'm sorry," Mikayla smiled apologetically.

"Oh gosh, don't be sorry. I didn't mean to overstep. I completely understand." Emerson put her hand on Micah's arm. "If you two need anything while you're here, please don't hesitate to let us know. I'll let my mom know to look out for you."

They chatted for a little while longer and then parted ways.

As Mikayla lie in bed recounting the conversation she hoped that Micah had missed the look of terror on her face. She knew he wouldn't be able to let it go if he did, and she was quickly losing her resolve to hide the truth.

One thing was certain. If he ever knew, he would never forgive her, and things between them would change forever

STRANGER

*M*icah had been angry with Mikayla in the past, and she had given him many reasons to be.

He had rescued her time and again from others, and from herself, always frustrated with her selfishness and her uncanny ability to get herself into trouble. He had sat with her in therapy, in the hospital, and even in jail once, but he had never imagined a day when he would never want to see her again.

She was his other half, and a life without her seemed impossible, but now as he thought about her all he could think about was how she had betrayed him. At first he hadn't wanted to believe she could keep such a secret from him. They had always told each other everything but as he sat at the bar, drinking his third beer, he was stunned at her ability to withhold such a momentous truth from him.

He was convinced he could never forgive her.

"Please don't leave..." Mikayla had cried as he stormed into his room and slammed the door. She sat on the floor outside of his room and when he opened the door, he nearly fell on top of her.

She cried out when she saw the worn out luggage in his hand. His refusal to invest in new luggage was a constant point of disagreement between them.

"No! Please. Don't go, Micah. Let's talk this out. I'm so sorry." Mikayla grabbed his arm. "Please. I'm sorry!"

"How can I ever trust you again? You've lied to me my entire life! You knew what happened, and you watched the pain I was in, and you didn't say one thing!" Micah's face was twisted in anger and grief.

"I'm sorry," Mikayla cried.

"You're sorry?" Micah stopped and stared at her, his face inches from hers. "You don't have any idea what it means to be sorry. I'm the one person in your entire life who has been there for you, even when you've screwed your life up beyond any recognition. But this is unforgivable! I can't even look at you!"

He stormed out, unsure if he would ever be able to forget how miserable she had looked.

"Izzy, shot please." Micah stared at the empty glasses that he had lined up in front of him.

"Another one? Do you think that it's going to help?" The Mizzen Mast had always been the twin's preferred drinking in the harbor. Tourists typically went to the new microbrewery that had opened a few years before, but Izzy's place suited him just fine. He felt at home there and Izzy was always good for company, even though at the moment she was looking at him, her brows knitted together and concern in her dark brown eyes.

She intimidated a lot of people with her dark makeup and piercings, but Micah had always found her to be the opposite. She reminded him of the lost souls he often met in the theater who were searching desperately for their place in the world, and he admired her grit. It wasn't often you met a girl with so many tattoos who played the cello as brilliantly as she did.

"I don' know…" Micah knew he was slurring.

"What's going on?" Izzy was always right to the point.

"It's… "

Micah heard the bell above the door ding and he turned around. He squinted his eyes, unsure, trying to decide if they were deceiving him.

Green eyes stared back at him.

He knew those eyes and his heart stopped.

"Micah?"

As he rubbed his eyes, he nearly fell off of his barstool, his foot sliding on one of the bags he had hastily packed in his escape from Mikayla. He caught himself on the bar and looked up, his face red, instantly regretting the last two shots he had done.

"Grace."

They stared at one another for a long moment, taking one another in.

He looked down and saw her tiny palm on his chest.

Always.

His voice echoed somewhere in the back of his mind.

"Grace... the usual?" Izzy's voice floated between them, and Grace nodded.

She sat next to Micah, her eyes never leaving his face.

"I... I...." Micah fumbled for the words.

"I should probably start..." Grace cleared her throat, tears forming in the corners of her eyes.

Micah nodded.

Grace opened her mouth as if to speak, but then closed it.

She looked over at the bar and grabbed her drink. She downed it in one long swallow and nodded at Izzy for another.

"You look good." She finally spoke, her voice as velvety smooth as he remembered it.

"You, too," Micah was being honest.

Her long blond hair was pulled back into a stylish ponytail, only a trace of makeup enhancing her beautiful features. He had always marveled at how naturally exquisite she was, never needing much compared to other women he'd seen all over the world. Even after all of the years that had passed, she was the same and his heart ached as he longed to touch her.

"Where are you going?"

Micah was confused.

Grace gestured to his bags and Micah let out a nervous laugh. "I was leaving. My... Mikayla and I got into a fight and I was going back... going to leave here."

"Where were you going?"

"Home... New York."

"Oh…" Grace took a long sip of her drink, averting his eyes. .

"I mean… I wasn't leaving right this second. I was going to stay for a bit." Micah tried hard not to slur.

"I hope you weren't driving anywhere." Grace gestured to his empty glasses.

"No." Micah shook his head, his expression very serious.

Grace laughed and Micah's heart leapt.

"Why are you here?" Micah blurted out.

Grace's eyes widened, a single tear slipping out of her right eye. Without thinking Micah reached up and wiped it away, the tension between them palpable.

"I moved here last year. I … always felt like this was home, even after…"

"Even after you left me?" Micah finished for her, his voice harder than he meant it to be.

"I didn't mean to…" Grace's voice faltered. "I never meant to leave you, Micah. I loved you with all of my heart. I didn't have a choice."

"What about after? You couldn't get in touch with me after? I had no idea where you were or how to find you. You just left without a word!"

"I tried, I swear. I tried to write to you. I tried to call you, but my letters came back unopened and when I called, your father told me not to call again."

Micah put his hands over his face as he tried to block out the betrayal from the ones he had loved the most. He'd wished many times that his father was alive because of the gaping hole he'd left when he died. But now he wished he was alive so he could ask what he ever did to deserve losing the love of his life.

Grace reached up and grabbed his hands, and Micah let her, marveling at how soft they still were.

They instinctively placed their foreheads against one another as they had so many times in the past, tears cascading down both of their cheeks.

"I'd always hoped you would come back," Grace whispered. "I came here, hoping you would one day come back for me."

Micah placed his hands on either side of her face and looked deep into her eyes. "I haven't been able to love anyone but you my entire life."

Grace let out a little cry as he enveloped her lips with his.

He wasn't sure if he would ever be able to stop kissing her as they stood wrapped around each other at the bar for what felt like hours, not caring who could see them. He paid the tab, and without speaking, she led him to a cab that drove them to a beautiful home on the north side of the harbor.

She kissed him fervently as they fumbled their way up the stairs. As they fell into the bedroom, Micah wondered if this was just another dream, and if he would wake up the next morning heartbroken as he had so many times before.

"Tell me this is real," she murmured as though reading his mind.

"It's real," He growled into her ear as he stripped off the last piece of clothing she was wearing.

As they fell into the bed their bodies already entwined, Micah cleared everything else from his mind and allowed himself to feel the happiness that only Grace had ever given him. He felt complete for the first time since they had been together last, his heart finally feeling as though it had found its way home.

MORNING

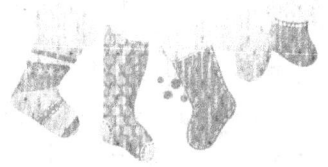

*M*icah stretched out his long body.

His tongue felt like it was coated in fur and his head was fuzzy. The sheets were cool around his naked body and he thought for a moment he could lay there forever.

Suddenly he bolted up.

Where am I?

He looked around the crisp white room at the fresh flowers that sat on the nightstand and the pile of books he didn't recognize. His heart pounded in his chest as he began to panic.

"Micah, how do you like your coffee?" A voice floated up the stairs.

Grace!

"Black."

He thought hard about the night before and memories of his fingers on her skin and her lips on his made him smile.

"What are you smiling for?" Grace's voice brought him to the present as she placed a steaming hot cup of coffee on the nightstand next to him.

"I'm just thinking about how I can't believe that you're here. That we're here."

Grace closed the bedroom door and sat next to him.

"There's something we need to talk about." Her beautiful green eyes bore into his and his stomach dropped.

"Sure. Let's talk." Micah took a deep breath.

A knock on the door startled them both.

"Mom, are you awake?"

Micah's head snapped toward the door.

Ophelia.

Grace put her finger to her lips, gesturing for him to stay quiet.

"Yes, sweetheart. I'm awake. What do you need?"

"Dad is on the phone. He wants to talk to you about when he's coming in. His plans have changed."

Grace's expression changed as Micah stared at her in disbelief.

"Tell him…" Grace's voice faltered. "Tell him that I'll call him in a bit."

Micah listened as footsteps walked away.

"Grace… You're married?" Micah threw off the blankets and searched the room for his clothes.

"No, Micah. It's not what you think. Please…" Grace spoke in hushed tones.

"I didn't know you were married. Was that our daughter?" Micah fumbled with his underwear.

"You know about… our child?" Grace stared at him in disbelief.

"Of course I do!"

"Why didn't you say something last night?"

"Why, Grace? Because I was in disbelief. Because I was drunk. Because I just wanted to touch you and kiss you and know that you were real. I didn't know that you were … married. Jesus!" Micah paced the room looking for the rest of his clothes.

"Shhhh… please." Grace begged. "I don't want her to know you're here."

"How were you going to hide me, Grace? What was your plan? Were you going to tell her that I'm the plumber fixing your bedroom toilet?"

"No, she goes to work in a half an hour and I was going to wait until then to have you … leave. I'm sorry, Micah. My life is a little… complicated."

"I'd say! So, what were you doing with me? Just using me? Was

I just a trip to your past to make you feel younger? You realize that I never married. I never had a family or kids or a normal life because I ..." Micah stopped, not ready to confess everything to her.

"Because you ... what?" Grace's eyes were suddenly rimmed with red, her chin quivering.

"Nothing... it's nothing. You're married and our daughter thinks that your husband is her dad. Does he even know about us? Does she? You must've met him pretty soon after you left if he thinks she's his daughter. What in the hell was I thinking?" Micah searched desperately for his last sock.

"She's not." Grace reached under the bed and pulled out his sock.

"She's not... what?"

"She's not your daughter, Micah."

Grace's face was wet with tears as she sank down on the bed.

He stared at her, absorbing her words.

"How is she not my daughter? Were you with someone else? I don't understand."

"Our daughter... Juliet ... died. She died soon after she was born." Grace's face crumbled as she buried it in her hands.

Micah sat next to her on the bed, the joy of his brief fatherhood stolen from him unexpectedly.

"How did she die?"

"They called it crib death. I was heartbroken, but I couldn't reach you to tell you.

"You named her Juliet... as in *Romeo and...*"

"Juliet. Yes. She was beautiful and I told her all about you and how amazing you were and how much you would've loved her if you could've known. She was loved, Micah. I promise you."

Micah put his arms around Grace and they held each other tight, mourning a life together they never had, and the life that was lost. He took in the feel of her soft hair on his cheek and knew that he was going to have to let her go again, this time forever. The agony of it drove a knife straight through his heart.

"This... has been a whirlwind of emotions that I wasn't expecting. I'm going to need to go now." Micah pulled away from Grace without looking her in the eyes. He knew that if he did, he might not ever be able to go

"Please don't go. I need to explain to you…" Grace held his arm tight.

"No, I can't. I can't take anymore truth right now. My entire life has been turned upside down and I've lost everyone and everything who once meant something to me. I can't, Grace. I'm sorry."

He grabbed his bags and ran out of the bedroom as fast as he could. He wanted to stay with her, and for a moment, he thought about how nothing had mattered when her lips were on his, but as he walked down the sidewalk he finally began to breathe again and a sense of relief slowly began to wash over him.

As Grace watched him from the window, she began to cry. There was so much more to tell him, but his entire life had been turned upside down and he was devastated.

She realized that she had no way of contacting him and took a deep breath. She knew what she would have to do and that a visit to Mikayla would be in order.

It was the last thing she wanted to do. Repeating her story again and facing the scrutiny she knew she deserved made her nauseated, but she knew she needed to do it.

She squeezed her eyes closed, forcing back the tears. She knew that she could cry all day if she let herself, but after spending the night with him and holding him in her arms, she couldn't wait any longer.

She needed to have him in her life again.

There was no other option.

SORRY

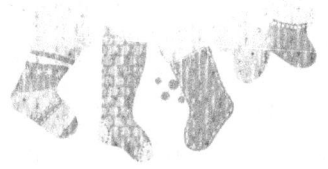

*M*ikayla thought about the last words Micah said to her and it shattered her heart.

He had packed in a whirlwind and left without allowing her to say anything else.

"I never want to see or speak to you ever again," he had said to her through gritted teeth, his eyes dark.

She hadn't been able to do anything else but cry.

The words played back in her ears over and over in her mind as she saw his face, twisted in anger. She didn't even recognize him but realized this was the brother she had been avoiding all of those years. She knew eventually that it would come to this even if she hoped it never would.

Even Heidi couldn't stop Mikayla's tears from flowing, though she refused to leave her side, pressing against her as hard as she could to remind her that she was there.

Micah refused to return any of her calls or texts.

"Please, please, please call me back. I am so sorry." Mikayla cried into his voicemail. "God, I'm so sorry, I would take it all back if I could."

Micah had been angry with her before but she knew that she deserved his wrath. She wished she had never told him and wondered what has possessed her to tell him the truth after all of this time.

Seeing Ophelia in the store had shaken her to the very core.

Deep down, she knew she couldn't hide the truth from Micah forever. It had been wrong to keep it from him for so long. His daughter, and likely Grace, were within a few miles of him, and he had no idea.

He was never able to stay angry with her for too long, but she knew this time was different. This time might just be the end.

Mikayla finally forced herself out of bed and walked into the bathroom.

She stared at herself in the mirror and was shocked at what she saw. Her hair was a twisted nest of unruly curls that looked as though they would be easier to cut off than to brush. The dark circles under her puffy eyes aged her by at least ten years.

"You're ugly, like your soul," she said to her reflection.

She slowly took her toothbrush out of the holder and slathered toothpaste on it. She brushed her teeth for what seemed like an hour, and when she was done, she realized that she felt a million times better.

Heidi danced around at her feet.

"Do you have to go potty?"

Heidi whined in affirmation and followed closely behind Mikayla as she walked to the door.

Mikayla shivered as the cold air hit her when she opened the door. It was unusually cold for November, and she was glad she had sent for some warmer clothes from Boston. She thought about her mom, and how they had never scattered her ashes, and Mikayla knew that she would never want her to do it without Micah.

Mikayla pushed down a sob. As she thought about the impending holidays, her tears began again. It would be the first Thanksgiving and Christmas without both of her parents, and now without her brother as well.

She had never felt so alone.

Even when she was alone, there had always been Micah. He had been her protector and had often saved her, even from herself. She didn't know how to manage life without Micah.

She didn't even know if she could.

She wondered if he had gone back to New York. She wanted him to stay in the harbor and look for Ophelia but she knew he wouldn't.

He would need time to deal with all of it in his head. He wasn't the kind of person who would show up unannounced and expect Grace to welcome him with open arms. He had been nearly mortally wounded when she left, and even though he knew it wasn't her fault, Mikayla knew that he would still be cautious.

She wanted a drink.

But she knew that if she had one, she might have ten, and that this time there would be no one to save her.

She wondered if that would be a terrible thing. She had done many awful things in her life but lying to her brother was the worst of the awful things. How could she deserve to live?

She'd never considered taking her own life before, but as she thought about her meds, she wondered how many of them it might take for her to fall into a peaceful long sleep...

Mikayla shook her head as though chasing away the thought of taking too many pills. She scooped Heidi up and decided to take a walk on the beach, despite the chill in the air and the fact that she wasn't really dressed for it.

As she walked she thought about the hundreds of times she had been up and down the beach, sometimes alone or often with her mom and brother. Martin had never been a big fan of sand between his toes, but on occasion he would tolerate it for his little girl who loved nothing more than to walk along the beach for hours collecting seashells and pretty rocks.

She had been her daddy's princess, until she gave up on him, and then he realized he had a son.

She looked down at the sand.

"Dammit, Daddy. Damn you," she cursed, angry tears coursing down her face. She had never told him that she knew what he had done, and she wished she had. She had never told anyone until she told Micah, and she wanted nothing more than to take it back. Even if she was living a lie, at least she would still be living it with him in her life.

Heidi whined as she looked up at Mikayla.

She bent over and scooped the small dog up and held her tight in her arms. "It's just you and me now, princess," Mikayla whispered in Heidi's velvet ears.

She wandered down the length of the beach and let the cool salty wind whip through her already tangled hair. She inhaled and thought for a moment that if she didn't have Heidi she might throw herself in the ocean. She would deserve the punishment of the ice-cold water and she needed to feel the pain.

Micah.

Micah.

He had to forgive her, but as his words played over and over in her mind, she knew he might not ever forgive her.

The thought of it made her want to sink into the surf and float away.

As she walked further down the beach she saw a tall figure walking in front of her.

As she drew closer she saw that the figure was walking down the beach hand-in-hand with two young boys. Her heart began to quicken with recognition, all thoughts of Micah gone for the moment.

Her breath caught in her chest.

It can't be!

"Mikayla Grey. Is that you?"

As she watched the familiar gait of the figure walking toward her, her heart began to pound wildly in her chest, and she felt as though she couldn't breathe.

She prayed for the sand beneath her feet to open and swallow her completely and wondered if it might be possible for her to disappear.

She froze hoping that if she did, she would become invisible.

"Mikayla!" The voice drew nearer. "I thought that was you. I can't believe it."

Mikayla tried her best to catch her breath as she turned around and faced a past that had once threatened to destroy her.

As the figure got nearer, Mikayla couldn't help but admire the strong physique and the muscular build. For a moment, she had a flash of her hands on those strong shoulders, and she felt the blaze of her cheeks as they turned red.

It had been many years since she'd seen him, and the boy she had once loved was now a man.

Their eyes locked. For a moment, time stood still and neither took a breath as they took one another in.

A slow sad smile spread across his handsome face that had only grown better looking with age. He had filled out, his t-shirt hugging him in all of the right places. Mikayla looked down at the two young boys who stared up at her with curiosity, their dark brown eyes identical to their father's.

"Mikayla." The sound of his voice still made her melt.

Mikayla nodded, unsure if she could find her voice. She opened her mouth, "Noah."

"This lady knows you?" the little boy on his right chirped, his tiny voice filled with curiosity.

"Yes, Connor. This is an old friend."

"She doesn't look very old to me," his brother piped up.

Mikayla laughed forgetting what that felt like. As she looked down at both boys a shooting pain went through her heart. If only, she thought, as she tried desperately to push the sadness away.

"Your sons." Mikayla smiled.

Noah nodded.

"Can I pet your dog?" the boy, Connor, said sweetly.

"Sure." Mikayla knelt down and Heidi sniffed the tiny human before sticking her tongue in his ear. Connor giggled uncontrollably. The other boy came around, letting go of his father's hand. "I want to pet her!"

Mikayla sat Heidi down on the soft sand holding her leash loosely as both boys sat next to her, gently patting her soft fur.

Heidi was in heaven, instantly in love with her new adoring fans.

"How... Why... I mean..." Mikayla stammered.

"The boys and I..." Noah cleared his throat, "the boys and I are moving home."

Mikayla's eyes widened. "It's been years since you've lived here."

"Yes, but I always considered this home. I spent the majority of my life here until..."

"Oh, I didn't realize that. Well... Welcome home." Mikayla knew her voice was too bright, too fake.

"What about you? What are you doing here?"

"I ... uh... Honestly, I have no idea. It's a long sad, awful story. You don't want to hear it. " Mikayla tried to laugh, her voice empty.

"Well... How long are you here?" Noah stammered awkwardly.

"For the foreseeable future," Mikayla smiled at Noah's awkwardness. "Where are you going to live?"

Mikayla looked around the beach and realized they were in front of some of the largest houses on the harbor. They made her beach house look like a cottage.

Noah looked at her as though reading her mind.

"We're in that one, over there," Noah pointed to one of the largest houses overlooking the harbor. Mikayla had always seen that house even as a child and wondered who would live there.

Mikayla smiled.

Noah had done well for himself. She'd always known he could, even when he didn't believe it for himself.

"Do you think you might want to catch up some time?" Noah shifted uncomfortably.

"Sure! That would be great!" Mikayla hated how happy her voice sounded and wondered if Noah would be able to see right through her like he once could. "I would love to meet your wife and spend time with your family."

"Mommy died!" Connor volunteered, not looking up from petting Heidi.

"Oh, gosh... I'm so... I'm so sorry." Mikayla looked at Noah's handsome face. His expression tried to mask his pain, his smile small and tight.

"It's okay... I mean, it isn't okay, but it's been almost a year. We've been trying to get past it but it's been hard. That's why we're... we just moved here."

" I am so sorry, Noah. I can't imagine how awful that has been for all of you." Mikayla nearly burst out in tears and suddenly felt selfish for feeling sorry for herself.

"Thank you," Noah smiled, gratefully.

"I truly am so sorry. If you need anything..."

Mikayla tried to hide the guilt that she had been feeling for being jealous of his undoubtedly gorgeous wife and mother of his two beautiful little boys.

"Thank you. This is the first time the boys have been happy in a long time." Noah smiled as he looked down at the boys who were content playing with Heidi. The princess never tired of all of the attention.

"You should get a dog." Mikayla thought about how Heidi always knew when she needed to be loved the most.

"I thought about that," Noah admitted. "Now that we are going to be settled somewhere, that might not be a bad idea."

Both boys perked up.

"I want a dog!" Connor said excitedly.

"Can we keep this one?" his brother asked looking at Heidi.

"No, Liam. This is our friend Miki's pup, but if you're really nice to her maybe she'll visit and bring Heidi with her."

"I would love to bring Heidi to visit you, Liam." Mikayla knelt down and looked the older boy in the eye.

"Yay!" Liam yelled as he threw his arms around Mikayla's neck unexpectedly, nearly toppling her over.

Noah reached over swiftly and steadied her and she could feel the electricity of his fingers on her arm. As they stood up she realized he must've felt it, too, as he pulled his hand away from her quickly.

"That's the first time he's seemed this happy since..." Noah choked up.

Mikayla teared up and tried to wipe the tears from her eyes. "They are beautiful boys, Noah."

"Do you think you would want to come down for dinner later? " he asked, almost embarrassed by his words. "I mean... we don't have much unpacked yet. Everything is in boxes and we'd probably just order pizza but..."

"Yes!" Mikayla said almost too quickly.

They smiled at one another and suddenly it felt as though the years had melted away. Mikayla didn't know how long they stayed that way but suddenly a cold wind blew and she noticed goosebumps on Noah's bare arms.

"I should get going, it's getting cold and you don't have a sweater on."

She knelt down to say goodbye to the boys.

"Wait! How will you know where I live?"

"It's easy. That used to be a good friend of mine's house a long time ago."

"Six o'clock then?" Noah asked shifting nervously.

"Six o'clock." Mikayla smiled as she turned away, knowing that her life was changed forever.

She turned and walked back to her house and felt his eyes on her as she did so. She tried to push down the happiness that threatened to bloom within. She didn't deserve to be happy when Micah was suffering.

As she approached the house, her heart started to pound. The figure sitting on the stairs, presumably waiting for her, looked familiar. As she drew closer she gasped, and her feet nearly froze in place.

Although many years had passed, Mikayla would've recognized that slender figure and the thick head of blonde hair anywhere. She paused and took a deep breath and braced herself to face the inevitable.

THREE WEEKS LATER

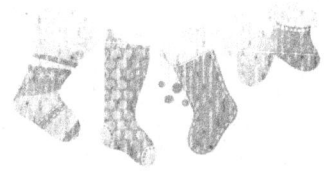

*M*ikayla hadn't talked to Micah for nearly a month and it was killing her.

It had been the first Thanksgiving without him and as she stared at her mother's urn, still sitting on the mantle containing the ashes that waited to be spread, she pushed down the emptiness in her chest.

Spending time with Noah and the boys had become the only bright spot in her life, and when he had invited her to spend Thanksgiving with them she had been surprised but grateful. It was the first time any of them had ever spent Thanksgiving in a restaurant, but it hadn't mattered to her.

She'd hesitated at first. She was struggling with too many demons, but when the boys looked up at her with the largest brown eyes and said, "please" she knew she couldn't resist.

Not only that but she didn't want to be alone.

She didn't do well when she was alone, and she realized that had always been her downfall as she had jumped from one relationship into another.

She was happy that Noah wasn't rushing into anything.

While they hadn't even come close to kissing he seemed to find comfort in her presence as she did in his. They were forming a friendship that filled in the gaps where the pain used to hide.

She realized that she had never had a male for a friend, but she found that the cadence between them remained slow and comfortable, hesitant yet hopeful. She needed that now more than she'd needed anything, and she told herself that if that was all that ever happened between them she would be happy.

She'd had enough drama and heartbreak in her life.

This was different. Special.

This was Noah.

She wished desperately that she could tell Micah about it.

As she lay in bed with Heidi who was resting her head on her chest, she thought about her brother and wondered where he was. There were only two weeks left until Christmas and the weather was unseasonably cold for Grey's Harbor. There was even talk in town about a nor'easter heading their way, possibly even on Christmas Eve.

She wished Micah was with her. She hated the thought of him at home in New York where it would be even colder.

She had tried everything to get in touch with him, but every effort was denied. She needed to talk to him and ask him if he had spoken to Grace. She needed to know if he was okay.

Grace had shown up on her doorstep unexpectedly the morning after Micah had left so angrily.

Mikayla would've recognized her old friend anywhere.

They had embraced, holding onto one another for a long time. As they pulled apart they were both sobbing. Words would never make up for the years of pain that being apart filled them with. While Grace had been Micah's lover, she had been Mikayla's only friend and she had missed her desperately.

"I messed up," Grace had said, falling against Mikayla. Mikayla had helped her into the house and they had talked for hours.

"Please... you have to talk to him for me," Grace had made Mikayla promise.

Mikayla had given Grace every bit of contact information she had for her brother, but she knew that if he was as hurt as Grace said he was, they might not hear from him for quite a while.

Even though she had talked to her brother nearly every day of her life, there had been times when he had sequestered himself away from her and she knew he was just catching his breath and regrouping. She was sure that was what he was doing now, or at least she hoped.

After Grace left, they talked every day. Often about Micah, sometimes about life. With Grace and Noah in her life, Mikayla felt like the brokenness inside was beginning to slowly heal, though she was afraid to admit it even to herself.

Still, with Christmas approaching, she was beginning to feel anxious.

"Micah, you need to call me. There's a lot you don't know about Grace. I know you're mad at me... maybe at her too, but call me. I'm your sister. dammit. I miss you." Mikayla left the eighty-fifth message on his phone. She had given up trying to sound calm and was considering her next move. She didn't want to contact the police, but she was beginning to worry that something had happened to him.

She kissed Heidi on the head as she tried to maneuver out from under her without disturbing the princess too much. Heidi let out a yawn and laid her head back down on the soft bed.

"Spoiled," Mikayla smiled.

Her phone vibrated.

"Lunch. Maeve's?"

"Sure. Are you bringing my buddies?"

"Not today. "

Mikayla was disappointed. Noah's boys gave her a joy she'd never felt before.

Connor was the youngest but had warmed up to her first. Liam had taken longer, but Mikayla realized that he was still desperately grieving and afraid to open his heart. Little by little he started to confide in her, mostly about how much he missed his mom, and her heart ached for him.

"I have a surprise."

Mikayla's heart skipped. She was intrigued.

"Okay..."

"See you at noon."

Mikayla smiled to herself.

She walked sleepily to the bathroom and looked in the mirror, leaning in closely to peer at her face. Her skin was clearer and more radiant than she remembered it being in a long time. No alcohol and no self-medicating looked much better on her. She'd even started doing yoga and running on the beach again and her lungs were already thanking her.

She brushed her teeth and mused about the surprise. She had a love hate relationship with them. As she continued to brush vigorously, her mind drifted to Noah.

The last time he'd given her a surprise it had been a gold shell necklace. It was the last gift he'd ever given her.

"For my beautiful girl," he'd said as he'd kissed her softly on the lips.

The memory was like a wisp she held onto and she realized she hadn't thought about it in a long time. She had worn that necklace every day for years and then she'd tucked it away, long forgotten.

She smiled as she subconsciously touched her lips and thought about his.

Mikayla shook her head. There was no way it was jewelry now. They were just friends, she reminded herself.

Just friends.

Still it had been a long time since anyone had given her a surprise. She tried to control the butterflies in her stomach.

He's not ready for a relationship and neither are you, she reminded herself.

She looked out of her window and saw the dark sky. The air had been much colder than usual and she was glad she still had her warmer clothes from Boston. She never thought she'd need them at the harbor but with the talk of an impending blizzard, she was happy she had tucked them away.

As she readied herself to meet him at Maeve's, she thought about Christmas. She had never spent a Christmas without him, and she couldn't imagine that he would stay away, no matter how angry he was. She'd hoped to hear from him by now but with his refusal to take her calls, time was dwindling for him to make it in for the holidays.

Emerson and her new husband, Ethan, had invited them to a Christmas party, and she was hoping that Micah would be home in time to go, but she was beginning to realize he might not come home at all.

As she finished getting ready, she closed her eyes and took several long and deep breaths.

Whatever happens will be fine, she tried to convince herself. But as she looked out of her window again at the uncharacteristically dark clouds looming over the harbor, she wondered if that could be true.

CHRISTMAS EVE

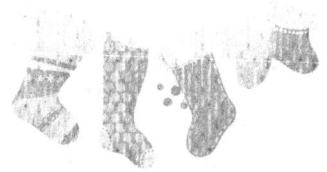

The nor'easter had been a strange phenomenon that took many in Grey's Harbor by surprise. They knew it was coming and did what they could to prepare, but few had ever seen anything like it before.

The town was sparkly with garland and ribbon and all of the lights they could hang, but a snowstorm was never in the plans.

With Mrs. Murphy's help, Mikayla had done her best to make the house as festive as possible, even though she didn't feel it in her bones. Christmas had always been her favorite holiday but her mom had taken care of most things, so she was grateful for Mrs. Murphy's help.

She had invited Grace, Ophelia, Noah and the boys to spend Christmas with her. Much to her surprise and happiness they accepted. She filled the house with as much Christmas as she could, but deep down she knew that without her parents and Micah, it wouldn't be the same as it had once been.

She did her best to push down the sadness even though she wanted nothing more than to let it surface and consume her.

With Noah and the boys in her life, she was learning she had much to be grateful for.

"Miki, is this for me?" Liam pointed to a brightly wrapped present under the tree.

"Liam!" Noah scolded, "That's rude."

Mikayla knelt down next to Liam and ruffled his hair. "I think Santa might have dropped that off here for you, but you'll have to wait to open it until a little later."

Liam nodded happily as he ran off to find Heidi who had been playing with Connor in the kitchen.

"You didn't have to do that," Noah chided her gently.

"I know. I wanted to, partner." Mikayla smiled warmly.

"Partner?" Grace eyed them mischievously as she took a sip of her champagne. "What's this about?"

Mikayla wished Micah was there. She hated sharing something so big without him knowing but since he still refused to accept her phone calls or texts, she had no choice.

"Well," Noah put his arm around Mikayla's waist. "I've always wanted to own a charter fishing boat company. It was my dad's dream and then it became mine. Now that I'm back in the harbor for good, the opportunity arose so I asked Mikayla if she'd like to partner with me, fifty-fifty, and she agreed."

"Oh my God! That's amazing!" Grace squealed, pulling Mikayla in for a big hug. "I'm so happy for you!"

"Me, too!" Mikayla's eyes shone brightly. Noah had surprised her with the offer at the Cathead and she had accepted on the spot. He had the business sense and experience, and she had the capital and the desire to learn. For the first time in her life she was going to do something she was proud of.

The only thing missing was Micah.

It became clearer to her with each passing hour that she wouldn't see him for Christmas.

With each passing day she had already begun to wonder if she had lost him for good and now she knew.

She thought he might consider forgiving her, but he hadn't even responded to Grace. He had decided to disappear, and Mikayla couldn't blame him. She'd already failed him so many times. Now that his heart was broken, she imagined it might take the rest of his life to ever forgive her for what she'd done.

As the wind howled outside rattling the windows, Mikayla shuddered. Even if by some miracle he would forgive her, there was no way he would make it in now. All major transportation coming in and out of Grey's Harbor had been closed off. There had been no flights in or out of Gilmore for nearly a week. Any hope left Mikayla had of spending Christmas with Micah was gone.

She fought hard to remain cheerful, especially for the boys. They had lost so much, she reminded herself.

As they sat down for dinner, Mikayla tried hard to remain present, but part of her floated away trying to feel for her brother somewhere in the world, alone, and without her, too.

"Can we open presents after dinner?" Liam looked up at Mikayla, his large brown eyes hopeful.

"Yes, but only one." Mikayla laughed.

"You mean there's more than one?" Connor looked at her, surprised.

"Santa still has to come so you'll have to open his presents in the morning," Mikayla chucked him gently on the chin.

Connor happily nodded at her. "Okay, Miki."

Grace leaned over and whispered, "You're good with them. Maybe you should consider having a few of your own one day."

Mikayla blushed as she motioned for Grace to be quiet.

As they ate, Mikayla looked around the table, proud of the little family she had formed. All of them a little lost, she had brought them all together at a time when they needed one another the most.

As they finished dinner, the doorbell rang, startling everyone.

Micah!

Mikayla jumped up and ran for the door, and when she threw it open she was surprised to see a roughened middle-aged man standing in front of her with several pieces of luggage.

"Micah Grey?" He looked down at a piece of paper in his hand.

"I'm his sister." Mikayla looked around him as though waiting for Micah to emerge at any moment.

"Oh. This luggage was supposed to be sent here for a Micah Grey."

Mikayla anxiously reached for the paper in his hand. Micah had sent it a week earlier!

"I'll accept it for him. Let me get my purse." Mikayla turned to go into the house.

"No need, Miss. He paid me really well to get this here. Merry Christmas."

Noah helped Mikayla carry the luggage in the house.

"This is his," Mikayla announced, staring at the worn out bags, a tear slipping down her cheek.

"So... his luggage is here, but where is he?" Grace tried not to sound as anxious as she felt. Ever since the morning he had left her bed, she tried closing her heart on the hope that he might return to her but just couldn't.

She had spent her entire life, including her marriage, trying to forget about the boy who had made his home in her heart and refused to leave.

Always, he had promised, and she had believed him.

Even after all of the years without him, nothing and nobody could ever come close to the love she had felt when she was with him. She knew she should have told him that first night that she had left her husband to move to Grey's Harbor nearly a year before. She could no longer stay away from the memory of the boy and girl they had once been, but he had never given her a chance.

She was angry with him for leaving and refusing to let her explain, but she was even angrier with herself. If only she'd left sooner, they could've had an entire lifetime together.

Still, she realized she had stayed for another love. For Ophelia, who she loved with all of her heart. When her daughter was old enough and she finally realized that her love for Micah was never going to end, she knew it was time to go home.

As she stared at his luggage she fought against the tiniest spark of hope. Even if he returned, there was no guarantee he might want her. If he'd felt what she had, he never would've left, she'd reasoned.

"That's the question," Mikayla's voice was full of worry as she stared into the night. The roads were horrible, and they were due for another round of snow before morning. "If he would just answer his damn phone..."

"I'm sure he'll be fine," Noah put his hand on her shoulder and she grabbed it instinctively.

"Who, Daddy?" Liam asked timidly.

"Miki's brother."

"You got a brother?" Liam seemed genuinely surprised.

"Yes. I do." Mikayla tried to smile. "He's a great brother, like you are to Connor and he is to you."

"Can we meet him?"

"I hope... I mean, yes... you can."

"Cool.... can we open our present now?" Connor's little voice made Mikayla laugh.

"Yes, of course you can," Mikayla tussled his hair. "You both can. Then, you'll have to get ready for bed because you can't stay up too late. Santa can't come if you're both awake."

Both boys ran as fast as they could to the tree with Heidi running after them barking and Noah chasing after them to prevent too much damage from being done.

"Do you think that he's okay?" Grace looked at Mikayla, worry brimming in her beautiful eyes.

"I've been wondering that since he left the first time. I certainly hope so." Mikayla grabbed her hand and squeezed it.

"I do, too."

CHRISTMAS DAY

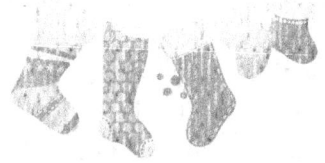

*M*ikayla woke up to a different type of silence than she was accustomed to on Christmas mornings.

As she rolled over and stared at the numbers 5-0-0 on her alarm, she realized that the silence of this Christmas morning held more anticipation and promise than anything she had felt in all of her adult years.

Her heart skipped with excitement as she pictured the boys snuggled up in the guest room with Noah, slowly waking and realizing Santa had come.

It was their first Christmas in Grey's Harbor and she wanted it to be special. Noah's house was still in shambles with redecorating and unpacking, and she had promised him that she would do everything she could to help him make it memorable for the boys. They had even made a call to Santa's secretary with the boys to make sure he knew where to bring the presents.

Mikayla couldn't remember having so much fun, and as she helped Noah put the presents under the tree, she allowed her heart to fill with the happiness she knew it deserved. She had become fond of her new little friends and she realized that the joy in doing something for others was what had been missing in her life.

"I just want to thank you." Noah's voice was full as he fought back tears after the last present had been placed under the tree. With the boys tucked snuggly into bed, Mikayla was happy to help with the presents. "Christmas was their favorite holiday with their mom, and I was worried that I would ruin that for them. But you've helped me make it... fun. Their last Christmas was the first one without her and it was awful. I don't think I could have even done this without you."

Mikayla fought the urge to throw her arms around his neck.

He's not ready, she reminded herself.

"You're welcome." She blushed.

"I have something that I wanted to give you, if that's okay." Noah pulled a little box out of his pocket and Mikayla's breath caught. "I didn't wrap it, but I wanted to make sure it was okay that I give this to you."

He opened the box and Mikayla gasped at the glittering compass necklace nestled inside.

"I remember getting you a seashell necklace once, but I thought this might be more appropriate. You've helped give direction to my life when I needed it the most and I just want you to know how grateful I am."

He took the necklace out of the box and unfastened it. As Mikayla lifted her hair, his fingers grazed her neck. He fastened it without allowing his eyes to leave hers and she realized she hadn't taken a breath.

"Thank you," she breathed.

He brushed her cheek softly with his fingertips. "It's beautiful, just like you. I'm so thankful you've come into my life again."

"I'm thankful for you, too," Mikayla threw her arms around his neck and when he kissed her, she knew that no matter how long it took for them to heal one another, she was never going to let him go again.

As she lay in bed, she wondered how long it would be until the boys woke up. She finally gave up on sleep and decided to get up. She picked Heidi up and carried her through the house so she wouldn't make too much noise.

As she tiptoed into the kitchen to make coffee, her heart stopped as she saw a lone dark figure walking through the kitchen.

Before Mikayla could stop her, Heidi leapt from her arms and ran toward the figure, but instead of growling, Mikayla realized her butt was wagging.

She flipped on the light.

"Micah!"

"Do you think you can get your killer dog off of me?" He had scooped her up and Heidi was desperately trying to assault him with kisses.

"Where have you been? We've been worried sick. We've texted and called and left message after message. Then your crappy luggage got here last night and you didn't come with it!" Mikayla forgot that he was supposed to be angry with her as she scolded him.

"I've been around, sister dear." Micah grinned. "Besides, I'm still pretty mad at you. In case you were wondering."

"Yes, but haven't you tortured me enough? Can't you put me out of my misery? It is Christmas after all." Mikayla burst into tears.

"Yes, it is."

"What about Grace? Are you still mad at her?"

Micah's face darkened.

"She's married, Miki. That's all. I don't do married drama, I never have. Not even for Grace."

"But she's not ... at least ... not anymore." Micah jumped as Grace's voice echoed from behind him.

He turned around and Grace's green eyes were staring directly into his.

"I'll leave you to it. We can resume our spat when you're done here. We have plenty of time." Mikayla smiled up at her brother before pulling him in and kissing him on the cheek, her eyes still wet.

Micah held her eyes and in that moment, Mikayla knew she was forgiven.

"Okay..." Micah turned his attention toward Grace trying to ignore how the hollow of her throat made his heart ache. "Now you."

"I'm not married. I moved back to Grey's Harbor hoping for

you. When I came back here, I filed for divorce from Ophelia's father and it was final last fall."

"Why would you do that?"

"Because ... I never stopped loving you. I didn't want to leave. I didn't want to lose you but we were young and I didn't know how to fight for you or even find you then. So, I came back here hoping for you. I know that sounds so crazy and stupid but..."

Micah took two steps and Grace was in his arms.

"I thought... I thought you were married and that..."

"No. It's only ever been you, my love. Only you. Always."

As Micah kissed her, he admitted to himself that Grace had never left his heart. His love for her had fueled him his entire life, and while he hadn't ever known if they would end up together his heart had always longed for her.

"So where have you been? We thought something awful had happened to you." Grace placed her hand on the side of his face.

"I was with ... family. They were helping me."

"What were they helping you with?"

Micah hesitated.

"I ... was going to wait and tell you but..." Micah ran his hands through his hair.

When he'd left Grace, he thought he could go home and settle back into his life, but everything had changed. Touching and seeing Grace and remembering everything they'd shared made him realize that his current life would never be enough. With or without her, he'd finally discovered the passion he needed in order to fulfill a life that was otherwise empty.

His anger with Mikayla hadn't dissipated immediately, but she had been a kid at the mercy of parents she desperately wanted to please. It wasn't her fault for keeping so many secrets from him. He knew how rare it was to feel the warmth of their father's approval and the desperation to keep it. Still, Mikayla had lived her life carelessly, and there was much she needed to answer for.

He wasn't ready to let her off the hook yet.

His return to the harbor the week before had fueled him with fire and purpose that he hadn't felt in a long time. He had been careful to keep himself hidden because the harbor was small and he didn't want anyone to know he'd returned.

Only Emerson and Lillian knew where he was and what he was doing. When the storm came in, he was thankful he'd done his traveling the week before.

He had planned to spend Christmas with Mikayla, but he hadn't expected there would be a house full of people, including Grace. Knowing now that she wasn't married changed everything.

"The theater." Micah couldn't think of anything else to say.

"Our theater?" Grace's eyes were wide.

"Yes. Our theater."

"It's a mess. I can't even bear to walk by it. My dad would be heartbroken to see what it's become." Grace's eyes welled up. She had loved the theater more than anywhere in the world, a place where many of her dreams were conjured and came true.

"I bought it." Micah reached for her hand.

"Y-y-you bought it? What... why?"

"I've spent my entire life chasing something, but I didn't know what it was. When I saw you, I realized that it had always been you, but when I thought you were married I knew the only thing left to do was to buy and restore the theater. It was the only thing left of us, and I realized that I needed to do it for me. For you. For us."

Grace's eyes filled with tears as she took in his words.

"So... does that mean you're going to stay?"

Micah nodded, his eyes wet as he pulled her in to him and held her tight.

"I love you, Grace. If you let me, I'll love you forever. I promise."

Grace tilted her head up and kissed him with her entire soul as though she would never let him go.

"Can you feel me in here?" Grace placed her tiny hand on his chest.

"Always," Micah breathed as he leaned his forehead against hers, finally feeling alive.

The patter of little feet and squeals of excitement burst through the house with Heidi right behind them.

"Merry Christmas." Mikayla handed Micah a steaming cup of coffee. "Black, like your soul, brother dear."

Micah kissed her on the forehead. "Merry Christmas, sister dear."

"Our parents would be happy to know that we're together today." Mikayla smiled apologetically.

"Yes, today ... and every day." Micah echoed.

"So, you're staying?" Mikayla didn't sound surprised.

"So, are you?" Micah nodded toward Noah and the boys who were excitedly opening presents with Heidi ripping apart the wrapping paper.

"Yes."

"Then I guess we've finally found our way home," Micah smiled, the first genuine smile he'd given her in a long time.

"Home." Mikayla smiled back allowing it to sink in.

As the brother and sister stared at the activity around them, they realized that the house had been sitting there for years, waiting for them to return.

They finally allowed themselves to be consumed with the love and hope they had been fighting against their entire lives, in the only place they'd ever found it.

In Grey's Harbor.

The End

Seaside Winter Wedding

PIPER MALONE

PROLOGUE

*G*abe jumped when the dogs' sharp barks jolted him back into the present moment. He was reliving the conversation with Mike and Kim not three hours earlier. Gabe could still feel Kim's warm hug and Mike's firm handshake. At the sound of Alex's car door closing, PB and Jay disintegrated into a wiggling pile of wagging tales and whiny barks.

"This security system is both ferocious and adorable," Alex said as she walked into Gabe's home with the freshly made key that he had given her last week. She bent to pet the dogs, her long blond hair falling around her as she greeted them one at a time and asked them how their day was.

"Hey! Welcome home. Uh, did you have a good day at the shop?" His greeting was the same, but Gabe could hear the hollow waver of his own voice.

Alex could too. "Yes," she replied, the word curling around her suspicion. "How was yours?"

Gabe shoved his hands in the pockets of his jeans. He was never good at trying to fake his feelings. That was part of the reason he'd avoided Alexandria Spencer for years in high school. He could never hide the depth of his adoration for her, even when she returned to Grey's Harbor after years away. Alex had blown back into town, and they worked together to rebuild Daisy's, her ice cream shop, and manage the family farm while her father was ill. It only took a day or so, but his high school crush roared to life with a meaning he couldn't define. Until now.

Now, when Alex decided to stay in Grey's Harbor permanently.

When she told Gabe she loved him.

And when he decided to talk to her parents about asking Alex for forever.

Gabe's fingers brushed the engagement ring he had chosen for Alex after taking into consideration her work at Daisy's and on the farm. The bezel-set diamonds would give her the freedom to wear the ring every day without fear of catching a raised setting on one of the animals or a piece of equipment, or have it caked with some ice cream ingredients. Once Gabe saw how the diamonds shimmered and sparkled from every angle, he knew it was perfect. Deciding to forgo the ring box when it made an obvious bulge in his pocket, Gabe kept touching the smooth metal ring nestled in his pocket, sending wild sparks of energy through him. He had been both edgy and elated for hours.

"Good," he said too quickly. "It was good. Are you hungry?"

"Always." She snorted as she followed him down the hall to the kitchen. "Hey, I got a call today from a company that's interested in Daisy's."

Gabe stopped abruptly and turned. "Daisy's? A company wants your ice cream?"

"That's what it sounds like. They'd like to have a meeting to discuss expanding the product line to grocery stores and other beach locations outside of North Carolina."

"Wow. That sounds like an amazing opportunity for the company."

"It's just a phone call for now. I don't want to get my hopes up too high."

Gabe saw the glimmer in her eyes and knew she had already envisioned herself cutting the ribbon at every boardwalk with a new Daisy's location for beachgoers.

"But," Alex continued, "we could have Daisy's To Go trucks in every city to support the brick-and-mortar stores."

"Well, if they came looking for you, then they must be smart investors." He could not let the dense rhythm against his sternum sway him from supporting her. Gabe wanted nothing but good things for Alex, but a very small part of him worried that this new life was a dream. The fear that he would wake up alone, with his life a little gray around the edges, was something he tried not to think about, but it haunted him.

"When do they want to meet?" Gabe busied himself with making plates loaded with baked chicken, mashed potatoes, and green beans. It wasn't fancy, but it kept Alex from having to stand at a counter when she had been working at the shop for hours.

"They'll fly me to New York next week."

The words made Gabe stumble. "New York City?"

"That's the one," Alex said as she reached for the plates. "This looks delicious. I'm starving. Thanks for making dinner." She took a bite of chicken and moaned around the savory morsel. "I've been trying to make waffles all day. I thought it would be cute to make ice cream cakes for Easter. I designed a rabbit cake but then wanted to give it a little something extra, so I decided to try making the rabbit ears out of waffles. Do you know how hard it is to make rabbit ears from waffles? I had random ears everywhere. I smell like I should be covered in syrup."

Gabe watched her devour the food, unsure of the right thing to say. He knew that offering support for a venture that could catapult Alex's business into stardom was necessary and well-deserved. But he wrestled with the fear that Grey's Harbor, that he, would never be enough for Alex and her big dreams.

"Look," she said as she lifted her hand and wiggled her finger, "waffle iron burns." Alex swallowed a mouthful, her deep brown gaze settling on him. "Gabe, what's wrong? You look pale."

He felt pale. He felt strange. "Uh, I think I'm going to step outside for a minute, okay?"

Alex nodded and Gabe moved for the door, a clammy feeling skating across his skin. He nearly closed the door on PB and Jay, who had dutifully followed him.

Three hours ago, Kim and Mike had given him their blessing to ask Alex to marry him. Gabe had a plan. It wasn't fancy or elaborate, but it was a future for them.

Alex would always strive for more. She had the Spencer genes that craved the adventurous things in life.

Gabe was grateful he found a way to sustain his life after years of rejection and abandonment from the family members who should have cared for him.

He sat on the wooden porch swing a little too hard, the metal chains jerking under his weight as his mind wrapped around the dread that, in this life, in this small town, he might be holding her back by asking her to stay with him.

"Gabe?" Alex called, her voice calm yet cautious. "Don't tell me nothing is wrong. Spill it. You're making me nervous."

"There's nothing to be worried about." He hesitated, and a look of open skepticism settled on her face. "Okay." He inhaled, uncomfortable about his own issues. "It makes me uneasy that you're going back to New York. I know you loved it there. I also know you want good things for Daisy's."

"Do you realize this could be a good thing for Spencer Farms too? If I can negotiate a contract that says Daisy's ice cream is only produced with Spencer Farms milk, the family business will have a lucrative market to pull from. We can push that revenue into Grey's Harbor and support our community in all the ways we want."

Gabe, embarrassed by his own raging fears, shook his head. "I didn't think about it like that." He exhaled. "That's a wonderful way to think about expanding."

Alex crossed her arms and popped her hip. "Now, tell me what's really wrong."

Gabe leaned back against the swing, running a rough hand over the back of his neck. "Are you sure you want to know?"

"Gabe, if we're doing this, then I need to know. You had no problem having me look at your rear end when one of the cows kicked you last week. If I can witness that, I'm sure I'll survive this. C'mon, out with it."

Gabe blew out a breath, tempering his emotions. "How long do you think you'll be there?"

"Two days at the most. Shorter if I don't like their business plan. I know this is still new for us, but . . ."

"This isn't a *you* issue, Alex. It's a *me* problem. I have loved you for so long, and the life we've started together is beyond anything I could've ever expected. It feels so good—"

"That you're worried it will go away?"

Gabe's eyes stayed fixed on the ground as he nodded in solemn agreement. "It's ugly and it's old stuff, but it's something I still struggle with." He looked up to face the woman he loved. "I talked to your parents today, and after that conversation, I felt good. But hearing that you have this opportunity shook that feeling."

"Okay, let's be clear about something: *we* have an opportunity. This deal seeks to benefit Daisy's and Spencer Farms. This is *our* chance to make great things happen. And, why are you talking to my mom and dad about us? Did they say something about me staying at your place?"

"No, nothing like that," he hedged.

"Are they trying to be your friend on social media?"

"I'm not on social media, City. You know that."

"Did Jay steal Dad's sandwich again? Because that's his own fault for leaving ham lying around."

"No, none of that." Gabe stood, pacing a bit before turning back to Alex. The pressure of keeping the secret felt too big to hold. "I talked to them about wanting to marry you."

The light playfulness that filled the guessing game deflated instantly. Gabe hadn't meant to propose so casually, but there it was.

"Oh." She breathed the word before swallowing. "And what did they say?"

"They said you don't deserve me," he managed to slide out with a snicker.

"Gabriel Barnes!" Alex laughed, then rolled her eyes. "Is that what this is? You're worried I'll stay in New York after you've made grand plans about us getting married?"

"Maybe," he said.

Alex walked toward him and wrapped her arms around his waist. Gabe felt a soothing wave of warmth push away his unsettled thoughts and bathe him in comfort.

"I tried to be in New York without you once, Gabe. You know how that turned out. I love you. I'm here with you."

"Alexandria, no one has ever tangled my heart as much as you. I'm sorry I freaked out."

"I'm glad you could tell me eventually. Next time, can we try to talk it out before you walk out? I was scared you got in your truck and took the dogs. I was minutes away from writing the next smash country heartbreak ballad."

"Deal." Gabe sobered and tucked his finger into his pocket. "This isn't how I wanted to do this, but since it's out in the open." He pulled the rose gold band that glittered with bezel-set diamonds from his pocket and held it up for Alex to see.

He watched her exhale, her bright brown eyes lighting with excitement.

"Alexandria Spencer, I have loved you since the first day I met you. Will you do me the honor of loving you for the rest of our lives?"

"Only if you allow me to love you for all of our remaining days and nights."

"Of course, Alex. Now, will you marry me?"

"Yes, Gabriel Barnes, I will."

CHAPTER 1

Seven months later

"Are you sure you don't want to come with me?"

Alex watched Gabe kick an invisible rock on the ground. "Nope."

In the days prior to leaving to meet with the Sunshine Sweets Inc. team, Alex could feel the rising tension everywhere. News of expanding her ice cream business spread through Grey's Harbor like wildfire. The town was happy. Her parents were thrilled.

News of their engagement added to the fervent excitement. Everyone in Grey's Harbor offered their congratulations. Customers who frequented the Daisy's To Go trucks shared their excitement and wedding day advice. Daisy's social media accounts were followed by bridal companies and wedding venues. Her business goals realized was one reason to celebrate; marrying Gabriel Barnes was cause for fireworks.

Unfortunately, her fiancé looked like he was ready to walk the plank.

Alex fingered her engagement ring. "I can show you Manhattan. We can catch a show. I know some great restaurants." She tugged at the hem of his shirt. "Come with me."

"I need to get things ready for the winter months here." He

looked across the open field next to the barn, where PB and Jay romped and snapped at bees that floated around tall yellow blooms. Alexandria Spencer knew her fiancé. Gabriel Barnes was avoiding her.

"My plane takes off in two hours, Gabe. Don't make me leave you like this." She reached up and touched the rough stubble dusting his jawline. "Tell me."

His chin puckered as he mashed his lips together. "It's just a lot to consider. Expanding the farm for national distribution of Daisy's ice cream is a massive undertaking. So is wedding planning."

"Well, we can push off the wedding until—"

"I don't want to do that, Alex. If I had the choice, I'd rather we get married first, then expand Daisy's."

She pursed her lips. "Well, we haven't talked about a date between the summer rush and the meetings with Sunshine Sweets. When do you want to get married?"

"You want me to pick a date? Isn't that a *bride* thing?"

"No, it's an *us* thing. When do you want to get married? Tomorrow?"

"You have a business meeting tomorrow. And I have the cows."

Ever since Alex's father had his heart attack, Gabe had assumed the majority of the daily operations of the farm. Her father had taught Gabe everything he knew about maintaining a successful dairy farm. He still offered supervisory assistance, but running Spencer Farms was Gabe's full-time responsibility.

"How about next summer?" she offered.

Gabe shook his head. "Too far. Plus, it's busy season for the farm and Daisy's."

"Next weekend?"

"Don't push me to the altar, City," he scoffed. "I'm not desperate."

Alex stifled a laugh. "Okay, the summer season closes in one week. We'll winterize the trucks mid-September. I'm sure the business world slows down during the holiday season. Let's plan for then."

"December? You want a winter wedding in three months?"

"I want any wedding where I'm marrying you. Besides, I've always wanted a Christmas wedding."

"Christmas Day or around Christmas?"

"Well, it will be nice to ride the festive spirit wave into the holidays. How about Christmas Eve?" Alex thought for a minute. "But we won't be able to have the ceremony at the church."

"Christmas Eve eve?" Gabe offered.

"That sounds perfect. Can you call the church and see if they have availability?"

Alex swore she saw Gabe blanch before he replied, "Sure."

"Great." She pushed up on her toes, kissing him. "Just so you know, I'm going shopping on this trip." Alex pulled him closer. "I might find some pretty honeymoon things while I'm there."

Gabe groaned. "Please do not tease me with the idea of lacy things when you are states away."

She kissed him, then pulled back. "I'll text you pictures."

CHAPTER 2

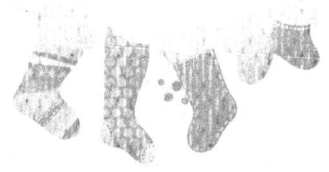

*G*abe bounced with the rhythmic pace of Nobel's canter across the open back pasture of Spencer Farms. Surveying the lesser-used farmland became part of his weekly responsibilities on the farm when Mike and Kim had been forced to reduce the number of cows years ago. Gabe loped Nobel along the fenced acreage, PB and Jay jogging close behind as he surveyed the fence for any breakage or signs of damage.

When he'd first come to the farm, the only thing that made him feel whole was riding out into the pasture with Mike and absorbing every piece of knowledge he had shared. For the first time in his short life, Gabe had the opportunity to see what a family looked like. He saw the value in home and relationships, and he realized he craved what others took for granted: a stable home.

Falling in love with Alex was a bonus. It was always from afar—first when she brought home boyfriends, then when she moved to New York City, but it was always there. He loved Alexandria Spencer even then. Now, after months of restoring her brick-and-mortar ice cream shop and creating a mobile business to distribute her homemade confection to beachgoers, they were living the life Gabe dreamed of as a child. They had the dogs, the farm, and now they were planning a wedding. Well, he was, anyway.

Gabe let his mind drift, trusting Nobel to steer them along the fence line. He thought about marrying the woman he'd dreamed of for years. He had been excited to propose, but envisioning their wedding day filled him with a peace he was unaccustomed to feeling. He thought about what vows they would be forced to say as Alex's request came to mind. *Can you call the church and see if they have availability?* Gabe didn't love the idea of getting married in a church, especially after being forced to meet with Pastor Clarke when he first came to Grey's Harbor. He just always felt a little closed in when he was asked to sit quietly for a specific amount of time. It made him antsy and, while he knew it was a little silly, he always felt like some spotlight was going to shine down from the ceiling and announce all the sins that peppered his youth before his father shipped him to live in Grey's Harbor.

Even if his past did come calling, he knew Alex would understand. She never balked at the sticky details of his upbringing. She knew that he was past it, and that was good enough for him. He needed to tell her his hesitations about getting married in the church —there was no reason to keep it a secret—but he wanted the opportunity to see if he could work through the issues alone.

Gabe thought about his hesitations, allowing Nobel to walk leisurely along the fence. There was nothing he could do to change what had happened. No one could erase the stains of poor relationships and bad decisions made in an attempt to survive another day. He did the only thing he could do: recognize that he wanted something better and fight to find it. He prided himself on finding someone to show him the way. Gabe was sure that Mike didn't know the depth of his respect. Whether Mike knew it or accepted it, he had saved Gabe's life.

Breathing in a fortifying breath, Gabe made a plan to talk to Alex about where they were getting married.

"If we get married in the church, can I trust you to not chew on a pew?" The normal dogged pant or collar jingle didn't follow when Gabe talked to PB and Jay. Pulling back on Nobel to slow his pace, Gabe looked behind him to see PB sitting down near where Jay was nosing at the ground, his stance playful as he bowed to whatever was just beyond the fence.

"Guys," Gabe called, "c'mon. Whatever it is, leave it." He knew enough to know that, if left to their own devices, they would never move on. Jay could never leave well enough alone, and PB was the ever-present spectator to Jay's antics. PB also reaped the rewards of Jay's affinity for stealing unattended sandwiches.

When the dogs didn't trot along behind Nobel as asked, Gabe circled back to herd them home. For shepherds with the skill of rounding up errant animals ingrained in their DNA, PB and Jay lacked the ability to keep themselves in line.

"PB! Jay! C'mon, boys. Before the sun sets."

Jay all but ignored the call, whimpering and nudging a pile on the other side of the fence. He was set to ignore the silent plea in PB's bright yellow eyes, but when he whimpered, Gabe dismounted Nobel. If Jay was the class clown, PB was the valedictorian, and Gabe had been with both of them long enough to trust their instincts.

"Okay, let's see what you have here." Gabe pushed past Jay's enthusiastic welcome to the party and reached through the fence. In the waning sunlight, Gabe hoped that whatever Jay found wasn't too dead, or if it wasn't dead, he hoped it wasn't too rabid.

He reached toward the dark pile of leaves and muck. Under the cover of his hand, movement and tepid warmth ruled out the possibility of a carcass. Gabe rationalized away the possibility of rabies when he didn't get a fight, and he quickly scooped up the animal to pull it through the fence. He recoiled at the stench clinging to it as he gingerly laid it on the ground. The musk of rotten leaves steeped in stagnant water made it clear that whatever this thing was, it had spent time in the river. PB and Jay moved in to inspect their find, tails wagging with happy inquiry. Only when Gabe heard the weak whimper did he take a good look at the stinky pile of brown.

If the puppy was three weeks old, it was lucky to be alive. Its brown fur was matted. Gabe rolled the puppy over in his hands, its weak limbs pushing against him as he looked over its skinny frame for any sign of injury. When the pup's dry tongue pressed against Gabe's palm, seeking any kind of nourishment, the memory of finding PB and Jay flooded his brain.

As a young man, Gabe had been discarded, just like PB and Jay

247

on the side of the road. The pair had been wild and wiggling, unlike the puppy that seemed only a few days away from death. Gabe couldn't let that happen. Even if she didn't make it, the pup deserved care and attention. She deserved the opportunity to be loved so much, any memory of her bad start could be forgotten. Gabe couldn't forget his past, but he helped PB and Jay live a happy life. He was determined to do his best for her. He held the pup close to his chest as he mounted Nobel, steering his horse back to the homestead.

"Well, guys," Gabe said to PB and Jay, "it looks like you just got yourselves a baby girl."

CHAPTER 3

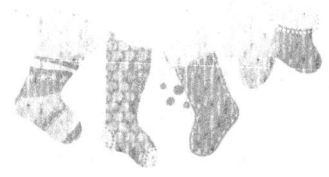

"*W*hat? You want to have a threesome?"

"Do not call me while you are standing in the middle of that chaos. You can't hear a darn thing." Gabe's voice pushed through the phone loud and clear. "Three dogs. We have three *dogs!*"

Alex snickered at Gabe's exasperation. She heard him right the first time, but she couldn't resist teasing him. "All right, you don't have to shout at me. I'm in the building now. Tell me about our newest addition."

"I don't think she's ours, City. Your dad is so in love with that puppy. He named her Carrots."

"Carrots?"

"Yes. According to your dad, carrots are a great side snack for a peanut butter and jelly sandwich. I didn't have the heart to argue. He looked so happy."

Inside the massive foyer of Sunshine Sweets Inc., Alex looked out at the bustling New York City street. From the warmth of the building, she watched swarms of people hustle through the cool November morning. Alex has been able to watch the decorations shift from spooky Halloween to bright and festive holiday cheer during her sporadic visits to the city. While she enjoyed the conference calls with The Team, she loved witnessing the festive change of the season.

Businesses were decked in garland and glittering lights. New York during the holiday season was a fairy tale come to life. So what if it was a fairy tale bustling with noisy cabs and hotdog vendors? To Alex, it was a magical scene.

"Gabe, you are very sweet, and I can't wait to meet Carrots, but I wish you were here."

She heard him snort a response, but she pressed on. "I'm sad I'm going to miss the tree at Rockefeller this trip. Every time, I feel like I'm seeing it for the first time."

Gabe grunted. "When is your meeting?"

"Fifteen minutes. I need to get up there." Alex pressed her thumb against her engagement ring. "Wish me luck."

"Always. Just remember, they are the ones who should be wishing for luck. You have everything they need, City. Call me when you're done."

Even over the phone, when he was crabby about her ridiculous love for a kinetic metropolitan city, Gabe had a way of soothing her worries. "I love you. I'll call you soon."

Ten minutes later, Alex was ushered into a conference room teeming with people.

"Ah, Miss Spencer. It's nice to finally meet you." A dapper gentleman cut through the chaos of the room, his arm extended in greeting. He had thick, dark salt-and-pepper hair and was dressed in a suit that cost as much as the monthly rent on her old New York City apartment. "I'm David Butler."

Mr. Butler—*David*, as in the CEO of Sunshine Sweets Inc.—was shaking her hand. Alex hoped her smile covered her shock. This was supposed to be a welcome meeting. An introductory meet and greet. A get-to-know-you coffee date. Not a fly-me-to-Venice-for-tiramisu seduction.

"Mr. Butler, I wasn't expecting to see you today, but I'm so honored that you're here."

"Please, call me David. I know this is a meeting with Sol, our project manager, and the team to talk about some preliminary ideas and strategies, but I wanted to introduce myself. You have quite a product, Miss Spencer. Thank you for sending the samples of your ice cream. Our last staff meeting was unusually quiet. It would be in my best interest to have your delicious treats at every meeting." His warm gaze never left hers as he spoke. The compliment was dressed in a subtle seduction that seemed very natural for David Butler.

"I'm happy to hear that everyone enjoyed them." Alex willed the happy flutter in her heart to slow down. She was one breath away from gushing at the praise. This was a meeting, and she wanted to make a good impression, not float down the river of compliments *David* was pouring. "It has always been a goal to create products for everyone to enjoy, regardless of their individual tastes. It's nice to hear that Daisy's product line was able to bring joy to your staff."

The warmth in David's smile cooled slightly as he absorbed Alex's words. "Yes, and that is why we're here today. We'd like more people to share in that joy." David clapped his hands together and faced the table. "Team, if you have not had the opportunity to meet Miss Spencer, now is the time."

· ✳ ·

"*W*hat's the good word, sweetheart?"

After hours of discussion with the Sunshine Sweets team, Alex was relieved to hear her mother's voice. She was also grateful to be in a city where she could wear her earbuds and engage in a conversation without getting side eye for talking to no one. "The good word is . . . *exhausted*. They wanted to know everything from product development to the To Go trucks."

"Product development?" Alex could hear her mother's fist on her hip. "Are they talking about making widgets or ice cream?"

Alex snorted. "After about an hour, I felt the same way. No one said the words *ice cream*. It was all so clinical. Daisy's is a cool treat, but it shouldn't feel cold."

"That's not your style at all, dear. How did you leave the meeting?"

"Sol, the lead manager on the account, is going to send me a draft of the contract to review. We have the option to suggest

251

changes and make updates. I was clear about keeping the primary production in Grey's Harbor. I gave them the numbers on expanding the farm. Gabe is confident we can accommodate more cows to increase production. I also suggested incorporating To Go vehicles that are eco-efficient."

Her mother paused on the other end of the line, causing Alex to hold her breath. "And?"

"And what?"

"And," her mother replied, "what do you think?"

Alex stopped rifling through the rack of lacy sleep sets. "What do I think about what?"

"About the fact that they're clinical about your coolness."

"Mom," Alex said with a lowered voice, "this could be *really* good for us. I mean really good. Since Dad's heart attack, I've worried about making sure you guys are okay—"

"Alexandria, do not ever let your father hear you say that. He'll fall over where he stands." She heard her mother sigh. Alex was sure if she had said the words in her mother's presence, there would be some admonishing finger waggling.

"You know what I mean, Mom. This might be the opportunity that provides a level of financial stability for generations to come. Think about the possibilities for the farm. Spencer Farms could be a nationally recognized name."

"Daisy's will be the name that everyone recognizes, dear. The Spencer name will be in little print next to the fat content label, also known as the stuff no one reads. I have always trusted you, Alex, but this has the potential for huge ramifications. Good and bad."

"I know." Alex couldn't get into the discussion in the middle of Gemma's Gems, an English boutique specializing in lingerie for everyone, regardless of age, size, or confidence level. "I was clear about what I wanted, and they seemed receptive."

"You have a brilliant mind, Alex, but please don't sign anything until your father and Gabe can look over it."

Alex bit her cheek to restrain the feminist rant that begged to free itself, but she knew her mother was right. If this contract sought to benefit everyone, then everyone needed to be included. "I know."

"Good. Now I need to talk to you about something." Alex could hear her mother moving through the house and the telltale creak of the third step leading to the upstairs. Whatever her mother needed to say, it was important.

"Is Dad all right?" Alex felt a familiar wash of panic. She'd been in a meeting with a potential employer when her silenced phone received the call that her father suffered a major heart attack. She fled New York with the fear that she might have missed the opportunity to tell her father she loved him one last time.

"Oh, he's fine. Your father is ridiculously in love with Carrots. I caught him talking to her like a baby while he was bottle-feeding her. Jay is jealous of his obvious affection for her. But, no, there's something else." She inhaled. "Russell is in town."

"Who?" Alex said, her attention drawn to a delicate deep-green lace lingerie set. The name sounded vaguely familiar, but she couldn't place it. "Should I know that name?" she asked, distracted by the possibility of dropping Gabe to his knees.

"You absolutely should, Alex. Russell Barnes is your future father-in-law."

"What?" Alex screeched in the subdued boutique. "Why didn't Gabe call me?"

"He just showed up. He's talking to Gabe right now. Dad and Gabe came in from the field and Russ was leaning up against Gabe's truck. Dad lingered for a bit, but then he came inside. It's been about twenty minutes. I just wanted to prepare you."

"Gabe never talks about his father." It was the truth. When she'd asked him about his family, Gabe had struggled for a week to tell her all the details. When all the information about the verbal abuse and neglect he suffered was out, he was jumpy for a while. After days of reinforcing that she was grateful he talked to her in the hopes to ease his jagged emotions, he simply needed to be told that she believed him. His tension relaxed, but they made a rule that anything related to his biological family would be dealt with together. No one deserved to suffer at the hands of someone else, and Alex wasn't going to allow anyone to disrespect Gabe. "Is Dad close by? Can he at least see him?"

"He's watching, sweetheart. We all are. PB and Jay haven't left his side. PB plunked himself down between Gabe and Russell like a furry dividing line." She hummed as if she was looking out the window, then her soft voice floated over the line. "I don't understand why that man won't just leave him alone. Gabe's been with us since his emancipation."

"But why would he show up now? Gabe told me he's seen him in town, but his father never bothered to see him."

"Gabe still has some family in town. Maybe word got to him and he's here to . . . I don't know. Forgive me, Alex, but there is not a single good thing I can say about that man. I just wanted you to be prepared."

Alex felt an ache deep in her chest. She was states away while Gabe was facing off with his father. There was nothing more she could do to help Gabe come to grips with his father's visit than talk over the phone. She needed to hold him, soothe him, or help kick the deadbeat's ass—whatever he needed, Alex would be happy to do. She needed that contract from Sol so she could get back to Grey's Harbor.

"Wait." Her mother's firm tone came through the phone, pulling Alex from her thoughts. "That's not true. Russell Barnes did one good thing: he made a wonderful son."

CHAPTER 4

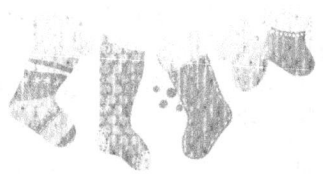

*G*abe couldn't think clearly. The stiff conversation with Russ lingered in his mind and deadened his limbs. Part of him felt the stains of his childhood resurface and taint the life he'd constructed with purpose and intent. Despite the fog he tried to cut through, one thing was clear: Gabe was grateful that Alex was nowhere near Russell Barnes.

He attempted to give Russ the benefit of the doubt when he saw him leaning against his truck, but he knew that the only reason Russ ever showed up was for personal gain. The prospects of money, a free meal, or witnessing someone else's drama for his personal amusement were the bright lights that drew Russ close.

In the rare moments Russ came to Grey's Harbor, Gabe had been able to avoid him. There was the rare occasion when Gabe heard his father's name whispered as he walked by. Two years ago, he had seen Russ's hulking figure moving around the farmer's market. Gabe left the market before picking up his order of pizza bread. He had abandoned his favorite football food for the son of a bitch who made him question everything about himself for years.

Now he had the balls to ask if Alex was making him sign a prenup before they got married.

You've been working this farm for years. It's only right for you to get your due from that pretty piece.

"Your due." "That pretty piece." When Russ reduced Alex to nothing more than a commodity, Gabe seethed. Russ knew nothing about respecting women, which was why Gabe never knew his mother.

Growing up, he'd struggled to find his place. A space where he could breathe and focus. He remembered the days when he would find anyone looking for a fight, desperate for an opportunity to pummel anything. If he felt pain, he could forget about the aching thoughts that circled: How could a father walk away from his only son? Russ left him in Grey's Harbor with his barely sober aunt in the hopes he would stay away from the speculative gaze of law enforcement. Even in the sleepy North Carolina town of Grey's Harbor, police seemed suspicious of him, aware that he was spawned from his family of liars and drunks.

Gabe fought against the invisible dragons of doubt and anger for months until, desperate for money to buy himself a way out of Grey's Harbor, he applied for a job at Spencer Farms.

Unlike any man he met before, Mike Spencer didn't question his motives or the fact that he struggled to look anyone in the eye. Mike only cared about two things: making sure Gabe knew the job and that Gabe knew he was doing a good job. The time Mike took to teach him the business was extensive, and the experience of being with Mike was monumental. For fifteen years, Gabe started and ended his days at Spencer Farms. Once he graduated high school, his entire day was spent in the pasture. It was a life he never anticipated. In the pasture, he was whole: mind, body, spirit.

When he returned to the Spencer homestead and found Russ waiting for him, a fine line of anger split the cool serenity of his world. He swallowed down the vicious command to tell Mike to stay away, instead opting for a reassuring nod to show Mike he was okay. Even though Mike took the cue, he lingered nearby. Gabe resigned himself to being respectful even when his gut told him to grab Russ by his shirt collar and yank him off the property.

He thanked every holy being that Alex was in New York and didn't see the slimy remnants of his past. The son of a bitch thought his fiancée was a commodity linked to the prize of Spencer Farms, as if she was something to be owned. As if he was in the relationship to reap the rewards of her family.

"Boy," Russ said, "how much are you standing to get out of this when this relationship is over? Besides, if she's not here, what makes you think she's committed to some Podunk farmhand?"

Mike must have overheard the conversation because he sent Russ on his way soon thereafter. When Mike tried to talk to him, Gabe couldn't hear the words. It was the swirling chaos of his own fears. Alex was in New York. Everyone knew it. He was starting to plan a wedding while his future bride was making big contracts.

Less than twenty-four hours after Russ invaded his world, Gabe was staring at a computer screen littered with pictures and websites for wedding planning. The images seemed to swim, the cigarette-roughed tone of his father's voice asked what his *piece* would like, and after he clicked one image, he was drowning in a sea of images of dogs wearing formal bow ties for weddings.

When he found a bow tie that matched the color of the flowers he was going to show Alex when she got home, an electric thrill zipped through him. He leaned back, satisfied he was moving in the right direction, when he looked at the clock. Holy shit . . .

He dialed Alex.

"How's the threesome working out?"

Gabe considered telling Alex that Carrots had chewed her pink work boots and had left various puddles around the house after Gabe finally resurfaced from wedding planning.

"Hey, why do they call it Pinterest when it's obviously a vortex?"

"Oh no . . . how many hours did you lose?"

"Years, City. I lost years."

"Did you find anything good on your voyage?" She snickered, and it made him smile.

"I think so. We need to talk about flowers and food."

"Did you call the church?"

Gabe felt the creep of dread. "No."

Even with miles between them, Gabe could hear Alex thinking. "Do you want me to call?"

"No. It just slipped my mind." Gabe knew better than to lie to

257

anyone, especially Alex. He had a hard time keeping her birthday present a surprise; telling her he didn't want to get married in a church was very different.

He heard a sound from deep in her throat that signaled more thinking, which was always a little dangerous for him. "How's everything at home? Any interesting news?"

"Nope."

"Are you sure?"

Sweat beaded under Gabe's shirt collar. Everything seemed too close. "How was the meeting with Mr. Sunshine?"

Alex sighed into the phone. "Amazing. I mean, it was a whirlwind, but David is such a nice man."

"You've had one meeting and you're dropping the formalities? Of course he's a nice guy. He wants your company."

"Easy, Barnes. We had a nice interaction and a wonderful dinner together. I met his wife, and we walked around downtown. It's so beautiful here, Gabe. I love this city. It's pure magic. I'm going to pick up the drafted contract tomorrow, but I scheduled a time to go ice-skating at Rockefeller Center."

"You can ice skate here, you know. Your frigid northern air has found its way down here and put a freeze on everything. I had to get the cows more hay."

"I would love to skate with you, but there's something special about New York."

"I see."

"Will you come with me next time? We have another meeting in two weeks. Come with me and you'll see."

"I have responsibilities, City. I cannot just leave three dogs and all the cows. There's no saying what will happen if I walk away from Pinterest for days. I might never recover."

"I think I have something that will help you recover and entice you to come with me." He could hear her amusement. "There are some amazing sights to see, but only if you join me next time. Put me on speaker."

He obliged but continued to call her bluff. "Oh yeah, like what?"

Gabe's messages pinged with a text from Alex. An image of her lean body covered in tiny strips of dark lace came into focus. He blinked against the rush of blood and lust and longing for Alex. For his fiancée.

"You come with me to New York," her voice flowed with seduction, "and this is the sight you'll see."

"Consider my bags packed, City."

CHAPTER 5

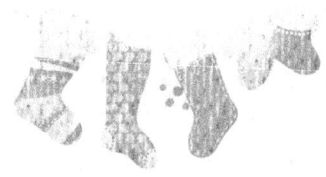

*A*lex knew, even from a very young age, she could trust her instincts. She knew her incessant fixation on food and how those flavors would translate to ice cream was strange, but also brilliant. Alex also knew that when her parents were hiding something, they were awkward and stiff. They were starched the instant she arrived home. She gave her father the draft of the contract she picked up from Sunshine Sweets on her way to the airport. She tried to look over the document on the flight, but she couldn't focus. Alex figured that allowing her father to offer his insights on the contract might help alleviate some of the stress.

As Alex recounted the conversation she'd had with Sol about the merger, Gabe was pleasant enough, but doted on Carrots. She could have sworn she saw PB and Jay share a snarky look when he picked the puppy up and cuddled her close. To his credit, Gabe was heart-meltingly adorable and distracted Alex from giving her parents every detail of her discussion with the Sunshine Sweets team. Gabe's ability to ride a horse, wrangle cows, and cuddle a runty pup made him super sexy, and her mind tried to battle against the low warmth in her belly.

Alex's mind lost the battle shortly after dinner.

"Do you still want to get married?" she asked, her head on his chest.

Beneath her, Gabe tensed. "Are you having second thoughts?"

"No, but I feel like everything here is out of sorts." She sat up, pulling the sheets around her chest and facing him. "I don't understand why everyone seems so strange. What happened here? I was gone for three days."

Gabe stretched his arm wide, then rolled to one side, propping himself on his elbow. "I don't know what to tell you, Alex. There's the farm, and Carrots takes a lot—"

Alex sighed and crossed her arms. "I know your dad is in town, Gabe."

Gabe shifted, his normally bright blue eyes turning cold and distant. "Russ."

"What?"

"His name is Russ."

"Okay. Your father's name is Russ."

"He's just Russ. He gets no other connection to me."

"Fine. Are you going to tell me about your conversation with him? Because my mom seemed to think his presence was significant."

Gabe pressed his lips together, the corners dipping under his consideration. "Hmm."

"Did you know he was coming into town?"

"No. I never know when he's going to show up."

"Why did he come to my parents' house?"

"To talk to me."

"About what?"

Gabe shrugged in response.

"All right." Alex leaned across the bed and flicked on the light. "Gabriel Barnes, you will not tell me that you still want to get married, then force me to pull teeth to get a straight answer out of you. If we're getting married, I think I should know what's going on."

"There's nothing going on, Alex. He's an SOB. Russ showed up, was his usual greasy self, and left."

"Yes, but what happened in between? What did he want? Did

262

you invite him to the wedding?"

Gabe jerked as if she had slapped him. "Hell no, I didn't invite him."

"Well, he *is* your father," she said quietly.

Gabe sat up, his frustration with their conversation evident in the deep lines of his face. "That man pawned me off to every lowlife relative with an open couch for years. He showed up to ask if we had a prenup that left me with a chunk of Spencer Farms. Is that what you wanted to know, Alex? How clear can I be? The man that I share DNA with disrespected you, your family's farm, and our relationship. Thankfully he stopped short of calling you my cash cow, or I would have had to punch my *father's* face."

Alex knew she hit a nerve the instant he began. She could count on one hand the times Gabe was so upset his blue eyes held an icy glint. She'd seen that same look when he saved her from being assaulted after the prom. Alex had witnessed that level of pain when she told him she was leaving Grey's Harbor and moving back to New York after they rebuilt Daisy's.

"He asked if we had a prenup?"

Gabe nodded but didn't offer anything more.

"What did you tell him?"

"That I get the dogs. You get the knowledge that you'll never have this"—he waved a hand over his body—"at your disposal."

"Dang. I lose the dogs?"

Gabe snorted. "Funny, City."

Alex could hear the weariness in his voice. "Seriously, Gabe, I know your family kicks up stuff for you. Can you talk to me about what he said?"

"I don't know what good it does. The more I think about it, the worse it gets. It's easier to accept that he's a waste and I'm better off without him."

"I think you are wonderful without him, but none of us are immune to those feelings. We all have stuff that haunts us. My mom called me after the meeting to tell me Russ had showed up, and before she could say anything, I panicked that something happened to Dad again. I felt all of it, the fear and the helplessness."

Gabe nodded. "I'm sorry you felt that again." He inhaled, his gaze drifting to the far side of the room. "Seriously, he's not worth discussing, Alex. I'll be okay in a few days. I just need to"—he exhaled—"accept."

She knew the conversation was futile. His jaw was set. Gabe's normally warm and loving eyes were distant, focused on something neither one of them could see.

"Well, if you ever want to talk about it . . ."

He looked at her. "He'll disappear soon. He always does."

Alex offered a soft smile of acceptance but felt the lump in her throat. The space he put between her and the situation with Russ felt cold and distant. When she flicked off the light, he held her close and she draped her arm across his chest. Alex inhaled the delicious scent of Gabe's soap laced with rugged scent of his masculine form.

She began to drift into sleep, lulled by the rhythmic flow of Gabe's breath, when her phone rang with her parents' ringtone.

They both shot up, Gabe scrambling for the light, Alex grabbing for her phone.

"Dad?"

"Hey, sweetheart, sorry to call so late."

"Are you okay?" Alex asked.

"Yes, we're fine, but we started looking over the contract with Sunshine Sweets."

"Okay . . ." Alex put the call on speaker so Gabe could hear. "What do you think about the contract?"

"I want to take more time to look over it, but it's generous. Beyond what I expected."

"That's great, Dad!"

"That's not everything, hon," her mother said.

"Alex, I've looked over it again and again," her father continued. "According to this contract, Daisy's will become the sole property of Sunshine Sweets Inc., who will determine the CEO, distribution locations, and commodities retailers."

Through her shock, Alex managed to form words. "What?"

She heard her father inhale before leveling his words. "I thought that might be your reaction. I didn't think you would make the choice to sever the connection between the Daisy's brand and you."

CHAPTER 6

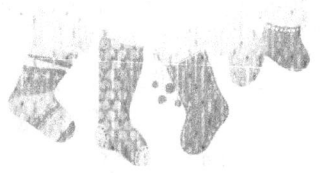

*A*lex stared at the contract and scoured her memory. At no point in the meeting, during dinner, or in the planning session did anyone on the Sunshine team counter her statements about the company remaining with her. No one mentioned that Spencer Farms and Grey's Harbor were not their choices for primary production and distribution.

The roiling awareness that the executives had duped her pissed Alex off to no end, but she pitted that feeling against the knowledge that Sunshine Sweets was offering her a way to help stabilize her family.

"Two and a half million is beyond what I expected." Alex knew that sneaky language and legalese was common in takeovers. She also knew that the first draft of any contract was extreme for the purpose of negotiation. She never envisioned or discussed passing Daisy's to another owner. She saw herself at the center of her business, helping Sunshine Sweets grow, along with Spencer Farms. She wanted to help steer the ship, not hand her bounty over to pirates. She also wanted to make sure the people sitting around the table with her never had to worry about paying a bill. She'd stayed in New York while her parents struggled financially. She didn't know they had to reduce their staff or the number of cows they had. Alex had missed the opportunity to help them and still struggled with the guilt.

She looked up from the documents to see her parents staring at her, waiting for her response. Her mother's typical warm greeting was tense. Her father's dark hair was pressed flat against his head, a habit Alex had only ever observed when he was stressed.

"They want everything." Her father's tone hovered between angry and exhausted.

"For a fat stack of cash." Gabe's voice held a harshness she didn't expect.

"That is a lot of money, honey," her mother offered. "You could do almost anything with that amount of money. Invest. Travel."

While Alex knew that her mother was attempting to be supportive, she also knew what her mother was actually saying. "It would be good, but can I live without the daily dose of Daisy's?"

Gabe broke in. "Could you live with selling out?" For a moment, Alex did not recognize her fiancé. Gabriel Barnes was bristling with anger.

"I'm not selling out." Her voice wavered under the assumption that he would think she would let it all go so quickly. "This is the early stage of negotiations. They're going to try to get whatever they want. This is business, big business at that, and we have a lot to gain."

"I thought your grand plan was to support Grey's Harbor. This has the potential to take all of that away. You might have the ability to invest and sustain a life, but what about the rest of us?"

"The rest of us? Gabe, *we* are us!"

His shoulders bunched and then rolled as he looked away. "The town, Alex. This is supposed to help the town."

"I still think it can," she said.

Gabe's gaze was drawn to the storm door, where PB and Jay sat with their noses pressed against the glass, whimpering and grumbling for attention. Even the dogs knew he was upset.

"Let's take care of the dogs, Gabe," her mother said. "I think we need a little break. If it's not too much of a heartbreak, I'll feed Carrots for you, Mike."

Alex fought her smile when her father finally reacted to something—the prospect of her mom stepping in as Mommy for Carrots. "Are you sure? You can bring her in here and I'll feed her. She gets wiggly when she's eating."

"Ah, yes. The telltale sign of a good eater. I've witnessed that for years," she said, patting Mike's shoulders and kissing his cheek. "We'll be just fine."

Alex and her father watched their partners leave. When they were finally alone, her dad pinned her with a look that she knew meant business. "Tell me what you think about this." He pointed to the contract, then her. "The real truth. No candy."

She exhaled, willing the tears to stay at bay. "Dad, this could be huge for us. That much money is—"

"Life changing," her father supplied.

Alex stood, reaching for both of their coffee cups. "But Daisy's has been . . ."

"Life changing?" he supplied again.

"With that money, I could set up our lives. We could make improvements to the farm."

"Besides the prospect of money, I don't know that anything else would really change for us. The things that continue to propel us forward will always be there. For me, that's making sure people get what they need. For Gabe, it's tending to the cows and bossing the hands around. Your mom, well, I can't name all the stuff she does, but she makes everything about life better, so that's her station. We'll have the cows as long as Gabe wants to manage Spencer Farms. Regardless, there will always be cows and chickens to tend to."

"Can we have goats?"

Her dad huffed. "Are we a dairy farm or a petting zoo?"

"Both?"

Her father pressed his lips into a thin line. "Alex, the way this contract is written, Sunshine Sweets is taking away your work. Gabe, your mother, and I will continue to work as we have always done, but this proposal alters everything in your world. This company is buying Daisy's. Once they do, you cannot have any part of them again. Are you willing to part with everything you've built?"

"Dad, this could set up my kids. They could have college funds before they're even born. I could make sure you and Mom don't have to worry about anything for the rest of your lives."

"Alex, you don't have to worry about your mother and me. We are fine."

"Dad, what if this opportunity passes us by? What if we'll never have the option to be this financially secure?"

"If we've never had the financial security this contract could offer, how will we even know if we like it? Money comes and goes, Alex. What stays is the work. You can sign this and set up your family, but what are you going to do every day?"

Her father no sooner asked the question and she pictured herself at the flagship Daisy's store. Alex was at Daisy's every day. That's what she did. Even when she lived in New York, Alex missed the feeling of creating new flavors of ice cream. She envisioned herself at her store, reliving her summers scooping cool, creamy delights for her friends and neighbors.

Alex suspected that her father knew her answer before she did. "I don't know what I'd do if I wasn't working for Daisy's in some capacity."

"Then this contract is—"

Before her father could finish, Gabe pushed through the storm door. "That's it. I'm not . . . I'm not accepting this. That contract is bullshit. There is no Daisy's without you, Alex. Either they negotiate to allow you control and oversight, or you walk. I will not stand by and let you give your hard work away. They don't get to reap the benefits of all you have to offer for a payout and a fancy dinner."

Her normally cool and collected fiancé was not helped by stepping away from the conversation in the kitchen. Alex concluded that he had been running his hands through his hair, causing swaths of chestnut stuck out in all directions. His cheeks, always bronzed from his hours in the field, hummed with the ruddy hue of his agitation. Gabriel Barnes was pissed because someone tried to mess with his fiancée, and his fiancée found that to be wildly sexy.

"I agree," Alex said.

Gabe stopped and straightened, absorbing the words. "Oh." He nodded, shocked at her acceptance. "Good."

"I'm going to call them today and decline this offer. If they still want to talk, we have the meeting in two weeks to discuss concerns and renegotiate. Since you're going to take over Spencer Farms when Dad retires, I need you to come with me. You can speak to the daily operations and offer your expertise on why Spencer Farms should be the model to begin expanding distribution."

Alex watched the warmth draw away from Gabe's cheeks. He swallowed hard before answering. "Of course. That sounds like a great idea."

CHAPTER 7

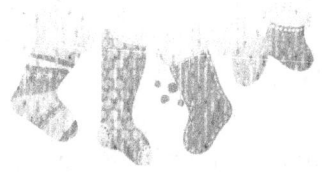

*a*lex stalled Gabe's forward progress. Then, with her eyes bright with excitement, she pointed to her left. "There. Look."

Gabe complied, his gaze absorbing the wide base of the iconic tree at Rockefeller Plaza, then traveling up its massive body. "There is no more guessing. You *are* a fan of big things."

From the corner of his eye, he watched Alex absorb the comment, her smile hidden behind the large cup of coffee she grabbed from a corner bagel shop. Since their arrival last night, she seemed energized, lighter. Her passionate energy had always been infectious, but as she shared moments of her life here with him, she became effervescent. It was easy to float along with her.

"Good thing it's Christmas trees and not other festive decorations," she said with a wink.

"Excuse me?" Gabe did his best to feign being wounded despite her laughter. "I am a human being, not some bag of meat for you to cavort with in luxury hotel rooms."

Alex sipped her coffee and hummed. "That bed is sinful. It's so soft."

"Yet firm, like your man."

"It's also huge"—she wrapped her arm around his waist and pulled close—"like my man."

The warmth of her proximity bled through the layers of coats and sweaters they wore on their morning walk. When he pressed his lips to the tender place below her ear and inhaled the scent of her skin, she sighed and softened against him. As she tucked closer to his body, Alex's lips found his. Memories of their evening in that large, luxurious bed—in the middle of a city he had been dreading, miles away from work, wedding planning, and responsibilities—came bubbling to the surface. While Gabe knew this morning walk was Alex's idea, he wondered how quickly he could change her mind and get her back to the hotel.

She pulled back, the glimmer in her eye giving him the slightest hope for a repeat of their seductive evening and her gorgeous body displaying the lacy bits of fabric she'd purchased to manipulate his sex-drenched brain. There wasn't anything he'd wouldn't do for her, period. He would travel to New York. He would participate in a meeting with the Business Butcher. Gabe started calling him BB after sitting with Mike, Kim, and Alex and highlighting all the ways in which Sunshine Sweets was determined to bastardize Daisy's.

Before Gabe met his nemesis face to face, Alex wanted to show him around New York and share her favorite places in the city. They'd arrived the previous evening in this chaotic flow of evening traffic. The streets and avenues were burst arteries spilling their contents of people, cars, and sounds in a never-ending flow. Now, everything was still. In the breaking dawn of a crisp December morning, before the beast of Midtown woke, she could share her passion for this place at a lower volume. While Gabe was enjoying himself, he appreciated her willingness to temper his exposure to this world.

"Did you get enough of *this* monster?" Alex asked, her smile too wide to hide.

"Of you? Or that monster?" he said, pointing to the tree.

"Huh." Alex's nose and forehead scrunched a bit. "If you've had enough of this monster," she said, gesturing to herself, "then we need to have a serious conversation."

"I guess now is as good a time as any." Gabe straightened his posture. "Alex, I love you, but I'm leaving you for Pinterest. She has everything I need, and she never goes on business trips."

"Gabriel Barnes!" Alex laughed, reducing her admonishment to fuel for his antics.

"I won't apologize for the hold she has on me. She pinned me straight through the heart. Vortex and I are eloping in the spring."

"You are no longer in charge of wedding planning." Alex tugged on his sleeve. "C'mon, let's walk this way to our next stop." She led Gabe around the massive tree, pointing out the ice-skating rink that would be filled with people trying not to break an ankle in a few hours, and through the Channel Gardens, a walkway filled with gold angels and enough lights to be visible from space. Holiday music poured from unseen speakers, and the icy crispness of the air made his eyes watery.

Alex was right. This was unlike anything he had ever seen before, or ever hoped to see. In all of the images he saw over the years of this place, the colors, sounds, and feelings would never be the same as this experience.

At the end of the path, Alex turned around, facing the way they had come. "Now look."

The evergreen seemed only slightly smaller in the distance, seemingly buffeted by the chorus of angels aiming their joyful noise toward its welcoming boughs. Gabe was struck with the splendor of it all. He loved the holidays in Grey's Harbor—the festive cere-monies and traditions of small-town life. But this . . . this was spec-tacular. Every inch of this place was covered in a fine sheen of shimmering gold and sparkling white.

"The first time I saw this, it took my breath away." Alex said the words to him, but her gaze remained on the tree. "The grit that makes this town great glitters during the holidays. It's magical."

"I've never seen anything like it." The wonder of it all struck Gabe. This town held unimaginable possibilities. Those possibilities could grab a person's attention and hold them so close that the life before the place seemed to fade away. He understood, even if by a fraction, how this place could call someone away from the quiet life of Grey's Harbor. Just as it had pulled Alex after high school.

"C'mon, we have another stop on the tour of *Alex's favorite New*

York landmarks." Her giggly voice and the light tug on his sleeve pulled him away from the worry that this town would be the place she craved even after they settled their life in Grey's Harbor.

Gabe followed her down the street, sneaking peeks at shop windows decorated for the holiday season. He did his best to follow the first rule she told him about navigating New York City: look like you belong. As he did his best to blend with the growing crowd, Gabe recognized the look of cool confidence his fiancée possessed. Alex had tackled New York City as a young woman from a country farm as she successfully completed college and launched a career. He was also impressed at her ability to navigate the streets that, to him, were indistinguishable.

"Here we are!" she quietly cheered as she bounded up the wide stone steps.

Gabe's vision climbed the heavy walls until they ended in tight spires that pierced the morning sky. "Wait." He grabbed for Alex, but she had already moved toward the door. "What is this place?"

Before he could get an answer, he rushed to help her as she struggled to pull open the heavy wooden door.

"Alex," he whispered, feeling a creeping dread as he followed her through a dark foyer and into a cavernous sanctuary, "you brought me to a church?"

"I just wanted to see if you'd burst into flames," she whispered back.

"You just wanted me here to *douse* your flames, City." Gabe looked around at droves of people coming and going. Some prayed or slept in the pews, while others seemed to be waiting. Yet more wandered through recessed alcoves along the walls of the sanctuary. "Why are we here?"

"I've always loved St. Patrick's Cathedral, and I wanted to refresh my memory of how it's decorated for the holidays so we can replicate it in the church for our wedding."

Gabe followed Alex down the center aisle. He could see her wonder and excitement. She couldn't see his dread three steps behind her.

Closer to the front of the church than he would have ever considered sitting, Alex tucked herself into an empty pew. He followed her and sat, hoping he actually wouldn't burst into flames.

"Alex?"

"Hmm?" Her gaze skimmed the pulpit.

"What if we didn't get married . . ."

Her cataloging of every minute detail of St. Patrick's halted. "What?"

"In the church." Gabe cleared his throat. "We don't *have* to get married in a church."

She narrowed her eyes. "Is that why you haven't called the church? You don't want to get married there? Why?"

"I think we could find someone who could perform the ceremony in a place that's more . . . us."

"Wait. You don't want to get married in the church?"

"Right."

"When were you going to tell me this, Gabe? We're getting married in two weeks."

He shrugged. "I thought the barn might be a great place. It's close to your parents' house and it's heated. And," he added with a raised eyebrow, "the loft."

Gabe watched Alex sink back against the pew, the words seeming to register in her brain like a freight train barreling down on a watermelon.

"You want to get married in *the barn*."

He knew the request was risky, but he couldn't stand in front of someone like Pastor Clarke—not again. "I can list all the reasons why, but not here."

"No, Gabe. It's here. You brought it up here. You are telling me here. We have three hours before our meeting with Sunshine Sweets, and I refuse to enter that meeting if we're not on the same page. Spill it." She crossed her legs and leaned back, coffee cup in hand, waiting for him.

Gabe blew out a breath, his cheeks rounding as he exhaled. Resting his forearms on his thighs, he focused on the ground and the coffee cup in his hands. He couldn't look at her. All he could do was explain.

"When I came to Grey's Harbor, my aunt made me meet with

Pastor Clarke every week. It was always in addition to confirmation class, Sunday school, and church. He was always a jerk. No matter what I did—volunteer work, cleaning, giving my allowance to the church—he never relented. I tried to tell him that the things my father and aunt said were not true, but he was convinced I was drinking and doing drugs. He didn't understand how a boy could be quiet or enjoy being alone."

"I always knew Pastor Clarke was a little strange, but I thought he was quirky. I wasn't sad when he retired."

"That's one way to put it." Gabe took a sip of his coffee. "People claim that religion is the one thing that can save you, but for some people, earning that salvation means damaging you in the process. My aunt hounded me about religion and the Bible but seemed to forget those teachings when she needed a drink. I never understood that, so I started going to the library and reading about other religions, and I showed Pastor Clarke what I found."

"What did he do?"

Gabe snorted a laugh. "He called me a devil child and said that I was the reason for my family's dysfunction. He told me that if I was compliant, everything would be fine. If I didn't do what my family told me to do, the devil would teach me the lessons I needed to learn."

"Holy shit, Gabe." There was a watery waver in her voice.

"I don't think you can talk like that in here, City."

Alex huffed a laugh and scooted close, wrapping her arms around his waist and snuggling close to his chest. "We'll get married in the barn and find an official you feel comfortable with."

"Thank you," he whispered before pressing a kiss to the top of her head. "I love you. And"—he gestured widely to the pulpit decorated with wreaths and candles—"we can make the barn look like this, just with fewer religious artifacts."

She sat up, pulling herself from his hold. Even with eyes shimmering, she laughed. "I love you, Gabe." She sniffled, wiping away her tears. "So much."

CHAPTER 8

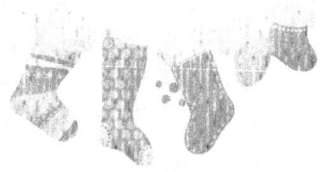

"*I*s he always that greasy?"

"Shh!" Alex smacked Gabe's leg under the table. "I think he uses pomade for that coif."

"I think it's ridiculous. The grease and the *coif*."

"Not everyone can pull off rugged, Gabe."

"Alexandria Spencer, that is a diversionary tactic and you know it."

Alex did her best to shoot Gabe *the look* and prayed he would keep his thoughts to himself or, at the very least, wait to share them with her until they were safely in a crowded restaurant, where she could enjoy his dry wit. She was also eager to be with him. Alone. They didn't have the time at St. Pat's to go into much detail about Gabe's revelation. When he told her about Pastor Clarke, she wasn't so much shocked as heartbroken. No child, regardless of their upbringing, deserved to be labeled by any adult, especially if that adult did not have the child's best interest in mind. Coupling Gabe's rocky start with someone determined to fulfill a prophecy was the perfect opportunity to damage a person for a lifetime. She knew that Gabe battled against his own history. She also knew they were on a path to create a new one.

Alex glanced over at Gabe, who looked a little stiff in the leather office chair. They had been ushered into the conference room by Mr. Sunshine himself. He shook Gabe's hand with too much bravado and clapped him on the back before expressing his delight at Gabe's presence in the meeting. According to David, they had *many things* to discuss. As soon as they were alone, Gabe asked if she had her list of objections to the contract.

"Is this part of the tactic? Make us wait in an office with too many chairs?" Gabe looked around the room, nodding his head.

"I doubt it." She turned to him. "Keep in mind that they're going to ask about what you do to support Daisy's."

"I know. I'll help them, but the nitty gritty info does not come until you have as much control in this merger as you want."

"Thank you," she replied, just as the door opened and a swarm of Sunshine Sweets staff entered the room.

David made brief introductions to new staff members on The Team and then left for another meeting. Alex felt a pang of sadness at the mention of his prior obligation. David had been so energetic and supportive of the merger; she held on to the very small hope that he would hear her concerns and absolve them. Upon his departure, she looked across the conference table and counted thirteen people on *The Team*, in addition to Sol, and felt woefully outnumbered.

She had one person in her ranks. When she looked toward him, Gabe met her gaze and Alex felt a wave of confidence. He may have held the cool, reserved look of her country farmhand, but Gabriel Barnes was ready for battle.

Three hours later, Alex flopped on the plush bed in their hotel room and groaned. "My brain is . . . gone."

"What the hell was that?" Gabe grumbled. "All I can hear is the chatter of people demanding to know how we pasteurize the milk for production." He snorted, lifting his beer bottle halfway to his mouth before stopping. "You know, they are darn lucky I didn't tell them to find a video on the internet or, better yet, encourage them to apprentice at a dairy farm. Mike would have never let me get away with that. He made me do the work because—"

"It's the only way to learn," Alex said, finishing her father's oldest—and truest—saying. "I wish he was here."

"Yeah," he agreed. "He would have had a few things to add to the conversation today."

"You think?" Alex pushed up on her elbow to face him. "Like what?"

Gabe swallowed and tipped the beer bottle toward her. "They didn't acknowledge a single concern you had with that contract."

"They took notes on the list I provided them."

"Right, but they never acknowledged that you were concerned about what the company was doing. Yes, they listened as you reviewed the ninety-five ways they tried to screw you over."

"It was twelve."

He waved away her interjection. "They never offered a statement like 'We'll look into that' or 'That would concern me too.' There was not a single moment when they asked how to make you feel comfortable with the contract. They took the info and pushed forward with their agenda, no mention of when or how your concerns would be addressed."

Alex flopped back on the comforter, allowing its marshmallow fluffiness to hug her. She wished it would swallow her. She needed a comfortable place to recuperate and think. "At least they're willing to bring in the farm. You seemed very engaged in the conversation with the dairy team."

Gabe rocked his head back and forth. "I'm not so sure about that."

Alex pulled herself from the poof cocoon to look at her fiancé. "What?"

"At no point in time did they mention Spencer Farms." He took a long pull of his beer. "They asked what I do and how I do it. There were questions about the breed and breeding of the cows and their diet. I gave them rough estimates of production time and how that could expand or contract based on the number of cattle." Gabe put his beer on a small side table, then sat back and crossed his arms. "They were interested in what I knew about how to effectively produce a dairy product for Daisy's. In my opinion, they were not inquiring about how Spencer Farms could be an asset in expanding the production."

The three-hour meeting had taken its toll on Alex's energy, but Gabe's observation made her blood pulse with renewed force.

"Production needs to stay with Spencer Farms," she said. "Using dairy from our cows makes Daisy's what it is."

"I tried to explain that. They didn't accept or refute the statement. I was just absorbed." He paused before moving forward. "I thought about something in that meeting, and I want you to hear it out."

She groaned. "Please don't tell me you think this is a mistake. At least not until we see the updated contract."

Gabe's silence was evidence enough.

"Really?" Alex couldn't help the pained whine. "You think this is a mistake?"

"I'm concerned about your business. I have faith that Spencer Farms will be fine. But it's you. I'm concerned about you."

"You sound like my dad."

"Your dad is a good man, Alex."

"I know. Go ahead." She braced herself. "Tell me what your thoughts are."

"Are you sure? I can wait until after we have the updated contract."

"No," she said with a sigh, "lay it on me. Let me wrestle with all the stuff at once."

"You know more about Daisy's than anyone else. Why are you giving the fate of this company to someone who doesn't understand even a fraction of it?"

"Gabe, it's the opportunity to be known nationwide. The money alone is life changing."

"Sacrificing the thing you have cultivated for years is life changing too."

"But the money, Gabe."

He shrugged. "Being someone who lived without money, I have a different view of that offer. Besides, money is out there. People have it, and they're willing to part with it for something they want."

Gabe was right. The lines for the Daisy's To Go trucks grew every week, as did her social media numbers. She even got a few online order requests to ship to people who couldn't get to Grey's

Harbor. For as strange as the process was, she was invigorated by learning how to ship her product with dry ice.

"I agree, but millions of dollars, Gabe. Millions."

He shrugged. "Great, we can buy . . . What do you want to buy? A boat? A fancy house with a housekeeper? It won't mean anything if you don't have Daisy's."

"You don't know that."

"I do know that, City. You came home after years away, and you were focused on two things: making sure your dad was recovering from his heart attack and making ice cream. I clearly remember someone staying up all night to churn ice cream and the gleam in that woman's eye the following morning."

He was right. Prior to coming back to Grey's Harbor, she hadn't realized how much she missed her life on the farm. She had her business, but she knew there was always the possibility of bigger things. She went to earn her degree, looking for more and more. She eventually realized that the one thing she was looking for was the one thing she left behind, and it was a tiny ice cream shop tucked in a sweet harbor town.

"Did I ever tell you about the time I did goat yoga?"

Gabe nearly choked on his beer. "Excuse me?"

"Goat yoga. It's where you do yoga with goats."

"Do they lead the yoga class or . . . ?"

"There's an instructor, and the goats move around the group during the session. They jump up on your back and bleat in your face."

"Why would you do that?" Gabe's face contorted with disgust. "They must have pooped on everything."

"They did, but it was okay." Alex inhaled. "One of the goats sat in my lap during Lotus pose." She laughed, feeling the same emotion from that moment. "He smelled like a barn."

"I'm sure that kicked up some memories for you."

She nodded. "I cried, Gabe. In the middle of goat yoga, I snuggled close to that little guy and inhaled every musty barnyard animal smell I could. He was a snippet of home I couldn't find anywhere else, and that memory broke me."

"Alex," he whispered as he moved toward the bed, tucking her close to his body.

"It was fine, but it was one of the moments when I realized Grey's Harbor held more for me than I ever realized. Smells, experiences, and food were all close, but nothing could replicate what we have in Grey's Harbor."

"Just like no other ice cream will taste like Daisy's."

"Exactly." She kissed his cheek. "Okay, now tell me your big thought."

"You're sure?" He waited for her to nod before continuing. "All right. To me, this merger seems off. There are too many cooks in the kitchen, and no one is taking direction from the head chef."

He held his breath and then exhaled. "I think you should expand Daisy's on your own."

CHAPTER 9

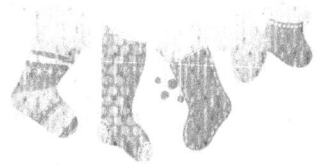

$\mathcal{A}$lex prided herself on strategizing a plan, then attacking. That was before wedding planning. Before she started working with Gabe to plan their wedding. Before she was sucked into Vortex and before all the shiny things captured her attention. She did her best to gather the essentials for a small ceremony, but there were so many pretty decorations for a winter wedding. Evergreen wreaths, candlelit receptions, holly and poinsettia centerpieces.

Her brain went into overdrive the moment she and her mother stepped into the bridal shop. On a normal day, she would not be so enamored with the lace and beads, but today she was looking for her dress. A dress that would complement the work she and Gabe had put into creating their wedding.

Alex met with Henry, a dapper gentleman that not only radiated style and elegance, but was the shop's most respected bridal consultant. She handed him a list of possible gown styles and fabrics befitting a Christmas Eve eve wedding. Henry looked at the pictures, then at her. Alex felt mildly uncomfortable under his gaze until he inhaled, his eyes flaring wide with excitement.

"Wait here, my dears," he said before disappearing between

rows of crinoline-fluffed gowns. Moments later, he reappeared and handed her the sleeveless bodice and full taffeta skirt.

"Thank you for this, but, um, it's pink," she said, balking at the gown.

He peered at her over the rim of his glasses and tilted his head. "It's blush," he replied. "Trust me. You'll see."

Alex agreed and stepped into the gown, her back to the tall mirror as she zipped and adjusted the gown, careful not to damage the delicate fabric.

The moment Alex turned to look at herself in the dressing room mirror, her doubt fled. She didn't believe her own eyes. In a gown she would have never chosen for herself stood a woman she'd never seen before. She saw a bride. The color of her cheeks and her own dark eyes deepened in the embrace of the blush pink gown. She felt shimmery, light, and unlike anything she had ever felt before.

Alex revealed herself, allowing her mother a glimpse.

Her mother hovered on the edge of tears and barely restrained excitement. "Do you like it?" she asked as she fluffed the full skirt, sighing as she circled Alex.

"I love it." Alex hesitated. "I never would have thought."

"Here," Henry said from an unseen corner. "If this wedding is happening soon, you'll need this." He stood behind her, wrapping her in the soft cotton lining of a faux-fur stole.

The synaptic nerves that made her brain a logic-driven monster faltered the moment the warm voluptuous wrap touched her bare shoulders.

"Oh my," her mother said. "Alexandria, you are simply gorgeous."

"Do you think Dad will like it?"

"Look at you, Alex," her mother admonished. "He would be a fool if he didn't. Gabe is the one you should be concerned about. I think he'll lose his mind, which means this dress is perfect."

"Told you so," Henry sang before excusing himself to help another bride.

Alone in the dressing suite, Alex turned to her mother. "Can I ask you a question?"

"I'm buying this dress for you, Alex. Don't worry about that."

"Thank you, but that's not what my question is."

With her mother's full attention on her, Alex felt the weight of her gaze.

"Oh, well, okay." Her mother moved to sit on one of the chairs reserved for family in the suite. "Go ahead. I'm all ears."

"Why did you and Dad let me open Daisy's?"

Her mother's posture softened a bit, her eyebrows coming together. "What do you mean? Why did we help you open the storefront?"

"Yes. I was so young, and you just plunged into this idea I had. Why did you do that?"

"Well, for starters, we were in a good place to take a financial risk. We got the storefront for a great rental price, and we made sure the business started out small and grew according to demand and what we—and, ultimately, you—could manage."

"Was the decision solely financial?"

"Finances are always a big part, but creating Daisy's was your dream, Alex. We had faith that you knew what to do. The more you studied business and marketing, the more we trusted your ability to get it done."

"But I left and it all fell apart."

"You went to college, and we didn't have the heart to make you choose between expanding your knowledge of the world and staying in Grey's Harbor. You came back when the time was right, and look at you now! You've expanded the To Go trucks, and now you're in talks to take your business even further."

"Okay." Alex turned and pulled her hair to the side. "Can you unzip me?"

"No." Her mother settled deeper into the chair. "Tell me why you asked."

"Gabe got a bad feeling about the Sunshine people."

"Of course he did, Alex."

"There was a point in the meeting where part of the team pulled Gabe aside and asked him about milk production and what he does to support Daisy's. He said they never mentioned Spencer Farms specifically, which was part of the deal."

"The farm wasn't mentioned in the first contract they sent over, so you can't blame him for being cautious."

Alex nodded. "He thinks I should try to expand Daisy's on my own."

Her mother didn't try to hide her amusement. "He wants you to franchise your own brand?"

Alex nodded.

"That's a smart move, if you ask me."

"Do you think I can?" Alex asked.

"Do you think you can't?"

"It's a big responsibility."

"So is starting any new adventure," her mother said. "That doesn't mean you don't try it."

"And what if it flops and we're homeless and destitute?"

"Has anything you've ever wanted badly flopped? You have a business, a college degree, a home, and let us not forget the biggest achievement to date: you got Gabriel Barnes to and from New York City without any major issues. He told me you took him to see the tree."

"We did. It was a nice getaway." Alex looked at herself in the mirror, trying to figure out if Gabe's suggestion was his way of empowering her or negotiating away from New York.

"Alex, no matter what you want to do, your father and I support you. You, Gabe, and the dogs will always have a home with us. As long as you want Spencer Farms, it's yours. You can take Daisy's to seaside towns up and down the coast or to Hong Kong if that's what you want. It belongs to you. Your father and I know it's safe in your hands."

Alex felt the tears welling up. "Thanks, Mom. I'm just scared about this whole thing."

"I know." Her mother stood up and rubbed Alex's arms. "You're allowed to be. You are also entitled to make any decision about your business that you want. There is no saying you have to take any deal right now."

"But what if another one doesn't show up? What if we never get a million-dollar offer again?"

"And what if you make your own million?"

Alex sucked in a breath at the ferocity of her mother's statement.

"Sorry for the delay, ladies," Henry called as he burst back into the room. "Now, what do we think about this gown?"

"I love it," Alex said.

"Wonderful!" Henry cheered. "Do you need a veil?"

"No, Gabe knows what I look like," Alex replied.

"She just needs that stole. She hasn't stopped petting it since you put it on her. Add it to the order, please," her mother said with a smile.

CHAPTER 10

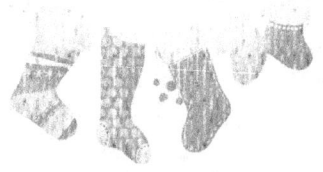

*A*lex pushed her hands through her hair. "How do card companies do it?"

"They have people who know everything about designing wedding stuff." Gabe hovered over her, his strong hands rubbing the tightness from her shoulders. "How is the program coming? Can you print this out? I want to look at it on paper."

She moved the mouse and clicked the icon, feeling the dull ache of her muscles and the sensitive patches of her fingertips. "You look at that, and I'll get back to the centerpieces."

Gabe looked over the page. "Looks good to me. Date. Time. You spelled our names correctly." He shrugged. "All the parts of the ceremony are listed. Yes, these are good. One more task off the list."

She nodded and stretched through a yawn. "Good. I'll look at it one more time tomorrow. For now, it's back to hot gluing more of my fingers than the evergreens."

Gabe had gathered discarded trimmings from the Christmas tree farm and wired them into wreaths. Alex's job was to attach the red bows. There were ten total. She had two done and scalded four fingers in the process.

"Why is hot glue so hot?" she said.

"I think *cold glue* doesn't possess the same laser focus. If someone wants to get a job done, they use hot glue. Cold glue? That's for grade-school crafts."

"Well this stuff is pulled from the bowels of Hades, it's so hot. I'm going to have scorch marks on my fingers when Eliza has us exchange rings."

"Nah, she'll be fine with it." Gabe's response was buoyant.

Since their meeting with the officiant, he seemed relieved. They'd met with Eliza for lunch and talked about how they met and what they wanted for the ceremony. It was a wonderful day, but Alex was exhausted and she just felt . . . off.

"Do you want me to help you so we can finish this up?" Gabe offered. "I'll handle the gluing; you can point and tell me what to do."

"Deal," she replied and followed him into the dining room, where the wreaths were laid out.

A text message pinged on their phones at the same time. Giving each other a quizzical look, they reached for their devices.

"It's your dad . . ." Gabe's voice trailed off as he scanned the message.

The hesitation made Alex scramble to his side, worried that her father might be having symptoms of another heart attack. When she looked at the screen, her tired eyes blurred, but she could make out the words.

I was worried about this. Incoming snowstorm.

Gabe tapped the link her father sent and looked at the forecast. There in bold white was the prediction she hadn't anticipated: snow. Sure, it was December and everyone loved a white Christmas, but it had not snowed significantly in Grey's Harbor in years.

"Well, it might be too early to really count on this." Gabe tucked his phone back in his pocket and looked at her. "Weather systems change all the time. Ready to glue?"

"You're not worried about that?"

He shook his head. "No. We're inviting a small number of people. Everyone is local. It'll be fine."

It didn't feel fine. It felt like one more thing. Centerpieces still needed to be created. They were a few songs away from finishing the playlist. She needed to finish writing her vows. The photographer needed a list of photo locations. Her wedding shoes needed to be dyed to match her dress. She still needed to figure out how she was going to do her hair. And, to make a stressful week even more daunting, Carrots had released her incessant need to chew on the very expensive ballet flats Alex bought for the reception.

While she was confirming, creating, and organizing, one nagging thought kept her from being completely swept away by wedding planning: Sunshine Sweets had been silent since their meeting last week. Even after she'd sent an email to Sol about their timeline for the wedding, he simply wished her well on her pending nuptials and said that the Sunshine team would be in touch.

It was eerie and a little unnerving. Prior to the last trip, there was a text or an email almost every other day. Alex tried to shake off the worry that the opportunity to stabilize her family was lost and that people were most likely celebrating the holidays.

"Hey, City?" Gabe's voice distracted her from her thoughts. "If this is too much, let's call it a night. I can see you're exhausted."

"No, it's fine." An incoming call pulled her away. "Who the heck is calling this late at night?" She looked at the number. "It's from New York," she said as she swiped the screen.

"Hello, this is Alex," she pushed through the phone with a smile on her face. She ignored Gabe's sour expression.

"Hi, Alex, it's Sol. Sorry for the late call, but I just got the word from David. He would like to meet with you this week. Can you fly in tomorrow or the day after? We found a few flights we can book for you."

"I thought the updated contract would be emailed, and I wasn't planning on coming up again."

At her statement, shock transformed Gabe's face.

"We're getting married in six days," she reminded Sol.

"Oh, that's right! Christmas Eve eve. Listen, we won't take much of your time; we want to discuss some of the adjustments we've made."

"Oh." Alex glanced at Gabe, diligently working on a wreath, and sent a small prayer that she could pull this off and celebrate her wedding and the holidays without worrying about the ongoing back and forth with Sunshine Sweets. "When is the earliest flight available?"

No sooner did Alex say the words than Gabe set down the hot glue gun and walked out of the room.

A brief agenda review and a round-trip ticket later, Alex found Gabe sitting at the kitchen table.

"When are you leaving?" he asked, looking down at his mug instead of at her.

"The day after tomorrow around noon. I'll meet with The Team on the twenty-first and be back home by noon the next day.

When Gabe didn't respond, Alex felt her stress level push against every aching nerve in her body. "Is there anything you need me to help you with before I go?" she asked.

"I don't think so. I'll finish the wreaths tomorrow. You did the programs and music. Food is ordered."

"Do we have a cake?"

Gabe roughed a hand over his neck. "I thought you were making an ice cream wedding cake."

"You want me to plan, create, and design a wedding cake in less than a week?"

"Don't, Alex." Gabe lifted his hand in protest. "Do not . . ."

"Do you know how much time that takes, Gabe?"

"As much time as building wreaths, planning flowers, and figuring out food?" His tone sparked a fiery pit in her gut.

"What is your problem? I thought we agreed to do this, Gabe."

"Exactly which *this* are you referring to? The merger or getting married or staying in Grey's Harbor?"

"What exactly do you want me to do? Postpone? They're calling me in to discuss closing this deal. We're almost through this. Let's just get this over with so we can move on."

"Move on? Are we moving on to get married? Is this an item on your already packed agenda?"

"Don't say it like that," she pleaded.

"Then should we postpone the wedding? I feel like you aren't into this."

"We agreed to this date. We were on the same page in New

York." She stepped away from the table, pushing her hands through her hair. "None of this should be this difficult."

"Then ask them to push back their takeover. They've taken this much time to figure out their plan. They can wait until next week."

"They aren't taking over, Gabe. I'm trying to do what's best for all of us. There's no need to be dramatic."

"I think you're mistaking my value of honesty for drama. I think that's exactly what they're doing."

"This is business."

"If they're so desperate for your business, they'll respect your request to postpone. They can wait," Gabe said.

"So can we!" Alex felt a rush of warmth throb into her cheeks. She watched a similar shade of ruby flow across Gabe's face and down his neck. His Adam's apple dipped as he swallowed, but he remained silent.

After a few minutes under his cold stare, when she couldn't handle the deathly silence a moment longer, he spoke. "You want to wait? Fine. I'll wait. But so will Sunshine Sweets. I'm willing to give one year. That'll give all of us plenty of time to figure out what we want."

His words sat on her chest, heavy and cold. "I thought we knew what we wanted." She tried not to let her voice sound weak, but she was so tired.

"Do we? Our wedding is in six days and you're getting on a plane."

"I'll be back the day before the wedding."

"Flying along the East Coast in winter is a gamble."

"It's only one day, Gabe. I can meet with them, get the contract, and fly home. You won't even know I'm gone."

"I always know when you're gone, City."

Alex mumbled a curse as she fought back her tears.

"I'll call around and order a cake or cupcakes or pie. Just tell me what you want, and I'll take care of it."

"No," she said with a sniffle, "I want to do it. I have enough time to make a rough design. Mom can help me make some fresh batches, and I can decorate it when I get back. I'll make sure it's ready."

Gabe's mouth formed a thin line. "If this is too much, we don't have to do this right now. I don't want to force you, City."

"Here's the most frustrating part of all of this." Alex wiped away her tears and drilled her fiancé with a fierce look. "You seem more confident in my willingness to marry you than you do in the decisions I make for my business."

"Let's be very clear, Alexandria. You said yes to me, and I will be honoring that. I am also honoring your decision to move forward with this negotiation. I trust you. I always have. I do not trust Sunshine Sweets. You need to be focused when you talk to them. If this is too much, then we need to reevaluate this plan." Gabe stood and moved toward her, but his warm, comforting touch never reached her. "I want you to be happy, Alex. With everything. Our marriage and your business."

"Then why do we keep fighting? Why does this feel horrible?"

"Well, what do they say about breaking eggs to make an omelet? Maybe in our case, we need a few hot glue burns to make a pretty centerpiece."

CHAPTER 11

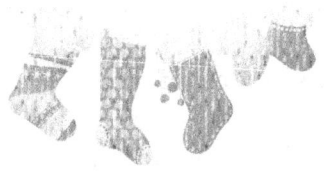

"*T*hanks for coming in on such short notice." Sol was a sashaying vision of holiday cheer. His green tortoiseshell glasses matched the festive tree on his sweater, and Alex muscled back the awestruck question, *Did you knit that yourself?*

"Thankfully, it's a quick flight," she replied, attempting to mask her exhaustion. She hadn't slept the night before. Gabe insisted on driving her to the airport, and when he kissed her goodbye, he told her he'd see her soon, and that was it. She fought the urge to run back to him the moment she was seated on the plane.

"Indeed," Sol said more to the heavy contract than her. "Everyone is off this week for the holiday, so it will just be you and me going over the accommodations and updates we would like to offer in response to your requests."

Sol flipped through the first pages and pointed out minor changes, ecologically sound modifications to production Gabe had noticed. "These were great ideas that came straight from your honey's mouth," Sol said.

"Gabe worked very hard to ensure Spencer Farms is good for the environment. He has made solar and wind power part of the farm wherever he could."

"Of course he did!" Sol's response was a bit too enthusiastic, even for eco-friendly business modification. "Okay, next we're going to go over your role with this company."

Alex sat up, looking at Sol's manicured fingertip directing her to the word. "Consultant?"

"Yes." Sol nodded, and despite the energy of the action, his hair —a russet helmet of perfection—did not move. "David would like you and Gabe to act as consultants."

"What does that mean?"

"We would reach out to you for guidance and support as the product line is expanded and distributed. You would help with making sure the flavors and colorings are true to the original small-batch recipes."

"What about Gabe? Would he consult on the dairy production?"

"Yes, he would." Sol pointed to Gabe's name and title.

"Does Spencer Farms have a role?" Alex knew that if Gabe was witnessing this conversation, he would be snarling.

"You will be pleased to know that Spencer Farms will continue to contribute to the Daisy's line, per your request."

"But we won't be responsible for the entire production?"

Sol looked at her as if she was losing it. "No. Spencer Farms will be compensated for their work, just as you and Gabe will be paid for your consultation services as Sunshine Sweets incorporates the Daisy's brand."

"How long will that process continue?"

"We will reassess progress as production and distribution grows."

"Okay." Alex felt like she wanted to ask more, but part of her didn't really want to hear his answer. "What does that mean for the farm?"

"Due to size and projected capabilities, Spencer Farms will be contracted for one year. Then, again, renegotiated if necessary."

"Wait . . ." Alex felt the punch of his words. "A year?"

"Mm-hmm." Sol's nod, accompanied by his tight smile, indi-cated that Alex's concern barely registered with him. "We attempted to explain this to Gabe during our last meeting, but he seemed, well, unaware of our business plan. I wasn't sure if he was going to be let go, so we didn't push the discussion."

"You were unsure if Gabe would be *let go?* Our business plan, the strategy I requested, was for Spencer Farms to serve as the primary hub of distribution. Gabe is a necessary component of Spencer Farms, just as Spencer Farms is integral to the Daisy's brand. I made that very clear to David."

"Yes." Sol's spine straightened as he spoke. "But according to our mock-ups, Spencer Farms will be unable to accommodate this product line at the capacity we have projected. As a result of this rearrangement, we have modified our offer."

Sol flipped over a few pages, pointing to the budgeted break-down of expenses and payouts. Alex scanned the document, stopping at the field Sol indicated. For Daisy's, the To Go vans, and the consultation services of both Gabe and Alex for one measly year was worth 3.2 million dollars.

Sol mistook her shocked silence for restrained approval. "I know! You can't do any better than that!"

Forty-five minutes later, Alex had emailed the contract to Gabe and her parents to review. She couldn't offer anything much, just that the changes were significant and that she would be in touch. A few minutes after the message was sent, her phone vibrated with a call. Alex felt every muscle resist her effort to silence the call. Mired in her heavy guilt, she thought it was a good idea to avoid conversation. She didn't know what to say, so silencing her phone felt like the best response.

She walked along Fiftieth and peered up at St. Patrick's Cathedral. On legs that felt rubbery, she scaled the steps and entered the building. She needed a quiet place. A place to think and plead with the universe to tell her something.

What was once money that could stabilize her family's future had exploded into life-altering resources. She envisioned expanding the farm and building a home for Gabe and their family. A family with children who would only ever know about Daisy's through pictures and stories. Her babies would never accompany her to beach spots. Alex's throat closed as she envisioned a little girl in a sweet sundress with Gabe's tanned complexion and bright blue eyes standing at the edge of the beach, ringing the bell to notify customers that the Daisy's truck was nearby.

She squeezed her eyes shut, willing the tears to stay trapped. Alex pushed back against the feeling that this was too much, that Sunshine Sweets was robbing her of what was truly hers. She thought about Sol's comment about Gabe's resistance, and an angry flare burst from her gut.

No, she thought, shaking off the spiraling feelings that had taken hold. *Figure this out, Alex. You can always figure something out.*

She pulled the contract from her bag and glanced around. While people sat and wandered through the church, no one was close enough to peer over her shoulder.

Alex flipped through the pages outlining the acquisition, the organizational chart where she and Gabe were listed as "consultants," and the paragraph detailing the subcontracting of milk and cream production to dairies across the country. The final page, the products page, caught her attention. In addition to Sunshine Sweets owning the rights to the names she created for her signature flavors, she was required to design, test, and present five additional flavors to the company within the first year of acquisition.

Five new flavors in one year? She thought about the feasibility of the task and shrugged. When she got in the zone, she could do anything. She'd updated the Daisy's menu in less time when she came home from New York. The timing, though . . . She flipped back to the organizational chart, where she and Gabe were listed as consultants for a year.

"That's convenient, isn't it?" Alex mumbled under her breath. If she didn't deliver the goods on their timeline, her consultation was no longer needed.

Alex scanned a few more lines before feeling a tightening in her chest. The section that outlined her rights as an owner was sparse compared to the rights Sunshine Sweets gained in the acquisition.

According to the contract, she retained the right to maintain her role of consultant as long as Sunshine Sweets found the relationship amenable. The next line made her stomach flip: *Michael Spencer shall remain the sole owner and proprietor of Spencer Farms Inc. and all its artifacts at the close of the contract with Sunshine Sweets.*

It never occurred to Alex that her father's farm – the *family* farm – would ever fall into the hands of someone other than her and Gabe. In previous versions of the contract, Spencer Farms was mentioned as a resource to support Daisy's, never as an entity that could become the property of Sunshine Sweets. The idea that someone, some big business, would even touch their family farm triggered an anger she didn't know she had. It felt wrong. Even though the terms were established to keep Spencer Farms safe, Alex's protective instincts flared. Those cows, that barn, the acreage, and all of its possibilities belonged to her family and no one else.

Heart pounding, she looked back at the document and gasped.

All materials, resources, and production processes necessary to create and maintain the signature ingredient list for all Daisy's ice cream flavors prior to and during the first transition year shall be the sole property of Sunshine Sweets, Inc.

In past contracts, her role was to work with the team and supply them with the necessary information. According to this update, she was no longer an integral role in Daisy's.

For her service as a consultant, they wanted her to share her work, then walk away. They wanted her recipes. All of them. Alex grappled with the idea of detailing her churning process and her method for testing and experimenting, and then handing that off to someone else. Sunshine Sweets would take her twist on her mother's berry cobbler, and it would never belong to her again.

Alex heard her mother's voice ring in her head: "If you think this is good, you should taste Alex's version. My pie is perfect for a cool evening; her ice cream is just right for a warm summer night."

She envisioned handing Sol the battered notebook she'd first started using to write down her ideas, and she fought back a sob. Her life, since she was sixteen, had been ice cream. She went to college, lived away from the farm, and ached for the one thing that had always been hers: Daisy's. Alex returned home and found not only the love of her life but her passion. Daisy's was her passion. Ice cream was her life.

And those city slick jerks wanted to strip every inch of her creative genius with a fat stack of cash.

No way in helllll. Whoops. Sorry, Jesus. Alex glanced at the pulpit and scrunched her nose. "Thanks for giving me the space to think," she whispered to any helpful being in the universe who was in earshot. She grabbed her bag, scooted out of the pew, and quickly walked out of the church with a fiery feeling in her chest.

She knew what needed to be done.

First, she needed to make a call.

CHAPTER 12

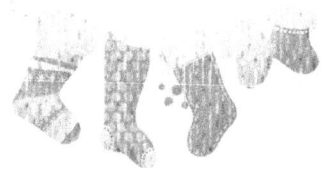

*A*lex's phone jitterbugged in her hand as notification after notification lit up her lock screen. How long had she been in the church? Missed calls from her mother and Gabe. Texts from Gabe and her father.

The two that caught her eye came from places other than her family—the weather app:

Storm system to pummel eastern shoreline of North Carolina.

And the airline:

Flights have been altered due to the increased threat of inclement weather. Please log in to review any changes to your itinerary.

Alex found a bench tucked among the massive angels in the Channel Gardens. She sat and reviewed her scheduled flight. A sigh of relief came over her when she saw that her departure and arrival times were the same, but a red banner across the top of the screen shook her relief. Her flight was headed straight for the storm.

She cursed under her breath, her fear fanning a wave of heat across her chest. She tapped the screen with shaky fingers, hoping she could find an earlier flight. After a few brief, frustrating moments, she grabbed her bag and ran toward the street. Alex held one hand out to hail a cab while the other tapped away at her ride-service app, creating an imaginary race between the two. When a yellow cab screeched to a halt unnervingly close to her, she wrenched the door open and gave the driver their destination.

She needed to get out of New York and into Grey's Harbor. She needed to marry Gabriel Barnes. Alexandria Spencer would figure out how to expand her business without a million-dollar buyout as soon as she and Gabe said *I do*. First, she needed to get on a plane.

CHAPTER 13

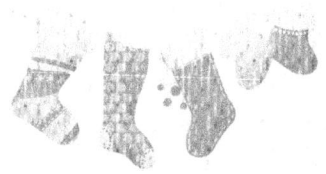

"*W*here have you been?" Gabe heard the screech in his own voice and paused. "I mean . . . are you okay? I was worried."

"Hello to you too," Alex snickered. "I just flagged a cab, and I'm on my way to the airport. I saw the weather report, but it doesn't look like my flight is delayed yet. How are things there?"

Gabe glanced around their home at the piles of centerpieces, wreaths, and candles everywhere. Then he paused in the middle of the living room and looked down at his last Pinterest-related DIY project. "Alex, I shellacked waffle cones with a matte glaze so we could use them as mini flower vases throughout the reception. This place is a mess, but that's expected. How did the meeting go?"

"It was interesting, but can I ask you a question?"

"I hope so."

"Do you believe in me?"

Gabe snorted. "I bought you a bus and had it converted it into an ice cream truck, Alex. I knew if I didn't, you would have pedaled your way around the shoreline until you sold enough ice cream to buy your own. If that's not faith in you, I'm not sure what is."

"Is that faith willing to sacrifice three million dollars?"

"They offered you three million?"

"For everything, Gabe. None of it would be mine anymore." Alex's voice was tight as she spoke. "They want my recipes. All of them."

At the sound of Alex sniffling, Gabe began to pace around the house like a caged lion. He knew she was more than capable of managing the city without him, but knowing she was alone and upset made his chest ache. Sunshine Sweets was trying to strip her of everything she'd created for their financial gain.

"The contract states that I can't make any of the flavors I create for them. The recipes are the sole property of Sunshine Sweets." Alex's voice wavered, then flowed into a low sob. "Our wedding cake is a Sunshine Sweets product."

Gabe stood stock-still. "Tell me you didn't sign the contract, Alex."

"No. Sol gave me forty-eight hours," she replied.

"Forty-eight hours for your legacy." Gabe couldn't keep the anger from his voice. "I know you've wanted this, but they don't care about Daisy's. They want to make money."

"I want to expand Daisy's, but not like this. If this was the right thing to do, I wouldn't hurt this much."

"That's because they're ripping out every good thing you've planted in your garden so they can grow it somewhere else. You don't need them, Alex. You have never needed them. They might have cash to throw at you, but you have everything they lack: determination and passion and killer ice cream flavors."

"Do you think we can do this without them?"

"City, you are capable of anything and everything. If you can figure out how to make rabbit ears for Easter cakes and a wedding cake in the middle of a snowstorm, you can figure out how to take your business all over the globe."

Gabe heard her relieved sigh. "I love you, Gabe. Are we still getting married in two days?"

He eyed the monstrous white dress bag Kim had dropped off earlier that day. "Well, you've got a dress waiting here and a groom that needs a bride, so yes?"

She giggled. "Perfect."

CHAPTER 14

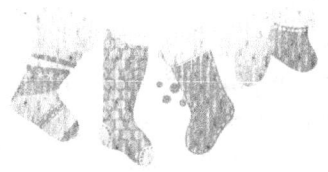

*A*lex did her best to pace her stride down the Jetway. She was eager to leave the plane but had no interest in mowing down the people who exited the flight before she did. Everyone seemed so collected. She had been stewing in the longest, largest internal hissy fit since the pilot's cool announcement.

The instant she stepped into the terminal, her phone pinged.

Why are you in West Virginia?

Of course, Gabe was watching her flight. He was on standby to pick her up at the airport in Grey's Harbor.

I like playing hard to get.

As soon as she saw Gabe read the message, her phone was ringing.

"Hilarious, City."

"Sorry, but I'm freaking out a little. I have no clue where I am and"—she paused, climbing up on a chair to give her a different perspective—"this place is a mess."

From her vantage point, Alex could see the arrivals and departures board changing by the moment. Green arrivals transitioning to yellow delayed notifications. Departures headed south updated to the dreaded red *Canceled*.

"Stay where you are. I'll come get you."

"How bad is the weather there?" she asked.

"There's about three inches on the ground now."

"No way. I am not having you drive out only to be stuck in a snowbank. What if . . ."

Alex jumped down from the chair and started to make her way through the terminal. Thankfully, the storm meant there were only sparse pockets of people in the airport. Once she got past the pack of disembarked travelers, she had the opportunity to navigate the long hallways quickly.

"Don't even think about it, Alex. No way."

She wondered for a moment if she and Gabe had achieved that level of connectedness where they shared a brain. "Why not?" she asked as she focused on the car rental kiosk. "You were going to drive here. Why can't I drive home?"

"I drive tractors and trucks and combines. You drive an ice cream truck."

"Do you doubt me?"

"Never, but I worry about you."

"You should worry more about my temperament after I'm forced to stay here. I'm pretty tough, but this lady draws the line at freshening up in an airport restroom."

Gabe was quiet on the other end of the line. Alex envisioned him pacing, his hand gripping his hair.

"Just let me try. They might not have any rentals; then you can figure out plan B."

Gabe didn't agree, but he did threaten to kill her if she ended up dead in a ditch from this *stunt*. He didn't want to hear that it was Mother Nature's fault, or that if she did end up dead in a ditch, she would haunt him because her love would transcend the grave.

She approached the counter, her heart pounding with unadulterated excitement and joy. This was an adventure, and she was here for it. She was on a quest to get to her prince.

"Hi! I would like to rent a car."

The young woman behind the counter held a firm and distant look. It was an unseen armor that people in the service industry wear to shield themselves against rude customers. "I'm very sorry, but our rentals have been secured. Maybe tom—"

"You there!"

Alex jumped at the shrill voice to her left.

The source of the demand, an elderly woman no taller than Alex's shoulder, leaned on the counter. Her fur coat looked a bit too fluffy to be faux, and the diamonds on her hand reflected like ice under a midafternoon summer sun.

"The vehicle you provided for me is not to my standards. The seats are cloth and I asked specifically for a luxury vehicle."

"Ma'am, I am sorry for the inconvenience, but given the storm—"

"Cancel my reservation! The concierge at my hotel will retrieve me, and I will find a method of transportation that is better suited to my driver's needs." The woman flung the keys on the counter and walked away.

Alex watched the woman leave, shocked at the dismissal, but then she realized her good fortune. She turned back to the rental counter. "I wanted to check one more time about any possible rentals?"

The woman behind the counter looked at Alex and then snatched up the discarded keys. "Well, miss, lucky for you we just had a cancelation."

Twenty minutes later, Alex could barely contain her excitement. The paperwork was filled out, her insurance was verified, and the car had an internal GPS system.

"Okay," the car rental rep said, "we are just about done. When will you be returning the vehicle?"

"Can I return it to one of your locations in North Carolina?"

The rep and the manager exchanged a glance. "I'm sorry, but our policy states that these rentals cannot be taken out of state. It is policy for the airport. If you were at an outside vendor, their rules might be different."

"But I need to get home tonight." Alex felt the waver in her voice.

"You can take it as far as the closest airport before crossing the North Carolina border, but that's as far as it will take you."

"Can I exchange it for another vehicle in that airport?"

"Same rules apply. You would have to be in the state."

"Can you modify your policy? This is an emergency. I'm getting married in two days. No." Alex looked at her watch. "I'm getting married tomorrow. On Christmas Eve eve. I need to get home. Please. I'm desperate."

The manager looked at her with a skeptical look. "We hear a lot of stories, miss."

"Listen, my name is Alexandria Spencer. You saw my driver's license. I own an ice cream company named Daisy's. Look me up on social media." She watched the rep flip through her phone, then turn the screen to verify if she had the right account. "Yes! See, that's me when I'm not gross from airplane funk. Those are my trucks. And," she said, pointing to the thumbnail images, "that's PB and Jay. They're Gabe's dogs, but they love me a lot. And that's Gabe." She gestured to an image of her fiancé holding an ice cream waffle sandwich up to his head for size comparison.

"I'm marrying that guy *tomorrow*. I was in New York because a business wanted to buy Daisy's, but the deal is awful, and I cannot sacrifice my dream for a huge cash payout. He loves me so much he put up with me negotiating this contract even though he knew that it was bad from the start. All he's ever wanted was for me to succeed. He bought me my first ice cream truck, and he opened a Pinterest account to help plan for our wedding. He made center-pieces and wreaths. Please," she begged. "Please help me get home so I can marry him."

The manager looked at Alex, then back at the phone. "Your dogs are cute." Then she looked at the rep. "Give her the keys."

CHAPTER 15

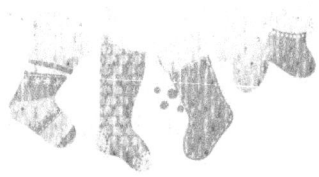

*a*lex did her best to sing along with the holiday songs on the radio, but no matter how many times she ho-ho-ho'ed, she was still terrified. The roads were dark and barren. The headlights illuminating the swirling snowflakes worsened visibility. While there was some comfort in driving a massive SUV designed to seat eight, she felt very alone.

When the GPS informed Alex that she'd be on a stretch of road for one hour, she was glad she connected her phone to the car's internal Bluetooth. She needed to hear a friendly voice, so she asked the goddess of AI to call home.

"Are you okay?" Gabe's voice filled the massive car's cabin, and Alex felt the slightest bit warmer.

"Yes. I mean, I'm still on the road, but it's lonely out here."

"Well, I offered to come get you."

She heard Gabe sigh and knew he was playing with her.

"I just wanted to hear your voice. What's new?"

"Well, the newest thing is that my fiancée is driving across the state in a snowstorm."

"Ha-ha," she replied. "Talk to me about stuff at home."

"Okay, well, your mom is bananas about decorating the

wedding cake. She took your sketch and has been in the shop until ungodly hours of the morning. She made fondant replicas of PB, Jay, and Carrots and set them on the different layers of the cake."

"Oh no. Is she cranky?"

"Worse, she's elated. She's singing and dancing around. She made our breakfast napkins into roses yesterday. Suddenly, everything is art. It's like Banksy and Van Gogh had a baby and they named her Kim."

Alex laughed and felt herself relax a bit. The tension in her shoulders eased for a moment until a gust of wind rocked the SUV enough to scare her. The storm was unpredictable and she could not let her guard down at all. She inhaled and refocused. "Okay, how's Carrots?"

"I need to break this to you now: Carrots is never going to live with us. Your dad is so attached to that dog, he is going to sue us for custody if we try to bring her home. He bought her a backpack."

"Why would Carrots need a backpack?" She envisioned the puppy with a wooden barrel hanging from her neck like a Saint Bernard in the Alps.

"No, he bought the backpack for her to ride in. We rode out to fix the hole in the fence, and he had her in the pack because, and I quote, 'she's too little to walk that far.' I'm lucky we were outside when I suggested Carrots stay with your mom because if we'd been in the house, I would've been moments away from the business end of his shotgun."

Alex's eyes teared, her heart heavy with laughter and the pressing need to feel Gabe's strong arms around her. "Gabe?"

"Alex?"

"I'm scared."

"I know, but I have faith in you. You can do this. You can do anything you put your mind to."

"Okay. I'm going to put my mind to getting home." Alex sniffed, willing herself to be strong. "I love you."

"I love you too." He paused for a moment. "I finished my vows last night."

"Oh yeah?" Her voice wavered, and she brushed away the thin line of tears trailing down her cheek. "Tell me about them."

"Get home and stand next to me tomorrow, and you'll hear every last word."

"Promise?"

"I do."

CHAPTER 16

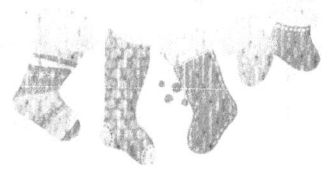

*G*abe was rocked from sleep by the sound of a fist against his front door. He squinted against the bright light flowing into the living room. PB and Jay bounded and romped toward the door as Gabe lumbered across the room.

"Hold on!" he called.

Mike and Kim were standing on the porch when he wrenched the door open. "Is she here?" Kim asked with more panic in her voice than he had ever heard before.

Gabe cursed himself for falling asleep. "We talked late last night, but that was the last I heard from her." He ran for his phone and looked at the blank screen. "Nothing. She didn't call you either?"

Mike and Kim shook their heads, looking restrained. Gabe knew it was not their style to lose their cool. Even when Mike had his heart attack, Kim was calm and collected. Now, she just looked scared.

"It's really bad out there," Mike said.

Walking over to the window, Gabe looked out over a new version of Grey's Harbor. Every inch of available surface was covered in snow. Thick snow. "How did you guys get here?" Gabe asked.

"Nobel," Mike issued. "I caught him rolling around in the snow this morning and figured he would enjoy the ride."

Gabe looked out over the side yard. Sure enough, Nobel was pressing his wide muzzle into the snow and pushing around fluffy mounds.

"We've checked on the neighbors and everyone is safe, but . . ."

"We don't know where Alex is," Gabe finished.

"I'm sure she'll contact us soon. She must have found a place to stay for the night and maybe her phone died." Kim's voice sounded optimistic, but her fear pushed through. "What should we do about today, Gabe?"

His mouth felt dry. Today he was supposed to marry the love of his life. The woman he had loved since their early teens. "I'm not sure."

"The storm has stopped everything. There's no traffic moving through town. Our first priority needs to be finding Alex."

"Yes, it does." Gabe flopped against the couch and looked at the people who took him in years ago. He wanted to say something, but he was lost. Around him, the world swam. His fiancée was missing. Their wedding day wasn't going to happen. He didn't know where to start.

A sharp pain pressed against his chest as he thought about the vows he wrote. If he didn't find Alex, he might never be able to say them. She might never be able to hear them.

"Okay." He felt his heart pound against his rib cage. "We need to contact the rental agency. I'm sure they have GPS on the vehicles. We can ask them to track the car and—"

From a distance, Gabe heard a low, bellowing horn unlike any vehicle he'd ever heard before. In the front yard, PB and Jay howled and bayed as the horn blew again, this time in succession.

"What the hell?" Gabe raced to the window and saw lights flashing yet moving down the street. He stared in awe as a massive snowplow pushed piles of snow as it made its way down the main street. The vehicle halted at the intersection leading to their house and blew the horn again.

Gabe watched Alex push open the vehicle's wide passenger door and assess the ground below.

"Wait!" he shouted before barreling toward the door.

Outside, he waved to her, calling her name. When she waved back, he yelled, "Stay there!"

He called for Nobel, who quickly came to Gabe's side. "C'mon, boy," he said as he mounted his trusty steed. "Let's get our girl."

CHAPTER 17

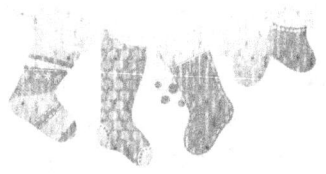

" *L* et me get this straight." Joy paused to secure a bobby pin in Alex's partially done updo. "He rode up to the snowplow on his horse?"

"Like a knight in shining armor," Alex said, her words sounding breathy. "I never knew what it felt like to swoon, but I do now."

"I still can't believe you got in a car with a total stranger."

During the retelling of that night's events, the color in her mother's cheeks drained. "Mom, there was no other option." Alex wasn't going to hear any arguments about it. She was faced with a problem, so she solved it.

For a long leg of the journey, Alex had followed the steady pace of a snowplow as it cleared a significant stretch of highway she couldn't actually see. She just focused on the lights and pretended she was the plow's caboose. When the plow exited the highway, she fought the deep snow.

About thirty miles outside of town, the stress of the ride had taken its toll. Alex had felt the tension in her shoulders. Her eyes began to drift shut. When she couldn't get warm, she knew she was at her limit. Exhausted and overwhelmed by the journey, she pulled off the highway and into a gas station. She turned off the rental, feeling the weight of her situation: She was an hour away from home, knee-deep snow covering roads that were no longer passable —on her wedding day.

In the calm respite of the parking lot, she thought about napping but decided it was entirely too dangerous. Instead, she opted for a slightly less dangerous option: gas station coffee. In the warm convenience store, three burly men in fluorescent jumpsuits lingered at the counter, chatting up the woman behind the register. As Alex perused the coffee selection, she overheard their conversation. Each had a route in opposing directions; one to the south, one to the east, and one along the shoreline.

The same fire that ignited inside her at the car rental blazed anew. She asked if she could hitch a ride to Grey's Harbor with the gentleman headed to the shoreline and explained her situation. Bart agreed to bring her along so long as she would not make him listen to pop music.

Bart didn't actually have the town of Grey's Harbor on his route, but after hearing her story, he offered to deliver her home. She invited him to the wedding. He declined Alex's offer, but did take a sandwich and then went to work clearing the town's streets.

Before he left, Bart gave Alex a hug and told her to be the most beautiful bride in this snowstorm. It was in that precious moment, huddled in the cab of the snowplow as they said goodbye, that Alex had decided that Bart needed more than just a sandwich. He deserved a signature ice cream flavor. If she had her way, everyone who helped make sure her marriage to Gabe happened today would get a commemorative flavor.

Joy sprayed one last spritz of hairspray and declared her done.

Her mother dusted finishing powder over her face. "Now we just need to get across the lawn without disrupting any of this." She gestured to Alex's face and hair. "Your dress is in the side tack room of the barn. We can scoot you in without anyone seeing you."

Alex, flanked by her mother and Joy, moved from her bedroom down the stairs. While Alex had never spent much time envisioning her wedding day, when she did, the location was never her childhood home. Thoughts of her special day hadn't involved the sweet scent of home or warm feelings like it did now, when she passed through the living room and saw the plump evergreen twinkling with lights. She floated on the memories of family and friends and her soon-to-be husband as they moved toward the back door.

When she entered the kitchen, a vision of the first time she saw Gabe when she came back to Grey's Harbor flashed in her mind. Alex stifled a laugh at her weak threat to beat him senseless with a slotted spoon for trespassing, when she was the one unaware of his constant presence. She reflected on the night she made flavors into the early morning hours, craving the satisfaction that came from creating something sweet, and then simply craving Gabe. Warmth swept across her face when she thought about the night she and Gabe gave into their long-held passion for one another.

The cold air from outside felt sharp against the warmth of her cheeks. Alex shivered in her light pants and shirt as she and her mother trudged through the high snow piles and into the barn. Inside the barn, Alex witnessed the handiwork of Gabe and her family. If their intent had been to create a sacred place for their vows, they achieved their goal. The places that needed to be swept had been tidied and decorated with evergreen wreaths and white pillar candles.

Wide tables filled with every imaginable bit of food lined both sides of the barn. In the clamor to get things ready, and with Bart's efforts to clear the streets, the town emerged from their homes and descended upon Spencer Farms. When her mother had told her that everyone was texting and calling to make sure the wedding was still on and to offer any help, Alex texted Gabe to make sure they had room on the guest list to accommodate everyone.

Inside the barn, to her delight, their small ceremony was now a Grey's Harbor event. The entire town gathered and chattered. Alex saw Maeve telling people where to set platters of food. She watched the guys from the brewery set up kegs in the far corner. She could hear the smooth sound of a master cellist and scanned the far corners of the barn until she saw Izzy Edwards deeply immersed in the piece she was playing. Alex smiled to herself. This place, their community, came to celebrate their wedding. She had never been so grateful for her hometown.

At the front of the barn, she found Gabe standing with her father and Eliza. Her heart skipped at the sight of Gabe in warm brown slacks and a crisp white button-down shirt. Deep navy suspenders framed his chest. Her father was working to pin his boutonniere to his shirt, Gabe looking only slightly nervous that he might be stabbed.

"They look so handsome," her mother whispered from behind her.

"Mom?" Alex turned to face her mother. "This is perfect."

"It is, and it's only just beginning." Alex's mother smiled, then pulled her in close. "C'mon, let's get you in this dress."

CHAPTER 18

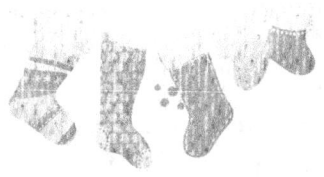

G abe looked at the tight cluster of flowers Mike pinned to his shirt. "Good?" he asked.

"Looks all right to me," Mike replied. "If it needs to be fixed, I'm sure Kim will let us know."

He chuckled and looked at the man who had been more of a father to him than his own ever was. "Thank you, Mike. For everything."

True to form, Mike lifted his chin and nodded. Without a word, he wrapped an arm around Gabe and pulled him close. "You have always been family, son. I'm glad it's finally official."

Gabe nodded and tried to respond, but everything was caught on the lump in his throat.

Mike clapped him on the back, his voice deep. "Okay, enough of that. Kim is flagging us down, which means"—he looked at Eliza—"we're ready."

"I am ready when you are," Eliza said, her warm smile triggering a rush of excitement through Gabe's body.

He nodded and took his place, reminding himself to let his shoulders relax and absorb the moment. Gabe looked across the barn at what felt like the entire town of Grey's Harbor. Despite the cold and the snow, they all came to help set up and celebrate. They trudged through knee-deep snow, yet they chattered as if it was a summer block party in June. His heart swelled with pride. These people, this community of friends, were his family by choice.

Gabe took a brief moment to calm his pounding heart, breathing through the emotion of the moment. When he felt a nudge at his calf, he smiled. PB and Jay, never ones to stay when told, each sat against a leg. He had furry groomsmen, and that suited him.

When the audience stood, Gabe blew out a breath. He knew Alex was going to be gorgeous. She had been a vision of beauty since the first time he'd laid eyes on her. Now, escorted by her parents, he felt his knees weaken at the sight of her. He'd pictured her in white or cream, not bathed in light pink, a color determined to magnify her dark brown eyes. Somehow, she managed to look light and airy. His bride was a whisper of spring breathing life into a cold, harsh winter. Alexandria Spencer was, as always, beyond expectation.

After Alex hugged and kissed her parents, Kim and Mike moved toward Gabe and shared the same affection with him.

"We love you, Gabe," Kim whispered in his ear. When she pulled back from the hug, she cupped his cheek with her hand, tears nearly letting loose.

Gabe turned to his bride, the feel of her hands in his flooding him with warmth and an unsteadiness he struggled to control. "Alex, you are beautiful."

She leaned into him, her fingers tugging on one side of his suspenders. "This," she said so only he could hear, "is a showstopper, Barnes. I need more of this in my life."

Her flirtation caught him, a laugh fell forward, and the rightness of the moment settled into him.

"Welcome, friends and family," Eliza began. "We have come together to celebrate the union of Alexandria and Gabriel. I sense from the energy in this room that this moment has been highly anticipated. I will ask this community of loved ones to share their heartfelt joy in this moment. Those who support Alexandria and Gabriel in the choice to share their lives together, please answer, 'We do.'"

The cacophony of responses—shouts, joyous cries, and even Mike getting PB and Jay to bark their support—had Alex brushing back tears.

Gabe was grateful for the time he took with Eliza to create a short but meaningful ceremony. After a blessing for him and Alex and then for the guests who joined them, they were called to recite their vows.

Alex smiled at Gabe as she turned to Kim, exchanging her bouquet for a piece of paper. Gabe saw the tremble in her hand as she straightened the folded note. He reached for her, cupping her hands as she held her vows. He watched her exhale a calming breath, then smile at him as she began.

"Gabe, you know that I have always been a little adventurous. I strive for the next big thing, the next goal in life. That drive shaped a teenage dream and sparked a journey to find the next step in creating the life I envisioned. I did not know that life was waiting for me in the one place I'd never dreamed it would take root, but it did.

"I left town to find a path that inevitably led me back home. I am so grateful you were here when I came back. Your ability to see the depth, the potential in me—and all things, really—gives me the opportunity to see the world through new eyes.

"I suspect that you always knew we were meant for one another. I am so grateful you waited for me to figure out that my happily ever after was working the farm in my own backyard. I know that you have always been my balance, the soothing breeze that calms my wild sea. Thank you for your patience, your calmness in chaotic storms, and all the possibilities our life together will bring. I love you."

In the onslaught of his emotion, Gabe could barely contain his response. Tears crested, despite his efforts to wipe them away. At some point, he stopped caring and just absorbed her words.

"Gabe, would you like to share your vows with Alex?" Eliza asked.

He nodded and pulled the copy of his vows from his back pocket. At Alex's little laugh for his storage location, he winked.

"Alex, it may seem cliché, but it has always been you. When we were kids, I admired your determination. I had the pleasure of watching you take a single idea and create a place for people to gather and share in the simple joy of ice cream on a warm summer day.

"Even as a teenager, I knew your spark would never be contained by any conventional methods. I also believed that your ability to take on the world would take you far from this place. I accepted that my life would be supporting you and your family through my work and dedication to the farm. The moment you came back, the instant we started working together, I felt a rightness settle over this place. I fought the feelings I held for you, but you stir something so natural in me that I do not have clear words to explain it. It's something different and new, yet constant and comforting. All of this, you and me and ice cream trucks, is beyond my wildest dreams. I was always happy in my station, but you elevated life to a new level.

"I hope you know that I would do anything to ensure your happiness. Partnering with me and accompanying me on this journey through life has undoubtedly ensured mine."

Despite their trembling hands, Alex and Gabe exchanged rings and basked in the applause of their friends and family as Eliza announced them for the first time as husband and wife.

EPILOGUE

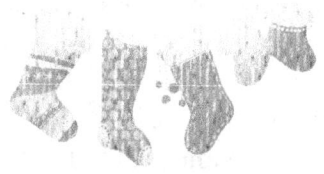

*T*hree-hundred and sixty-six days later

"I was hoping for a repeat." Gabe's voice sounded wistful as he looked over the backyard. "Thank goodness we have pictures."

All of the chaos leading up to their wedding had seemed to melt away the moment she walked down the aisle. Even a year later, after reliving the day through their photo album, the excitement felt as fresh as the snow that had fallen that day.

"We do," she confirmed. "Hey, can you help me for a minute. I need help deciding on the colors for these pint graphics."

"Did you ask Bart about his favorite colors?" Gabe asked as he refilled his coffee cup.

"I did," she replied, looking at the message from social media. "He said, and I quote, 'I like the colors on my beer can.' How do you suppose we do that?"

"I guess we could do a red, white, and blue hometown hero graphic," Gabe offered with a cool shrug of his shoulder.

"How do you do that?"

"Do what?"

"How do you just suggest something that is so right, while I've been up all night worrying that Bart is going to hate his specialty ice cream flavor."

"He's going to love it. He's one of your biggest contributors on social media." Gabe took another drink from his coffee cup. "Okay, enough work." He held out his hand. "Come sit with me and tell me all the reasons you're on the naughty list this year."

Alex laughed and took his hand. "Are you playing Santa again?" She let him lead her into the living room. They flopped on the couch, admiring the massive Christmas tree nestled in the corner.

Since she didn't have time to decorate last year, Alex felt she deserved to splurge. Every conceivable branch was dripping with ornaments. To her delight, fans of Daisy's had started sending ice cream ornaments. When she and Gabe did a live social media spot, he made the mistake of mentioning that she got all the ornaments. They had been inundated with cow, barn, horse, and dog ornaments ever since.

"Merry Christmas Eve," he said.

"Merry Christmas Eve," Alex replied, her giddiness growing. "Can we share one present today?"

"Always eager for the good stuff, aren't you?"

"Oh yes," she replied. "Okay, me first. Pick a gift for me."

She watched her husband leap over the pile of gifts under the tree and giggled as he made a show of claiming that each wrapped gift was for PB or Jay or Carrots.

"Whew! I'm glad I found one. I was worried for a minute." He moved a large, rectangular gift to the center of the floor. With one end on the ground, the top of the package touched Gabe's waist. "I don't think I can safely get this to your parents' house tomorrow."

She scrambled off the couch and kissed him before tearing at the paper. It took a moment for Alex to realize what the gift was, but when she did, her vision blurred. "Oh my goodness."

Gabe had collected the media spotlights, the newspaper clippings, and photographs printed throughout the past year as she launched Daisy's beyond Grey's Harbor, and he'd had them framed for posterity. Her efforts to expand distribution through their community's resources were highly supported and well documented.

For Alex, it was easy to accept that she accomplished a task and quickly moved on to the next, but Gabe put it all under glass so she would never forget.

"Do you like it?" His voice wavered ever so slightly.

"It's the best," she replied, her voice watery with emotion. "You are the best."

"Good," he said with a satisfied smile.

She lingered a bit over her gift and then placed it where she could admire it until they could hang it in her office.

"Now," she said, "your turn."

"Okay," Gabe settled back on the couch. "Gift me, City."

She nodded and attempted to look serious. "Do you remember our last trip to New York?"

"For the Thanksgiving Day parade? Yes, it was pure chaos. Thank God we had a hotel room to watch the balloons go by."

She giggled, remembering his excitement over the Snoopy balloon. "I got your gift on that trip."

Gabe paused. "Okay." He thought for a minute. "When? We were only there for three days."

"It was a short trip."

"Yeah," he said as he moved and set his coffee cup on an end table. "We were together the whole time and we barely left the hotel room."

Alex sat across from him, trying her best to keep her smile hidden. "That is very true."

"And you got my gift then?"

"Uh-huh."

"Where is it?"

"Right here." She lifted her hands in a *Ta-da!* flourish.

"No way, City. I got the gift of you last year."

"Oh, I promise." She couldn't help her giggle. "There's more."

Alex's true gift was witnessing Gabe's reaction as he thought through her riddle. When he realized that they had made his gift together, his excitement was palpable. "Are you pregnant?"

She nodded. "I am."

Gabe wrapped his arms around Alex, holding her close.

She could feel the shudder of his emotion roll through him and felt her own cresting wave of joy.

"Best gift ever," he said, emotion straining his voice.

"I thought so too. Merry Christmas, Gabe."

PURCHASE THE GREY'S HARBOR SERIES

Click the Book Covers to purchase the books you are missing

Five Tales of Love and Romance
by the Sea

GREY'S
HARBOR

curated by
THREE QUILLS PRESS

A Grey's Harbor Story

HOPE
ADRIFT

LARK GRIFFING

MEET THE AUTHORS OF GREY'S HARBOR CHRISTMAS

LARK GRIFFING

Lark Griffing is all about stories of adventure and romance. Whether writing about a recent widowed women discovering life in a teardrop trailer or a teenage girl dealing with evil spirits in her aunt's ancient house on the cliffs above the sea, Lark sets the story in motion and the reader is never really sure where or how it's going to end. Often that reader gets a surprise they weren't expecting, and Lark likes that.

Lark Griffing is a dabbler. Her hobbies are many and varied, from SCUBA diving to backpacking, kayaking to knitting. You never know what you're going to get on any given day if you hang with her.

Her husband and boys are used to her running off in all directions, and they humor her because they know that with Lark, an adventure awaits them. The only members of her family who are not up for the fun are her tabby cat, Dickens and her golden doodle, Maggie. The two of them would prefer staying curled up together holding down the fort until Lark comes bursting back through the door.

Keep up with Lark at her website: www.LarkGriffing.com

faccbook.com/larkgriffing
twitter.com/Lark_Griffing
instagram.com/LarkGriffing

J.C. WING

J.C. Wing is a multi-genre novelist whose works include *The Color of Thunder*, *The Gannon Family Series*, the *Goddess of Tornado Alley Series* and a collection of short stories, personal essays and poetry titled *Acquainted With Butterflies*. She wrote *The Key* and *Nine Ladies Dying*, both novellas, and a thriller called *Next Day Gone*. Currently, she is one of several authors contributing to the ongoing *Grey's Harbor Series*.

As an indie author, J.C. publishes under Black Cat Press, her own imprint. She manages Wing Family Editing, and her co-workers include Mouse, a cranky but lovable twenty-pound cat, and Tara, the drama queen of golden retrievers.

J.C. is an eternal optimist and a friendly sort. She smiles a lot … but she is silently correcting your grammar. She doesn't mean to. She's an editor. She can't help it.

Keep up with J.C. Wing at
http://www.jcwingandthegoddess.com/

facebook.com/authorjcwing

twitter.com/writer_jcwing

instagram.com/writerjcwing

JENNIFER SIVEC

Jennifer Sivec writes beautifully broken stories with heart.

She is attracted to and writes stories with characters that are complicated, flawed and completely imperfect. Her books are often a reflection of life, encompassing difficult subjects such as cancer, addiction, abandonment, and abuse. She writes with a raw, complex, yet hopeful approach often weaving tragic stories with honesty and grace, creating unforgettable characters.

Jennifer has been writing since she was in the fourth grade but didn't publish her first novel until 2014, and has been writing non-stop since. Her passion for reading and sharing stories gives her perspective and peace of mind.

She lives in Ohio with her husband, two boys, and three dogs who create balance and levity for her. She loves her crazy life and wonderful readers, and is grateful for all of it, every day.

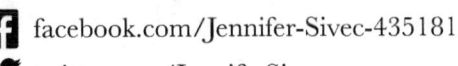 facebook.com/Jennifer-Sivec-435181503228103

twitter.com/JenniferSivec

instagram.com/jennifersivec

PIPER MALONE

Piper Malone is an award-winning author who writes stories about strong, driven women and their swoon-worthy heroes. Her novels enchant readers with deeply romantic tales infused with passion, friendship, and laughter.

She is a reader of all things. Lover of dark chocolate, adventures, and pet adoption. Devotee of face masks, curling ribbon, and stationary.

Piper is a mother and teacher with a serious love for car karaoke, buttercream icing, and her dog, Swiss.

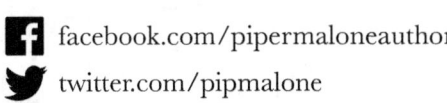

facebook.com/pipermaloneauthor
twitter.com/pipmalone
instagram.com/pipermalone

www.ingramcontent.com/pod-product-compliance
Lightning Source LLC
Chambersburg PA
CBHW072121250626
47159CB00007B/2525